SILVER TONGUE DEVIL

STACEY MARIE BROWN

ALSO BY STACEY MARIE BROWN

Contemporary Romance

How the Heart Breaks

Buried Alive

Smug Bastard

The Unlucky Ones

Blinded Love Series
Shattered Love (#1)
Broken Love (#2)
Twisted Love (#3)

Royal Watch Series
Royal Watch (#1)
Royal Command (#2)

Paranormal Romance

Darkness Series
Darkness of Light (#1)
Fire in the Darkness (#2)
Beast in the Darkness (An Elighan Dragen Novelette)
Dwellers of Darkness (#3)
Blood Beyond Darkness (#4)
West (#5)

Collector Series
City in Embers (#1)
The Barrier Between (#2)
Across the Divide (#3)
From Burning Ashes (#4)

Lightness Saga
The Crown of Light (#1)
Lightness Falling (#2)
The Fall of the King (#3)
Rise from the Embers (#4)

Savage Lands Series
Savage Lands (#1)
Wild Lands (#2)
Dead Lands (#3)
Bad Lands (#4)
Blood Lands (#5)
Shadow Lands (#6)

A Winterland Tale
Descending into Madness (#1)
Ascending from Madness (#2)
Beauty in Her Madness (#3)
Beast in His Madness (#4)

Timeline

Collector Series
Ends Here

FAE WAR
Darkness Series Ends here

Eastern Countries secede
from Unified Nations 1 year
after war.

Battle with Stavros/Stone of Fal
2 years after Fae War.

Croygen Leaves,
returning to piracy.
Lightness Series Ends here

The substance called necter
is discovered 5 years after Fae War
and 15 years before Savage Lands.

Wars between Fae and
Humans in the Eastern
intensify.

Istvan finds Dr. Rapava's work.
Starts experiments.

Savage Lands starts 20 years
after Fae War.

Prologue
Croygen

The wind off the sea tangled through my black hair, salt coating my lips. The sensation was so familiar it slid over my skin fitting like a glove. At one time I was a feared pirate with the likes of Blackbeard, Ned Lowe, and Samuel Bellamy, a relic of the golden age of piracy before humans ruined everything fun, pushing us fae back into the darkest corners. Though for fae, piracy never truly ended, we simply got better at hiding it. It was a struggle to stay hidden in a world of developing technology to keep humans from discovering fae walked among them.

That was no longer the case.

The wall between the Otherworld and Earth had fallen.

Long before that, I had lost my crew, my ship, and my dignity. Disappearing from the world in which I no longer fit, I found people who had me believing once again in family. A home. There I found a rare gem, a beautiful girl I could see myself loving… but in her death, the man I was becoming died with her.

It woke me up. Made me see.

I was a pirate.

My home was the sea, my love was my ship, and my desire was for adventures and riches.

My dark eyes slid back to my friends standing together on the shore, the people who claimed me as theirs watching me sail away. I had thought I had finally found peace. Happiness. But that time was over.

I lifted my arm up to the sky, then tapped my heart six times, one for each of them—Zoey, Ryker, Annabeth, baby Wyatt, and even that furball monkey-sprite, Sprig. But it was the last tap that made my throat close up, reminding me I could still feel. It was for the girl full of fire and life, who had grown up before my eyes and had become a stunning, bold-as-brass woman. Lexie. My lil' shark. Losing her broke something in me, making me realize I was not meant to love or be domesticated.

The Silver-Tongue Devil, the man who seduces your wife, cuts your throat, and steals your money all at the same time. That's who I truly was.

Something deep inside me ripped into shreds as I turned away from my family and friends, agony clawing up my throat, but I kept my gaze on the horizon, the haze of magic thick in the air.

The barrier between Earth and the Otherworld had collapsed, and technology and modern life had come to a halt.

It was time for the pirates to command the seas again.

Yo ho… it was a pirate's life for me.

Chapter 1
Katrina
5 years before the Fae War

"Joder!" *Fuck!* He bellowed, his fingers digging into my hips, his head curling back into the silk pillow. His lids squeezed shut, and his mouth locked open as he spilled inside me. Another long, deep moan radiated from his chest.

A drop of sweat trailed between my breasts, and I tipped my head back, enjoying the rush of pleasure rolling through me as my own body slipped quietly into a climax. Sucking in air, I tried to stay in the bliss for a moment more. It never lasted long. Never enough.

I didn't realize how much I needed even this small release. My worries and stresses had been building up, twisting me in knots. I didn't always go this far, but when he kissed me, I knew he would be an excellent lover. And I needed nothing more than to let off some steam while still getting work done.

"My god." He spoke English, but his Castilian accent was thick. His expression was open as he stared up at me in utter awe. "That was…" He gaped, licking his lips, his eyes drifting down to where we still connected. "I have never felt

3

anything like this before. Jesus, your pussy… it is absolute magic."

Little did he know how true this statement was.

"Thank you," I hummed, leaning down to brush my lips over his, knowing he would be drifting off to sleep.

"You are so beautiful." His fingers threaded through my long, silky black hair, pulling me against his chest. His lips skated over the curve of my neck, tipping my head to the side.

My lids squeezed together as I relished the feel of his teeth scraping my skin, tasting me. Why not appreciate it? He definitely was getting something out of this too. The best sex of *his* life, which he would never be able to match again.

"One of the most striking women I have ever seen." The man cupped my face, his brown eyes meeting mine. "Your eyes. They are bewitching. Never seen anything like them before."

I lowered my lashes hungrily, knowing full well the power my almond-shaped eyes held. Yellow irises with bright green rings around the black pupils. My dark lashes only made them burn brighter. To humans, they were a phenomenon because they didn't understand the truth of what made them that way. That I was not like them.

At one time, I had been ignorant of the influence my looks could generate, the sensual way I moved and the untamed aura around me. Now I understood how to use it to seduce prey. It was survival of the fittest. And I planned to come out the fat cat.

Literally.

Petite-boned and only five feet four inches, I was usually waved off as nothing of consequence unless they wanted something pretty to fuck. Half Polynesian and half German, my looks got a lot of attention. I was a feather in the cap of any man who lay with me, and they patted themselves on the back.

This man was no different. Human men didn't see me as any threat.

Fools.

They had no idea the prettiest things out there were the most dangerous. I was not their prey; they were *mine*.

"When I saw you, so young and beautiful"—his mouth moved back over mine—"I had to bed you." He breathed me in, the kiss turning needy, licking a spark of desire through my blood again. I never seemed to be satisfied. Never quenched, no matter how many lovers I had.

My slight frame, oval face, and flawless skin suggested I was young, maybe early twenties, which made the many *old* men I had after me kind of disgusting. Little did they know I was far older than all of them combined, and eras from now, I wouldn't look any different.

"I wanted you too." I kissed him back, feeding his ego. His chest heaved with gratification, the pheromones casting over him, bleeding into his veins, the high from his intense release drowning him in blissful fatigue. It was over-whelming for humans.

I wasn't lying. I wanted him… but not for what he thought.

The sex was a bonus.

He walked into the club dressed in the finest suit, his chest puffed and arrogant. He was handsome, with soft, unworked hands and glossy hair. The foreign accent and gold watch around his wrist screamed wealth, begging for every con artist in the place to set their sights on him.

He was the kind who couldn't see past his own entitlement and superiority, thinking he was the only one in this part of the country making shady deals, never believing someone like me would be anything but tripping over myself to be noticed by him.

He was very good-looking, with dark, wavy hair, umber

skin, and dark eyes, but the constant smirk on his mouth was twisted and told me he knew it.

He was nothing more than a job.

He exhaled again, his lids sliding closed. My lips feathered over his as he sank into slumber, a smile curving his mouth.

"Sweet dreams," I whispered, peering down at the beautiful man. We hadn't bothered to learn each other's names. Not that he would have gotten the truth from me. He had been more fun than I thought, but after so long, my bar wasn't very high.

Waiting one more beat to make sure he was fully asleep, I slid off him, scrambling off the bed. I pulled on my knickers and top, ready to pretend I was returning from the toilet if he happened to stir. But in my experience, they didn't wake up until long after I was gone.

My eyes darted around the room. The hotel he was staying at fit his stature, catering to wealthy patrons who wanted to stay anony-mous. The space was decorated in rich colors, dark teak woods, and expensive local silks. Indonesia was teeming with people like him, exploiting the black market as piracy multiplied hourly in this area. Though, I missed the good old days of true piracy.

Slipping out the lock picks from my pants pocket, I snuck to the closet. I knew there would be a lockbox in the cabinet. He wasn't so wealthy to have the hotel hold his possessions in a private vault. He'd trust his items would be safe near him.

The wood door creaked open and snapped back as he stirred. My heart thumped against my chest. He rolled onto his side, facing my direction, then he sighed contently, snuggling into the pillow.

Air exited my nose, and my stomach coiled up like a snake. Pinning my focus back on the box, my fingers pinched the lock picks, sliding them into the keyhole. Human-made safes were pathetically easy to crack.

After I twisted and clicked a pick into place, the lock popped open. My chest fluttered with excitement as the door swung open. The thrill never got old.

"Fuck. Yes," I muttered, a huge smile curling my lips. I spied stacks of bills, women's jeweled rings, and a necklace dripping with diamonds.

This could set my crew for months.

A creak sounded behind me—the hotel room door opening.

"Oh darling, I had to come back early from the spa retreat. Nadine was making me positively craz—" An English accent hit my ears as the woman stepped into the room, stopping dead in her tracks. Beautiful and young, her ring finger was decorated with an expen-sive gold band and diamond ring, making me groan inwardly.

Fucking bastard was married.

Her eyes widened with horror as her gaze went from my barely dressed form to the naked man in bed and back to me.

"What is going on?" she screeched.

The man jolted awake in confusion, floundering, peering around, trying to figure out what was happening.

"You cheating bastard!"

His eyes turned as round as hers, his attention snapping between us.

"*Mi amor*! It is not what you think!" He leaped out of the bed, his naked body still covered with arousal.

I snorted.

"Not what it looks like? I'm not stupid! My father warned me about you, saying you would cheat on me every time I turned my back. I should have listened!" Her voice hit piercing levels, her glower coming back to me, pausing on my hands. Shit. "Wh-what are you doing with those?" She

7

pointed at the box in my grip. The man spun around, his lids narrowing.

"I'm gonna let you two lovebirds work this out." I snapped the lid closed, standing up.

It was a blink. A heavy pause before everything exploded in commotion.

"Thief!"

Time to go.

It had been a while since I had to escape sans pants. I snarled at the memory of the slivers I got in my backside last time.

"Help," the woman screamed. "We're being robbed!"

"Thief! Thief!"

Their cries rang like a bell through the hotel, stirring everyone within the walls of this resort.

The man grabbed for a gun he had hidden in his nightstand as I swung for the window, opening it. The warm breeze opposed the air-conditioned room.

"Hurry! She's getting away," the woman called down the hallway, pulling my attention to four huge guards with weapons running toward the room.

"Stop!" the man bellowed, pointing the gun at me.

Now it was really time to go.

Tucking the box to my chest and crawling out the window, I paused on the sill.

"Thank you for a most entertaining night." I winked. "And the fuck was pretty decent too."

His mouth dropped at my bluntness and audacity, the gun loose in his fingers. Desire smoldered in his eyes, a slight satisfied smile picking at his lips.

"What are you doing? Get her!" His wife bounced and squawked like a parrot I had once known.

The guards burst into the room, spotting me, then lurching forward.

I blew the man a kiss before leaping off the sill, my ass dropping painfully onto the roof covering the lower rooms. A puff hurtled from my lips, my skin tearing as I skidded down.

"She's escaping! Go around to the front!" Hollers echoed from the room, nipping at the back of my neck.

Scrambling to the edge of the roof, I leaped again. Soundlessly, my feet hit the ground, my hands gripping the box more firmly. My gaze moved around, seeing perfectly through every shadow. Not as well as I could be, but still 100 times better than any human.

The people on the streets didn't even gape at a girl in her knickers and singlet. Skulking through these streets was a common occurrence around here.

This place was a lesser-known hub for piracy than Singapore. But the Strait of Malacca was a gold mine for attacking oil tankers and getting goods from the west to the east. The vast wealth up for grabs around Indonesia was too tempting to ignore, drawing all types here to reap the benefits, which was why hotels of this caliber were guarded with hired mercenaries.

"Stop!" a deep voice ordered. Boots hit the steps as a bullet pinged off the wall near my head.

They had no chance of getting me. Even staying in this form, I could slip out of sight, darting away before they could even blink.

My legs moved me easily down the lanes I knew better than anyone, dodging and weaving. Of course, I'd be a lot faster in my other form. The only problem was I needed my hands to carry the loot.

Weaving down alleys to move closer to the water, I slipped through a door, then downstairs, upstairs, and through another door. I finally climbed the steps of an abandoned building, hidden away from human eyes in this town.

"Secret code?" a voice asked at the same time a gun was put to my temple.

"Really?" I rolled my eyes.

"You never know. I should fully inspect to see if it's really you." A man's voice nipped in my ear, his hands sliding down my hips. "Caught in your knickers again, Kitty-Kat?"

Only one person was allowed to call me that.

"Fuck off, Gage. And get your hands off me." I twisted my head close to his mouth; the coyness in my tone was laced with warning. "Or you will have one ball missing by morning."

"Back off, Gage." A deep grumble came out of the shadows as the man strolled up to me, no doubt spotting my healing cuts and bruises, taking in my lack of clothing and the scent of sex billowing off me. A flutter of sadness graced his face before he schooled it into a neutral expression. I tried to pretend I didn't see his hurt every time I came back from a night of "letting off some steam" and that I didn't feel his disappointment and pain.

We knew each other too well not to recognize what the other one felt. We had been children together. He was the only one here I truly trusted entirely with my life. He found me again after my father was murdered. Had been by my side since, helping while our crew expanded and assisting in developing my plan to take to the high seas and find the man who killed my father, who destroyed my life.

"Kat." His violet eyes tracked me as I strolled past him, heading into our hideout. He walked next to me.

"I think with this, we can finally afford to get back on the sea." I handed him the box. As he peered inside, I exhaled. My dream of captaining a ship was so close I could taste the salty air on my tongue. "With you by my side, we can get a ship." I nudged my friend. "We can track him down…"

"He hasn't been spotted in decades." He peered at me, slight annoyance in his gaze. He didn't grasp my obsessive need for revenge. "Maybe he's already dead."

"Oh, he's out there. And I will track him down for what

he did to my father. For what he did to me." My lip lifted in a snarl, my mind trickling back to when pirates controlled the seas and *the Silver-Tongue Devil* was among the most revered. There was a time when I had adored him, thought the world began and ended with him.

"And, Killian, not only will I find him... I will *kill* Croygen."

Chapter 2

Katrina

The 1700s - The Golden Era of Pirates

The sun sparkled off the clear blue water, the warm sun already trickling sweat down my back. A seagull glided overhead, coasting toward the island not too far away. It was one of those perfect days, and all I wanted to do was jump overboard and swim in the cool water.

"Katrina!" My name was clipped, yanking me back to dark eyes narrowed on me from my teacher. "Pay attention!"

"Sorry, Master Yukimura." I bowed my head, adjusting my stance and gripping the bamboo stick in my hand. The boy across from me snickered. When I stuck my tongue out at him, his response was to do the same back.

"Katrina..." Master Yukimura frowned.

I had been scolded a lot lately because I wasn't very "ladylike," as if when I turned twelve, I was supposed to act like a proper girl. I had been raised on this ship with all men, running around, playing tag and hide-and-go-seek, scrubbing the deck, and climbing the shrouds and masts.

It had never been a problem until now.

"Posture straight!" Master yelled at both of us, tapping

12

my back. "Get into strike position." He circled us, correcting any tiny thing he saw wrong. Sometimes we would train for hours just to get our breathing and stance right.

It started as something to keep us busy, the only two kids on the ship, with abundance of energy. Yukimura started teaching us Kenjutsu and Kendo, sword fighting techniques from his homeland, probably so we'd stop annoying him, but along the way it became a daily occurrence. Something both of us took seriously.

"Let's see if you can get one hit in this time, *Kitty-Kat*." Violet eyes sparkled back at me, a grin hitching his mouth.

"Shut up, *Leo*," I taunted back.

"Don't. Call. Me. That." His lids narrowed, his shoulders rolling back, his jaw tightening. I always knew how to rile him up. He *hated* his real name. His father's name. He hated anything that had to do with his past. A reminder his father neglected and abused him, basically throwing him out on the streets at six years old. He was put into a poorhouse where his supposed best friend, Hazem, tried to kill him in his sleep because he was the favored kid, being far better at pickpocketing, and getting extra helpings and attention. The orphanage owner, a dirty gambler, taught all the kids to steal to pay their way. He was the best thief there, and Hazem was jealous. He still bore the scar where Hazem stabbed him.

He ran away and stowed away on our ship.

That's where Captain found him, down in the hull. A dirty, half-starved, scrappy kid. He had survived most of his life stealing and pickpocketing to feed himself. Instead of throwing him off at the next port, Captain made him crew. We became instant friends. He'd been with us for about three years now.

"Oh, sorry, *Killian*." I smirked, lifting my bamboo sword.

"Emphasis on the first part, Kitty-Kat." He grinned mischievously back, bringing his sword up to mine.

He had such a killer instinct to survive, to do what

needed to be done, that it wasn't long before he was given the name Killian, meaning "little warrior" in Gaelic. And it stuck. A rebirth of the boy.

With a dark mop of hair, violet eyes, and sharp features, he should have belonged in the high seelie court as the son of a royal fairy or something, not a poor boy from the slums who was now a pirate.

Most of the prostitutes who the crew would bring on for the night already gawked at him with interest. At fourteen, they saw the potential, what he'd look like when he got older. Or they'd tease us about being boyfriend and girlfriend, which made me uncomfortable. Killian was my buddy, a brother to me. Though I could feel the change in the way he looked at me, touched me, and brought me little gifts.

Master Yukimura gave the order to engage just as the captain of our ship stepped out onto the deck, the air in my lungs fluttering as my eyes drank him in. My cheeks burned, and I had a funny feeling in my belly, like thousands of tadpoles were swimming around. I would fight to the death for my captain, but something was happening to me lately. After I caught him with one of his women, watching what he did to her, I couldn't stop my cheeks from flushing. I got all squirmy, wanting to wear something less boyish than breeches and a dirty linen shirt, like those pretty ladies I saw on the mainland. The ones he would wink at, and though they would act outraged, I could see them looking back, their eyes heated.

I wanted to impress him.

I wanted him to *see* me.

Watching Captain out of the corner of my eye, Killian and I clanked our bamboo swords against each other, shifting in swift, fluid motions. The problem with training alongside someone every day was that we could predict each other's moves and had learned to get out of them. But when the captain appeared, my attention got all blurry. The edge of the bamboo stick hit my arm.

Dammit.

"Strike for me. Come on, Kat. You're making this easy," Killian bragged, circling around, forcing me to turn with him. I noticed most of the crew was watching us, along with the captain. "You're fighting like a *girl*."

Those were combative words. And he knew it.

"Oh, someone's mad," Killian teased me. "You're growing whiskers."

My face burned with humiliation, my teeth clenching as embarrassment burned through my muscles. I was coming into fae puberty. I couldn't fully shift into my cat form yet, but I would start to change without my control. When I got emotional, I'd start growing claws and whiskers, and shiny black fur sprouted out of my skin in patches.

It was mortifying.

Grunting, I leaped forward, my stick clanking down on Killian's weapon, my tiny frame coming at him. Killian recently had a growth spurt, and he towered over me now, and I was angry he was so much bigger than me.

Being tiny didn't mean I couldn't beat him. Slipping around him, I tapped my sword at his side. "Strike for me!"

"Barely." Killian's smugness flared my temper. My father said I got it from my mother. She was Polynesian and petite like me—and a total spitfire. Her stubborn temperament was legendary. But that came with being cat-shifters. We were temperamental creatures.

Killian and I moved across the deck, my ire rising with every hit he got on me. His bamboo stick hit me right in the middle of the stomach.

"Yes! Won again." He winked at me. "Sorry, Kitty-Kat."

Anger fumed under my skin like a volcano. All eyes were on me, but I felt the captain's the most. Rage bubbled up until a cry rose from my throat, sounding like a howl. When I lunged for Killian, daggers sliced into my body, my bones cracking. The taste of heavy magic and the salty air clogged my throat.

Every sense sharpened to almost painful levels. I could hear a single seagull miles away, see a fly up on the crow's nest, and smell the pungent odors of fish, seaweed, sweat, and moldy wood.

The clothes I wore fell off me as my body shifted. I had only done it partially a few times, and it had made me want to throw up. Pain coursed through my bones, forcing me to stop the shift and return to my human form.

On my hands and knees, bile burned at the back of my throat as I coughed and hacked, my body shaking with the abundance of magic still volleying through me. Taking huge gulps of air, I tried to center myself, to swallow back the vomit in my esophagus.

Breathe, Kat, I ordered myself.

Then I noticed the silence. The feel of the ocean breeze on my bare skin.

Lifting my head, I discovered every crew member staring at me, my clothes pooling underneath me.

"Katrina!" My father called my name as he pushed through the throng of onlookers. Rushing to my side, he grabbed the shirt I had been wearing off the ground, covering me with it.

"Get back to work!" Captain bellowed out. "Now! And if I see one of you looking over here, I will cut your throats myself!"

The crew dissipated in a hurry since he was a man of his word.

"Kat...?" Killian gazed at me with sorrow, his hand reaching for me.

"No." I scrambled back, tucking into my father, hauling the shirt tighter to me, only feeling humiliation and shame. Everyone saw me naked. Saw me lose control of myself.

"Killian." Master Yukimura pulled him back, trying to lead him away.

"I'm sorry." Killian swallowed, his head bowing toward Yukimura.

"Put this on." My dad whispered in my ear, and I quickly yanked the shirt back over my head. "Come on. I got you." Dad helped me to my feet, my muscles feeling wobbly and weak. He held me tight as we went back to our cabin below.

My father was the first mate, second in charge if anything happened. That gave us a few more allowances than the rest of the crew, such as a private cabin with washrooms and my own bedchamber. Nothing fancy, but it had been my only home for as long as I could remember.

My mother died when I was one, trapped in a house fire. We lost all our crops, home, and property. My father barely escaped with me. With no other way to support us, he took to the high seas, something he had done before he met my mother. He worked hard, earning respect from one of the most feared and revered pirates.

The *Silver-Tongue Devil* of the Sea. He was notorious for talking *any* woman out of her knickers, especially the wealthy married ones, seducing them while he robbed them blind before they even knew it. A gentleman in one room and a cutthroat bandit in another. I noticed he preferred not to kill anyone, but if challenged, he had no problem declaring his dominance.

He could be ruthless and cruel. But the women seemed to thank him more for it. I had seen too many wanting to leave their husbands and sail away with us. This used to baffle me... but something changed. I was beginning to understand.

"Kat." My father's rough hands cupped my face as I sat back on my bed. "Are you okay?"

I knew he meant physically, not emotionally.

"I'm fine." I drew away from him, not wanting anyone to touch me, my skin still humming with energy.

17

Strained silence filled the room, another thing I had noticed lately. My father and I had always been close, but since I started going through fae puberty, it had become awkward.

"*Kätzchen.*" *Kitten.* My father called to me in his native German tongue. "I wish I knew what to do. How to help you." His voice was thick. "Your mother would know. She would be so much better at this than me."

My father, Fredrich Roth, was half-fae, which was rare because humans didn't know fae existed. Not that his father had been aware his lover was fae—or that he had a son. But my father was very low on the magic spectrum, whereas I took after my mother. She had been a cat-shifter too.

"I don't know if this life is the best for you anymore."

"What?" My head bolted up. "What are you talking about? I love it here. This is my home."

"*Katze.*" *Cat.* He stood to his full five feet, eleven inches. My father had light blue eyes, blond hair, and pale skin that belied how much time he spent in the sun. I took more after my mother, but you could see my father's roots in me too. My unique heritage got me a lot of looks. "You are no longer a little girl. You should be at school. Getting a proper education. Learning how to control your abilities. I mean, cats don't even like water."

"That's not always true." I folded my arms. "Please, Father. I don't want to go anywhere. I want to be with you. Master Yukimura is teaching me how to breathe, how to keep myself calm and focused. To control myself. Please don't make me leave."

My father's head bowed, his head dipping in acceptance. I knew he didn't want me to leave either. After my mother died, I became his entire world. And he was mine. My father was compassionate, quiet, and brilliant. He was the captain's counterpart. He ran this ship day-to-day, keeping the books, handling the money, and dealing with all the business stuff. If my dad had magic, it was his mind. His brain worked so differently from others, able to solve any problem in seconds. Sometimes he would forget a world existed outside of his books and ledgers, getting stuck in his thoughts.

"*Promise me* you won't send me away?" I pressed my hands together.

"*Katze.*" He tilted his head, knowing what I was asking. To a fae a promise was binding. Not something you could break like humans did.

"Please, *Vater.*" *Father*, I pleaded in German.

He took in a deep breath. "Okay, I promise." I don't think my father ever said no to me.

Before I could respond, a knock hit our main door, my skin prickling like I could feel who was on the other side. His magic was palpable, his presence felt far before he entered a room.

My father strolled to the front door while I hovered outside my bedroom.

"Captain." He dipped his head, opening the door wider, letting him enter.

"Rotty." Captain stepped in. Everyone called my father Rotty, going off the last name Roth.

Captain's dark eyes slid to me, tunneling through me, making my skin flush and the tadpoles in my stomach spin like crazy. I tugged at the end of my linen shirt, feeling practically naked, my cheeks burning.

His gaze snapped back to my father. "Can I speak to you in private?"

"Of course," my father replied. "*Kätzchen*, go in your room." My dad nodded for me to retreat. "Shut the door."

With a frown, I did what he said, though they seemed to forget my hearing was exceptional.

"You already know what I'm going to say. We've been through this before." Captain's deep, raspy voice created shivers across my shoulders.

19

"Yes, but I can't. She is my little girl. All I have left."

"She is no longer a child, Fredrich. And we can't keep pretending she is. This is not an appropriate place for her anymore."

Hurt and utter betrayal sank into my stomach at his words.

"She needs to be in a proper girl's school, not on a ship with a bunch of horny fae men who drink, fuck, swear, and thieve."

"But, Captain—"

"No. This is not up for debate anymore, Rotty. The crew has taken notice of her. And she is throwing off *potent* pheromones, which only tap at their baser needs. We are at sea for weeks with no other women on this ship." Blood pounded in my ears listening to him talk about me, my skin itching with magic as emotion swirled inside my chest. "And after the incident earlier… I *can't* have her here anymore. It's for the best. For everyone."

"No!" Resentment and rage flooded me, pushing me through the door as I screamed at them. "I won't go!"

"Katrina," my father yelled.

Captain slowly turned to me as if he knew I had been listening the whole time.

"You can't make me leave!"

"Want to bet?" His gaze leveled on mine. A challenge. A threat.

"Katrina, please go back into your room," my father snipped, as if I was being rude to a guest. But the captain wasn't a guest. This was my family. The only one I had ever known. And Captain was acting like I was some nuisance. Like I didn't belong here. Like I wasn't one of them.

He was someone I would lay down my life for. Who I thought cared about me. But I was nothing to him. Easily swiped away, same as all the other girls.

"I'm not going!" I put my hands on my hips, my chin high.

"She leaves tonight," Captain ordered my father, heading for the door.

"I'm not! Tell him, Father. You promised me you wouldn't send me away," I cried out.

"He might have." Captain opened the door, looking back at me. "But *I* didn't. You leave tonight."

That night my life shattered before me. Everything I knew was taken away.

It was the last time I saw my father alive.

And it was the first time I swore vengeance on the Silver-Tongue Devil. I stole his most prized possession that night, stuffing it in my bag, the signature coat he never took off. I wanted him to feel loss, to know who took it, to come after me.

But he never did.

So it became my mission. I would take *everything* away from Croygen like he did me.

I would become the pirate *he* feared.

Chapter 3
Katrina
Five years before Fae War

The moonlight glistened off the ocean, the slight breeze tangling through my wet hair, which reached my lower back. I leaned on the rail, taking in a deep breath. The ocean was the only place I found true peace. It was odd for a cat to love the water so much, but it was the one place that felt like home.

Our hideout was in a dangerous area, but it gave me views of the sea. The boats bobbed and swayed against the docks, begging to be set free. Like wild horses, ships were meant to be out on the water, not tied to a dock as captives.

My ears twitched as a figure moved up the stairs, his familiar scent reaching my nose. Killian could always find me anywhere.

"It's time, Kill." I stared at the sea as he stepped in next to me. "I can feel it."

"I hate him too, Kat. I'm disgusted I still have his mark on my chest." He patted at the spot. Croygen had those who declared their loyalty to him tattooed. It was a feeling of pride to the crew; it meant you were part of the family. I had been jealous when I was younger that I wasn't part of the group. "You know I want to destroy him, but Croygen won't be easy

22

to take down. He's been off the radar for a long time. What makes you think you can find him?"

"Because." I turned to look at my best friend. "He *will* find me." Killian's eyes tracked mine, dropping to my mouth for a beat. "I will become the most notorious pirate." I glanced back at the sea, trying to ignore what I knew Killian wanted, what he had wanted since we were children. "His ego will bring him out of hiding. He won't be able to stand another one claiming his title."

"Piracy is not what it used to be, not like when we were kids." He faced out to the sea, nudging his shoulder into mine. "I don't want you to be disappointed, Kitty-Kat."

"Ugh." I groaned. "For a kid who used to fight for survival in the streets, you've become soft." I rolled my eyes. "What happened to *Kill*ian? The boy who used to be so fearless."

"I saw what was truly out there." Killian turned toward me. "You didn't. I was the one in actual battles, where I witnessed men shit and piss themselves before Captain cut off their heads while you were learning how to read and write and wear fancy dresses."

"You think I wanted to be?" I whirled back on him. "I had to! I was forced to leave the ship. My home. I ran away from the school six times before I got expelled."

"And it was better you did," Killian snapped. "You don't want to know what it takes. I lived through the fall of piracy, when they were putting our heads on stakes and hunting us down like animals. Hanging and torturing us. I watched everyone die on our ship that day... where *your father* got murdered by his supposed friend. Croygen put your own father's dagger through his heart. I saw him do it." He swallowed hard. "You live in a fantasy, Kat, where you're sailing around the world like it's a fucking cruise. It's not like when we were kids!" His eyes flashed brighter, letting me see the real power behind them. "You weren't there when we got scurvy or syphilis. At sea for months when no breeze came in. Stop believing you're going to live some fairy tale out there!"

"I'm not!" My voice sounded more like a yowl. "I know what it takes. And I am willing to give anything to avenge my father. I will live forever with the guilt of never getting to see him again. Never saying goodbye. Croygen took that from me. He took everything, including you. I will not stop until I find him. He will pay for what he did."

"You're obsessed with revenge on Croygen." Killian grabbed my wrists, pulling me closer to him. "What about what's right in front of you?"

"What are you talking about?" I swallowed.

His head tilted, his gaze burrowing into me. "You know what I'm talking about. You aren't that dense."

I sucked in. "Kill..."

"Fuck, Kat, I've been in love with you since we were kids!" His arms went out. "That's not a secret. And we could have everything if you opened your eyes for a moment. If you gave *us* a chance. We could have all you ever dreamed of. A home, a family, love. There is nothing I wouldn't do for you."

"Wh-what?" My mouth parted, not ready for him to say the words out loud, though I already knew how he felt about me.

He pulled a small object out of his pocket. My attention landing on a familiar jade stone in his palm, he had gotten me when we were kids. I had left it behind when I departed, probably thinking I would be coming back.

"Remember when I got this for you? Gods we were so young. But even then, I knew." He smiled fondly at the small trinket. "I've been carrying this with me forever now. Waiting until the right moment to give back to you." He squared his shoulders, his violet eyes setting on me. "Kitty-

Kat..." He tugged me closer. "You are the first girl I have ever loved... you are the *only* girl I will love."

"Kill—"

He cut me off, his hand cupping the back of my head, pulling me to him. His mouth came down on mine, his soft lips devouring, parting my lips with his tongue.

My brain went into shock.

This is my buddy, my best friend... kissing me.

There were moments I imagined us together, but something always stopped me. He was family to me, something I held far more sacred than a lover. Those were easy to throw away.

His mouth moved hungrily, and for a moment, I let myself believe we could be more. That I could give up my revenge to find peace and happiness with Killian. That I could love him.

But my heart knew I couldn't, not the way he wanted.

"Killian." I pushed away, shaking. "Stop."

His frame stiffened, his head jerking back.

"You are my best friend. A brother to me."

"A brother..." His jaw crunched down, his nose flaring, his fist curling around the gem in his hand.

"Feelings only mess everything up. You know that. That's why the crew never crosses the line." It was one of my rules, unless they came in a mated couple like Polly and Dobbs.

"Crew?" he spat, his arm flying out motioning in the direction of where the rest of the group was. "I'm not just fucking crew, Kat," he bellowed. "Who was the one who came to find you, stood by your side through all the ups and downs? Who watched you fuck your way through each port? Who always has your back?"

"So, you think you deserve sex for that?"

"Oh, my gods." He gripped his head in frustration. "You are so daft. So single-minded in your lust to get Croygen that

25

you can't see anything else, even if you hurt those who love you the most. Don't you want more than this?"

"Yes!" I spat. "That's what I've been working toward. I want everything."

"No, you want revenge. That's not everything."

"I want to live free, to experience life. To have wealth we never dreamed of, to have power, to have it all. To live by no one's rules as we sail the seas. I'm tired of being broke, barely getting by day by day. Being some poor man's wife or raising a family doesn't interest me. I want *more*, Killian. I thought you did too."

He jerked back like I punched him.

"I didn't mean—"

"No. I get it. I'm not wealthy enough to love or fuck."

"That's not what I meant!"

"That's exactly what you meant." He took another step back from me, his expression tight. "I have loved you for so long, thinking one day you'd look up and see me. But no matter what, I was never going to be good enough for you…"

"Kill, that's not true."

"Your fixation on Croygen? It never went away, did it?"

"What does that mean?"

"It means you were pining after him when we were young and still are today. And not because you hate him. Shit, Kat, you stole his favorite leather coat and treat it as your most cherished possession."

Even living on the street, that jacket was the one thing I held on to no matter what. A reminder of what he did, what I lost, and who I would avenge. I fantasized about when we finally battled face-to-face. I'd be wearing his coat, and he would understand the meaning as he died by my hand.

"I mean, he's all you ever talk about, then and now." Killian shook his head. "While I've been the poor pathetic boy running after you, hoping for any scraps you throw my way."

"Killian… that's not true at all."

"Yes, it is." He dipped his head like he had made a decision. "I can't do this anymore."

"Do what?" Panic fluttered up into my lungs.

"Be this guy." He inched farther away from me.

"What? Be my friend?" My voice dropped in terror, feeling like the ground under my feet was being pulled away. I could always count on Killian. He was all I really had in this world anymore. "You are my family."

"No, I'm the rug under your feet." He shook his head. "I love you, Kat. So much. It's why I have to leave."

"What?" Terror pitched through me. "Don't you *dare* leave! We can talk about this."

"I'm done talking. I'm done watching from the sidelines." He headed for the stairs.

"Killian?"

"One day you'll come crawling to me, when I'm the one swimming in riches and power." He paused on the top step. "Bye, Kat. Hope you find him, get all you dreamed of." Killian went down the stairs, leaving me frozen in utter shock. The idea of Killian leaving me had never crossed my mind. Panic and terror bubbled up, running after him.

"Killian!" A sob racked through my vocal cords. "Killian!" I tore through the hollowed-out building, ignoring the rest of the crew by the fire pit, who peered at me with curiosity.

Could I love him? What if I tried?

I followed his scent, screaming his name. As fast as I was, Killian had learned to be faster, his powers sometimes astounding me.

Dashing out into the street, I looked around. "Killian?"

No, no, no… don't leave me. I'll give us a chance!

He was my lifeline. The one who kept me together.

Circling around, desperation and grief heaved my body when I could no longer feel him near.

Killian was gone, and something in my gut told me it was for good.

Collapsing on the cement, I sobbed, my wails curving my body over itself.

My best friend had left me. My father was dead. I had nothing and no one.

It was only me.

Maybe I could have loved Killian. Perhaps this is what I need to figure out. Killian deserved so much happiness, but I could not give him what he wanted right now.

After my father died, my heart perished with him. It was empty and cold. It craved vengeance. It sought the blood of my victim to fill it again, to pump life into my veins.

I couldn't love anyone until I fulfilled my vow to my father. +Until Croygen became another victim to the Davy Jones's locker.

I would not rest.

I would become the most ruthless pirate, and I would seek my revenge.

Chapter 4
Croygen
Two years after departure

The muggy air made my shirt cling to my skin, the fans overhead and the slight breeze from the ocean doing little to ebb the stuffy heat in the packed tavern. A large figure crashed against my table, forcing me to grab my drink before it spilled. His attacker appeared, peeling him off and punching him again, flinging his body onto another table across from me.

The fight was probably over something stupid. No one here, including the bartender, would stop it. Let them wear each other out until they both forgot why they were brawling in the first place.

Or kill each other.

Either option was probable. Especially here.

"Fuck off, bloody eejit," the giant bearded Scotsman across from me muttered into his cup, scowling at the men. "Was shit this bad back then?"

"It was worse," I replied. "We were just a hell of a lot younger then. We *were* those assholes." I motioned to the pair.

Scot snorted into his drink. "Yeah, I remember skelping ya pretty good."

"Think your memory is faulty, my friend." I rolled my shoulders, settling into my chair.

The Scotsman was probably the only person I trusted out here. He had been with me for a long time. His alliance to me had never wavered, which was rare in this profession as a "tradesman." Even when I disappeared, giving up piracy after the fall of the Golden Era when pirates like Blackbeard, Ned Lowe, and Sam Bellamy reigned over the high seas. I took a sip of whiskey, trying to appear relaxed like I was any other person enjoying the evening, though I was aware of everything here. Shifting under my dark lashes, my gaze darted around the space, keeping tabs on every single person and interaction.

This wasn't a place tourists would find themselves since the island of Salt Cray, part of the Turks and Caicos Islands, had become the new "Port Royal" for the modern wave of pirates. It ballooned after the wall between Earth and the Otherworld fell. Human technology crashed, and fae were now known to humans, throwing the world into chaos.

Chaos was fertilizer for piracy. A vacuum in our world that was ripe to take advantage of. Should my connection to the rulers of the Unified Nations make me feel guilty about doing so? If it did, I drank it away, as staying in the neutral area was my nature. This territory was still owned by the British, which was under the umbrella of Lars and Kennedy, but separate enough to give me the excuse I was just helping Lars *distribute* his new technology to a wider audience across the globe.

I was a pirate, and I needed to remember that, and not who I was before I got domesticated by Zoey and the rest.

When I left piracy, lost and alone, I met a woman I considered my soulmate. For a long time, I pursued her. Did *anything* for her, convinced she would see it too and love me. Little did I know she not only loved someone else, but someone I now considered a friend. She was such a con artist it took me centuries to see through her shit. She twisted me up so much, but I kept going back for more.

"Never again," I muttered into my drink, taking another swig.

Amara had found me when I was at my worst. I had recently lost my ship, my crew, and my reputation. Everything I had known was gone. She had made me believe I was everything I thought I lacked at that time. I fell for her hook, line, and sinker, trailing her and her lover, Ryker, constantly being her whipping boy in all her schemes. It wasn't until I met Zoey that I started to see clearly. Though Ryker and Zoey were meant to be together, I think I fell in love with Zoey too. At least I fell in love with her friendship, with finding a home, a place where I belonged. For the first time, I truly felt like I had a family with Zoey, Ryker, Annabeth, Wyatt, and even that furball, Sprig.

But it was Lexie who seeded hope in my soul I hadn't possessed in a long time.

Lexie was Zoey's younger foster sister. I met her when she was twelve. She had been through devastating tragedy and loss far beyond her years. My little card shark was feisty and bold. But of course, she was a child. I was protective of her and wanted to keep her safe. I never thought of her as more than that. But over the years, her gaze lingered on me, her teasing got more nuanced, her smile more sensual. Lexie grew into a stunning young woman. I fought it for a long time, but against my will, I started to look at her differently. She was fearless and brave.

For a moment, I believed I could be a good man.

Then I lost everything.

Again.

All the stars in the sky went out. Life held no more joy or wonder. And being around everyone made me feel trapped.

Locked in a cage I couldn't see out of. The only thing I longed for, the only thing putting oxygen in my lungs, was getting back to the sea. Being as far away from that life on land as possible.

Zoey, with her powers, still had a way of finding me, jumping in and checking in every few months, but no amount of pleas turned me around. And after a while she stopped trying, letting me be.

A pirate was not meant to be landlocked. Our *first* love was the ocean, and I made a vow that would be the only love I would ever have.

"Well, if it isn't the infamous Silver Tongue." A huge, blubbery man with bristle-like whiskers stumbled up to our table, drunk. His tusk-like teeth revealed he was a walrus-shifter. "Didn't think you were still around. Funny, I thought you were supposed to be the most revered pirate at one time. How the mighty have fallen."

"I'd shut your trap, *Wally*," Scot sneered, setting down his cup. "*Awa' an bile yer heid.*" *Get lost.*

"You're no longer the king out there," the man slurred, motioning to the docks. "You're nothing. Someone else has your title now."

I can't say my reentry had been smooth. Things had changed a lot since I left, and though piracy had somewhat returned to the Golden Era because of the fall of the fae wall, it still was a modern version. It took me a while to find a crew, regain my sea legs, and start getting my name out there again. To start reminding people why I was once revered.

"Shut. Up." Scot's muscles tensed, his broad shoulders puffing up.

"It's fine." My voice was smooth. The man looked too drunk to pick up on the tightness in my vocal cords. "He has a right to speak freely." I had a casualness about me that put people at ease. Little did they know that was when I struck. "So, who's the man daring to take my title?"

There was only room for a few of us at the top, and I had to ensure my return was known among us thieves.

Wally let out a laugh, sounding like a strange knocking noise. "Oh, you have been gone a while."

My hand gripped tighter around my glass, anger bubbling up my spine. His claim made me feel stupid and out of the loop. Not a sentiment I enjoyed.

The man wobbled, leaning closer, curling his fat fingers for me to do the same, as if he was sharing a secret.

"Captain PIB might have two huge guard dogs around all the time, but she'll cut your throat with the heel of her boot before you can even blink."

Scot tipped back in slight surprise. We weren't sexist; it simply wasn't common for a woman to get into this business. There had been a handful throughout history; most were far superior pirates, but today it was still male-dominated.

Wally glanced over his shoulder, like even speaking would manifest this woman.

"She's ruthless. Most who challenge her have either lost their ship and treasure or did not come back alive." He spat as he talked about this woman. "She's supposed to be as beautiful as she is deadly, and I've heard even her prisoners beg to be in her bed. That her pussy is so magical, they plead for her to take whatever she wants as she fucks them."

Shifting in my seat, a prickle of resentment burned up the back of my throat. That used to be my MO. I could seduce and talk any woman out of her panties. Queens to nuns, duchesses to bar wenches, and everyone in between. The wealthy noble women, bored with their husbands, were the easiest and the most profitable back then. Many would follow me back to the boat, addicted to the high I gave them, wanting to run away with me.

Sex wasn't just sex with me. It was an experience.

Not that I had gotten back to my ways in that area yet. I

still felt dead inside, a shell of the man who used to fuck like it was a sport. And won every time. Sex was a game to the wealthy. Chess. The women weren't idiots; they understood what my play was, and I think they got off on the forbidden by hurting their cheating husbands—at least in their pocketbooks.

I hadn't become celibate by any means, but it was more transactional now. I didn't find much joy in it past the immediate release.

"Why do they call her PIB?" He wiped at his long whiskers, sprouting out like a weedy mustache.

"PIB?" Scot chuckled under his breath. "Yeah, sounds really scary."

"P-I-B," the man spelled out.

"What the fuck does it stand for?"

"Puss In Boots."

A laugh coughed up my lungs. "Like the story?"

"Don't be fooled." The man stumbled again, losing his fight against the drink. "I hear the coat she wears is from the skin of all her dead enemies and the boots she wears can slice people in half."

Scot snorted, shaking his head. The pirate world exaggerated with wild tales, most encouraged by the pirates themselves to spread fear. Blackbeard was good at that. He had tales spun so tall cargo ships would surrender before he got up to them. He got wealthy and didn't have to do a fuckin' thing because his unstable, ruthless reputation was so notorious. Well, that and a little glamour.

Blackbeard had been unseelie. Dark fae, though that had nothing to do with good and evil. Most of the seelie I knew were cruel SOBs. Blackbeard had lost his way at the end, getting too caught up in this alter ego, the very reason for his demise. Born Edward Teach, Blackbeard had been kind of a friend. If pirates had friends.

I still missed that crazy fucker.

34

"So where is this little Puss in Booties?" Scot leaned back in his chair, amused by this tale. "Sounds like my kind of woman."

The man sucked in, peering around nervously. "I wouldn't be saying shit like that."

Scot groaned, rolling his eyes. "Go on your way, Walrus. We don't have time for your fairy tales." He swallowed his whiskey, standing up, probably looking around for a woman he could take his energy out on. With a ship full of men, except my navigator, Tsai, who was ancient even by fae standards, we took advantage of our time on land.

Vane and Zidane were already off somewhere getting their dicks wet, going straight to the brothel when we arrived on shore. Corb and Tsai were left back on watch.

"Don't say I didn't warn you." Walrus downed more of his beer, slopping it on himself. "She rules the high seas in the east. Even the Somali pirates won't fuck with her."

The Scotsman stopped, his gaze darting to mine.

I had no respect for modern-day pirates. We may have been ruthless and cruel in our time, but there was honor among us, respect, democracy on our ships. A sense of pride in our raids. And we tried not to kill if possible. The Somalias were cold-blooded killers. Pitiless. Only greed ruled them. They bowed to no one or nothing.

"Somali pirates?" Scot repeated. "You sure?"

Wally nodded his head, his whiskers moving around nervously.

"Sounds like this pussy has some teeth." I lifted a brow, making Scot chuckle.

"I'm off to find one *without* teeth who can swallow like a sucker fish." Scot strolled toward a group of women who smiled coyly at the giant brute. I was comfortable enough to recognize he was a good-looking man. Most of my crew were, which had us gaining notoriety from the "pirate chasers." They were a group of mainly women who hung around taverns and other places we did, wanting the adrenaline rush we provided as the ultimate bad boys. Bragging rights to say they had been with one of us. We were rock stars of the sea.

"She's got teeth, claws, daggers in her boots, a terrifying crew, and two pit bull-shifters who guard her twenty-four-seven," Wally continued to ramble. "She'd kill you before you even knew it."

Slowly standing, my tall frame towered over the walrus, though he far outweighed me. In a blink, his head slid down onto the table. With my blade at his throat and my palm squashing his head, he puffed a grunt from his throat.

"You ever disrespect me again, or I'm using your blubber to light my lamps this winter." The threat tinged my words, my knife cutting enough into his neck to make him whimper.

"She might control the East *for now*, but *I am* the king of the Western Hemisphere. You understand me?"

He tried to nod, only pushing the blade in deeper. "Y-yes."

"You tell everyone you know that the Silver-Tongue Devil is back," I barked as he grappled for air under the pressure of my blade. "Or I hunt you down and gut you, then feed you to the sharks while you slowly die. You got me?"

"Y-y-yes."

"Say it louder."

"I-I understand!" Warm liquid trickled onto the floor, his piss trailing down his leg.

Disgusted, I pushed away from him, wiping the blood he left on the knife over his shirt, before I slammed the rest of my whiskey down and headed out into the night.

I should have killed him. Showed my irrefutable dominance here. But that had never been my style, though I was afraid times had changed too much while I was gone. The talent of my tongue, whether it be in bed, battle, or politics, wasn't enough anymore.

The water crashed against the shore, and the black flag flying from my mast flapped in the wind. Taking a deep breath, I gazed out at the water when my shoes hit the end of the pier.

I knew what I had to do. It was all I had left.

I would become the king again.

I needed to claim the western trade before I went for the east.

But eventually, the Silver-Tongue Devil would lap up this Puss in Boots.

Chapter 5
Katrina
Present

The Revenge bobbled softly in the bay as I stared off at the city skyline. The rhythmic sounds of the wood flexing and swaying against the bay tide were a siren song. The noises a ship made were familiar, instantly easing my shoulders, which seemed to ride high a lot nowadays.

I was the master of my own ship. The captain. A feared pirate. Notorious around the world.

I had almost everything I ever wanted. But be careful what you wish for.

Not that I would trade it for all the world, but piracy was not the same as it used to be. Modern times had erased much of the charm of pirate life. Most of the East had split off from the Unified Nations, turning it into the Wild West, bringing back a taste of the old world. However, pro-magic technology was slowly filtering in from the West.

Now the same black-market devices I may use could be wielded against me. It upped the game a lot and had you looking over your shoulder, constantly worried you were about to step into a trap. My crew members were the only people I trusted, and to be honest, I didn't completely trust all of them.

There wasn't a day I didn't miss Killian, probably the only person besides my father who I had trusted implicitly. I thought about him a lot, wondering where he was and what he was doing. I hoped he was happy. He wasn't meant for this life. Not like me. It was in my blood. In my DNA.

My lust for revenge, my need to be the greatest pirate, overshadowed everything—including him. And as much as I loved him, missed him, and wondered if I should have run after him, I knew I had made the right choice.

I was a pirate, not a wife. My only love was the sea. And I vowed to keep it that way.

I used my time on land to let off steam while robbing another wealthy aristocrat blind. Being a cat-shifter came with perks. I actually did have a magical pussy. An aphrodisiac, lulling them into a deep sleep after the best sex of their life. Though most didn't even begin to scratch the itch for me. One that was always there, never quite satisfied.

"Captain?" Gage's voice came up behind me, and I turned to see him reboard *The Revenge*. "President Tanvik has arrived. They are done packing the carriages. Both Ruby and Dobbs confirmed seeing the box being loaded into the second carriage." Gage moved behind me, where I leaned on the railing of my ship, staring at the dull lights of Singapore. Once a grand metropolitan city, bright with electric lights and high-rises, it was now a shadow of itself after the fall of the barrier. The magic from the Otherworld destroyed all the human technology, sliding us back in time. The Unified Nations under King Lars and Queen Kennedy were flourishing with new technology, while the East seemed to fall more and more into the Dark Ages.

The Emperor of Singapore walled himself up in luxury as the rest of the city fell into disarray. Only a few dozen firebulbs burned through the city, giving the once beautiful place a seedy, shabby feel.

"India's president is in a caravan. Two carriages, moving toward the emperor's grounds. We need to strike before they get to the palace."

President. What a joke. The title was a false flag so the citizens would believe they still had a say in their ruler. Yet so many seemed to happily comply after the Fae War, willing to forgo their rights for a so-called strong ruler. Humans were so scared of fae rule that they chose dictatorship with humans, thinking it was better.

Idiots.

It didn't take long for the corruption to seep in. Most of the ruling class doing dirty deals to keep their positions, throwing their own people under the bus, letting them starve and die so they could stay on top.

Only five years since the wall between Earth and the Otherworld dropped, and this new meshed world was in utter chaos and division. It presented an opportunity for rulers to give up all democratic notions, taking control and dividing most of the countries that seceded from the Unified Nations between fae and human rule. It was a battle every day, and no one was winning. Human leaders formed alliances with those they might have considered enemies at one time.

Politics was a dirty, deceitful, corrupt, disgusting business… and that was coming from *a pirate.*

President Tanvik from India and Emperor Batara were some of the dirtiest.

But it was Batara who was the cruelest.

"Guards?"

"Thirty or so."

"Only?" I paused, a slight alarm triggering. Usually, leaders traveled with legions, paranoid about attacks from those who'd had enough of their tyranny.

"Tanvik has been known to do that. His arrogance has made him think he's invincible."

Something still nettled me, but I pushed on, glancing at my second-in-command. Gage had been with me from the beginning, stepping into Killian's place when he left. Boisterous, touchy, flirty, a pain in the ass, and beyond arrogant. But he was also smart, quick on his feet, and could steer a ship out of the tightest situations. He had my back, never showing his doubt in front of the crew, even if he didn't agree with my decisions.

"Everyone in place?"

"Zuri and Moses are in position." Gage nodded. Zuri was Swahili and Dutch, giving her an appearance as unique as mine. As an earth fairy, she had a connection to the land like no other, able to track and feel vibrations through the soil. Out on the water, she could sense land days before any of us saw it on the horizon.

Moses was an Egyptian water fairy. These two were my yin and yang, working together but also at each other's throats all the time. They treated each other like brother and sister, their tempers always flaring.

"Polly and Dobbs are set to come around the back," Gage confirmed. "I will join them."

"Ruby?"

"I put Ruby on lookout duty. If anything looks off, she will warn us. The rest are ready at our signal."

I hated little Ruby being anywhere near this, but she was not staying back. The girl might be twelve, but she had been through more than most. She suffered untold loss and hardships before I found her half-starved on the streets.

Something about her fierce nature reminded me of Killian at the same age. That was why I brought her on the ship and made her part of the crew like Croygen had with Killian.

41

My lip lifted in a snarl. I would not allow myself any positive thoughts of the man who destroyed my life.

I gave the skyline one more glance. Tonight could be the night I went down in history, stealing a fortune no one could even fathom in this day and age.

"Okay, let's go."

Gage nodded, tension in his face. He was nervous—and rightfully so. Emperor Batara was known for his sadistic ways. He didn't just kill. He made criminals an example, torturing them in the slowest, nastiest way possible in the city square. He ruled with an iron fist, and one of the human leaders who thrived in this new world because there was no freedom here anymore.

Those who visited him were forced to bestow riches on a man who already owned the entire country. He did not understand or care about the poverty and devastation right outside his palace walls. He barely ever ventured out.

It was a risk, but I didn't get to be a revered pirate for not taking chances. And this was a gold mine.

I peered over at the twins, who were never far away from me, giving them a nod. They instantly moved out and off *The Revenge*, sniffing at the air, their weapons loaded, ready to fight or protect me at any cost. The dog-shifters were both at least six feet, three inches, with beefed-up physiques, dark-brown mohawks, and covered in tattoos, piercings, and scars.

Sexy, but fucking frightening too. And their bite was far worse than their bark. They didn't talk much, but when they did, their howls had grown men pissing themselves.

Typhoon and Hurricane—Ty and Cane—were pit bull-shifters, but they also had some German shepherd in their genes, which made them superb fighters and protectors. I had "saved" them from a trading ship, which carried rare fae to be put into underground fighting rings. They had been starved, beaten, and abused.

The pirate carrying that cargo was a nasty piece of shit. No one seemed to be able to bring him down, even the deadly Somali pirates. Until me. I relieved him of his duties, his cargo, and his life.

After that, Ty and Cane pledged their alliance to me. They were fierce, deadly, threatening, and utterly faithful to me. Just the sight of them had people running away. And with so many out to get me now, they were a great asset.

Following behind the twins, I debarked, sneaking up the pier to Singapore's dark and dingy streets. The boys slipped into the alleys, taking lead while Gage took the rear, keeping me in the middle. The four of us glided effortlessly through the darkness, unseen. Tonight was a risky mission. The foreign rulers were always well guarded as their caravan would be burdened with money, jewels, and art, as well as gadgets from the West.

President Tanvik was supposed to be carrying a rare diamond. The worth would set up my crew and their families for the rest of our lives and turn us into living legends. We hoped to relieve him of this heavy burden before they reached the gates.

My tall lace-up boots moved quietly across the pavement, my long leather jacket flowing behind me. Both were prized possessions because one reminded me what this all was for, and the other kept me on the path toward it.

A neigh from a horse and the creak of carriage wheels clattered down the alley to us, letting me know how close they were. When cars became useless metal scraps after the barrier fell, we reverted to horses and buggies. Trains didn't even work. I heard the king of the Western Hemisphere was working on getting transportation up and running in his country, but we were in the Dark Ages here, making it a haven for thieves.

Ty peered out of the alley, giving his brother a look

before he darted across the lane to the other side. Cane moved one alley over from his, and Gage was down a few from us, spreading us around the approaching caravan in a circle, closing them in from all sides.

Down the dim lane, the two carriages were surrounded by guards. With what Tanvik was carrying—such a renowned jewel—you'd think he'd have his entire military. Maybe he thought he was untouchable or that it was better to slip under the radar, not gaining as much notice, but my intuition prickled at the back of my neck.

"It will never steer you wrong if you learn to trust it. Hone it." A voice whispered from deep in my memories, causing me to shake my head, resentment and anger taking its place.

The prize at the end of this was too much to turn away from because *I* was the one being paranoid.

The clicks of horseshoes drew near, and the thrill of our ambush hummed magic under my skin. The adrenaline always triggered my need to shift, but I learned to restrain myself over the years. The humiliation of that day when I was young still echoed through me. Scarred me. I was now so in control of my feline side that I never shifted unless I determined it so.

Anticipation hung in the air, the twins waiting for my signal. One nod from me and there would be no turning back.

The carriages were so close. My moment was now.

The knot in my gut tightened. I brushed it away, giving my men a clear nod. No turning back.

Typhoon slipped out, his blade silently crossing a guard's neck, making him a sacrificial lamb as Hurricane and I came from the other side, doing the same. Moses and Zuri advanced from the opposite side while Gage, Polly, and Dobbs approached from behind, eliminating more of his soldiers, stopping the horses and closing in around them.

It was a few seconds before the guards realized what was

happening. Their comrades fell around them, and their warning resonated in the air like bells, screaming of an attack.

My gaze caught on one soldier lying on the street whose helmet had fallen off. Apprehension shot my attention to all the guards, and I picked up on more details. The men were not Indian; they looked to be from here.

Were these Emperor Batara's men? Where were Tanvik's soldiers? Why wouldn't he bring his own? Leaders never left their land without their own troops.

I had no time to think, my sword clanking against three guards coming at me. Twirling and stabbing, my movements were ingrained in me. Master Yukimura's lessons were as much a part of me as my cat was.

Gunfire popped in the air, accompanied by the clank of swords and screams of death. Blood sprayed across my face as I slipped closer to the carriage, the three men falling to the ground one by one, my blade dripping with the same red liquid.

"Captain!" Ty moved next to me, cutting through men blocking us from the treasure. "I got you. Go!" He nodded at the first carriage. We learned Tanvik always rode in the first one because so many leaders chose the last carriage; he liked deflecting.

Going for him first would stop his men. His life on the line would entice them to back off so we could take the treasure off their hands easier.

Darting to the carriage door, I ripped it open. A man sat inside dressed in a gold silk embroidered kurta and pants. His wide, fearful eyes met mine, sinking everything to the bottom of my gut.

Oh, fuck.

Although this man's body type was similar to the president's, his white beard was fake, and his youthful eyes and Asian features told me this was not the leader of India.

His features wouldn't be noticed from a thousand yards away.

Deflection.

"No," I whispered under my breath, already beelining for the carriage right behind while Cane dragged the young man from the first one. But holding a knife to his throat wouldn't be the threat we thought it would.

Gage cleared the way to the second carriage. I yanked the door open and spotted the trunk Polly and Dobbs had noticed being loaded on.

Leaping inside, my hands shook because of what I already knew. I flung the top open, dread dropping on me like an anchor, rushing all the air from my lungs.

The box was empty.

My mind couldn't accept what was right before me, that I could be tricked, my ego in denial of my folly. But it was all in front of me.

I hadn't even doubted the intel we got about Tanvik's arrival. He was rumored to have the gem, and bringing it to Batara for an alliance made sense. Everything had been laid before me, and I had gobbled it up, thinking I was getting the drop on them when it all had been a ploy. I was the one fooled. And I lead my crew straight into this ambush.

"This is a trap..." My voice came out softer than I wanted as my plan crumbled like my confidence. I was the best of the best. This wasn't supposed to happen to me, and deep down, a nagging voice told me Croygen would have never let this happen.

Moving to the door, my only thought was getting my men out of there. "Gage... it's a tra—" My words died on my tongue while I climbed out of the carriage, silence surrounding me. There were no sounds of battle, like everyone was frozen in place.

Gage held his knife to a soldier's throat, but his attention was over my head. Twisting around, I followed his gaze to the top of the carriage.

A gasp got trapped in my lungs, acid torching up the back of my mouth.

Batara's principal guard, Gou, stood on top. His curved katana dripped with blood. Gou was a fae who had no problem working for a human if the pay was right. He took a vow of silence a long time ago, but he needed no words. He was notorious for his skill with a blade, rumored to be an old twelfth-century samurai who slaughtered thousands without a thought.

But it wasn't him that curdled terror and grief in my lungs.

Gripped by her neck, Ruby's lifeless body dangled from his hand, her throat cut ear to ear, her dead eyes staring right into me. She was supposed to be safe. The job as scout was away from the fight, but Gou found her.

I swear I could hear her wonder how I let this happen to her. What kind of captain was I to not be there when she needed me? To let her die so brutally. Alone.

My heart screamed out her name, but only a whimper made it to my lips.

Gou's expression didn't change as he chucked her at my feet, his dark, beady eyes locking with mine. His sword, still caked with Ruby's blood, went into the air, and a noise came from the lanes, chilling me to the bone.

Batara's troops flooded in from the alleys. Hundreds of them, their war cry piercing the air.

I had gotten us out of a lot of close calls and tough situations. For once, I knew that would not be the case.

Gage and I glanced at each other, understanding in his eyes too.

"Never go down without a fight." He shrugged, his blade still at the man's throat. "Fight or die trying."

I struggled to swallow.

"For Ruby," he said.

I nodded. "For Ruby."

"Been a hell of a ride, Captain," Gage said before dragging his knife over the man's esophagus, dropping his body, declaring to the rest of my crew and our enemies that we wouldn't go down without a fight.

Turning away from Ruby's body, I swung my sword with a grunt, putting all my emotions into taking down as many as I could with me.

Soon I would be joining her.

Kicking out my leg, the blades in my heeled boots slid out, slicing a man's stomach in half before twisting around and stabbing another. Their gurgling screams barely registered as I onto the next few.

They kept coming, more and more. Even if they were human, there were far more of them than us, nipping at our energy and wearing us down.

A familiar voice bellowed, and I craned my neck to the side. In the darkness, Dobbs went still, his eyes growing wide. Then his head tipped over, falling off his body before the rest of him collapsed to the ground. Gou stood behind him, holding his sword.

He killed two of my crew. My family.

My gaze locked on him.

He was mine.

He disappeared into the throng of moving bodies. As I advanced in his direction, my boots stumbled over Polly's body, her heart stabbed through. So full of life a few hours ago; now her dead eyes stared blankly up at me.

This was all my fault.

I had been set on this mission, determined no matter the danger, like it would finally make me more famous than the Silver-Tongue Devil. His legacy still overshadowed my own;

so blinded by ego, consumed by revenge, I led my family into slaughter.

The itch to shift, to sink down to a small cat and slink away, buzzed over my skin, but my pride would never let me do it. I would die with my crew. Fighting.

In my peripheral vision, a figure moved up next to me, and without fully looking, I knew who it was.

I was a dead woman.

Gou's ancient magic skimmed my skin, his bloodied sword set to kill me.

Fuck.

All my work, all I fought for, and this was how I would die. A bragging right for Emperor Batara that he could bring down the illustrious Puss in Boots, solidifying his power as a pirate hunter. A fae killer. He would be feared and revered.

I couldn't even make a move before Gou's sword twirled in his hand, the handle coming down on my skull with a thunk.

"Captain!" one of my men called for me, but I could no longer see, and sound slipped away like water through your fingers.

Everything went black.

Pain stabbed through my skull, jolting me awake with a groan. It was a moment before I remembered what had happened. Before consciousness slipped back to me, allowing memories of fighting… of death…

Of Ruby, Polly, and Dobbs.

Oh, gods, they were all dead because of me.

My heart lurched against my ribs, forcing a loud gasp to burn up my throat. My nose burned, and I blinked from the light, confused about where I was and that I was alive. Slowly my senses picked up the gilded room around me and the small but stone-faced man standing over me with a bitter-smelling cloth at my nose. His likeness was painted on the portrait over the fireplace and adorned everything in this city.

Terror sunk to the bottom of my gut.

Emperor Batara.

He folded the handkerchief away, stepping back, his gaze rolling over me.

"To finally meet the infamous woman pirate raiding my seas." His timbre, cold and stilted, was woven with fury. Visually, he was nothing special. A small-framed man, he had dark but graying short hair and obsidian eyes set in a face that never showed emotion, never letting you know how much danger you were truly in. I wasn't afraid of humans, but for him, I made an exception.

He had me chained to a chair, the goblin metal leaching into my bones, keeping me from shifting or moving. Goblin metal was the nearest thing to kryptonite a fae had.

"What do they call you? Puss in Boots?" He tugged at the cuffs of his expensive suit. "A vulgar name, but what can I expect from someone like you? The worst scum of the earth."

Not answering, I drifted my eyes over the space. The room was trimmed in gold and draped with rich reds and elaborate chandeliers. Asian-style motif wallpaper, elegant, curved furniture embedded with ivory, and rich handstitched rugs cost three times more than my ship. All fit for an emperor, enjoying his finery while his people starved.

Both exits in the room, plus the window, had two huge guards loaded with weapons stationed at each post. They stood so silently they could have been mistaken for statues.

Even if I could shift into my cat form, I wasn't slipping out so easily. Humans had learned quickly how to level the playing field, how iron ripped magic from faeries, and goblin metal or druid magic basically crippled all fae.

"As you see, there is nowhere to go," Batara spoke, his gaze never leaving mine. I could feel the emptiness behind them. How insignificant my life was to him, which made me wonder why I was here and not dead already. "And if I wanted you dead, you already would be."

"Where is the rest of my crew?" What has left, anyway. I swallowed, my jaw locking so I wouldn't betray my devastation—little Ruby's slit throat, Dobbs's headless body, Polly's dead eyes staring at the sky.

In this line of business, emotions were something you learned to hide, to not let anyone see your weakness. My expression was blank, but my grief tore at my chest.

Were Gage, Typhoon, Hurricane, Zuri, and Moses still alive?

"You are a hard woman to track." Batara moved confidently around the room. "I have some of the best spies in the world, and they still could not pin you down."

I said nothing, my steady gaze watching his every move.

"It's why I had to set up this elaborate affair." He pulled a cigarette out of his silver case in his jacket pocket. "You should be honored. I have never had to put on a show for anyone before." He lit his cigarette, taking a drag. "But I knew you could not resist. To have the notorious *Blue Moon of Josephine,* once worth over 48 million dollars. What is the worth today?" He tipped an eyebrow at me, taking another puff.

"Close to 80 million," I replied.

"Yes." He dipped his head. "What a thief could do with that kind of money."

"Yes, like help feed the starving people in this city. Or provide clean water. Rebuild. So many things I would do."

He stabbed out his cigarette, his lids narrowing on mine. "Let's get to the point, shall we?"

"About time."

His jaw twitched, and his shoulder tightened as he approached me.

"You are only alive because I have a deal I wish to present you."

Acid pooled in my stomach. Nothing good came from "deals" with men like him.

"My only son, the heir to all my fortune and title…" Batara inhaled, and for one second, I thought emotion crossed his eyes, but it was gone before I could blink.

Batara had several daughters, but only one son. And in this sexist, misogynistic world humans still clung to, it was his son who would get everything. Not his daughters.

"My son is not well." His jaw clenched, and I could tell how much he hated exposing this flaw to me. "Since he was a boy, he has battled leukemia."

I schooled my expression. This was news to me. His son, though sixteen, had never been photographed or caught outside the city walls. Now I knew why.

"We thought we cured it, but it has come back."

My mouth stayed firmly closed, and I wondered why he was sharing this and what it had to do with me.

"Your name has come up over and over as the best in the world to find lost treasure."

"You want me to find you treasure?" I blinked at him. "You don't have enough money to pay for treatment here? That gold statue could buy the entire hospital." I gestured with my head; my hands still pinned behind me.

"You see, this treasure is not gold or jewels." A strange look glinted in his eyes. "It is *far* more valuable than all the diamonds and money in the world." He came closer to me, his voice dropping very low. "Especially to us humans. Especially to my son, who is no longer responding to treatments."

My mouth was ready to get sassy, to say something smart-assed back, but I couldn't forget who he was, what he was capable of. And though it pissed me off to no end, I didn't have Croygen's silver-tongued ways. He could say anything and get away with it. My strengths were in other areas. I wasn't going to sleep with Batara, and I couldn't kill him right now.

"Being fae, you are aware of the power of fae food." He strolled slowly to his desk.

"Yes, but it was all destroyed when the wall fell." Before our worlds collided, if humans found their way into the Otherworld and ate or drank fae food, they could never eat human food again. Nothing else but fae food would satisfy them, pouring magic into their system. It became an addiction. All they craved. They would slowly go insane without it if they went back to Earth's realm, starving themselves until they died. The upside was that eating fae magic turned them more fae-like. They were cured of all diseases and sicknesses, lived for centuries, and were much less fragile than humans.

All pure fae food was lost when the barrier dropped. Humans who heard this tale had been searching the globe for something like it, coming up empty.

"You know it doesn't exist anymore. It won't help your son."

He pressed his fingers into the top of his desk, taking another breath. "What if something is out there like it?"

"Like fae food?" I shook my head. "There's not. Nothing survived. Earth nullified all that type of magic."

He cleared his throat. "There are whispers about an object found after the Fae War, which bestowed humans with immortality, strength, and magic. Curing them of disease and weakness. In other words, it turned them fae without the side effects."

"It sounds like wishful thinking to me, a fairy tale, and I live in a world of myths and legends."

"There is a scientist who is convinced it is real."

"Then he's a quack."

"I do not believe he is, and he is not the only one claiming its authenticity," Batara stated. "I believe it is real.

You will find this object." A muscle twitched in his cheek, anger flaring his nose. "And bring it back to me."

"You want me to find something that is nothing more than a story? That might not exist?"

"This is not up for negotiation. Your survival depends on it."

My catlike eyes glided over the room, my magic pushing against the goblin metal, feeling the threat to my life rising. Did I have enough energy to shift? To escape all the obstacles and slip out of this room? I couldn't hide under the sofa forever, and no doors were open to get away.

"I see we are still hesitant. Then let me raise the stakes. A ship is essential to a pirate, is it not?" A smug smile hinted on his face as he grabbed a folder out of his desk.

Bile burned up the back of my throat.

"Your ship, *The Revenge*, is now being boarded by my men." His dark eyes met mine. "I'm holding it as collateral."

"What?" My heart sank. It wasn't just a ship to me. It was a symbol of my success. My home. My entire world. It carried everything which meant anything to me. The last letters my father ever wrote me before he was murdered. A necklace from my mother. "You can't take my ship!"

"I just did."

"How the hell do you expect me to find this object for you, then?"

He strolled to me with the file in his hand. "I will allow you the use of one of my boats." I flinched at the term *boat*. It was always obvious who didn't breathe the sea air in their lungs as they used those terms interchangeably.

"My crew?"

"They are also being held as insurance."

"What?"

"Those who lived anyway." He smirked. "Though with every moment you hesitate, the other five will be the ones who are penalized. Brutally."

Fear and dread slid over my skin, ramming my pulse in my ears, my stomach rolling with vomit. Yet I hung on the number. Five were still alive.

"You will be crewed with *my men*." Batara tilted his head with a cruel grin. "I need to know you will stay on task, *Puss*." His gaze ran over me as if he suddenly realized I was a woman. He was notorious for his concubines and not being very nice to them. "So you won't do something foolish." He leaned into my face. "I hold everything you have. And if you have any doubt, I will take it all from you if you disappoint me." He stood fully up, nodding at a guard near the door.

The buff man walked up, a piece of cloth in his hand, and placed it in Batara's.

Batara peeled the fabric apart, lowering it for me to see clearly.

My stomach knotted, my throat tightening. I had seen a lot in my time. Death up close was brutal and pitiless. I had learned to curb my gag reflexes. But laying on top of the handkerchief was part of a bloody ear, with an earring I recognized.

Gage's.

At least I knew he was alive, and Zuri, Moses, and the twins were captured too.

"A token for you to remember what is at stake," the emperor stated. "I need your vow that you will locate the object for me."

My throat dipped, going dry. Promises and vows were binding with fae. And he knew it.

"Pirates pull in a big crowd when I publicly execute them," he threatened. No doubt he would torture and kill the rest of my family.

"They are to stay unhurt and safe?"

"If you get me what I want. Yes. Everything will be returned to you. And I will look away when I hear of your raids in the future."

There was no choice here, but the words struggled on my tongue.

"I-I promise."

Smugness filled his eyes as he moved in very close to me. "I own you now. Your life, your ship, and your men depend on you to locate it and bring it back to me."

"What am I even trying to find?"

"A magical *nectar*."

Chapter 6
Katrina

Crates of food and supplies were being loaded onto the emperor's gaff cutter. The ship was smaller than mine. Fast, but it resembled every other ship out there. Batara wanted my voyage to be covert. To appear as an average trading ship passing through, covering up my real objective.

Finding this nectar.

Batara's information didn't include exactly where in China it was supposedly located. It was a big country, and he didn't have much to go on. All Batara told me was the first stop would be Hong Kong. From there, I had to figure it out.

What the hell had I gotten myself into? What the hell was this nectar, anyway? How did you even know what to look for? The chances of finding it were slim to none...if it even existed.

And everything was riding on it.

"Shit," I muttered to myself, sensing eyes on me, my skin bristling.

One of Batara's men stood not too far away, openly observing me, his aura screaming he would slice my throat at any moment if I blinked wrong. And I had no doubt he had orders to do just that. I could see no way out of this for me and would most likely be killed in the end.

Even with all I worked for, all I sacrificed, I would never fulfill my purpose—to avenge my father. I would die knowing Croygen was still out there, alive. I could think of nothing worse or more cowardly than a man turning on a friend, his first mate. My dad had been nothing but faithful to him.

The thought of my own crew burned tears behind my lids, but I blinked them back, knowing better than to show emotion. Privately, I mourned the ones I lost and set all my determination on saving the ones still alive.

Another of Batara's look-alike men yanked the plank from the pier, nodding curtly at me behind the helm.

Fear trickled over my skin, my body itching to shift, but I shoved it back. The moment I pulled out of this bay, my safety would fall to the depths of Davy Jones's locker.

They could do anything to me. I was at the whim of Batara and how much "freedom" he was giving these men to keep me in line. And because of my binding vow, I had to continue forward.

Released from the docks, the gaff cutter glided out of port. My gaze twisted to the side, taking in the last glimpses of *The Revenge*. The ship was breathtaking, the epitome of a pirate ship, the black flag with crossbones flapping in the wind. I could feel it looking back, wondering why I was abandoning it.

My heart ached. That ship was my soul. My blood, sweat, and tears.

And now it was being held hostage, like my crew.

Swallowing, I coasted the cutter out of the harbor and into the bay. The dozen men Batara sent with me worked the rigs, preparing the main sail or setting up below, with two staying to watch over me.

With Hong Kong being my only lead, I set my navigation toward the east, the wind blowing my hair back, the smell of the ocean the only thing calming my thumping heart. In all the different scenarios Gage and I came up with for the mission earlier, this was not an outcome I imagined: sailing to China in the dead of night to find a nectar to save the emperor's dying son.

The dim city lights grew further away, unsettling me. The possibility of never seeing my men or ship again blurred my vision for a moment. The weight on my shoulders pressed down on me as we headed into a stretch of the Singapore Strait renowned for being the most dangerous here. The Somali pirates waited to pounce on the heavily laden merchant ships not far from Batam Island. Normally, they left me alone when *The Revenge* came into port. But in this merchant gaff cutter, we were easy prey. A newborn calf walking into a lion's den.

Keeping most of our sails down until we hit the open ocean, we slowly coasted through the still waters. A strange shiver ran down my spine. Deep into the witching hours, my body was tense; my ears perked at every movement and noise. My intuition was honed, my senses high. As much as I despised Croygen, he taught me a lot about trusting my instincts and believing what my gut told me.

"Come here, little Katze." A memory came to me of the captain motioning for me to stand at the helm, calling me the way my father did. I was no older than six, on a night much like this, clear, warm, and still. *"Take the wheel."*

"Really?" My eyes opened wide, and I ran up to him, not giving him the chance to take it back. *"I want to be a pirate just like you."*

"Just like me, huh?" His eyebrow tipped up, a corked smile lifting his lip. *"How about you become an even better pirate?"*

59

I blinked in awe, my little girl mind thinking no one in the world was better than him.

"Do you know what a good pirate has to have?"

"A ship?"

He let out a laugh, the sound making me smile wide.

"That helps." He crouched down. "But you know what makes a pirate better than others?"

I shook my head.

"This." He tapped at my chest and stomach. "Instinct and intuition."

"In-tow-u-sian?" I tried to repeat his word.

"You know that sensation in your tummy when you feel something but can't see it? When you get prickles over your body and get scared? Like it's trying to warn you of something?"

I nodded.

"That is your intuition. Your gut telling you something is off. Sometimes your eyes can't see. Our vision can trick us, but your hearing, your sense of smell, little Katze..." He touched the end of my nose softly. "It will lead you. Your cat instincts will make you an incredible pirate. Even better than me. It will never steer you wrong if you learn to trust it. Hone it."

I had worked a long time to perceive things my senses had yet to pick up, to acknowledge the nip at the back of my neck, a bitter smell of danger in the air like a fragrance, an itch crawling over me.

As it was doing now. My skin slithered with awareness of a threat as our cutter slipped deeper into the strait. The land on either side was filled with darkness and hideaways.

The hair on the back of my neck prickled as the high-pitched whine of a shoddy motor powered by a homemade battery filled the air. Since standard engines no longer worked, we had to come up with solutions and a means to propel our boats at faster speeds than wind.

The Somali pirates were the first to covet the idea of using makeshift batteries. They would come in as a horde, a handful of small boats, spreading out and surrounding their target, boarding the ship on all sides like an infestation.

The buzz of their familiar motors echoed in the dark now, heading toward us.

"Fuck." I curved the wheel to take us closer to the shoreline, hoping to give us a little more time and only one side to attack. "Somali pirates coming in on the starboard side! Load the cannons and be ready to fire!" I yelled at the men because we were sitting ducks. The breeze was low tonight, and we weren't far enough to pick up much speed.

Batara's men took my order, some pulling out their automatic rifles and lining up along the side while others darted to the cannon room below. We only had four cannons, two on each side, leaving the front and back exposed. If they got too close, the cannons would be useless anyway, volleying far beyond the danger.

That's what the Somalis were trying to achieve. Get close before we could use our cannons on them.

The wail of the boats grew closer, my heart hammering in my chest as I tried to steer the ship, getting us near the shore where we would only be vulnerable on one side but also not run us aground.

Bangbangbangbang!

A rip of bullets echoed in the night, pinging off the ship and tearing into the wood. Batara's men fired back at the shadowy shapes on the water, but with every second, they got closer, some even approaching the bow and the stern of our ship.

Boooom!

A cannon thundered from below, firing into the darkness, blasting my eardrums. The splash of water as it crashed into the bay told me it missed. Cannons were hard to aim, and if you didn't know what you were doing, they could be very dangerous.

I had no trust these men had a clue how to actually fight pirates. They were trained to protect and kill with their hands and legs, but this was a different kind of combat.

My fingers gripped the helm, trying to keep us steady as we skimmed the rocks underneath. I was good at sailing, but Gage was the one who could weave us through every dangerous spot with his eyes closed. I preferred to be out with my crew, fighting. It gave me a better understanding of everything going on and how to react.

Batara left me weaponless, providing me with a crew who had no clue what they were doing against pirates who would slice our throats without a thought.

Bullets pelted the air, the sounds of battery-operated motors zooming around to the port side. Their tiny boats were able to go into shallow water, while we couldn't.

I cranked the wheel the opposite way, trying to pull away and prevent them from gaining access. Up ahead, a schooner glided toward us, probably already aware they were about to be in the middle of a raid and were trying to get around us and the hell out of the way.

Booom!

Another cannonball shot out, walloping the water, which sprayed like a fountain. The pirates had slipped past the line, too close for the cannons to do any damage.

Screams and orders came from below on the port side. I tried to yell at Batara's men, but no one heard me or cared. A crew had to be in sync, have trust, know our plan of defense during an attack and how to adjust in a blink. `No one trusted or respected each other here, everyone taking charge, but no one leading.

Several metal hooks were tossed up from boats below, fastening onto our railing as the pirates climbed up, breaching our ship. Once they reached the top, we would be screwed.

But it wasn't a pirate attack that thumped at my intuition, spearing terror through my gut. Bitterness sat on the back of my tongue, prickles daggering into my neck. I could feel it happening, my ears picking up the sizzle of the cannon being lit below my feet, the muffled clank, the ball jamming within the walls of the barrel.

For a moment, the world went still.

BOOOOOOOOOOM!

The backfire from the cannon exploded from the belly of the ship, tearing through the wood, blasting from the inside out like a back draft and shredding everything into pieces.

The explosion hit my body like a train, punching me off my feet. I flew through the air, losing all my senses as I tumbled, hitting the cold water with a painful slap. Everything went numb, my mind protecting me from the onslaught of agony, making me want to close my eyes and sleep.

I sank, letting go, allowing the darkness to swallow me and lead me where there was peace and no pain. It was always how I thought I'd die, in a battle, my grave far below, at the bottom of the sea.

But imagined I'd go down with *my* ship.

After I honored my father's memory. Avenged him.

"Katze." My father's voice came into my head, speaking to me how he did when I was a child. *"Wake up, my sweet girl. Don't give up. You must fight!"*

My eyes bolted open, the sudden need for air clawing at my lungs, my arms and legs pushing through the water, pulling me up to the surface with a brutal gasp. I tried to breathe in air, greedily sucking it in.

Fire reflected and danced off the water, and debris sprinkled across the bay along with bodies. I took in the wreckage burning a dozen yards from me. The emperor's ship was nothing but firewood, a giant hole in the side allowing water to slowly tug it down, the ship sinking along with most of Batara's men and a lot of the Somali pirates.

I could play it safe. I could swim back to shore, head straight to the emperor, and tell Batara what happened. He'd probably set me up with a new ship and crew within an hour. Locked under his restraints even more. My life on the chopping block. Controlled.

Or…

Play dead. Find this "nectar" on my own.

Along with his crew, he would likely assume I had been blown up, my body eaten by the fish and sharks.

Batara may have said I could have everything back once I returned, but I knew his type. He would continue to hold the crew and my ship over my head or kill me once he got this object. Even if such a thing existed, the only way for me to come out on top was to be the one who found it first, and then I would hold the power.

My attention went to the beautiful schooner I spotted earlier, gliding closer. A handful of shadowy figures perched in the rigging and on the ship's rails, staring at the fiery debris, which was nothing more than a floating tomb.

A smile played on my mouth. While their attention was diverted, how easy would it be for me to climb aboard from behind, shift into my cat form, stow away until they debarked, and slip away into the dead of the night with no one knowing I was even there?

Not like I hadn't done it before.

I was small in life and petite in cat form, making it so easy to hide. My dark, inky coat, which was the same color as my hair, blended with the shadows.

Swimming around, my fingers glided against the ship's rough surface, turning my nails into cat claws and sinking into the rope ladder that dangled from most ships of this nature. They were for those who went overboard, giving them a chance to save themselves and climb back up.

"Fuck, that's a fire. Anyone pack the s'mores?" a man's voice joked as I scaled the rope, my head peeking over the rail. I counted five figures, three at the railing and two up in the rigging.

"Should we check for survivors?" another one with a Scottish accent asked.

"No." A low, deep voice came from the quarterdeck, hidden behind a sail.

A shiver ran down my spine. That one word was filled with power, his voice rich and gravelly, causing the back of my neck to tingle. My instinct pegged him as the captain. His magic and power oozed from him.

Sopping wet, I carefully swung my leg over the rail, my feet softly padding onto the deck. I needed a safe space to shift, then I could tuck myself away.

Men's voices muttered back and forth as I tiptoed behind the wall where the captain's quarters usually were, slipping up to a few large barrels, probably full of gunpowder or fresh water. Tucking myself behind them, I closed my eyes, trying to ebb the stress, pain, and exhaustion from my body, my frame shifting.

My soaked clothes fell into a puddle around me, my wet boots and prized jacket easier to get off as my feline frame wiggled free of the fabric. Leaping up on top of the wooden container, my tail swished back and forth while my gaze darted around, my pointy ears twitching, picking up the men's voices even better. The smell of the sea, of burning wood, oil, and corpses, dominated the air. I jumped down, keeping to the shadows, following the wall to the stairs which led to the rooms below. Below the captain's quarters were private chambers for his high-ranking crew. The cannons took up the rest of that level. The level below would usually house the rest of the crew near the galley, but the crew here seemed bare bones, and the rooms all looked like they were being used. Heading to the kitchen and storage, I went to the farthest corner of the ship toward the bow, curling myself into a little cubby where I would never be noticed.

The explosion had rocked through my bones, and my achy muscles were waking up after the shock. I longed for a ray of sun to curl under, to feel the healing rays heat my black fur and absorb into my body. But I was in a dark, windowless room that smelled of rotting wood and brine. Tucking my tail over my eyes, I wiggled deeper into the little hiding spot, letting sleep take me under.

When I awoke, it took me a moment to remember where I was, my sight cutting through the dimness, making out the clear shapes of the storage room I was in, recalling the ship I stowed away on. Seagulls and lapping waves resounded in my ears. Yawning, I got up and stretched my limbs out, curling my back up and down, my muscles stretching and pulling. I was still sore, but being in my cat form healed me much faster.

Poking my head out of the cubby, my cat ears homed in on any sounds close by. No boots walking overhead or vibrations of a person nearby. Not one indication anyone was on board. The ship tipped back and forth gently, telling me it was not only in shallow water, but probably tied up to a dock.

Slipping out farther, I padded tentatively to the doorway, bits of daylight streaming down from the stairway, appearing deeper in color than I figured for morning. Smells of eggs and bacon drifted from the galley, but I could tell it was no longer fresh, a hint of breakfast still clinging to the surfaces.

Scurrying up the stairs, I got to the cannon and private room level, my heart tapping faster as my eyes took in the purplish-blue glow coming in from the opening to the main deck. *What time was it? How long had I slept?* Fae, when severely hurt, went into a coma-like state to heal. It could be hours, weeks, or months, depending on the severity of the injury.

I darted up the last set of stairs, the sun setting far in the west, the evening already stripping the sky of red and oranges, showing I had been asleep for well over fifteen hours.

Panic pushed my limbs faster toward where my clothes were hidden, the window of time to escape crashing down on me. Jumping on top of a barrel, my attention went out to the port the ship was docked in, taking in the skyline of Singapore. My ship was visible in the distance, but my flag had been taken down. The emperor's banner now flapped from the mast, a cruel reminder of what was at stake. He wanted people to know he owned it now. That he took it from me. And if you were a pirate, he'd be coming for you next. I wanted to reclaim it, to sail it right out of here, but I knew I couldn't. He needed to think I was dead. Stealing it back would only bring his fury and army down on me. Plus, I was good, but I couldn't sail it alone.

It was dangerous to reenter Singapore, but I needed supplies, money, and a small one-manned boat to escape Batara's clutches while I regrouped. Singapore was the best place to steal those things.

My attention zoomed around again, peering for any kind of threat or person strolling close to the pier. I closed my lids, taking in a deep breath, my body responding to my order to shift back.

When I reopened my eyes, my naked body was perched on the container, my senses readjusting and centering back into me.

Reaching down behind the barrels, I gathered my clothes, the items reeking of seawater, drying stiffly in the hot weather. Standing up, I pulled them up to my chest.

"I wouldn't move, lass." A gun cocked against the back of my head, terror freezing me in place. "Unless you want to lose more than your *claes*." *Clothes.*

Terror pumped through my veins, the end of the gun

pressing hard into my scalp. How did I miss him? I didn't pick up his scent or hear him.

"Toss your *claes* to the side and put your hands up, lass."

"You have to pay for peep shows in Singapore." I wasn't anywhere near a prude and had been caught naked more times than not. It came with the territory of shifting and leaving your clothes behind, but I wasn't a huge fan. It made me feel vulnerable.

"Looks like the show is making house calls." His Scottish accent revealed he had been away from his motherland for a while. "I said drop 'em." He cranked the safety off, the sound clipping in the back of my ear.

Tossing my boots, jacket, and clothes down onto the deck, I put my hands up. "What are you going to do? Pat me down, checking for weapons?" Batara made sure I had none left.

"From the looks of it, you are a walking one," the Scottish man scoffed. Leaning over, he swiped up my clothes.

"How sweet." I took the chance, turning around to face him, ready to use my figure to get what I wanted… which was to get the hell off this ship.

The tall brute of a man kept his expression locked down, but his throat bobbed as I fully faced him. He was a man you'd stop to do a double-take. Tall, broad, with the signature reddish hair and beard you'd imagine a Scotsman to have. He wasn't the faerie kind of beautiful, but he had the rough, dark fae look. The "I'm a rugged pirate" kind of thing going on. Probably pretty good in bed. Definitely a man I could let off steam with. Maybe more than once.

His gaze went over me, and I let my smile curl over my mouth.

"What are you doing here? I know you ain't some *hoor*, so don't lie to me." He checked the pockets of my pants with one hand, keeping his gun pointed at me with the other. "I didn't see you come aboard. How did you get on here?"

He was probably left behind to guard the ship. But I hadn't smelled or sensed him. How I missed this big guy was beyond me. Maybe the explosion rattled me more than I thought.

A high-pitched call came from far down the pier, momentarily gaining his attention. His shoulders stiffened, and he tossed back my top. "Put that on."

Gladly doing as he said, I pulled the tank over my head. Shifters got used to going without underwear a lot. Just another item we lost too many of. Got expensive.

Boots hit the plank, walking steadily up onto the vessel. Three more men came into view, coming aboard the ship, their heads swinging toward us.

"Well, well." A sexy, dark-haired man sauntered closer, licking his lips. About average height but fit, he appeared in his mid-twenties. He looked Spanish, with dark eyes and hair and a mustache and light scruff. He seemed very aware he was "pretty," his clothes more fashionable than any of the others. I had no idea what he was, but his magic flared off him. "Scotsman, are you hiding her from us? You guys doing some kinky role-playing? Mind if I join?"

"*Haud yer wheesht*, Vane." *Shut up*, the Scotsman muttered. "I found her sneaking around."

"A thief?" Vane's dark eyebrow went up.

"What the hell would she be thieving half naked?" Another man, with a hint of a Jamaican accent, came up next to Vane. Around the same age, slightly taller, his arms rippled with muscles. He had long dreadlocks and dark skin. He was so utterly flawless my eyes kept going back to him. He was rougher than Vane, but even more striking.

"Well, she's stealing my breath away." Vane winked at me, openly gawking. "What a stunning thing you are."

I had played with so many men like him before. Their egos gave me all the fuel I needed to con them.

The third man was a foot taller than the Scot. The least

attractive out of the gorgeous group—he had to be at least half cyclops—the beefy, silent man rose over seven feet, with curly light-brown hair and one large blue eye in the middle of his head. Even with one eye, cyclops were known to have incredible vision and could see far out. The perfect bodyguard, though he did stand out in this area.

"Captain seen her yet?" the Jamaican man asked.

"No, he hasn't returned," the Scotsman replied. "Zidane, put her in the brig." He nodded at the man, giving me the clear impression the Scot was second-in-command.

"How about you put her in my cabin? I will keep her locked up until Captain arrives." Vane drew his tongue over his lip, his gaze rolling over every curve of mine.

The Scotsman shot him a glare. "Captain decides what happens to her."

The man with the dreadlocks, called Zidane, stepped up to me, pulling out his own weapon. "Come on." He grabbed my arm, hauling me to the stairs down to the brig.

My gaze circled around. I knew what I had to do, but that meant leaving two of my most valued items. The long-worn leather jacket, which reminded me every day of my purpose, and my specially designed, knee-length boots, which had blades in the heels—the only weapons I had left.

Turning into a cat and racing off this boat before they could lock me up was my only hope. Brigs were also purposely designed with iron and goblin metal to keep fae confined.

Zidane's hand clutched my arm tightly, and his gun pointed in my direction, making my heart pound.

My lids closed as I exhaled deeply, demanding the change to happen. My bones cracked as I shifted, Zidane losing his grip on me as I transformed in a blink. My four paws landed on the ground with my tank.

"Holy fuck!" he yelled in shock. My feet scrambled away, beelining for the plank.

Bang! Bang!

Bullets cut through the wood near my cat form, forcing me to zigzag and dart in different directions.

"Get her!" a voice yelled, turning back, taking my focus from my escape for one moment.

Just as I tracked, my tiny frame rammed into a wall, or what felt like one, toppling me backward and scattering my brain. Unable to get up fast enough, I felt a man's hand pinch the skin behind my shoulder blades, and he lifted me to his face.

Dark, almond-shaped eyes the color of a moonless night stared into mine, the edges flickering with the stars. They were pure dominance, evoking many feelings.

At one time, I had loved them.

Worshipped them.

Shock knifed through my gut, adrenaline pumping fear into my blood and shifting me from my cat shape to human. The sudden weight between his fingers caused my naked body to crash to the ground at his feet.

"A cat thief." His gaze slid over me, not at all shocked that a naked girl was before him. "How cliché." His voice was deep and smooth, though the power stung my skin like he poured whiskey over me. The timbre stirred up all the things I recalled about him. Calm, sensual, carnal, and slightly cheeky, he could ruin your world in all the right—and wrong—ways. "Do you know what I do to thieves?"

I peered up at the man I had been hunting. The captain who destroyed my life. The pirate who killed my father.

"No, but it can't be any worse than what you do to your friends." I clenched my teeth. All the emotion he whipped up in me turned into abhorrence.

Revenge.

I had finally found him.

My nemesis.

Croygen.

The Silver-Tongue Devil.

71

Chapter 7
Katrina

Dusk outlined his tall physique; the man was even more broad and toned than in my memories. He was a greater thief than I was. The kind who stole your thoughts, your breath, and your sanity. I had forgotten how sensual and rugged he was, my heart pounding at his nearness.

Shadows cast his face in darkness, his eyes sparking like the stars were waking up. He loomed over me, making me feel like I was still a child. A girl easily enraptured by the seductive pirate.

I had experienced his rare moments of kindness, the times he'd teach me something about sailing or fighting, opening my eyes to what the world could offer, the power I could wield. He showed compassion to a young boy starving on the streets, making him part of the crew, giving us both a family, a home, a place in this world.

And then he shattered all my illusions, waking me up to the reality of this world. The cruelty. Not only turning his back on me but murdering my father. Killian had seen Croygen standing over my dad, using my father's own blade to stab him through the heart.

That kind of betrayal was unforgivable.

"Who do you work for?" Croygen tilted his head, his arms folded over his black T-shirt, his long hair knotted back. He wore black boots, cargo pants with a leather belt, and even in this heat, he wore a signature pirate coat, looking modern, but even sexier. "Who sent you here to spy on me?"

"Work for?" I blinked up at him, my hand covering my bare breasts. *Did he not recognize me? Did he not know who I was?*

For a split second, Croygen's eyes dropped to my chest, his nose flaring before he jerked away, searching out behind me.

"Her clothes." He grunted the order at Zidane. He came up beside me, handing me the tank I had left behind when I shifted. Zidane's lids narrowed on me with annoyance.

I swiped the tank from his hand, pulling it on as I stood up, my head only coming to Cryogen's chin.

Tugging the fabric to my thighs, I glowered back at the Devil. "What makes you think I'm not trying to rob you?"

"And where, may I ask, are you stowing away these treasures you are pilfering from me?" The side of Croygen's mouth quirked up, his hand motioning to my mostly naked body, the rest of my clothes still in a pile near the Scotsman. "Will I have to pat you down and make sure you're not hiding anything in secret places?" The tip of his tongue glided over his lip, his gaze sliding over me with a smug smile, letting me know exactly what he would do. "You know they call me the Silver-Tongue Devil for a reason."

A deep, pounding pulse struck between my thighs, heat suffusing my cheeks, my nipples pebbling. My spine went ramrod straight at my body's needy reaction, opposing the disgust seething in my head. At one time, all I wanted was for him to look at me like he did the older women. I didn't understand the simpering looks they shared between them until I was much older—the language of desire, of sex. A wordless consent that left claw marks down his back.

73

Croygen's attention traveled to my breasts, a heated glint flickering in his eyes at my body's response.

Keep calm, Kat. You know the power he has with his words. Play the game he isn't even aware he's in.

He didn't recognize me. The last time he saw me, I was twelve. This could work in my favor. If he discovered my identity, he would figure out why I was here. Take away my advantage of surprise. But if I pretended to be an admirer, easily seduced by him, playing on his ego, I could get close.

Close enough to kill.

Pushing through my aversion, I moved closer to him like I wanted him to search me any way he saw fit. His crew moved with me; their guns raised as if I was some big threat.

I was. But not yet.

"You know who I am, don't you?" Croygen craned his neck to look down at me, not backing away from my nearness, his ego puffing his chest.

"Yes," I purred. The sound was an aphrodisiac, even to fellow fae. "I very much know who you are." Tucking a strand of hair behind my ear, I lowered my gaze, dipping my lashes down coyly. "I'm not working for anyone. I just heard the no-torious Silver-Tongue Devil was in port." I glanced up, subtly biting at my bottom lip, familiar with the power I had over men.

His gaze went to my lips, but he was good enough to hide his emotions. Croygen might know how to play the game, but he wasn't any different from any other arrogant male I had come across in my time.

They all bowed.

"I wanted to see if the legends about you were true." Every seductive word made me feel ill, betraying my father. Betraying myself. I loathed him with every fiber of my being.

Back in the day, Croygen had many women try to sneak onto the ship. Most were found hiding, naked, declaring their love for him as though he was some god. This angle I was playing was completely believable because it had happened all the time.

Croygen's eyes met mine, and the air in my lungs hitched. If it was even possible, he had gotten even more gorgeous since I last saw him. Still, his eyes held a hardness, a seriousness that was never there before. Somehow it made him even more formidable. Thrilling.

I detested him for it.

"So..." He leaned in so close his mouth almost grazed mine, his voice gravelly and low. "You came here to see if I lived up to the hype?" He tucked more hair behind my ear, exposing my neck. Leaning into me, his breath glided down my skin. "If my tongue could lick through you with a verse, make you cry out in prose, provoke a shudder with a sonnet? The *Devil* would only break you in the end... and you'd beg for it."

My skin flushed, my breath struggling to move in and out of my lungs, my body shivering as he whispered roughly against my ear, depriving me of all thought except the desire sparking something deep inside.

He leaned back, his dark gaze going to mine. I didn't move. I didn't respond, unsure what I would do if he touched me.

Something in his eyes flickered, but it was gone before I could figure it out. A slow, arrogant grin pulled up the side of his face, his full lips parting in a scoff. "I'm not that fucking stupid." In a blink, his entire disposition flipped, his expression now cold and guarded. "Corb, pull the gangway." He nodded at the cyclops.

"What?" I exclaimed.

"But we're leaving port," the Scotsman countered.

"Yes." Croygen's focus shifted over to me. "And now she is our prisoner." He started to stroll deeper onto the ship. "Whoever she is spying for will learn not to let their pets roam free."

"You're kidnapping me?" His men moved around me. The huge cyclops he called Corb towed in the small plank, then stood guard, making sure I didn't get away this time.

What the fuck just happened?

"Kidnapping is such a strong term. Picking up a stray is more like it." Croygen lifted a brow at me. "Vane, take her below to the brig. Zid, Scot, Corb, prepare the ship for sail." He turned for the helm. He stopped, his gaze drifting to where Scot picked up the rest of my clothes, pausing on the jacket in the Scotsman's hands.

Fear poured down my throat, sizzling like acid in my stomach.

Would he recognize it? Connect the dots between us?

The jacket I wore, one of my most prized possessions, was his.

The night he sent me away, I took it. Wanting a piece of him, wanting to hurt him, and wanting a reason he would come for me. Hunt me down to claim it back. I naively thought it connected me to him. Like a rope I could hold on to, and he would heave me back in.

He cut that link and left me in a girl's school to rot. Where I was never accepted, even by the teachers. I was beaten, starved, and humiliated daily. I ran away, living on the streets.

That was also the last night I saw my father alive.

That jacket held my revenge like a sponge. My hate was woven in its threads, my hurt absorbed into the lining. With every kill, every rise in the ranks of piracy, I wore it like it would punish Croygen.

His attention went over it briefly before he turned away, showing no recognition of the item he used to wear. It strangely pissed me off. I had held onto it like a battle cry, and he didn't even recollect it was his at one time. Another thing forgotten. Thrown away.

He probably didn't even remember me. If he did, it was a distant memory, something you had to be reminded of, while I lived and breathed him every day. He was the fire in my lungs, the motivation in my veins. I had been planning my retaliation from the moment he kicked me off his ship. And it was nothing to him.

My father. Me. Killian.

We were scribbles in the margins.

Vane grasped my arm, tugging me forward, my gaze catching on Croygen at the helm right before we descended. His feet were wide, his hands on his hips, pushing his coat back away from his body, showing off all the weapons hanging from his belt. His sword, the one Black Beard gifted him was still at his side, reminding me of how many times I used to hold it, pretending to battle foes, and find treasures on the high seas.

My attention went to the smaller weapon above that. My world tipped to the side, my insides feeling as if he just stabbed me with one of them.

On his harness was a gold-hilted dagger, the unique carving and design reflected in the last dying rays of twilight.

I knew it better than anything.

Because it had been my father's.

"Get comfortable, *Bella*." Vane slammed the cage door to the small cell shut, the goblin metal already nipping at my energy. Locking the cell, he clipped the key ring to his belt.

"No food or water, no call to my lawyer?" I glared at him through the bars.

Vane's smile curved over his face, his eyes light with humor, making him even prettier. He shook his head, nearing the bars. "You're a feisty thing, aren't you?"

"Cats have been known to claw and bite."

"Sounds like a good time to me." His eyes floated down my barely clad frame, his intention clear over his features.

"Vane, stop stroking your knob and get your arse up here," Scot bellowed.

Vane smirked, his eyes never leaving me. He didn't feel threatening, just the type that was driven by sex and beautiful things.

"I'll return soon, *Bella*. Maybe you can sharpen those claws on my back later." He winked before walking away, his body lithe as he leaped up the stairs.

I stared blankly at the dim room the brig was in, deep in the ship's bowels, the sounds of the vessel and its crew members setting sail far above me.

Of all the ships in all the oceans, I happened to climb onto Croygen's. The man I had been pursuing since I was a girl. Fate or chance, this was the opportunity I had been dreaming of. Except, of course, it came at the worst time, my oath to Batara weighing heavy in my gut.

My revenge needed to be soon and swift. My promise was already starting to tug on my soul, demanding me to fulfill my obligation the farther I went off course. I had no time to play the long game. I needed to find a way to escape this cage, slice Croygen's throat, and slip away.

The image of Croygen standing on the quarterdeck, his hands on his hips, looking like the pirate I recalled from centuries past, haunted my memories. The one I would stare at in wonder. Dream about. Scribble notes about in my diary. He was even more intimidating, more dominating, than before because whatever youthful joy he had when I knew him was gone now. As if life had broken him.

Good, I thought. Wearing my family's heirloom as a trophy was an insult to the man who had been his faithful servant and friend for years. Pirates weren't known to have true allegiance to people, but in my silly young heart, I believed Croygen was different. That those he let in close were his family.

I was a stupid fool. He had no loyalty to anyone but himself.

He needed to die.

My attention went over the holding cell, my stomach twisting in understanding. I was fucked. The bars on the cage were thick and so close together that even if I could shift, I wouldn't be able to get through them. Only four by seven, the small cell held nothing I could use, just goblin-painted bars and the floor.

The ship rocked forward, swaying the craft freely as it left the pier. Once again, I left this dock as some kind of captive. Except this time, I had little control over what would happen to me. And if Croygen found out who I was, would he duel me? Kill me outright? I thought I once knew him, what he would do, but this man held no honor. He was capable of anything.

"Those who seek darkness only find darkness." A woman's scratchy, accented voice came from behind me, causing me to leap around with a cry.

A short silhouette stood in a doorway at the other end of the room. The figure shuffled slowly toward me. The old woman seemed like she could be a hundred years old if she were human, buried under blankets and shawls until she almost looked hunchbacked. Down in the belly of the beast, it was cooler, but the humidity still sneaked through from outside, yet she still clung to the layers, trying to keep warm.

The small fae woman hobbled up to me, letting me see the details of her face. Round and heavily wrinkled, as if she wore every year of her life, it displayed Asian features. She had only a few teeth left, and her thin gray hair was tied back in a bun. But it was her milky eyes that had me sucking in.

Thick cataracts blinded her completely, turning her entire pupil grayish-white.

"Who are you?" I glanced around, wondering why a ship full of men had this ancient lady tucked down here. "Are you a captive too?"

"Criminal to many, but captive of no one." As she spoke, it sounded like English was not her first language. "My time for being hunted is long past."

"Hunted?" I blinked at the frail thing; nothing about her looked criminal or dangerous in any way. Yes, some could fool me, but she wasn't running away from a threat anytime soon.

"To see me, you wouldn't think so, huh?"

"Sorry, no."

"I was once young and pretty like you."

"How do you know I'm pretty?"

"Youth is beautiful. So many take it for granted. Waste it. Think they are too ugly and fat when one day they will wish for the beauty they once hated." She inched closer to the cage, her white irises burrowing into me. "I may not have my sight, but I can see everything. What has happened, and what is still yet to come. I see…" She tapped at her head. "I know *all*. I see what you are running from, girl. What you seek…"

A flush of fear washed over my cheeks, feeling like she really could see through me. "Are you a seer?"

She moved her face an inch away from the bars, the creepiness of her eyes chilling my skin, and her mouth opened to respond. "Nah, I'm just fucking with you, girl." She cackled like a little kid. "The youth are also really dumb. So gullible and easy to manipulate. Take one look at me and buy that shit hook, line, and sinker!"

I blinked at the sudden turn, my head wagging. "W-who are you?"

"They call me Tsai." She tugged her shawl tighter around her.

"Tsai?" My forehead furrowed. "Why does the name sound familiar? Wasn't there a pirate by that name? Cheung Po Tsai?"

She jerked back, her sightless eyes staring straight at me. Her throat bobbing.

"Tsai? Are you taunting our hostage again?" Vane sprang down the steps, a grin on his face, one hand holding a flask of water. "You freaked out the last guy so bad he pissed himself."

"Fragile little bitch." She snickered, clearly finding it hilarious.

"You are a menace." Vane swung one arm around her shoulder, kissing her head. "Captain needs you on deck."

"Captain needs a good wank too, but I'm not running upstairs to do that for him either," she huffed.

"Then it's only me you offer those to?" Vane playfully winked at me, telling me he was teasing.

Tsai made a noise, her hand batting him away before slowly heading up the stairs to the top deck, her bones creaking along with the wooden steps. I stared after her in bewilderment.

"You get used to her." Vane followed my gaze with a shrug. "She's a handful and can rob anyone blind because they think she's some sweet old lady who needs help to cross the street." You could hear the admiration in his tone. "That woman is ruthless. Complete troublemaker and the best navigator in the world."

"Navigator?" I guffawed. "She's blind."

"She's been sailing the oceans longer than most of us. Knows more than all of us combined. Plus, she doesn't need to physically see the world to know how to get through it. Sometimes instincts are more dependable than sight." Vane's words reminded me of what Croygen taught me so long ago.

"You sound like your captain."

"How would you know what my captain sounds like?" Suspicion drew his brows in.

Oh. Fuck.

"I mean, you sound like *a* captain." I curled my mouth into a flirty smile, hoping to distract his ego from my slipup.

"That's my plan, *Bella*." He moved closer to my cage, licking his lip. "Want to be part of my crew?"

"Let me guess, I'd be first *mate*."

"I promise you will be the first, or at the very least, the second I mate with every night."

I rolled my eyes at his sexual joke.

"Here." He shoved the water between the bars into my hands. I purposely ran my fingers over his, locking eyes with him. In this world, you had to learn everyone's weakness. Money, power, sex, ego, love. It was usually the same few. And Vane's dick was his.

Men were men, fae or human, and you had to work with what you had.

Casually my eyes drifted over to the keys hanging from his belt, the ones that would free me from this cell. If I gained his trust, or at least his lust, and got close enough to him, I could use that.

"Thank you." I took the bottle, staring him down, letting a low vibration come up the back of my throat.

He transferred his weight to his other leg, cupping his pants and adjusting himself. I don't think he realized his response was probably in direct correlation to my purr. At different frequencies, it could calm, attract, frighten, and heal.

"I'll bring you something to eat later." He cleared his throat, his attention heavy on the bare parts of my skin. "And later you can show me your kitty again." He winked, leaving no mistake at which one he meant.

I fought hard not to roll my eyes again. The sexual puns about my "kitty" were endless and never original.

Puss in Boots was supposed to be an insult, which was exactly why I took it on as my moniker. I wanted to claim it, take it back, own the rights to it. To give it a different association. To not let them have the power, belittling me as a pirate.

I made sure anyone overheard trying to disrespect me either dealt with me or had a run-in with Ty and Cane. Unless I decided it, none made it out alive.

My title came with respect and fear now, and only the ignorant or the foolish slighted me.

Only someone as arrogant as Croygen would underestimate me.

Sitting down in the middle of the cell, the only thing I could do was think.

Plan my escape…

Plot my revenge.

The rocking of the ship fluttered my lids closed, and the creaking of the wood surrounding me hushed me to sleep like a lullaby.

My stomach rumbled as I curled up into a ball. My bladder ached, and fatigue from the goblin metal made it hard to stay coherent.

Hours had passed since Vane had left. The silence above told me most of the crew had likely gone to sleep, casting a peacefulness over the ship. By the temper of the sea under me, it was a calm, windless night, allowing the schooner to drift quietly through the darkness.

I was trying to stay awake, to have my wits about me, ready to act out my plan if given the chance. Every pirate ship had a dinghy. A small boat used to run to and from land when the ship couldn't get close enough. That would be my escape plan once I killed Croygen. I'd keep to the shallow waters, far out of their reach. There was a vast probability that his crew would come for me, but they would have to find me first, and if they challenged me later, I would fight them too. My plan was to silently take Croygen's life, slip away into the night, and be long gone before anybody woke. All this hinged on someone coming down here, giving me the opportunity to escape.

As if I summoned him, my ears picked up on the vibration of boots, the tapping of feet hitting stairs. I jolted up, rising to my feet as a figure came down the stairs.

"*Bella.*" Vane grinned at me, holding a plate of food and more water. "Did you think I forgot about you?"

"I didn't know you *could* think." I purred through my sharp tongue. It was hard for me to play the damsel. I never did it well, which was one reason I was punished more often than not at the boarding school.

Vane's smile widened, his gaze dancing around me, strolling up to the bars. "Showing me your claws already, *gata?*" Cat.

"Thought that's what you wanted?" I tilted my head, keeping my voice low and flirty.

Vane scoffed, his gaze swinging back to me, just as playful.

The food in his hand caused my stomach to growl loudly.

"Bet you are hungry."

"And I really have to pee," I replied. "Lack of food, water, bathroom breaks, even a blanket. I can't say you guys will get high ratings from me. My stay here has been less than satisfactory."

"Guess you will have to take it up with management."

"I plan to." Far more than he thought.

Vane held up the plate of food next to the bars,

suggesting I push through and take it. Anxiety prickled at the back of my neck. I needed him to open the cage. That was my only way out of here.

"You don't want to feed me yourself?" Sultry, suggestive, my lids lowered on him.

"I'd rather lick it off you." He flirted back, but he didn't reach for the keys hanging on his belt. "But you'd have to take a bath first, *gata*. Then I'll eat whatever you want." By his impeccable appearance, I could tell he took hygiene to the extreme, which wasn't common in the pirate world. Not that they were dirty like they used to be back in the day. But it wasn't easy living and working on a boat, and you wouldn't look like you came off a runway.

Vane seemed to defy that. Clearly, his name held more than one meaning.

"Then lead me to a bathroom." I moved as close to the bars as I could. "I will be deeply grateful."

"As much as I would love to, *Bella*, I'm under strict orders not to open this door."

An alarm batted against my ribs. Working hard to keep it from showing, I twisted my face in a pout. "Please, I have to go really bad. Just to pee. That's all I ask. Unless you want me to go right here." I looked straight at him. "And I'm figuring it's you who'd have to clean it up." I wrinkled my nose. "Do you really want to clean up cat pee? You know how that strong smell sticks on you." I laid it on thick. It was true, but only in my cat form when I wanted to spray and make my presence clear.

He flinched, his chest rising with disgust at the thought.

"It would never get out of your clothes." I motioned down to him, my legs squeezing together, wiggling around like my bladder was about to explode. "I'm going to pee now if you don't take me to the bathroom."

His forehead wrinkled with doubt, his eyes casting back at the stairs as if the captain would be standing right there.

"Pleeeaassee." I vibrated my voice, not with desire or fear, but calm. To ease his anxiety. The voices in his head were telling him to follow his captain's orders. Glamour didn't work on fellow fae like it did on humans, but the endorphins I put out could take the edge off.

He sucked in, setting the plate of food on the table nearby. "Okay, but I will be with you every step, and if you make one wrong move, I will cut your throat, *Bella*. No matter what the captain said." His expression turned serious, his hand pulling at the keys on his belt. "You understand?"

"Yes." I nodded.

Vane reached down, unclipping the keys from his belt while I continued my charade of being in utter pain. Not that I had to pretend all that much.

The sound of the key turning in the lock soared my heart up into my throat, my muscles locking down. Preparing. Waiting.

Timing was everything

It was a split second. My teeth ground together as my hands wrapped around the toxic metal, gritting back the agony tearing through my limbs as I rammed the door into him with all my might.

The bars smashed into his face, cracking the cartilage in his nose. He stumbled back with a cry, and I pounced, taking his thin, fit body to the ground. My fingers went to a spot on his neck, pressing down. His body thrashed against mine, my thighs clamping down, holding on while he wiggled and grew weaker under me. Pinching the carotid arteries more firmly, I felt his body go lax, falling unconscious under me.

"Your captain taught me that move." I patted Vane's cheek, climbing off him. He was maybe five feet, ten inches and thin, but solid muscle. Straining, I pulled him into the cell, shoving him inside and relieving him of his gun.

"Sorry, pretty boy." I slammed the door and locked it. I

did feel kind of guilty. Vane actually seemed like a nice enough guy. Obnoxiously hypersexual, but that appeared to be just him. The stereotypical Latin lover. But I couldn't allow him to wake up and get to me before I fulfilled my mission. "It's not personal."

But it was personal with Croygen.

Slinking up the stairs, I cautiously listened for any other movement. During the night out at sea, there was usually one who stayed up on watch while the rest slept. At this hour, the one most likely on watch was now locked up in the brig.

The calm lapping of waves kissed the side of the ship, the rigging tapping in rhythm to the very light wind. It was one of those perfect nights. The moon headed west, although dawn was still hours away, and everything was tranquil. Typically, on a night like this, I would stroll quietly, lost in my thoughts, staring off into the dark ocean, watching the moonlight glittering off the water.

My happy place.

But it contradicted with what I was about to do. For centuries, I had been plotting this, waiting for my chance, and it all seemed anticlimactic. I had devised hundreds of scenarios over time, but this wasn't one of them. I didn't come on in battle like some movie, covered in blood, screaming for my father's revenge. I came silently and calmly like a lapping wave, sans pants and underwear and only wearing a tank.

A knot tugged in my stomach as I crept toward the captain's quarters, but I shoved it away. Nothing would stop me now.

My bare toes padded over the wood, slipping up to his door. My skin prickled like I could feel him on the other side, my entire body sensing him. Twisting the knob, my heart leaped when it unlatched. Another thing I knew about Croygen was he never locked his door, the result of a childhood fear of being locked in a room and drowning. Relieved that quirk of his hadn't changed, I opened the door slowly and quietly, using every catlike quality I had, silently entering the room.

A slight squeak barked like an alarm, my body stilling, oxygen holding in my lungs, my gaze darting to the far end of the dark room. My pulse beat in my ears as I scanned the shadows for any movement, my gun ready to fire. But nothing stirred.

Slipping fully inside, I closed the door with a soft click, moving deeper into the room, so glad my sight was excellent in the dark. I captured every detail of Croygen's chamber, and the simplicity of it caught me a little off guard.

He used to love grand things, not a peacock or obnoxious, but he enjoyed the money that flowed in. Croygen's style of clothing had always been low-key; his leather or velvet jackets were his signature pieces. But his room was where he had displayed his wealth. Velvets from Eastern Asia, silks from China, tapestries from Paris. In his quarters, he was king. He used to have a long mahogany table from Spain, filled with drink and food for his guests, a huge sleigh bed dripping in dark silk sheets, and sparkling chandeliers over priceless rugs and art on the walls. It was a lair for his women, intimidation for his competitors, and an insult to the governments trying to bring him down.

But this room was humble. No table for private guests, only an old desk, two chairs, and a wall full of books and charts behind shatterproof glass. There were closets, a door to a private bath, and a platform king bed lined up along the wall of windows, giving stunning views of the sea outside. No silks or tapestries, nothing to suggest Croygen was the king of pirates. Though I would not be fooled. One can change their outfit, but not their spots.

Creeping closer, I spied Croygen asleep on his back, his arm tucked under his pillow, his head turned away from me. The thin white cotton sheet pulled up just above his hips wasn't hiding anything.

Involuntarily my breath sucked in, my body responding to what I was seeing. Heat slid down from my cheeks, pulsing hard between my thighs, making me very aware I had no underwear on. For a moment, I couldn't move, my twelve-year-old crush transforming from innocence to something completely different. Grown-up. Filthy.

Croygen was gorgeous. His face was angular with a sharp jaw; the beard only added to his sensual appearance. His features, especially the shape of his captivating eyes, suggested he had some Asian ancestry, though I knew almost nothing of his childhood, only bits and pieces he let slip over the years.

His body had always been tall and lean, but he had bulked up a lot during our years apart. His muscles corded over his figure, leaving no fat. Tattoos covered his arms and chest, most of them new. My attention trailed down his torso, a deep V-line disappearing under the sheet. His cock, thick, long, and hard, was outlined clearly under the cotton.

My innocence back in the day would have turned me away with an embarrassed squeal. I wished that was how I felt now.

Desire surged, along with the sudden need to climb over him, slide my pussy down his shaft, and ride him until I couldn't breathe. My body trembled at the notion, drowning me in the craving. The yin of my hate battled with the yang of my need.

What the hell was wrong with me?

I had been so enamored with him. Boldly wrote in my diary that I would be the one to marry him. When I grew up, he'd be mine.

Now I was grown up, and the only thing I planned to do was kill him.

Yet, I stood still, watching him and wasting the precious seconds I could have used to execute him and escape.

Out of the corner of my eye, something glinted off the

moonlight. I twisted my head to a hook on my left. Hanging from it were his jacket and belt, which displayed the gold handle of my father's dagger.

All the desire I had experienced a moment ago turned to pure, red-hot rage, coloring my vision. My blood boiled with fury, striking out everything else. Pain and grief set fire in my gut.

It called to me, the perfect end for the pirate. To die by the very blade which killed my father. My revenge complete. Just.

I reached for the dagger with my free hand, the gun in the other, the decorated handle fitting into my palm like it was made for me. Ripping it from its holster, I swung around, ready to bury the blade in Croygen's throat, giving him only a few moments to understand who I was before I sliced his neck all the way through.

I swung with precision, the tip of the blade about to kiss his neck, when the sound of a gun cocked against my ear, a barrel pressing into my forehead.

Shock froze me for a moment, my attention shifting down to the man on the bed. His dark eyes stared into mine, a cheeky smile hinting on his mouth.

As if he had been waiting for me.

"Nuh-uh," he tsked, his throat bobbing against the blade. "Not so fast... *Katze.*"

Chapter 8
Croygen

Sleeping with my door unlocked over the years turned me into a light sleeper. It might be easier to just lock my damn door, but the panic of being trapped inside with no way out harbored in my chest, rattling around like a ghost, the screams that would never go away playing in my mind. A rogue wave took my family—everyone but me—that fateful night. As though I was kept alive to be punished for eternity because I was the one who wasn't trapped in my room. The one who disobeyed his father.

I'd rather sleep light than not at all. Not that I was sleeping tonight. My brain had been buzzing around insistently.

The girl's eyes. So unique and stunning. I remember being entranced by them even when she was a small child. Her face, voice, and mannerisms were altered, but the more I dug into my memories, the more I saw *her*.

I tried to push it away, the tight sensation in my gut, disgusted by what I had said to her, what I was thinking, while my dick was still hard as a rock.

To be fair, I didn't know who she was. Then I saw her jacket. *My* jacket. The one I still tried to match centuries later, never finding anything that fit me like that one had.

I had been furious when it disappeared, ripping the ship apart trying to find it.

Yet I still couldn't reconcile the tiny child I used to know with the woman locked up in my brig now. The one who had my entire body standing on end the moment she rammed into me. Her curves, her face, and her voice... the sultry feline way she moved.

There was no fucking way it was the same girl.

It couldn't be.

That's what I wanted to believe anyway. Especially because she acted like she knew my reputation, but not me. That told me she was a liar or just a common thief. I trusted neither.

But I trusted myself less.

Whatever temptation I felt for the sensual woman needed to be bled from me. I would not let her see she had any power over me. I decided not to go to the brig and find out for sure who she was, no matter how badly I wanted to.

All night I fought against a current, not daring to drink since my inhibitions would crumble. She stirred up old feelings, memories I tried to forget. Guilt and remorse I buried deep.

Lying here, my cock throbbing, I was absolutely repulsed by myself. I tried to go to sleep, ignore the temptation below me.

When my door squeaked open, I was certain it was her. Her magic skated over my skin, twitching my cock with excitement. My mind skimmed back to her thin, muscular legs, her thighs barely hidden under her tank, her hard nipples exposing themselves under the fabric. Her stunning face and eyes, and the hair my fingers twitched to thread through.

My response pumped anger through me. I was sickened by my indecent thoughts. No matter what she had grown up to look like, at one time, Kat was a twelve-year-old I thought of as a niece. A young brat, full of vigor and gumption.

You're a sick fuck, Croygen.

Aware of every move she made toward me, of the heat coming off her, I ground my teeth together.

When she reached for Rotty's blade, she erased all doubt about who she was. She recognized her father's weapon.

The little kitty had come for retribution.

Because I slept with my door unlocked, I always kept a weapon under my pillow.

She swung the knife for my throat. When the blade touched my jugular, I whipped out my gun, cocking it and pressing it to her forehead.

"Not so fast...*Katze.*" I looked into her yellow irises; the vivid green rings around the black pupils widened in shock at her pet name. It was what Rotty called her. "Do you really want to do this? Drop the gun." I nodded to her other hand, swallowing against the blade as it cut into me, surging adrenaline through me. Which only hardened my cock, making it almost unbearable.

Her breath stilled in her lungs. "Ho-how?"

"You think I didn't know who you were?" I fudged the truth a little, acting like I had been one step ahead of her the whole time. "*Katrina Roth.*"

She inhaled sharply, her expression shifting from disbelief to anger.

"Good. Now you know why you are dying tonight." Her voice was low, the vibration rubbing over me like it was her entire body while she pushed the knife in more firmly.

"I don't think you'll do it."

"You want to challenge me, pirate?"

"I prefer to go by tradesman now."

She blinked at me with confusion, hitching a grin to the side of my mouth. "I can pull this trigger before you could even break my skin." I pressed the gun harder to her head. "Drop your weapons and let me get up, or drop the gun, keep the knife, and climb into bed with me. Your choice." The last statement came out of my mouth without thought, and my body stiffened as I tried to act like I didn't just say that to her. What the hell was I thinking? She was a little girl when I last laid eyes on her.

Her nose twitched, her throat bobbing, and for a second, she seemed to consider the options.

"You think you can talk to me like all your other common whores?" she hissed. "That I don't know exactly who *you* are?"

A strange, uncomfortable sensation tightened my gut, the judgment of my past flowing over me.

My nose flared. Pushing against the blade as it cut shallowly into my neck, I sat up, lowering the gun in my hand, my lids narrowing on her. "You got it wrong, Kitty-Kat." She stumbled back as I rose to my feet, my naked body towering over her petite frame. Faster than she was expecting, I yanked the gun out of her hand, tossing it across my bed where she couldn't reach it. "They weren't the whores..." I leaned closer to her face, the blood from the knife trickling down my neck. Her eyes widened as I stopped barely an inch from her mouth. "*I was.*"

I never slept with actual prostitutes. Not that I had anything against their profession, but I didn't see the purpose. I had hundreds and hundreds of wealthy women of all ages, races, and influence begging me to be in their bed. I was the one who profited, stealing or receiving huge donations, which made me the whore. And I had been fine with it for a long time. It was who I was, my signature, my moniker. I had no guilt, no shame, and I still had manners.

Then I lost everything, going down a dark path where I met a woman with even fewer morals than I did. I fell for her hard, loving that she had no scruples and wasn't bowing at my feet. We were Bonnie and Clyde before they even existed, stealing, running dirty deals, always onto bigger and better payouts. Until I realized her having no ethics meant her feelings for me were also on that list. Amara had me on a tight leash for years, giving me enough to keep me holding on while she was in a relationship with another man.

I was thankful she was out of my life, but I still hadn't forgiven myself for allowing her to take so much of it. For making me hate who I'd become.

Then Lexie came into my life. Beautiful, fierce, and loving. Like Kat, I had seen her grow from a kid to an adult. And for one brief moment, I thought I could find peace again.

When she was brutally killed in front of me, any hope or light I had left disappeared.

Now with Kat, I was further reminded of the pain and guilt I carried for my sins.

"Cut me, *Katze*." I grit my teeth, suddenly okay with the idea that she would be the one to end me. She had every right to. "If you are going to do it…" I grabbed her wrist with my free hand, pushing it harder against my throat. "Then do it."

She swallowed, her chest rising and lowering rapidly, not moving a muscle while fire danced behind her eyes. The desire to watch me bleed out was written on her features. "What did I teach you?" I regripped her arm, more blood trickling down to my chest. "If you hesitate…" My fingers pressed down hard on her tendons, weakening her hold. In a blink, I whipped her around me, her ass slamming into my cock, my hand forcing hers to hold the knife against her own neck, my mouth skimming the back of her ear. "You die."

She let out a gasp, a shiver running violently through her. Everything right and wrong slipped away, my body reacting to the feel of her. Her tank had pushed up, and my cock nestled against the seam of her ass.

Fuck.

Lust washed over me like lava, scorching through me until I couldn't think. I went still because, with only one *tiny* motion,

I would be inside her. I knew how fucked up and wrong that was, but my cock ached to move, to thrust into her pussy and take everything out on her, letting her punish me back.

She remained still, our chests heaving together in a static frenzy. I could feel her heat pulling me in like magic, her wetness, and I struggled to keep from acting on my desires, which was rare for me lately.

Since Lexie, I had felt nothing. Even with some woman wrapping her mouth around my dick or riding me, nothing ebbed the pain. Filled the hole in my chest. Brought me back to life.

"Captain," a voice bellowed. Scot pushed through my door, half-dressed, a gun in his hand. Vane was right behind him, his eyes black and blue, nose crusted with blood. Weaponless.

Scot came to a stop, his eyes widening at the scene before him. Then his shoulders eased, his head shaking like he expected this. Vane almost looked like he was ready to collapse with relief.

"Captain—"

"Vane, shut the fuck up," I muttered, not moving an inch from her. They could see I was naked, but from this angle, they couldn't tell I was about an inch from sliding into her. With the way Vane and Scot both looked at her, I wanted to do it. To fuck her in front of them. Bury inside her and release.

Marking her.

As if she could feel my thoughts, sense the alpha need in me, a puff of air only I could hear hit the back of her throat, her muscles quivering against me.

What the fuck are you doing? Get your dick away from her. She's Rotty's kid!

Sucking in, I pulled away. My blade was still against her neck, but I wasn't pressed into her.

"Sir, I'm sorry. I was just going to let her go to the bathroom."

"Vane, I'm about to use this knife on you," I growled, my cock angry, craving to settle back into her heat.

The faster I got this girl off this ship and away from me, the better.

"Scot, take her back to the brig." I lifted the knife, pushing her toward him. Everything changed in a beat. Twirling around, Kat wrapped her foot around my calf, whipping me off my feet. My ass hit the wood with a thud, the knife falling from my fingers. The tiny girl leaped onto me, snatching up the weapon. I sucked in as her bare, wet pussy slid down my torso, making me groan. She pointed her father's blade right at my heart.

In a blink, her body went up, hissing and clawing at the air as Scot lifted her off me. The blade clanked next to me.

"I will fucking kill you, Croygen, for what you've done!" she bellowed, thrashing in Scot's grip, trying to get back to me. "I will slice your throat, dagger your heart, and then eat it like catnip!"

Dragged kicking and floundering, her hollers echoed back to me all the way from the belly of the ship.

"See?" Vane exclaimed. "She's a lot more powerful than she looks."

"Vane." I clenched my jaw, staring at the ceiling. "Get. The. Fuck. Out. Now."

Vane reacted instantly, hustling through my door, giving me a moment.

I continued to lay still. My mind and body were at war. Taking in a deep breath, I tried to rein in my emotions. To get a grip on myself.

Kat had almost skewered my heart… And I had never been harder than I was right now.

Centuries earlier, I had ordered Katrina off my ship because she was starting to wreak havoc with my crew.

It seems nothing had changed.

Fifteen minutes later, my crew sat around me in the galley, minus Corb, who stayed above on duty to watch the horizon as dawn breached the sky. Scot was on my right, Tsai on my left, while Zidane, looking bleary-eyed and irritated, shook his head at Vane.

"Tonight we had a breach of duties," I stated. All eyes swung to the man in the back holding a bag of frozen peas to his face. "My direct orders ignored."

Vane slunk down in his chair, a frown on his face, placing the icy bag directly on the growing lump on his forehead and eye.

"And I was attacked in my personal chambers." I had thrown on a shirt and pants, but every inch of my skin still sensed the "attack" and itched with awareness.

"Not my fault!" Vane held out his arms, the thawing bag dripping in his hand. "She bewitched me, I swear!" Vane's Spanish accent grew thicker when he got upset.

"A coatrack would bewitch you," Tsai huffed.

"She had to go to the bathroom. What was I supposed to do?" Vane grumbled, placing the peas back on his eye. "Let her pee right there, smelling up the place?"

"You are seriously the worst pirate." Zid rubbed at his forehead.

"I don't think I'm to blame for this at all." Vane sat up, motioning around. "You are the ones who put me in charge of a beautiful, half-dressed woman. You know I have no willpower against them."

Scot chuckled under his breath, his arms folded, his head bowed and wagging. "He has you there, Captain."

Agreement rumbled through the rest of the skeleton crew.

"Yeah," I blew out. I had pretty much asked for it. Vane actually was a good pirate, but beautiful things were his Achilles' heel. Normally, he leaned toward women but was open to all pretty things, especially when they were flattering him.

"Zid and Scot, you will both take turns seeing to our prisoner." It was strange calling her that. Katrina had been once part of my crew, my family, but I couldn't trust she wouldn't try to kill me again.

"Wait, you're taking me off?" Vane exclaimed. "I swear I will do better."

Laughter boomed through the room.

"She swishes her tail in your direction and Captain will have a dagger in his gut by noon." Scot shook his head. "We can't trust you alone with your own reflection."

Vane huffed, slumping back. His bruises were starting to heal, but his pride would take a bit longer. He knew he fucked up and was lucky to be left only with the punishment I'd be assigning him this week, like swabbing the deck, cleaning toilets, and working kitchen duty.

In the past, I might've marooned a crew member for this kind of mistake. I had even killed one for less. In this new era, humans were aware of the existence of fae, and it was causing more hate, violence, and division in a world already struggling. Trustworthy people were few and far between, so you held on to them. Fought for them. Something Zoey had taught me.

My mind flickered to a group of people half a world away, knowing every day they waited for my return. Almost five years had passed since I sailed off. I had missed Wyatt's first steps, his first words, his first day of preschool. But I couldn't bring myself to go back; the reminder of all we had lost was too much. Though no matter how far I sailed, Lexie's blood still stained my skin. The memory of her dead body in my arms still haunted me. The nightmares still woke me up screaming, as if it was happening all over again.

And not once could I prevent it.

The half-strighoul, half-seer called Zeke was the one who murdered her. A science experiment born in Dr. Rapava's labs, made with Zoey's viable eggs, created a whole new *unnatural* species. Almost invincible, smart, powerful, strong, they were still out there somewhere. Creatures who shouldn't exist.

One day I would hunt Zeke and all the others down.

"Captain?" Scot nudged me, snapping me back to the present. "What are your plans for her?"

"I don't know yet." Rubbing my head, I let out an exhale. "Though I can't release her."

"So, we're gonna keep her prisoner?" Zid sat up. "We can have pets now?"

I glared at him, shaking my head.

If older Kat was anything like her younger self, she was stubborn, determined, and would not give up until she got what she wanted—which seemed to be my death. Letting her go would only land us right back here, and there was a good possibility she would succeed next time.

"She'll stay a prisoner until I figure out what to do with her. Right now she's not my first concern." The whole reason we were even in the east was to reestablish ourselves here, making it known the Silver-Tongue Devil was back and ready to claim his title again. "Did anyone hear anything in Singapore about this PIB or *The Revenge*?"

I knew *The Revenge* belonged to this infamous PIB and her crew. As I took back the Caribbean, all I kept hearing were larger-than-life myths about her. How her bodyguards would tear you into bite-size pieces. With only the heel of her boot, she could make you mincemeat, killing hundreds of men, including well-established ruthless pirates. Her first mate was the best sailor in the world. And how she could seduce, fuck, and rob better than I ever had.

Okay, I was man enough to know *that* was what bothered me the most. I mean, I worked decades for the reputation. No one had come close, but now it was being taken from me?

It was an outright challenge.

"Several people claimed they saw the ship in port a day ago, but the one they swore it was now flies the emperor's insignia," Zid replied.

"The crew?" Scot asked.

"Disappeared," Vane piped up.

"If Batara took it, the crew is dead," Zidane stated, his fingers twirling around a blade, looking half-bored as always.

"We came all this way and got dressed up for nothing?" Scot scratched at his red beard with a snort.

My mind kept wheeling around as they continued to talk about what they heard, prickles tapping at the back of my neck, crackling over my skin. Something didn't add up to me.

"We still need to make our mark. But in the absence of this Captain PIB, we can easily gain control. Make sure the Somalia pirates know who is boss." Vane tossed the peas aside, blood still crusting his swollen nose.

"Aye, right," Scot declared in response to Vane.

"Fools." Tsai's voice popped my head up. "And people think I'm the blind one." Her white gaze went right at me. "Pussy right in your face and you guys still can't find the clit."

"What the fuck, old woman? Why do you think the women keep coming back?" Vane spouted out. "I know exactly where it is!"

"Do you? Seems to be sitting right on you and still you're all oblivious." Tsai spoke directly to me, a twitch in her lips. "Puss and her boots…"

Oh. Holy. Shit.

The jacket, the boots… a pussycat down in my brig.

No fucking way.

"I want to be a pirate just like you." A memory stirred into my head. She was no older than five or six.

"Just like me, huh? How about you become an even better pirate?"

I jolted for the stairs. The need to confirm what I already knew had me running out of the galley. Darting inside my chambers, I went straight to where I had put her items. My old, long leather coat, worn from time and sea salt bleaching, it appeared like a patchwork of skin.

Sucking in, I grabbed the boots hidden behind the door, my fingers fumbling as I touched the heels, seeing the blades hidden in them.

"She's supposed to be as beautiful as she is deadly... I hear the coat she wears is from the skin of all her dead enemies and the boots she has can slice people in half."

"Captain, what's going on?" Scot came into my room, Vane and Zid right behind.

"Fuck." I dropped the boots, pushing past them, beelining for the brig. It had been in my face, but I hadn't let myself see the connection. To me, she was still Katrina. *Katze.* Kitty-Kat.

Not my rival.

Not the one I came here to challenge. To eliminate.

My bare feet padded loudly on the steps to the cell, my men trailing after me, no doubt feeling my anxiety, not knowing my past had collided with my present.

As I walked down the stairs, Kat stood, her muscles locking up. She seemed to sense my mood as well. My narrowed gaze went over her, seeing her in a whole different light. It was there all along. I hadn't let myself even consider it because of who she had been to me. The young, bold-as-brass little girl who used to play and sword fight on my deck with Killian. Who used to look at me with stars in her eyes. I had let my ego dominate, not allowing me to see the woman before me *now*. Who she grew up to be: a fighter. A seductress. Smart, clever, powerful, and strong. The most feared pirate in today's age.

The same one who wanted to kill me.

"So, *Katze*." I strolled up to the bars, my head tilting to the side, my gaze roaming down her body. "Or should I call you Puss in Boots?"

Chapter 9
Croygen

Her upturned eyes grew wider as she tried to swallow back her gasp. Her yellow and green irises went horizontal for a moment before she reined in her emotion.

It was all the answer I needed.

"You think I wouldn't figure it out?" Even without Tsai's push, I would've eventually. "I want to say I'm shocked, but really I think I'm proud."

"Proud?" she repeated through her teeth, her lids tapering on me.

"You have made quite a reputation for yourself. The Caribbean is abuzz with rumors and tales about this infamous Puss." I leaned even closer. "Her skills in sword fighting and thieving have made her the most feared pirate in the east. Why wouldn't I be proud? I am the one, after all, who taught you everything you know."

My crew let out sharp inhales, unaware of our past connection. Scot had been with me the longest, but he joined me after Kat had left.

Kat folded her arms, her smile curling her lips. "The greatest teacher I've *ever* had, the one who taught me to be the pirate I wanted to be. The person I wanted to be." She moved close to the bars, our faces only an inch apart. "Was Master Yukimura."

A low scoff pushed me back with amusement, my head shaking. "Haven't changed, have you, *Katze*?"

"Haven't changed?" She arched up her brow. "I'm nothing like that idealistic, naive girl I once was. You know, the one who used to be enamored with you. I wised up to that childish folly the moment you threw me away."

My jaw gritted at the disgust in her tone. The hatred. Because I deserved it. But in no way would I let her know that.

"Not enamored with me? Really?" I countered, lifting my eyebrow. "You've just spent the last few centuries trying to become the best pirate out there, am I right?" I gripped the cage, my face even with the bars, showing her how the metal didn't affect me. It did, but not like others. I had spent so much time being held prisoner by Dr. Rapava, being injected with goblin metal, tortured and tested on, that I had developed a higher tolerance than most. I was able to touch it and be around it much longer than other fae.

"*All* because of *me*. Every thought and breath has been about *me*. Dreaming about me, practicing what you'd say when you finally saw me again. Tell me I'm wrong, Kitty-Kat?"

"Dreaming about *killing* you." She swung her hand forward, her nails shifting into longer claws. I leaned away, a laugh bubbling in my throat.

"You had your shot, and you hesitated." I licked my lips, my mind going back to the feel of her straddling me, the fierceness in her eyes. "You won't get the chance again."

"So sure of yourself, aren't you?" She seethed. "The moment you look away, the moment you let down your guard. I will take everything you took from me. My fath—"

The sound of heavy feet pounding on the stairs distracted me, cutting off whatever Kat was saying. Corb ran down, his eye wide, his deep grunts filled with alarm. Cyclops could make sounds, and their grunts expressed a lot in tones, but they couldn't speak. I had taught everyone our own version of sign language to be able to communicate. His fingers formed a signal.

"Somali pirates?" Zid exclaimed at the same time the sound of machine guns pinged off the side of the ship.

"Fuck!" My feet were already racing for the stairs as Kat yelled for me.

"Let me out! I can help."

For a moment, I debated. She was an excellent fighter, but I didn't trust her. She could easily turn a gun on me instead.

"Where am I gonna go? Join them?"

"I wouldn't put it past you," I clipped, rushing for the stairs.

"Croygen!" Her voice grew fainter as I ascended up to the deck. "You fucking asshole!"

The buzz of battery-operated boats hummed around us like bees. Their boats were tiny and low-tech, but they made up for that in quantity and sheer determination. The Somalis had nothing to lose. Most of them understood if they went out, they most likely wouldn't come back. Their own lives or those of others were of no consequence to them. They were pitiless and cruel, overwhelming you like cockroaches.

"Cover the starboard side!" I ordered, pointing at Zid and Vane since the pirates had gotten too close to bother with cannons. Twenty or more boats swiftly surrounded us, blending in perfectly with the ocean in the dawn light.

Times had changed since the mid-seventeen hundreds, but many of the ships out now remained the same because technology had gone backward, falling into the times before electricity, cars, and computers. King Lars had a team of scientists, engineers, creators, and wealthy donors working on getting products to function in this new magic-boosted world, but not fast enough.

We were sitting ducks.

The pirate's automatic guns tore into the wood of the ship as they sped closer, the front ones already prepping to toss their hooks and board my ship.

Scot, Corb, and I covered the stern and port side of the ship while Tsai went behind the helm, maneuvering us away from the attack. The woman may be blind, but centuries of experience made her the best at what she did. The woman had a photographic memory and could recall every inch of this ocean. She knew the alignment of the stars in the sky at any time and place, and she knew when a storm was coming by the smell of the air.

With such a small crew, it was easy to be overwhelmed. My reputation in the Caribbean had stopped anyone from coming after me, but they had no such honor here. All probably way too young to even know who I was.

Bang! Bang! Bang!

Blasts fired in the morning air, my adrenaline pumping as, one by one, I shot every soul who tried to get close to my ship. They were relentless. Their buddy would fall dead next to them, and they'd be covered in his brain matter, but they'd shove him aside and take over what he could no longer do.

"Captain! There are too many!" Scot barked down from me as dozens more clumped around, metal hooks flying up to catch onto our balusters. He fired his gun and sliced at any rope attached to us at the same velocity.

Dread slid down my throat, knowing he was right. The precious seconds I wasted reloading my gun cost us.

"Hold down for a moment!" I yelled back to Scot, darting for the mainsail. No motors meant we were entirely dependent on the wind to move. The breeze was light this morning, but I hoped it would be enough.

"Tsai? Be ready!" I dropped a sail, watching the wind catch in it. It wasn't a fast escape, but it was a lot harder to board a moving ship. We drifted forward, forcing some of those down below to fall into the water or to try to keep speed with us.

I could only leave it in Tsai's hands to get us out of here.

Gunfire and yelling throbbed in my eardrums. I was unaware of the bullet slicing through my arm until the searing fire touched my nerves, jerking me around.

A handful of pirates had scaled up from the bow, climbing onto the deck and shooting at us.

It was like my past came back to life, the day that haunted me. Recalling the screams, the smells, the taste of black powder and sea salt on my tongue.

The day I lost everything.

I would not let it happen again.

Anger flared up, my brain shutting down and switching into attack mode. Yanking my sword from my belt, feeling the magic, the legend of Black Beard hum through it, I let out a warrior cry, defending my home, my family. I had also been taught by Master Yukimura when I was a boy; the man had been part of the Han dynasty in 206 BCE and had later mentored Genghis Khan.

He was another I lost that fateful night, causing more guilt to weigh on my shoulders.

Twirling and spinning, bullets bounced off my blade as I moved toward the intruders, none of them understanding the skill or admiration of fighting with a sword. Back in my day, whether you lived or died, there was honor in it. The one with the most proficiency won. It was the way of the fae for a long time until the worlds came together; now fae were picking up human behaviors. Lazy and easy. Guns took no expertise or brain power. Just point and kill.

My blade swiped down and sliced up, bodies falling, but more and more came—an endless parade of desperate people trying to stay alive in this new world. To be the one to come out on top. Or at least survive another day.

The warmth of their blood squirted over me, along with the spray of ocean water, as our speed picked up. My men defeated the raiders, a sense of pride and hope billowing in my chest as we beat them back.

Vane punched up his arm at our clear win. Some of the boats drifted away from us, their batteries not powerful enough to keep up. "That is how you do it, am I right?" He knocked into Zid's shoulder. Zidane, of course, looked neither happy nor displeased. The man was the coolest I had ever met under life-threatening experiences. And we had many of them.

Using my sleeve to wipe the blood off my face, I motioned for Corb to toss the dead bodies over. "Nothing like a pre-breakfast attack to get the heart pumping." I shook my head.

"Uh, Captain?" Scot spoke from his place on the port side, his attention on the water.

"Zid, how about cooking us up some of your fritters and fried plantains?" I pointed to him. They all took turns on kitchen duty, but Zidane was by far the best cook, pulling in skills from his Jamaican roots.

"Captain!" Scot's voice rose, and I jerked my head toward him, my light mood dipping at the anxiety on his face.

Running up next to him, I took in the sight. Dread lumped into my stomach, my adrenaline spiking up again.

A few boats continued to follow us, too far to shoot at them. That alone wouldn't have been alarming if it weren't for the two men in the front boat. They held a whale harpoon gun. One large enough to take down a sperm whale. They could sink us if they hit right, tearing into the side of the ship.

The sound of its release punched through the air, howling to us in a blink.

Like the arrow had driven through my own skin, I felt it crack through the hull, the harpoon digging into the belly of my beast. Right where Kat would be.

The metal embedded under the wood, connecting the pirates to us. Other boats grabbed onto the rope, pulling themselves closer.

"Fuck!" I shouted. "Scot, come with me. Everyone else, shoot these motherfuckers!"

Scot and I barely hit a stair as we raced down to the hull. My eyes adjusted to the darkness, finding the glint of the harpoon in the wall only feet away from Katrina's cell. Air gushed from my nose in relief at seeing Kat was unharmed.

Our eyes met across the room, hers reflecting what little light we had in the dim room. "You okay?"

She nodded as Scot and I headed straight for the harpoon, the metal claws cutting deep into the wood, making it a great anchor.

"How the fuck do we get it out?" Scot searched around for anything to help us.

My own gaze hunted the room for an object, my brain trying to come up with a plan.

"You have to cut it out," Kat spoke up, and I turned my head to her. "It's like a tick. It will keep embedding itself unless you remove it.

"You mean cut a hole in my ship?"

"You *already* have a hole in your ship." She gestured to the harpoon, a trail of water seeping in.

"We will flood," Scot snipped back.

The sounds of gunshots popped off as the pirates got closer.

"Not right away." Kat rolled her eyes as if she was done with our stupidity. "At least then you won't be taken over by pirates and lose your whole fucking ship. I've dealt with these things before. Trust me."

She was right. We had to cut it out. But I had nothing that could be used to remove it.

"Do you have dynamite?" Her stunning eyes met mine through the bars, glowing brighter than usual. There was no denying Kat was devastating. One of the most beautiful women I had ever seen.

"Are you feckin' serious, lass?" Scot's arms went out. "Dynamite? You want to sink us right here?"

"Yes. *Dynamite.*" Her gaze stayed on me like she was communicating a deeper meaning, the word triggering something in our past.

"Blackbeard," I muttered, the curve of her mouth saying we were on the same page. His reputation for being crazy and ruthless was well-earned. He used to stick small candles of dynamite in his beard to scare the crap out of his enemies. The man was insane, but he was also brilliantly clever. A good man. Kat had sat on his knee as a baby, thinking he was some version of Santa Claus with his booming laugh and red cheeks.

His kink—playing with dynamite—taught me there were ways to control it.

Whipping around, I moved to the storage cupboard, digging into the items we used to break into vaults, chests, and safety boxes. My hands wrapped around several dynamite candles tucked inside.

"Fuck, I can't believe I'm doing this," I muttered.

The gunfire and yells from outside were almost right on us. It was now or never.

Grabbing a metal bucket off the floor, I shoved it in Scot's arms. "Hold this."

"What are you doin', Captain?" Scot peered at me with trepidation.

"Doing something stupid as fuck."

"How about you don't?"

"We have no choice. I'm not losing my ship. Not to these fuckers." I dug for a lighter in my pocket. I no longer smoked, but I still had a habit of flicking the lid opened and closed, oddly calming me down.

"Kat, get into the furthest corner and cover your head." I turned back to Scot, grabbing the bucket back. "Do the same."

"No." He gritted his teeth. "I'm fighting for my home too."

I knew Scot well enough to not argue with him, and by the sound of voices on the other side of the hull, they were here.

Lighting the fuse, I tossed the dynamite into the bucket, slamming the bucket over the tip of the harpoon and holding it to the spot. It was the only way to contain it, but fuck, it was going to hurt.

Scot pushed down on the side with me, both of us closing our eyes, waiting for the spark to detonate.

Booooom!

My body flew back, crashing into the opposite wall, my skin feeling like it was being torn from my hands and face, my head cracking into the wood. My ears rang, my head flipping around while darkness tugged me down. I forced my lids to stay open to see daylight spilling through the hole we created, water splashing in. It was large, but high enough that I hoped we could limp to a port if the waters stayed calm.

The harpoon was gone.

We did it. Not only was it gone, but every pirate nearby now floated face-first in the water, their boats destroyed.

A groan made me lift my head higher. I pushed myself up, trying to stay conscious. Scot was feet away, blood gushing from his head and burn marks over his skin, but he stirred awake, his eyes fluttering open.

My gaze went over the room, everything torn to shreds.

"Kat?" I shot up, my vision blurring, my ears still echoing with the blast, almost tipping me over. Blood trailed down my face, my skin black and tight in places, but I was numb to any pain. "Katrina!" Fear whipped through me before I saw her still balled up in the corner of the brig. At my voice, she lifted her head to peer back at me. Scratches covered her face and arms and her nose was bloody, but nothing serious.

Relief washed over me. The goblin metal actually kept her safe, holding strong against the blast.

"You all right?" I waded through the wreckage, getting to her.

She nodded, flinching as she got to her feet. My gaze drifted over her anyway, making sure she was in one piece. The little clothes she had on had holes from small debris hitting her. I turned to Scot. "You good?"

"Aye." Scot nodded, wincing, his hand pressing against his head wound. "Shocked that bloody worked."

"Don't we say that about everything we do?"

Scot scoffed at my remark, nodding. "Aye."

"Captain?" Vane screamed from above, his footsteps pounding down the stairs. "You alive?"

"Yeah," I replied as Zid and Corb made their way down to the hull, looking around at the destruction before them, their eyes wide.

"What happened?" Zid peered at us.

"We got rid of the problem." I nodded toward the hull.

"You did this on purpose?" Zid shook his head. "Solid plan, Captain... put a hole in the fucking ship." Zidane motioned to where water spilled inside, the floorboards already covered by half an inch of water.

"Did you have another plan?" Scot snarled, getting into Zid's face. "I didn't think so. So shut the fuck up and never second-guess your captain again. He just saved all our lives."

Scot was protective of me. Loyal. I knew my crew was faithful to me, but the big Scotsman was one who would go above and beyond.

"Hey." I backed Scot off, the men glaring each other down. "Now is not the time." I used my sleeve to wipe the blood from dripping into my eye. "We need to get to the closest port and fix the hull before we sink." We were traveling to Jakarta. It was another big "tradesman" territory, so it was a good place for dirty business and a port we needed. "Zid, you and Vane, patch this hole with a tarp the best you can. Corb, I need you on watch. There might be more following us." My attention shifted to the girl in the cage and the water lapping around her ankles. The jail was compromised. "And Scot, handcuff Ms. Puss here and bring her to my cabin." I winked at her scowling face and strolled away. When my orders were being followed, I headed back up to speak with Tsai.

Four hours later, we hobbled into Pangkal Pinang, the capital of the Bangka Belitung Islands. Before the Fae War, it was a contrast between poor and wealthy. The beaches were full of resorts and tourists, while those living here worked hard to keep afloat. Now it was mainly empty and impoverished, most heading to places like Singapore or Jakarta to make money after the tourists stopped coming while the older and stubborn stayed put.

It was all the help we would get around here, my ship taking on more and more water. Sailing into a canal, the docks mostly abandoned and collapsing, we found one still in use. An older human gentleman pushed up from the broken chair he was sitting on in the hot, blaring sun, his expression twisting up like we were bothering him.

"Zid?" I flicked my chin at the man approaching our starboard side. Zid was the best at languages, and though I knew over fifteen, I didn't want to deal with haggling the price for using this dock.

Zidane leaped off, communicating with the man. Instantly the man's head swung in a firm no, while Zid's head was shaking at whatever he said. Eventually, Zid nodded, both in agreement, before Zid climbed back aboard.

"He says he knows people, a place we can find provisions, and supplies to fix the hole."

Everyone "knew someone." Bait and switch, cons, and hustles had magnified since the war. Hard to not be taken by them, but what was a pirate but a con man himself? Except here, we had little choice. Our prospects of getting our own materials were slim.

"Vane and I could check it out." Zid squinted against the brutal sun, not showing any other sign he was experiencing the insufferable heat like the rest of us.

"Last time you checked something out, you ended up at a brothel."

"The best information source you can find," he responded.

Snorting, I folded my arms. "Helps if you bring that information back instead of staying there for two days."

"That was one time, and that was Vane," Zid grumbled. "Couldn't leave a man behind. Isn't that one of your rules?"

I laughed, shaking my head, dipping into a shallow nod. "Fair enough."

"When was the last time you got laid?" Zid lifted a dark brow. "Getting a bit tense there, Captain?"

My attention flittered to my cabin door like a magnet. Quickly I snapped my attention back, my mind recalling the last time I let off some steam.

Fuck…when was that? Not remembering the last time I got laid wasn't a good sign. Not like me. My memory was a steel trap. Helped me in many situations, and the women always figured the small details I recalled were because I was really listening to them. I cared. And I did, but not the way they wanted.

The only thing I wanted to do right now was sleep and let myself heal a bit. But at the thought of Kat in my room, my dick hardened.

Tightness strangled my chest, a force drawing me to my room and urging me to run from it at the same time. I still couldn't believe the sensual, clever creature being held captive in my cabin was Rotty's daughter. The tiny pipsqueak, whose eyes flared with fire and were set with determination, battled those twice her age and size. Challenging the world, she let nothing stop her, and I had no doubt she could do it. She was fierce, strong, and wild.

A thud of realization hit me, and I stepped back with sharp understanding.

Lexie.

Katrina.

The same qualities I had seen in *Katze* were in Lexie at the same age. Was that why I was so protective of my little card shark? The fact I saw Kat in her? Not sexually, of course. Even the thought made me sick. That was the last thing on my mind. She and Annabeth were barely teenagers when I first met them, and that was all I saw. But Lexie had that extra spunk. Confined to a wheelchair most of her life, she learned to fight with words, with her mind. It wasn't until much later, when Lexie had grown up, that a slight shift happened. And honestly, I don't think I really grasped what I felt until I watched her die in front of me.

Had I been in love with her? For a moment I thought I could be, but now I wasn't sure. It never had a chance to get there before being taken away. I loved her, though; it was impossible not to. Far older than her years, Lexie was a diamond that sparkled through the rough.

I mourned the loss of a friend. Of what could have been. Of a spark that was stolen from the stars.

A part of my family was now missing, and I felt it was my fault. I told her I'd protect her. I'd keep her safe, no matter what. I failed. And she was killed.

I knew deep down that was partly the reason I stayed away from Zoey and Ryker's home. The look on Annabeth's face and the devastation on Zoey's after losing their sister... because I didn't protect her.

The grip on my lungs squeezed tighter, my gaze going back to my door. I had thrown Kat off my ship, her only home, sending her off to boarding school. I had to; it was the right thing to do at the time. But not helping her understand why was cold and cruel.

I hadn't protected her either. I ignored what I had done, the pain I caused both her and Fredrich. The irreversible damage I would later cause them both.

When Lexie came along, was I trying to make up for Kat through her?

"Vane and I will head out now." Zid stepped around me.

"No." I turned with him, my head wagging. I needed to get off this ship and as far away from Kat as possible. "I will go."

Zid's forehead pinched. "Really? You sure?"

"Yes," I stated. "People need to know I am back, and we are not to be fucked with." I squinted up at my flag. *The Silver Devil* was printed on the banner flapping from the mast. "I miss the days people feared this flag." It had been a long time since *The Devil* or the pirate who captained it had made his position known. My name was of legends and stories, but they needed to be reminded I was real and there were reasons I was once feared.

Maybe I am too old for this shit. I thought coming back to the pirate life would fill the part of me I lost in the battle with Stavros and the Stone of Fal, when Zeke put a spear through Lexie. With all the deaths from the war, and then the battle to keep our country from the Stone taking Lars and Zoey or Stavros's dictatorship, something died in me.

I thought I would find it on the ocean. This was where I belonged. Some days when I sailed, the wind against my face, the sun setting, glowing the sky with warmth, my soul felt replenished. Then other days were like this. What the fuck was I doing all this for?

I ached to see my family, to hear their voices, Wyatt babbling in the background. Even that talking rat with fur. I snorted. The memory of Sprig riding the back of Matty, Zoey and Ryker's border collie, through the house like a cowboy always cracked my shit up.

That monkey-sprite was fucking annoying, *but...* I rubbed at my chest, at an emotion I wanted to shove far back because there was no way I missed the little fucker.

None.

I instructed my crew to watch over Kat, making sure Vane was on the opposite end of the ship. Scot and I turned, making our way off the dock, heading for the only place you'd find the type of help we were looking for.

A seedy, criminal-infested tavern.

Chapter 10
Croygen

The air was tainted with the smell of food prepared with spices from various stands combined with manure from the horses pulling buggies as Scot and I made our way to the local pub. No one had learned to switch their mopeds to battery yet, pushing time even farther back in this area.

"Looks like the place." Scot nodded at an unconscious man, a bottle still in his hand, in front of a shack. A bar, restaurant, or any type of market here wasn't what you would picture. Probably someone's garage, a patchwork of makeshift buildings squeezed together and converted into spaces between chicken coops, laundry, and a few convenience stores. Here the legitimacy and safety of the shaky buildings and bad wiring weren't ever questioned because they didn't have laws or rules to keep them in check. It was whatever you could come up with to make work. Their poverty level was a stark contrast to the West and was made even more so after the fall of the Otherworld, taking away most modern conveniences.

Only a few heads turned our way when we strolled into the bustling space. The lack of windows kept the room dark and slightly cooler than outside, but that didn't take away the sun radiating off the tin roof, making sweat slide down my back. My eyes drifted around the seedy garage-turned-bar, filled with people getting drunk off cheap liquor and waiting for an opportunity to get out of this port.

Scot and I approached the bar, our eyes always moving around the room, aware of everything. Gauging and assessing the type of people in here.

"Well, well... if it isn't the Silver-Tongue Devil and the Scotsman." My head jerked toward the woman's voice on the other side of the bar. *"Sudah lama tidak bertemu." Long time no see,* she said, acting as if she had seen us an hour ago.

I blinked at the woman I had known centuries earlier, when I was the King of the Sea.

"Bulan?" Her name meant The Moon, her face as round and as lovely as one. Barely reaching five feet, her young, sweet appearance and huge brown eyes blinking innocently at you were all a sham. She was what the Indonesians call an Orang Bunian. Their intense glamour showed them as pretty and humanlike, and their scent of French fries and adorable stature lured humans like moths to flames. They also were said to abduct children, which was total bullshit.

Though Bulan did use her powers to "befriend" and glamour humans to hand over their money and jewelry to her, getting them to pay ten times the amount for something because they were so enamored of her adorable, sweet appearance. The woman was a crook. Shady as fuck, and why I think we became good friends.

"Little Moon Pie." Scot winked at her, causing her lids to narrow. "I've missed you." She'd have killed most people for calling her that, but she seemed to let the big ginger get away with it. *"Och."* Scot shook his head. "How long has it been?"

"January 1733," she replied instantly, like it was yesterday.

My teeth crunched together at the date. It had been a dark time for me. I had lost everything by then. Sailing away from the destruction I left back in the Caribbean, heading for the East, I continued to rain havoc in my wake across the globe, bleeding out and causing more heartache and damage to everyone I crossed.

One of those times produced a daughter I never knew I had until a few years ago.

Rez.

Her mother, Mareza, was a siren I bedded during my lost, dark, drunken, selfish state, searching for something to ebb the pain. I didn't even know she was pregnant when I left, moving on to the East.

Rez was grown, didn't need me, and happily mated to West, a Dark Dweller, yet it still hurt that I hadn't been there for her growing up.

Bulan grabbed a whiskey bottle, pouring us a drink, recalling what we liked.

"Like old times. Some things haven't changed." I smiled at my old friend.

"Some things have." She peered around at her establishment, her nose wrinkling. "But we adapt and survive. Make do, even when times are hard." She gripped our drinks, her lids tapering on us. "Now, I don't want any trouble from you two. Got it?"

Scot and I nodded at her demanding tone.

"Now pay me or fuck off."

"Same old Bulan." I yanked out my wallet, tossing money on the table. She slid the drinks in front of us with a huff and walked off to help others.

"Ach, for a wee thing, she's kind of terrifying." Scot picked up his drink, turning to lean against the bar. "Sounds like someone else we know." Scot looked out, a smirk on his mouth. I snarled at his implication, taking a huge swallow.

121

"One shackled up in *your* cabin, barely dressed, and stunning. But here you are—as far as you can."

"You think I'm running away? *From her?*" I coughed out, defensive ire heating the back of my neck. "A teeny ball of hissing fur? Please." I snapped, flipping around to watch the room too.

"Not what it looked like last night when she had you on your back, straddling you."

"Fuck off. That is disgusting. I knew her as a child."

"She's not a child anymore." His tone was filled with meaning, as if his mind conjured carnal thoughts of her right then. "Not for centuries."

Fury flared up into my veins, and I whirled on my friend, getting an inch from his face, my voice ice. "You lay a finger on her or even think of her in any way, I will fucking kill you."

Scot's eyes widened slightly, his eyebrows going up. I was known for my easygoing personality, being blasé and a little bit of a smart-ass. It's what made me good at what I did. People didn't expect the one joking with them to turn around and slit their throat, taking their money, their wife, and their ship.

Three years ago, that changed. After the battle with the Stone and Stavros, where Lexie and so many others were killed, my temper rumbled violently. A squall under the surface.

"Her father was my second for a long time." I continued to spout. "My frien…" I trailed off, realizing what I was about to say and that I had no right to call him that after what I had done.

"Yes, I remember Rotty." Scot had only been a member of my crew four months before it all ended. Another one I saved from a horrible situation. He vowed his life to always be faithful to me. And even when I disappeared, he tracked me down, never going back on his word.

"Let's talk about Rotty." Scot took a drink. He was the only one who knew the story. The only one who had been there, lived, and heard what truly happened that night. I confessed on a drunken, guilt-filled night when he had to coax Rotty's dagger from my fingers so I wouldn't end it all right there. "I'm sure he would love that you have his daughter chained up instead of letting her go."

"You think I should let her go? She wants nothing more than to kill me."

"Thought she was just a teeny ball of hissing fur?" Scot grinned at getting a rise out of me.

"She's also the infamous Puss in Boots. *My enemy.*" I turned away from him, having had enough of this conversation. "She's lucky to be alive at all."

"Sure." Scot laughed, which grated on my nerves.

"Shut the fuck up." I gritted, nodding out to the room. "Go find supplies, labor, and any leads on smuggling or royal ships passing in the area."

While I was a revered pirate sticking it to the man on most days, I still tracked down smuggling ships filled with black-market items from the Unified Nations, the umbrella King Lars and Queen Kennedy worked under to bring all the countries together in alliance. Many countries in the eastern bloc gave a big fuck you to them, declaring they wanted independence. Independence, my ass. It was an excuse for the power-hungry tyrants to rise. A fight between the elite humans and fae to become the next dictator, gaining all the wealth and privilege while most of the people suffered.

The irony in getting Lars's items back from thieves was that he made sure I was compensated for my piracy. Not much different from how piracy usually started under monarchs before we turned on them. And did I also sell some for my own profit like I did back then? Fuck, yes. After all, I was a *tradesman*.

Scot shot back the rest of his drink with a grunt and did what I asked, leaving me alone at the bar.

Taking a drink, my agitated mood didn't ebb, and I knew deep down where it stemmed from.

"Goddam cat," I muttered, guzzling down a huge gulp, my mind lost in my thoughts.

"Shut up, mate. You're full of shit," a man with an Australian accent spoke next to me, pulling my attention.

"I'm not," another man replied, his accent so light I couldn't pick up exactly what it was. "I swear to you it's real. I heard even the king of the Unified Nations is looking for it."

Lars? My ears perked up, the men capturing my full attention as I continued to drink like I was just enjoying the late afternoon and not eavesdropping at all. Sliding my eyes quickly to them, I spied a stocky man with grayish skin and gray-blue spotted hair slicked back, reminding me of a tiger shark. The Aussie's wide side eyes and broad nose resembled a hammerhead shark.

Shark-shifters.

"Fuck off," Hammerhead replied with a huff. "There is no way... all that shit was destroyed when the fae wall came down. Someone's pullin' your fin, mate."

"No." The tiger shark man growled. "It exists." He took a drink. "My brother worked with a scientist in the Georgia Territory. Someone brought them this magical substance, which didn't die after the wall dropped. Testing it, they found it even more powerful than fae food, curing diseases, giving humans fae-like qualities and almost eternal life. It would be the greatest discovery ever... and probably the most destructive. Humans would burn this world down to try and get it, and fae will do the same to keep it away from them." He downed the rest of his drink. "And if the king is seeking it? It might be too late."

"But your brother and this scientist have it?"

124

"You don't fucking get it," Tiger snapped. "They've disappeared. I last heard from him over three weeks ago when they were leaving Hong Kong to go up north, and I haven't received news from him since. That's not like him." His voice tightened. "In my gut, I know something's wrong. I could hear it in his voice. He told me he felt like they were being followed. That people were after them." Out of the corner of my eye, Tiger turned to his buddy. "I need your help. You can navigate the waters better than anyone I know."

"Navigate? Where?"

"Shanghai, China," Tiger responded. "I'm going to find my brother... and this object they call the nectar."

My eyes cracked open to the blazing morning sun, and a pounding boomed inside and outside my skull.

"Fuck," I grumbled. Squinting, I lifted my head, cringing as the sound of hammers hitting wood vibrated through me. "Ouch." I rubbed my neck, stiff from falling asleep in a deck chair. The sound of the men Scot had hired to rebuild the hole in the ship echoed from below.

I enjoyed drinking but no longer set out to get drunk. Last night we stayed out until the wee hours of the morning, stumbled back, and I passed out in a deck chair.

But even as drunk as I got, the conversation I overheard at the bar kept coming back to me. Most of me wanted to chalk it up to bullshit talk, a yarn his friend was weaving together from paranoia and over exaggerations. But the man's tone when talking about his brother was so serious and terrified it was hard to ignore.

If Lars was looking for something, wouldn't I know? At least more than this random guy would. Not that Lars told many about his plans over the years. His ego was the reason he almost lost his throne to Stavros, why Stone took over his mind and body. Why Lexie was killed.

This whole "nectar" thing, which gave humans fae powers, seemed impossible after the fall of the barrier, destroying that type of magic. It sounded like complete bullshit. Yet something dug into the back of my neck, burrowing in and not allowing me to let go of the idea.

"Sleep well?" Tsai shuffled in next to me, her body a carpet of blankets even though it was boiling out.

"I could have used you as a pillow," I mused, motioning to her layers.

"And I could have used an orgasm last night, so we're all cranky for different reasons."

"Tsai…" I rubbed at my face, trying to block out any images wanting to attach themselves to that claim. "It's too early."

"I'm just saying someone was trying to avoid his cabin," she baited me. "The lord of the manor too scared to face the tiny kitty cat inside?"

"Fuck off. I'm not scared." It was the second time I had been accused of that. My fingers tangled through my hair, wrapping it up off my face as I got to my feet.

Tsai snickered, enjoying my annoyance.

"Oh, men. And they think I'm the blind one."

"You know, old woman, I could toss your ass off this ship if I wanted." I strolled to the railing, peering down at the workers below, Vane and Zidane instructing them.

"Go for it." She grinned, showing some of her teeth. "Love to see you boys be without me for a day."

We could, but we wouldn't want to. Tsai was embedded into this ship, into its bones, and into us. No one knew the true legend who lived among us wasn't me.

"Though someday you will, you know." She saddled up

next to me at the railing. "I'm of the old world, which is disappearing every day. And when it finally goes, I will go with it."

A growly noise of refusal came up my throat.

"You cling to what was, Croygen, not what could be." Tsai's tone softened. "You are a good man, but you have trouble letting go. Guilt, ideals, people. What you think you deserve. Holding on to what is toxic and pushing away what is good."

"What do you mean, holding on to toxic?"

"Amara?"

"I'm not with her. Haven't been for years."

"Yet she still is embedded in your mind. Holding you back."

Exhaling, my shoulders slumped.

"So, I'm gonna say this once, my dear boy." She lifted her hand to touch my face. Then hit me with it. "Stop being a dumbass!"

"Jesus!" I tried to duck out of the way as she swung for me again.

"I'm stuck on a ship with a bunch of morons." She tossed her arms up at the sky in frustration. "You thought we were getting all sentimental and shit. That I was sweet-talking you. No, you ass. While you've been finding every reason to avoid her, even sleeping like a dog, the girl has come down with a fever."

"What?" I twisted my head to her. "A fever?"

Fae didn't get fevers. We didn't get sick. Though goblin metal could affect fae, weaken us, and give us something resembling human flu.

"Is she okay?"

"Why don't you go see her for yourself?" She wagged her head like I was a simpleton.

Glaring at the old lady, I turned and stomped to my cabin. Locking my shoulders back, I blew out a breath as I opened the door. It creaked open, the salt-soaked wood making the hinges sing. My eyes adjusted to the dim room; the shades closed over my windows. Kat's body was curled over some blankets in the corner, her head tucked away, her wrists cuffed around a pole. The goblin metal kept her lethargic and too drained to shift.

My boots hit the floor quietly as I inched closer to her. "Kat?"

No response.

Her breathing was light and fast, her frame twitching and jerking as if she was freezing.

"I swear, if you are faking this, I will tie you to the rudder." She didn't respond, continuing to spasm. Maybe cats were even more sensitive to goblin metal? Or maybe her injuries from the explosion were worse than I thought.

"Kat?" I crept closer, still weary of this being a trick, that she'd leap up and try to attack me. Double checking her arms were latched to a post, I squatted beside her. "Katrina?" My fingers drifted over her silky hair, reaching under until I cupped her chin, lifting her face to me.

Air caught in my lungs, my shoulders jerking back.

Her fevered yellow and green eyes peered up at me with anguish.

"Shit," I hissed when fresh blood trickled from her nose and eyes.

Feeling Tsai there at the entry, I turned to her. "Go get Zid and Scot!" Scot was the closest we had to a medic, while Zid worked more with plants and organic medicines.

Panic had me fumbling for the keys in my pocket, finding the ones that unlocked the cuffs.

"Croygen." My name barely made it out of her mouth, turning into a pained groan, like her insides were tearing her apart.

Unlatching her, I yanked the cuffs off her wrists, my arms curling underneath her, lifting her body and carrying her to my bed. Her skin burned into mine, yet it shivered at the same time. Lying her gently down, I hoped to see some relief since the goblin metal no longer touching her, but her body didn't stop shaking.

"Captain?" Both Zid and Scot came into my cabin.

"She's sick. Help her," I ordered them, a flurry of panic starting in my gut. She looked awful, as if she would stop breathing at any moment. "I took off the cuffs."

Scot pushed in next to me. His hands moved over her face, feeling her sticky, hot skin to examine her.

Zid leaned in closer, his head wagging. "This isn't goblin poisoning."

"Then what is it?"

"I don't know. I've never seen anything like this before." His lips pinched.

"I have." Scot's hands left her. He stood up, glancing at me. "With you."

"Me?" My forehead wrinkled. "What the fuck are you talking about?"

"When I found you in New Guinea."

Pausing, my mind stumbled back to what he was talking about. It was so long ago and such a hazy period, I barely recalled anything from that time. I had almost died because of my stubbornness. When I had enough of Ryker and Amara shoving their lust in my face, I left, saying fuck you to the pledge I made to the Viking. And then I turned my back on him, trying to get as far as I could, pretending my promise to him was something I could walk away from.

It was when I discovered what happens when an oath is disregarded. Going against it shredded me from the inside out. When Scot found me, I was so out of it I didn't remember much. But from what he told me, the condition I was in was exactly like this.

My gaze dropped to her, fully taking Kat's symptoms,

seeing all I went through happening to her. The agony and unbelievable torture. "Holy shit."

The longer it was ignored, the worse it got. How many times did I think I'd turn away from my duty even after that first time? Believing I was stronger. That I could break it. That I could forgo my commitment to Ryker. But, fuck, the magic always seemed to know.

There were two types of obligations.

A life owed or...

A *promise.*

And no fae did either unless they were stupid, i.e., me, or there was *no* choice.

"Kat..." I ground out, my throat dropping to my stomach. "What the fuck did you do?"

Chapter 11
Katrina

Voices muttered around me, my sight little more snapshots of blurry faces. My consciousness slipped further and further away, trying to separate itself from my body. Every molecule burned and twitched in pain, pleading to crawl from under my skin.

When I was young, entering fae puberty, I had the equivalent of human growing pains. A combination of restless body syndrome and unbelievable spasms through my muscles. But ten times worse because I was also trying to shift and adjust to a cat form as well as a growing person. The pain was torture since it wouldn't let up for hours, sometimes days. They were so bad I used to throw up.

This was a thousand times worse.

The agony of this hell gurgled moans up my throat, the excruciating aches keeping me semi-conscious and thrashing to find any kind of relief, never letting me fully disengage.

"Katrina?" said the only voice to cut through the noise, the only one I held on to like a life raft. "*Katze?*" I was left stranded in nothingness, and the rope to pull myself out of this dark hole was out of reach. The voice was home, it was security, and I struggled to reach for it. To grab hold. "Kat, open your eyes." The tone grew more tense, only adding to my own anxiety. I wanted to ease it, to do what he asked, but I couldn't. "Zid, can you do something?"

"If this is from a vow she made? Then no. That shit is from the gods and goddesses. You don't mess with that stuff."

My body flopped to the side, air struggling to get through my endless whimpers, hot and cold chills flushing my skin. I was on fire, melting from the inside out while at the same time shivering as if I was freezing to death.

I wanted death. Peace. I wanted it all to end.

"Someone fucking do something!"

My body leaned toward the voice every time it spoke, it ebbed the pain a little. As if my mind could forget the agony and focus on it. I needed it. Craved it like nothing else.

A sob broke free from my throat. Forcing my lids to pry apart, I took in only hazy outlines before they shut again. "Croygen." The name came from out of nowhere, my voice barely audible. I had no understanding of what it meant, but I knew it. It was embedded in my DNA, written long ago on my bones.

"What do ya want us to do?" an accented voice replied, no one seeming to hear me.

"Anything! She's fucking dying."

Gods, I needed him closer. To touch me.

"We need to find a healer."

"Och, a healer can't touch this magic. This isn't something you can take an herb for. You know this," another boomed back. "The best healer in the world isn't going to save her. The only way to relieve it is to fulfill the oath. And we have no feckin' idea what that is."

More agony twisted my body, and a flood of cries came from my gut, begging for relief. I needed my anchor, the voice that soothed the pain. I tried to lift my hand, my muscles refusing to respond to my order. His name was a whisper in my mouth, but it couldn't make it past my lips.

I was sinking.

"Kat?" The voice I craved was right there. Opening my lids just a little, dark, sultry eyes greeted mine, his hand brushing back my sweaty hair. A low moan hummed in my chest. A single moment of numbness. "Tell me what you did. I can't help you unless you tell me."

My dry lips rolled together, and I strained to get my vocal cords to work. To respond to him. Energy drained from me with every blink, my lids drooping, pulling me back into the darkness.

My response curled in my mouth, and using the last bit of my strength, I pushed it out, hoping they heard me before I slipped away.

"China."

Chapter 12
Croygen

It was a whisper, a faint hymn on the breeze, the single word barely escaping from her.

"China."

Katrina's body went limp, giving over to the pain, leaving me unsure if I heard right or not.

"China?" Zid repeated next to me. "Did she say *China*?"

Standing up straight, my hand still tingling from touching her, I ran it through my hair. I had no idea what trouble she got herself into, but I knew If I didn't respond fast, she would go into a coma and possibly never come out of it.

This was why fae never fucked with promises and oaths. They carried deadly consequences if ignored.

For a brief second, my gaze went over her. Knowing this fierce little girl grew up to be a badass pirate made my chest seize. The thought of never hearing her voice again, having those cat eyes on me and seeing her smile, was unthinkable. Even if we spent the rest of our days trying to hunt the other down and kill each other, I needed her to live.

For Rotty, I told myself. I owed him that.

"We set sail in three hours!" I ordered, striding for the door.

"Wee chance of that!" Scot huffed. "They are still working on repairs of the hull. It's gonna take at least a day."

I whipped my head back, my hand on the knob, my tone low and threatening. "Then I suggest you get in there and help speed it along."

"Captain, that's impossible," Zid countered.

I reacted without thought, my hand going to my sword, slamming Zidane into the wall, the blade against his neck. "I gave you an order," I uttered between my teeth, already feeling the trickle of shock at my actions. "I don't want to *hear* 'it's impossible,' I want to hear 'yes, Captain, right away, Captain.'"

"Cap?" Scot spoke behind me, a slight reprimand in his tone, but I kept my gaze locked on Zid.

"Did I make myself clear?"

"Yes, Captain." Zid's jaw clenched, his chin lifted, but he dipped his head. My easygoing nature sometimes gave them the impression they could walk over me. Now and then, I had to remind them who I was. My crew was family, and I preferred to keep it more or less democratic, but I was still the one in charge.

Releasing my crewmates, I marched out of my chamber and headed for the helm, where Tsai waited, as if she already knew my plans.

Behind me, Scot shouted for the hired men to pick up the pace, getting Vane, Zid, and Corb to help with the progress.

"I swear, old woman, if you already know where we are going, I will toss you over the side to see if you float."

"Declare if I'm a witch?" She smirked, getting my reference. "No, my boy. You're simply not all that hard to figure out. What your next action would be. You'd like to think yourself cavalier and venal, but I know you, your past. What you do for those you love, especially when they are in danger."

135

"Love?" I scoffed. "Let's bring it down a hundred notches. It's barely tolerance."

"Did you not purposely turn yourself over to that lab to be tested on, not once, but twice, for love?"

"I need to stop telling you shit when I'm drunk," I muttered. "And with Zoey, it was because of the oath. I had to follow her." When Ryker's powers shifted to Zoey, the vow I had made to him transferred to her. She became who I needed to protect. To track down into the depths of that vile hell.

"You would have done it anyway." Tsai shook her head, both of us knowing she was right. "And Lexie wasn't an oath. You went willingly."

I flinched at Lexie's name being said out loud. In my head, I had grown accustomed to it, but audibly it was like a knife to my chest. "She was a young girl. I wasn't going to let her go by herself." My defensive anger crawled up my throat.

"All I'm saying is you have a good heart. And that makes you the best pirate... and the worst."

"Think it's time someone went for a swim." My annoyance level shot up my shoulders. "See how nice I am when I leave your ass behind?"

"Worst doesn't mean bad."

"Yes, it does. That is the very definition."

"It just means sometimes you make decisions with your heart, not your head."

"You got five seconds before you are going off the plank."

"My, my, someone needs to get laid."

"Tsai..." I rubbed my forehead, the blistering sun only adding to my pounding head. Fae didn't get hangovers—our bodies' metabolism burned through alcohol too fast—but I drank enough last night that I might be the first. "Do you have a point?"

"I know you want to help her, but I have a bad feeling about heading to China."

"How do you know about China? Are you a fucking clairvoyant?"

"No, it's called eavesdropping."

"Eavesdropping? You're half-deaf."

"I used a glass."

"That's called spying."

"More like snooping."

"Tsai." I pinched my nose, taking a deep breath. "If you're not a seer who can see the future, your *bad feeling* holds no weight."

"Men tend to end up dead when they ignore a woman's intuition." Her lips thinned. "Look at my husband, for example."

"Which one?" I snorted. "Both are dead because you were by far the better pirate." If most knew the true identity of who I had navigating my ship, one of the greatest woman pirates of all time, we would become the stuff of myths and legends—more than we already were. My ship would become a celebrity sighting, relentlessly gawked at. None of us wanted that, and I respected Tsai's privacy. The desire to live out her life quietly. "We are leaving the moment the repair is done. Have this ship ready to disembark." I started to turn.

"Croygen." She said my name so rarely that I swung back around; her expression was serious. "There is a power, something I've never felt before, ahead of us." Her cloudy white eyes darted back and forth like she was searching for something. "I feel that if we go, not all of us will return."

A flicker of anxiety swelled in my gut, but I quickly shoved it back, exhaling deeply. "That is no different from any other time we venture out to sea." I shrugged a shoulder. "The risks of being a pirate."

Sweat pooled down my back, my shirt long gone, my muscles aching as my hammer pounded in the nail, putting up one of the last boards. The day was brutal, and all of us were shirtless, sweaty, and smelly. I wasn't someone who stood on the deck, dictating from a perch. I was right there in the trenches with them. A good leader was next to their soldiers in a fight, not on the hill watching. You got harder workers when they saw you doing the work as well.

Plus, it was a good outlet for my anxiety. The need to run to her bubbled under the surface, pushing me faster with every moment that passed as she was only getting weaker the longer we stayed here. The blood from her nose and eyes still stained my hands, driving me to push forward every time I wanted to take a break.

Kat's pained howls echoed louder in my head than the pounding of hammers. We built from the bottom up, both inside and outside the hull, the last planks being set in place. As the final nail sunk in, a loud cheer boomed from all the workers, waving their tools in the air.

"Fuck yeah!" Vane clapped his hand on my back, holding up his hammer in celebration. "We *nailed* that in no time!" He bumped my shoulder, laughing at his cheesy pun. "I say this calls for celebratory drinks."

"Untie us from the mooring," I ordered Vane, tossing my tool down and taking off up the ramp, already dictating orders to my crew. "Scot, pay the men. The rest of you, get us ready to sail. Now!"

Tsai was already at the helm waiting for Vane to release us from the docks and Corb to pull anchor, pushing us back out into the canal and turning us northeast.

I had been so focused on getting the ship back together, I

was able to curb my constant pull toward Katrina. But now the need overtook me, and I jogged for my cabin, swinging open the door. The instant I unlatched it, the cool air brushed my sticky skin, and terror braided down my esophagus. The smell of blood and sweat filled my nose with a sharp bite. A tingle of magic soured the air. If agony had an odor, it would be this. She would suffer a long time before she died, but it didn't take away from the emergency of her predicament now. I was lucky to have Scot. He saved me from going completely into a coma. I had heard some went brain dead, never coming out of it.

"*Katze?*" I crept to her, watching her chest take in short, shallow breaths, like a cat panting. Her hair took on a fur-like quality, her ears more pointed. Her body naturally wanted to protect her, going into her animal form, but she no longer had the energy to shift.

Grabbing a cloth and bowl and filling it with water, I pulled a chair up to the bed, perching on it. Blood crusted her eyes, nose, and mouth, sweat glistening off her flushed skin. She looked so small and fragile. For that moment, an uncontrollable, almost irrational wave of protection crashed over me, a growl vibrating deep in my bones. It was primal. And if anyone stepped into this room, friend or foe, getting too close to her, there would be hell to pay. The need to attack, to tear into them before they could reach her, had me sucking in sharply.

Shaking my head, I leaned over her, boxing up whatever the hell came over me and locking it away.

"Hey," I brushed the damp towel across her forehead. "We're setting sail now." The moment the promise knew she was back on track, it would start to ebb. I learned that when Scot found me. When he was able to get me on my feet, leading me back to Ryker, the pain eased up quickly, disappearing the moment I resigned to the idea of my role with the Viking.

This magic was so intricate and nuanced that it

understood intent, not just actual distance. I could have sat next to Ryker, and if I had done nothing to help save his life when he needed me, the same result would have happened.

One more reason we didn't fuck with this shit. The gods and goddesses of old were twisted assholes. They loved pain, torture, sex, and blood.

The ship surged as we pushed off from the dock. The landscape through my large window changed as we backed up, turning toward the sea.

A low cry came from Kat, her limbs twitching violently.

"You're going to be okay." Reaching out, my palms pressed down on her arms. A zing ran up my hands as her body eased. This time a low moan purred from her as if my touch filled her with relief. The sound shot straight into my dick, an electrical charge forcing me to pull away. The moment I did, her face scrunched up, her legs kicking out, whimpering.

What the fuck was that?

"Shhhhh. It's okay." I inhaled before cautiously laying my hand on the side of her face, sensing the same zap. I kept my hand there, brushing through her damp hair, instantly quieting her. I used to be awful at caring for people, but it was another thing Lexie taught me. She suffered a lot after all the things Dr. Rapava did to her. I spent hours either trying to make her laugh or trying to soothe her, willing to do anything so she didn't feel pain anymore.

The ship creaked when we hit the main ocean, breaking against the waves as we made our way out of the canal. My gaze got lost in the backdrop of the stunning water glinting off the lowering sun. The ocean had a way of calming me instantly and making me feel I was right where I was supposed to be. Getting lost in the view, I didn't realize a good chunk of time had passed.

I suddenly noticed how quiet she was. My head lowered as I realized my fingers were still threading her hair. Oxygen sucked through my nose. Kat's bright yellow and green eyes unabashedly stared at me, bare chest and all, as if she had been watching me for a while.

I pulled my hands away from her and cleared my throat. "You're awake." I shifted away from her, standing up. "Feeling better?"

Her intense gaze stayed on me, her tongue sliding over her dry lips. She took a few seconds before she nodded.

The moment she did, something clicked in me. The irrational response I had earlier shifted to her. I wanted to attack and scream. All the fear I had been holding curled into fury, bubbling up my spine, singeing and melting away all my humanity.

"What the fuck did you do, Katrina?" My shoulders rose along with my voice. "You are so fucking lucky Scot recognized what was happening to you!" I motioned out my door. "Otherwise, you would be brain dead right now!" I started to pace. Weak, she struggled to sit up. "Did you make a fucking *promise,* Kat?"

She flinched at my question.

"Did you?"

Her mouth stayed shut.

"Tell me!" I bellowed.

She still didn't respond.

"Oh, no, you don't get to go silent now." I motioned to my hands and arms. "See this? This is *your* blood all over me."

She touched her face, patting at the dried substance around her eyes and nose.

"So you don't get to pull the 'I can't tell you' bullshit with me. I had to pay double for the men and triple the price for materials to get this ship fixed *today*. For *you*!" I gestured down to the hull. "I swear to fuck, Kat, you better explain to me, as someone who knows better, why the fuck would you make a vow?"

"Because I *had* to." Her voice broke but came out sharper and louder than I expected.

141

"You had to?" I folded my arms. "Did someone save your life and you foolishly vowed your life back to them?" Yeah, I did. I was exactly the kind of idiot back then who would do that.

"No." She slid off the bed, her legs wobbled, but she forced herself up to her full height, which was still barely anything. "Let's say I didn't have a choice and leave it at that."

"That's adorable. You think you're gonna get off the hook?"

"Just drop me off at the next port, and we can go our separate ways like you wanted from the beginning."

A huff of air blew out of my nose as I strolled closer to her, using my physique to shadow her, my crossed arms almost touching her. "That's not how this works, Kitty-Kat."

Her lids narrowed, her chin jerking up. She was weak, wobbly, but even with blood, sweat, and tears dried on her face, she was still such a force. Still breathtaking. And that made me want to punish her. To show her that even after all these years, with all her training and plans, I was still the king.

"And I know you too well. You will never let me go. You've been after me for too long to walk away. You know nothing else." A smug grin tugged at my lips when she bristled at my statement. Her own anger billowed off her, bumping against me. "So, you are going to tell me everything. And I mean *everything*."

"Fuck you," she hissed.

"Think you tried that already." I inched even closer.

"I haven't even gotten close to fucking you yet," she challenged, our faces only inches apart.

"Promises, promises."

Her chest heaved in and out, her cheeks flushed with anger.

"What's wrong, Kitty-Kat?" I smirked because she didn't like the nickname. Killian was the only one she didn't get mad at, but something about her now made me want to push every button. Pick at every scab.

Something told me she wanted to hurt me back. Her energy rolled down my vertebrae, binding around my dick. Violence pulsed in the room, both of us walking a fine line. I was overwhelmed with the desire to kill her... or grab her roughly by the head and kiss the fuck out of her.

"Captain?" Scot stepped into the cabin.

I treaded quickly back, sucking in through my nose. Fuck. I was about a breath away from doing something very, very stupid. This was Katrina, Fredrich Roth's little girl. I knew her when she was younger than when I had met Lexie. It was sick. It didn't matter if she was grown-up now. She wasn't to be touched or looked at.

"Yes?" I spoke to my second, but my glower stayed on Kat.

"Tsai has set us north but needs to know where in China. It's a pretty big fucking place."

Kat bit her lip, her gaze sliding to the side.

"You're not getting off this ship anytime soon." I didn't take my eyes off her. "And sorry, little kitty, but you owe us. We saved your life. We're in this now. It's us, or we take you back to Singapore." I tilted my head. "I have a feeling you were trying to get away from there for a reason. It was your ship in the harbor, wasn't it? With the emperor's flag on it?"

Her nose flared enough to give my theory credit.

"Thought so."

"Are you blackmailing me?" She scowled at me.

"Nothing you wouldn't do to me." And she knew it. Hell, Katrina would probably do far worse to me.

"Tell me why and to whom you made this promise. And where in China we're going."

She shifted on her feet, struggling a bit before she sighed. "I don't know."

143

"Don't know who you made your vow to?" My brows went up.

"No." She peered between Scot and me. "Where exactly in China. I just know whatever I'm seeking is there."

"What are you seeking?" Scot came up next to me.

She sat back on the bed, her shoulders drooping, giving up the fight to hold her secret. "I got into a little trouble back in Singapore." Emotion flashed over her face. "I was arrogant and reckless, letting my crew suffer for my shortsightedness. Long story short, we walked into a trap and were ambushed by the emperor's men." She swallowed. "Some of my crew were killed; the others… were taken as hostages."

My head dropped forward when I realized where this was going. Batara was a vindictive asshole. He had a vendetta against pirates because he didn't appreciate others taking the riches he believed were his. He would torture them in the main square in the most humiliating and gruesome way.

"Instead of torturing and killing them all, we made a deal."

"Fuck, lass." Scot rubbed his head. "You made a vow? To *that* man?"

She nodded. "He had my ship, my crew. My entire world. Everything I worked for. All the things that meant anything to me. I *had* to."

"What do you have to do in exchange?" Dread built up through my chest like a wall.

"It's crazy." She shook her head. "It's not even possible to achieve. He's so desperate to cure his sick son he has me chasing after a myth. Now I'm stuck, and I have to go after it."

"What do you have to go after?" Scot prompted. "Treasure? He doesn't seem like he needs any more."

"No, it's not money. It's an object… something he called the *nectar*."

Nectar. The word slammed into me.

"I'm going to find my brother... and this object they call the nectar."

"Holy. Fuck." I stepped back in shock, feeling I had been hit with a mallet but had yet to recognize the blow, my brain still swimming in disbelief. The conversation I overheard at the bar last night replayed in my head. I had blown it off as intoxicated embellishments, as nothing more than a bullshit story, which was how most gossip and rumors started—a drunk loudmouth in a bar.

"What?" Scot turned to me. "What's wrong?"

I shook my head, dumbfounded, slowly raising my gaze to Katrina. "You aren't the only one who's after it."

"What?" Kat stood up. "What do you mean? You've heard of it before?"

"Yes." I nodded, glancing at my first mate. "Scot, go tell Tsai I have her destination."

"Where?" Scot asked.

"Shanghai."

Chapter 13
Katrina

"Shanghai?" I parroted, watching the large Scotsman stride out of the room, instantly reacting to his captain's order, while my head spun in utter confusion.

What the fuck was happening?

The moment the door clicked behind Scot, Croygen's dark, erotic eyes slid to me, his gaze intense. My legs wobbled under my weight, forcing me to lean back on his bed to stay upright.

"I don't understand. How do you know that? How do you even know what this nectar is?" My voice came out fainter than I expected.

"I just do." Every syllable was purposeful, filled with danger. "I need you to tell me *everything*."

Ire slithered up the back of my neck. "Not before you tell me how you know about it!" I snapped back.

Croygen's eyes darkened, if that was even possible, his shoulders setting back. "Kat..."

It was a warning. A threat. One I knew all too well from my childhood, when I would watch some new crew member or captive not picking up on the change in the captain's tone.

They always figured it out too late.

But I wasn't some dupe he could command. I was his rival. A pirate to be feared. My idol had fallen from grace, and I would never be the little girl who revered him again.

I could never forget he was the man who killed my father.

Straightening my spine, I overrode the fatigue holding my body ransom, the glaze of sweat and blood covering my skin. "You can't order me around, Croygen. I'm not your subordinate."

A small grunt was my only warning before he advanced toward me, faster than I expected. My reflexes were slow from exhaustion, and he slammed my back against the bedpost. A gasp hitched my lungs when he gripped my jaw, jerking my head up to him.

"Not how it works," he rumbled. His ripped bare chest pressed into the thin tank I wore, rubbing against my breasts, pouring heat down my spine. My defenses rose, trying to block my reaction, deny anything but absolute abhorrence. "You know there can't be two captains on a ship. So, either you are crew, *Katze*, or you are my *prisoner*."

My nose flared because I knew that. It would be the same on my ship as well. I had a problem going back to being *his* crew.

"Then I guess I am a prisoner," I snarled. "I will never bow to your orders again."

A smirk lifted the side of his mouth, his grip on me tightening as he moved in closer. "Want to make a little wager on that?" He pushed against me, raising my tank past my thighs, the fabric of his pants parting my folds. My muscles locked up, and I had to fight to keep a moan from escaping.

Croygen's fingers pinched my jaw, sparking heat into my nerves. His hips curled into me, dragging over me again. My lashes fluttered and my thighs parted, a slight arch curving my back. Cat-shifters were known to be sexual. The moment we hit puberty, we were "in heat." And unlike real cats, it wasn't only for a season. It was constant, and why I always had to let off steam, which had been far too long for me now.

I was horny as fuck. That had to be the reason for my response to the man I despised. *My father's killer*. It. Had. To. Be. I wouldn't accept anything else.

"How fast I could have you bowing to my *every* demand, Kitty-Kat." His mouth almost touched mine, our breaths mingling, his voice raspy.

"Not a fucking chance," I spat back. The hollowness of the statement boiled more anger in me. I hated weakness; I hated that I hadn't killed him yet. I hated that I stood here, frozen, because he still had this strange power over me.

He should be dead. My vengeance complete.

"Though you will bend to mine." A malicious grin curved my mouth as I wrapped one leg around him, bringing him even closer and making sure he could feel my heat, the power and magic I knew I could induce.

His muscles flexed, a jolt running through him, his massive erection getting even stiffer against me, pushing so hard against his trousers, his jaw snapped together. His hand dropped from my face, going to the post over my head as if he was trying to stay upright.

His eyes flashed, a grin forming on his mouth. "Oh, kitten, you are not ready to play at my level." It took a lot to provoke Croygen, but I had witnessed times when he snapped.

Death came with a ruthless, beautiful smirk. Even staring into the eyes of a murderer, I understood how so many went willingly into death. Croygen was sultry and carnal, flipping something in one's brain which hit on one's most perverse desires.

The depraved thought of him pounding into me as he choked me to death had my heart thumping in my ears and shivers burning up my skin.

"Do not forget who I am." One hand fell from the post, moving down my frame, his fingers gripping the thigh on his hip, yanking me into him. My teeth crunched together, sweat gathering behind my neck. He leaned his face into me. "What I am known for." His fingers glided to the space between my inner thigh and pussy, hinting at more. A broken noise stuck in my throat, raw need washing over me, my hips curving, forcing another grunt from me. "And why I am a legend."

I had always been in charge when it came to sex. When, where, and with who. They begged me. They were the ones on their knees.

Now, with a hint of his touch, tears built behind my lids, the ache so deep I could feel a plea forming in my mouth.

"You may be a recognized pirate now, even a renowned one, but you are nowhere near my level, *Kitty-Kat*," he muttered, a ghostlike touch brushing over my folds. "I will *always* win."

His two fingers parted me, sliding into me. My mouth opened on a cry; my body jolted like I had been electrocuted. A surge of magic blasted up my spine, bucking me. He sucked in sharply, a choked sound tearing out of his throat, his own body shuddering as if he had experienced the same thing.

"We are set for Shanghai." The door swung open, Scot's tall frame sauntering in. Both of us scrambled away from each other like thieves getting caught. Yanking down my tank, I sucked in, smoothing my features to appear normal. Unflustered. "If the winds stay right, we should be there in a week," Scot muttered, his eyes darting from Croygen to me suspiciously.

When the door opened, reality hurtled into the room like a tsunami, shattering whatever trance Croygen seemed to have put me in.

Holy fuck. What was I about to do?

Scot snorted, shaking, seemingly seeing right through us. "Do I need to have a babysitter around at all times?"

149

My actions in my own head were bad enough, but seeing them through someone else's eyes branded me with dishonor, especially because I could still feel Croygen's fingers touching me, like they had burned into me.

"Shut up." Croygen barked, fury thick in his timbre. Shame. He wouldn't look at me, his expression tight with anger. "Take her to the crew's showers. Get her a change of clothes. Have the crew convene in the mess hall in twenty minutes." His order was brisk as he stomped toward his private bathroom, slamming the door behind him.

Scot turned to me, his eyes glinting with mischief. "What are you doing to our captain, Kitty-Kat?"

"Don't call me that," I ground out.

He huffed in humor. "Follow me, *ciabhagan*." His Scottish accent thickened as he motioned me to follow him.

"And that means?"

Scot didn't answer as he led me down to the crew level to the showers. Scot flicked his head at a stall down at the end. "I'll get you some clothes to wear."

"Thanks." I started to turn away.

"I knew your father briefly." His claim stopped me in my tracks, whipping me back around. "He was a good man."

I blinked at Scot.

"What happened that day…" He swallowed like he shouldn't be telling me this. "It really fucked Captain up. He went to a very dark place for a long time."

The anger I lacked earlier came sprouting up like weeds with refreshed energy.

"Dark place?" I lifted a brow. "He murdered my father, his right-hand man, in cold blood. He hasn't even touched the darkness I plan to bring to him."

Chapter 14
Croygen

The jeers of my crew batted me like the howling wind outside, the ship rocking as Tsai directed us around a tropical storm, the motion making my whiskey spill out of my cup.

"Oi!" Scot whistled, silencing the others. "Let the captain speak."

The change in direction and my plan to take us to Shanghai was not going over well with Zid, Corb, and Vane. Corb grunted his opinion as Vane and Zidane yelled theirs.

"Why would we head to Shanghai? Don't we have a price on our heads there?" Vane exclaimed.

"Didn't know you were such a coward?" Scot folded his arms.

"Que te jodan!" Fuck you! Vane lurched for Scot.

Zid grabbed his collar, yanking him back. "Calm the fuck down." He shoved Vane back into a chair, annoyance showing along his jaw. His serious gaze returned to me, demanding I make it clear why I had a change of heart.

Kat's presence was palpable even though I had Scot lock her in one of the windowless crew bedrooms downstairs, double-checking for anything she could use as a weapon. My slipup earlier, my loss of right and wrong, of any reason, banged like a drum in my chest. What made me so disgusted with myself, so ashamed, is that I was forcing myself to feel guilt. To keep reminding myself I had watched her grow up.

One time was bad enough, my feelings for Lexie shifting slightly, but this was even worse. And I was not that type of man.

The memory of Lexie the last night before the battle, the way she linked her hands with mine, her beautiful brown eyes sparking with desire, a desperation to her words.

"Spend the night with me."

"I don't think that's a good idea, lil shark."

"Tomorrow we might die..." *She pressed on, never taking no for an answer.* *"I don't care about right or wrong or some notion you have in your head about why this can't happen. I love you, Croygen. I have since the day I met you. And if tonight is all we have, I want to spend it with you."*

"Captain?" Zidane's voice snapped me out of my thoughts, pulling me back to the present.

Rubbing my head, I exhaled. "Yes, we have a bounty on our heads in Shanghai." Most pirates did. If Emperor Batara was known for his cruelty, Emperor Ju was going for most diabolical. He was old-school in his torture, taking up methods from Vlad the Impaler and Genghis Khan. All these men relished that they no longer had to play nice in the human world. The moment the fae were discovered and the worlds merged, they seemed to feel they had a right to be as horrible as they needed to be to keep humans "safe." Total bullshit. Ju impaled more of his own people than anyone else for not paying their taxes.

His views on pirates were even worse than Batara's. And he didn't like me much.

"Maybe if you hadn't fucked his wife." Vane huffed.

Yeah, I did that.

"And then his eldest daughter the same night."

"It was her twentieth birthday." I shrugged. "I couldn't say no to the birthday girl."

"You really are a sick fuck." Zid dropped into his seat with a laugh.

"You think you should talk, Zid?" I lifted an eyebrow. No one on this ship had any room to judge.

"With all our lives at risk, give us a good reason why we're going back there?"

My gaze went to Scot, his chin dipping subtly.

Inhaling, I breathed out my answer. "Katrina."

Confusion wrinkled the men's brows. Corb, always the silent, unemotional one, even appeared baffled.

"Kitty-Kat?" Vane spoke.

"Don't call her that." I shot back, my voice lethal and deadly, jerking him back in his seat. A strange, protective vibe itched my shoulders because she hated others calling her that name. It could be intimate or demeaning. The fact that Killian could use it had always made me somewhat jealous. They had this bond, two kids growing up on a pirate ship together. It was not hard to see that he was completely enamored of her. And when I forced her off the ship, his admiration for me grew into animosity. Over the years, it turned to hate.

And in this world of cutthroat monsters, I couldn't have any mistrust among my crew.

"Katrina made a vow," I reported. "To Emperor Batara."

Zid and Vane sucked in while Corb made a grunt of surprise.

"Why the fuck would she do that?" Vane sat up in his chair.

"To save her crew, her ship, and her life," I replied, taking a sip of whiskey. "He has her going after something to cure his sick son."

"And don't tell me… it's in Shanghai?" Zid ran his hand over his dreadlocks.

"Okay, so we drop her ass off, and we go on our way." Vane lifted his hands. "Right?"

I wish it were that easy, but even when my mind told me it was the best option, I couldn't bring myself to agree with the plan, something locking my jaw shut.

"What is she even looking for? Why can't he get it in Singapore himself? Or have Ju ship it to him? They are allies." Zid leaned over his thighs, no doubt realizing this was more than I was saying.

"That's the thing. What she's looking for…" I peered at my entire crew. "Might not even exist."

"What do you mean, it might not exist?" Vane wagged his head in confusion.

"In desperation to save his son, Batara has her looking for something called *the nectar*."

"Nectar? Like in flower nectar?" Vane asked.

"Nectar as in the gods." At Tsai's crackly voice, I turned to the blind woman stepping into the room.

"I know you're old and senile," Vane said as he turned to speak to her. "But that shit is a myth and would definitely not exist now that the wall has fallen."

"*Boy*, I may be old, but it only means I have seen much more than you, have experienced things no one would believe. Look at me. I am said to be a tall tale myself. Myths always stem from some truth." She shuffled closer, continuing. "In the ancient folklores, ambrosia was the food or drink of the gods. This was often depicted as conferring longevity or immortality upon whoever consumed it. From it, the fae race was born, separating humans from fae and driving a violent jealousy and fear between them. Humans pushed fae into hiding by slaughtering them by the thousands. The gods were furious, and because of their anger, vindictive. If a human accidentally came into the fae world and had any fae food or drink, they would become addicted. No human food would nourish them, no drink would quench their thirst. They'd wither away and die painfully if they stayed on Earth. To live, they became the very thing they used to fear and had to join the fae world, never to leave again."

"Okay, but we don't have a fae world anymore, nor fae food." Vane lifted one shoulder, pulling my focus from Tsai.

"Yes, it was all destroyed when the barrier dropped, but there are whisperings that on the night of the Fae War, all that magic, death, and blood was like a sacrifice to the gods, creating a substance so potent, so concentrated, it became even more powerful than the gods themselves. Death couldn't even intercede."

"Okay, old woman, you have finally flown the coop, haven't you?"

"You know I can still kill a man with just my thighs while I'm fucking him."

"Ahhhh!" All of us cringed, making her snicker.

"Come on now, I'll need to drink that image out of my head for the next month." Scot rubbed at his forehead.

"How do you think I know all this? Men enjoy talking in bed while I'm riding them raw."

"Stop!" Vane held up his hand. "Please. Stop."

"You are all so fragile." Tsai swished her hand at us. "Perfectly normal for older women to be sexually active."

"Older?" Vane huffed out. "You're several millennia old or something!"

"Can we get back on topic, please?" I could feel a headache coming on. "What are you saying, Tsai? That this rumored substance is the nectar they are seeking?"

"Yes."

"It would be the only thing that could cure disease, give them an extended life and fae abilities. Humans have been hunting for its equal for a long, long time," Scot added. "Could you imagine the money and power one would have if they found something to do all that?"

"But it's a story, right?" Vane glanced between all of us. "We're not seriously thinking about going after something that probably doesn't even exist?"

Corb grunted in agreement.

"What if it's not?" My eyes slid to him. "I've seen things I could never explain." Like Ryker carrying the Stone of Fál, one of the treasures of Tuatha Dé Danann, which was supposed to be a myth too.

"True." Zid nodded. "I was on the field five years ago, fighting in the Fae War. I saw a man get sliced in half, and a moment later rise from the dead, completely healed."

Vane's attention went over us all, noting no one else seemed to be pushing back.

"You got to be kidding me?" He folded his ankle over his knee. "Let me get this straight. You want us to sail into a place that, if caught, we will be tortured and brutalized, getting a rod stuck up our ass—"

"Don't act like you wouldn't enjoy it." Scot scoffed.

"I like the ones that don't also come out my throat as I slowly die for weeks."

"Think of how many women you'll have to fight off if we find the most coveted object in the world." Zid knew exactly how to taunt Vane. "Riches beyond your dreams, the finest jewels and clothes, and dining at the most prestigious places."

"I don't know, my dreams are pretty extravagant." Vane curved an eyebrow.

"I'd prefer it to be unanimous," I stated, though I knew I was doing it anyway, with or without my crew. I was a pirate. We coveted treasure; we craved adventure. It wasn't because of the petite cat-shifter. It was all for selfish reasons.

"All opposed?" Scot requested, no one speaking. "All in favor?"

"Aye!" All except Vane. We all turned to him, waiting.

"Fine." He huffed. "Aye."

I had no idea how I was going to go about this. Getting into Shanghai was dangerous enough, but where would I even start looking for this item? There were a few black-market sellers I could talk to, but every person I spoke with was another person who might want to join in on the treasure hunt. And I already had one too many in my way.

Kat might be the reason I even knew of its existence, but she was just as much my competition. She needed to take it back to Batara, but I would be the one to take it from her.

The humidity crept up on the ship the closer we got to land, robbing us of the breeze we had out at sea. The skyline rose higher, a tidal wave of skyscrapers, concrete, and metal. Everything made me shiver with revulsion. It smelled of millions of people stuffed in one place together, like death and poverty. A prison of lost dreams and memories of a day that would never return. Not with Ju in charge.

So many countries thought pulling away from Lars and Kennedy and forming their own authority would show strength. Except the rulers seemed to use it as a way to control and money grab, forgetting that nations trade and function together, not separately. The people were in favor at first, getting behind these autocratic rulers, only to find it was not the utopia they thought it would be.

It was hell.

Making our vessel appear as much like a trading ship as we could, we still veered for a quieter port off one of the nearby islands, then took a smaller craft into the city. Ju had a tight rein on what was going in and out of his ports, always on the lookout for bold pirates daring to fleece him.

Fear was not an emotion I experienced much, and I would never show if I did, but my nerves wrapped tightly in my gut because of how much we were putting on the line. How quickly this could all go wrong.

"Captain?" Scot's voice spoke behind me, but it wasn't him who caused the prickle at the back of my neck. My awareness of her was a tide, moving out and back in. A cat ready to pounce. My shoulders tensed, keeping my gaze straight ahead. I had stayed clear of her most of the journey, drinking in my cabin until I passed out each night so I wouldn't go down and see her. The need was always there; the craving kept me restless. Even sleeping, I got no rest, the vixen slipping into my dreams.

Barricading myself, I slowly twisted around, showing no mercy.

Kat's stunning eyes caused my teeth to crunch together, raking anger through me. Dressed in Tsai's pants and deck shoes, she wore one of my old black T-shirts tied up. Her long dark hair curtained around her like a cloak, shining in the early morning rays.

I wanted to hate her, to dismiss her as I do too many who cross my path, friend or foe. Yes, she was the daughter of an old crew member. Yes, I had watched her grow up. Yes, she was stunning as hell. But she was still my enemy. Here to slit my throat when I let my guard down, no matter what truce we had.

I could never forget, no matter her size, that she was Puss in Boots, the ruthless pirate who drew you in only to cut you down. She had killed some cold-blooded, savvy, well-known pirates already.

With my own methods.

158

"Katrina," I said formally, not sounding at all like me. "You look much improved."

A sardonic smile hinted on her lips. "All thanks to you, *Captain*." She tilted her head. "Or do you want to be called *master*?"

Fuck.

Her screwing with me only hardened my cock more, dropping all pretense, my rage building under my skin. With Scot behind her, I stepped into her so she had nowhere to go. Her breath hitched up her throat, her spine knocking into the Scotsman. She locked down her response, keeping her expression blank, lifting her chin to me.

"Don't push me, Katrina." I gripped her chin, getting only a breath away from her. "I'm about a hair's breadth away from locking you back in the hull and chaining you with goblin metal while I go searching for this nectar myself."

She stiffened, pushing away from Scot, getting even closer to me. "You do, and you will find your neck smiling by morning."

"You're adorable." My gaze purposely rolled over her as if she was insignificant and clawless. "You forget I taught you everything you know, little cat."

"Master Yukimura trained me. All I learned from you was betrayal, cruelty, and how to *fuck* to get what I want."

Heat expanded my veins, burning me from the inside, pressure seizing my chest at her statement. Anger frosted the edges, coating the jealousy, lust, and guilt rumbling underneath. A picture of her riding someone flamed up possessiveness, locking up my muscles.

My nose bumped hers. "And who do you think trained me?" I replied, shoving the image down deep, using my ire as fuel. "There isn't a move you can make that I don't already know." I stepped away. "Prepare for port and get the dinghy ready for the two of us," I ordered Scot.

159

"You don't want us to go with you?" Scot frowned.

"Too many of us to recognize. It will be just Kat and me."

He shook his head. "Captain?"

"That's an order," I stated firmly. "Get her some breakfast before we anchor."

Scot nodded, about to turn around, taking her with him.

"Kat?" I called her name, her head twisting back to me. "If you renege on our truce, be sure my punishment will be much more ruthless than you ever dreamed up."

Her jaw clenched, lids narrowed as she turned away and stalked off. Her wrath was so vivid I could taste it on my tongue, causing my body to tighten, getting off on her rage.

My gaze was so fixed on her retreating form it took me a few moments to realize Scot was standing there, staring at me.

"What?"

Scoffing, he rubbed his bearded chin. "I have known you *a long* time, and in all those centuries, I have seen you with a lot of lasses, including Amara." He wagged his head. "But I have never seen you as fucked as you are now." He strolled away before I could respond, his statement echoing in my gut, riling up resentment and defensiveness.

Fuck that shit. I would never be fucked over by a woman again. Amara was a mirror of me then. Opportunistic, seductive, with no morals or boundaries. We were too much alike, but I stupidly believed it made us perfect together, bringing out each other's worst side at a time I didn't want a conscience. I didn't want to remember all I had lost, what I had done. She played me like a fiddle, using me, stringing me along, bringing me close again only to stomp on what was left of my black heart.

Finally, I had seen the error of my ways, and now I was ashamed of my weakness. I vowed I would never let it happen again. Especially with a foe whose father's blade hung on my belt.

Pirates weren't meant to be with one person. Our love was the sea, the adventure, tasting and sampling everything all over the world. Gaining riches, killing, and plundering.

And that was the way I wanted it.

The sky rumbled with an early afternoon thunderstorm, suffocating the air with humidity and adding to the stench in the streets. A mix of spices, food, garbage, feces, body odor, and rats.

"Stay close," I muttered to Kat from under my hood, pulling her in tighter, my attention on anyone bumping into us, the streets bustling with activity around us. I had seen Shang-hai grow from a new trading post to a pirate haven, rocketing to the top when it became a major exporter of cars, phones, and computers. When the wall fell, magic destroyed all of it, plunging Shang-hai into dark times, splitting the rich and poor even more.

Nowadays, it was yet another city becoming a shadow of itself as the elite took more and more, ignoring everything beyond their own needs while the working class suffered under the heavy hand of greed and cruelty.

It was scary how fast prevalent cities could fall in the aftermath when their communist tendency went full force or they returned to the "warlord era."

The crowded, dirty sidewalks, filled with horse carriages and wagons, were lined with skyscrapers, a strange mix of the old world and new. The extreme between the haves and have-nots was prevalent, the poor now back in rags, trying to make a small living in the streets while Emperor Ju and his rich friends lived in excessive wealth away from the poverty-stricken people he forced to be here. And every year, more and more joined the impoverished, becoming another statistic.

The less money and opportunities there were, the more cutthroat a place became, everyone trying to claw a little higher up the ladder, trying to survive.

Keeping our heads deep in our hoods, a cloth across our nose and mouth to not only block the stench of horseshit and sewer, but to keep our faces hidden, I steered us toward the area even most criminals and Ju's police stayed away from. The area was run by the Chinese mafia, who controlled the black market, which included almost everything. Ju had made many things illegal—alcohol, porn, drugs, prostitution, weapons—pretty much anything wanted by the people. But in doing so, he drove the need higher. Restricting people only made them more desperate for it.

Especially anything which lets the people escape this hell.

"This way," I muttered in Kat's ear, tugging her down an alley, the thunderclouds darkening the passage in deeper shadows. The air changed, even in the humidity, and the hair on my arms prickled. Every person working a cart we passed, hanging around smoking, was watching us. Nothing happened in this area without the Triads knowing. The deeper we went into their territory, the more hostile eyes were on us. My connections here were old because I hadn't been in these parts in a long time, but I had no doubt Duan Ru was still here. The man had been around as long as Tsai, and he was the person you went to for information.

Tension wormed up my back as I kept my head forward. I was aware of everything around me, sensing figures following us to the pub which, funnily enough, was called "Smugglers Inn," a criminal haven since the early days of piracy.

"We're being followed," I whispered to Kat, holding her firmly on one side, my grip on my weapon on the other. I picked up our steps a little, trying not to act like I felt threatened by them.

As the pub came into sight, a string of men, loaded down with guns and swords, stepped in front of us, blocking our way, jolting me to a stop.

"Shit." I hissed under my breath, pulling Kat to a stop with me as more of these guys surrounded us, making me twitch with tension. The need to protect her, to keep her safe, forced my body slightly in front of hers. "Stay quiet. Let me handle this," I muttered to her. Besides being able to slip away into the shadows, my talent to get myself out of any predicament with a flick of my silver-tongue was my forte.

"Not looking for trouble," I spoke. "Just wanting to get a drink. Meet up with an old friend."

"You have no friends here." A man pushed through the throng, stepping out in front.

Shit.

The man was all of five feet, six inches, a little fatter than I recalled, but still had the same sharp eyes and scar on his upper lip.

One I put there.

"Yeo…" I grimaced. "Look at you now."

"Croygen," he snarled. Our paths had crossed lifetimes ago when he was an errand boy for the Triad boss. He was smart and ruthless and clearly worked up to the top. Lucky me. "You dare step into my city?"

"Was your name on the welcome sign? Sorry, I must have missed it under the layer of horseshit."

He glowered at me. "I have waited for this day, and then they told me you were here."

"I'm so flattered you missed me." I put my hands on my chest. "I've been feeling so low about myself lately, so you don't know how much this means to me."

"Shut. Up." He stepped closer. "The first thing I'm going to do is cut your tongue out and hang it alongside your head."

"Please hang it so it displays my left side." I twisted my head to him. "It's my better side."

"Kill him."

Yeo's men lurched for me.

"Stop!" Kat's voice yelled next to me as she yanked down her hood, showing her face.

Yeo's eyes widened, the first emotion I had ever seen on him. In a blink, he held up his hand, speaking in Chinese. The men came to a halt at his order.

"Katrina?" He gaped at her.

My head snapped back and forth between them. Her gaze flicked to me with a smirk before turning to him.

"Hello, *tomodachi*." *Friend*.

"Baobei." Treasure. He opened his arms, wrapping her in them.

What the fuck was going on?

"What are you doing here?" He pulled back, his gaze going to me with hatred. "With him?"

"Him?" She glanced back at me, an eyebrow curving up. With one word, Katrina could seek her revenge. End her connection with me right here. He would gladly kill me where I stood, and she could order it to happen.

I swear I could see the moment she debated the options, a smile curving her lips.

"Unfortunately, I need him. So, I can't have you killing him right now." She sighed like it was an inconvenience. "We need to be under your protection while we are here. Both of us."

Yeo's icy features locked on me for a moment, the scar at his mouth twitching before he dipped his head in agreement to her demands.

"Only because you ask, Katrina." He spoke directly to her. "You are both under my protection, *baobei*. You have my word. But no trouble." He pointed his finger at her. "No fighting. And I have to take your guns. It's the law here."

"Still old-school, huh?" she teased as his guards relieved us of only our pistols, leaving our blades.

"Only way to keep order. Plus, guns are human laziness the fae are picking up on too easily. We used to kill with honor and die with pride." I had never seen this man show a shred of emotion or empathy, gutting a father in front of his child, but he treated Katrina like a goddess. "And, *baobei*, you don't need anything more. You are one of the best fighters I have ever seen."

"Thank you." She kissed his cheek.

He gestured for his men to recede, glowering at me as he strolled off, his gang clumped around him.

Twisting to Kat, I shook my head. "What the fuck—"

She was in front of me in a blink. "You ever treat me like a subordinate again, I will cut out your tongue myself," she muttered calmly, but her anger oozed out. "Do not *ever* forget who I am. I'm *not* the little girl you once knew, a girl who needs to be protected and saved. I have dropped leaders of lands to their knees, taken out dozens of fighters at once as they pissed themselves and pleaded for my pity." She stepped back. "And never forget I just spared your life." She whirled to go into the pub.

"How do you have Yeo wrapped around your finger?" I shot at her. "You sleep with him?"

She stopped as thunder shuddered overhead, rain pouring down, soaking into my clothes.

Slowly she turned to me, her glare filled with anger, disbelief, and disappointment that I asked her that. "No," she spat. "But I am the reason he is the leader of the Triad now." She flung open the door and marched inside.

I stood still in a mix of shock, fear, pride, and relief.
And my dick was harder than stone.
Shit… Scot might be right… I might be truly fucked.

Chapter 15
Katrina

The Smuggler's Inn was in the heart of the Triad quarter, accommodating all stereotypical criminals and pirates who needed a place to hide. Crowded, dark, old, smelling of stale ale, body odor, and debauchery. It wasn't necessarily the place I liked to hang out, but in this area, we didn't have a lot of choice. My face was known among Ju's men, and I would be a great catch for Emperor Ju. If I were caught, Batara would find out I was still alive, and I wanted to avoid that at all costs.

There was no denying my insecurity walking in this time, pulling my hood back up. Normally, I burst through the doors, Hurricane and Typhoon flanking me while Gage took the front. Zuri and Moses had my back, Polly and Dobbs trailing in after, making people shrink back in fear. The absence of my crew stabbed the truth in my gut, driving me forward. Reminding me why I was here with Croygen, working with my enemy instead of killing him.

Croygen came up behind me, his presence nipping at my skin. Biting down on my lip, I ignored how my body responded to his nearness, how thin the line was between wanting to strangle him and wanting him to push me up against the bar and make me come on that wicked tongue of his.

I shook my head at that last thought, recalling how close he kept me to him the whole way here. The audacity he had, treating me like some girl he could order around, helpless and unskilled, not an equal partner or a feared pirate in my own right.

Yet how fast he stepped in front of me, guarding me…

No, Kat. I hissed at myself. *He treated you like a child.*

"Two Yamazaki 12 Years Old whiskeys," I ordered at the bar, heading for a table by a window as the rain poured down. Croygen lifted an eyebrow as he took a seat, making sure he could see the entire room. "What? Has your taste changed?"

"No." He leaned back in his seat, pushing off his damp hood and retying his hair back. "Just surprised you knew that."

"You used to share a bottle with my father every time you returned after being in this area." For some reason, I couldn't look at him as I recalled a memory. "I remember I was almost ten. You and the crew went whoring while my father stayed to watch the ship. You came back with a bottle, smelling of perfume and covered in hickeys."

Croygen's gaze felt heavy, a force that pulled mine over to his. He watched me boldly, peeling away the layers of my walls, seeing way too deeply.

"That bother you, Kat?" His voice was so low, it vibrated through me. Thankfully the waitress dropped our drinks on the table, taking my focus off him. Downing a swig, the rich whiskey burned the back of my throat, sliding into my chest. Yeo made sure he had the best black-market items in his section, the only area in which you could get alcohol.

"Answer me, Kitty-Kat."

My head jerked to him. He knew he could get my attention by calling me that.

He leaned forward on his forearms, his long fingers sliding around the rim of his glass. "Did it bother you I came back smelling of other pussy?"

"Fuck off," I grumbled, taking another sip, my body flaring with heat. At that age, it had been innocent jealousy, a little girl's crush. Now violence stormed up my thighs, churning in my stomach with intensity.

A cheeky grin tugged at his mouth, his tongue sliding over his lip after taking a huge gulp of his drink, his gaze never leaving me.

This man was intense, his power hard not to fall under no matter how much you fought it. No matter what he had done to you. No matter how he destroyed your life.

"Tell me about you and Yeo."

"Why?" I brushed my hair behind my ear, leaning back in my seat. "Does it *bother you?*"

"It might."

His answer startled me, the glass pausing at my lips. I lowered it, glancing away. "We were both on the rise up in our careers. Xiao, the last Triad leader, was making things difficult for me. He didn't respect women, nor was he willing to work with a woman pirate. I eliminated him so Yeo could take his place. Something which benefited us both. Now I have someone who will forever be in my debt."

"Damn," Croygen scoffed. "Little did I know *Katze* would turn out so ruthless."

"There is a lot about me you don't know."

"So it appears." He took a drink, his gaze fixed on me the whole time, my core pulsing under his watch and the aura he exuded.

Were we flirting?

I jerked my head to the side, scanning the crowd. "Who are we looking for?"

"Don't worry. He'll find us."

I inspected the pub, low murmurs and bursts of laughter permeating the small room. Some women stood in the corner, clearly here to *entertain* for a price. Each time I came, it got seedier and more crowded. A multitude of people searching for a way to dull the harshness of life, to find an escape from the endless suffering of Ju's stranglehold. Drinking away the idea that they probably once supported Ju's claim to the throne, happy that Shanghai would be independent, a stronghold against the West and against fae leaders. Only they became the very thing they feared they would—victims of an extreme fascist regime.

"I am curious." Croygen played with his glass, spinning the inch of liquid left in it, waiting for my full attention.

"About?"

"Killian."

The name was a jolt to my spine, and I was not ready to hear it from his lips. A flash of lightening flickered the dim firebulbs in the room, and I concentrated on them, not responding to Croygen.

"I mean, you two were inseparable."

"Until you forced me off the ship," I shot at him.

"I know he kept in contact with you." Without reacting to my jab, he continued, "I would have thought he'd be velcroed to your side, pissing around you at the mere mention of my name."

My fingers pinched the cup, stirring in my seat.

"He was in love with you." Croygen tipped his head to the side, gauging my response. "You had to know that."

"Is there a point to this?"

Croygen's eyes were unrelenting, and I hated his power to make me squirm. "Not at all surprised he ran straight to you after he left. He would've followed you into hell. But he's not here," he stated. "Why is that?"

I shrugged, trying to cut this conversation short.

"Listening to how he spoke about you, you'd think you would be happily married with a gaggle of babies by now."

"Then I guess you don't know me at all." I glowered at him.

"Wrong, *Katze*." He leaned forward. "I know you *better* than anyone else. You were never something to rein in. You were as wild and free as the sea."

"Is that what you thought when you forced me into boarding school? Having to leave my father and the only home I ever knew."

"I had to." A frown creased his head, finishing his drink before signaling to the server to bring us another round. "You were no longer safe."

"Safe?" I sputtered. "I am capable of taking care of myself."

"Not then." He shook his head. "I will not apologize for protecting you and my crew."

"That crew was my family too."

"Yes, and that would have been forgotten the moment they could no longer fight the pheromones you were putting off."

"Don't give me this bullshit that a man can't control himself and it's all the woman's fault."

"No, we are completely to blame. But you were a cat-shifter going into puberty on a ship full of fae men who were sex-deprived, drunk, and half-insane already. I wasn't going to risk anything happening to you."

I would never forgive him. His choice altered my life forever, and he had no right to decide for me.

"Don't worry. You weren't the only one to hate me." He nodded as the server set down another two drinks. "Killian's animosity was enough for both of you."

"He told me about that night," I said without thinking. "The night you stabbed my father through the heart." My hands began to shake, and I gripped the mug harder to control them. The awareness I was so close to my father's murderer, someone we both trusted.

"Is that what Killian told you?"

"Do you deny it?"

"Not everything is black and white."

"See, that's where we differ. My question is only black and white. Yes or no, Croygen? Did you kill my father?"

Croygen stared at me, his mouth parting, when a figure slipped smoothly into the seat next to him. I was startled by how soundlessly and quickly the old man moved, and I reached for my blade. Croygen scarcely gave me a look, but somehow I understood we were not in danger. I released my grip on my dagger.

"Croygen." The small, gray-haired man bowed his head at my companion, his stern face and stiff body gave the impression he was not someone to joke with. He was all business. Something about him made you feel he fit better in the time of the first dynasty.

"Duan Ru." *Scholar*. Croygen ducked in respect. "Getting slower, my friend. I have been here for at least a half hour now."

"I had business," he replied curtly. "I knew you docked this morning; you are lazy and arrogant."

Croygen snorted, "Good. I'd hate to start changing."

"What do you want?" Duan Ru scowled.

"Always good to catch up with you." Croygen prodded at the old man, then caught my eye, his expression losing all his charm, turning serious. "This is a different kind of request." He took a breath, trying to phrase his words. "We are looking for something. Probably will have no idea what I'm even talking about." He exhaled. "We are searching for what is called *the nectar*."

The old man went still; his only movement was his lids blinking. "No." His voice came out low, his brown eyes darting around the room. "Do not say that word again in here." His gaze subtly scanned around. "There are always eyes and ears."

"You know what it is?" Croygen's eyebrows lifted.

"Forget you ever heard of it. Forget everything about it." Peering around us as he stood up. "I cannot help you." As quick as the man sat down, he slipped out of his chair, disappearing into the crowd.

"O-kay." I peered back at Croygen. "Was that normal?"

"No." Croygen still stared after him, a contemplative expression on his face.

"Well, that was a bust."

"No." His finger tapped at his mug, his dark irises snapping back to me. "Quite the opposite. It gave more legitimacy to it. I have known Duan Ru for a long time, and he's never been afraid of anyone or anything. Tonight he was afraid of something." He tipped his cup to me before taking a drink. "I think we are going in the right direction."

"But we need more to go on."

"Yeah," Croygen agreed, examining the bar. "But we need to be very careful. I have another contact who might know something. She hears a lot of gossip."

"She?" I failed to keep my tone even. "Let me guess, one you are acquainted intimately with?"

"It's like you know me." He winked.

I rolled my eyes, a disgusted huff coming out.

"Be careful, Kitty-Kat. Some might think you're jealous." A sultry smile pulled his lips.

"Far from it," I huffed, rising, needing to get away from him. "Going to the bathroom. Think I need to wash the residue of your ego off me." I turned for the hallway.

"Believe me, you will need more than a rinse if I released my *residue* on you." His comment was mumbled, but I heard it loud and clear, clenching my fists as I strolled for the toilet. A flash of what he was insinuating went through my head, his cum spilling on my stomach, marking my skin as he pushed back inside me.

A growl of anger unfurled in my throat. Slamming into

the bathroom, I leaned over the sink, sucking in a deep breath, hating how this man could still get to me. I should know better, be stronger, be immune to his charms and devilish tongue. But when the man you used to fantasize about is turning his seduction on you, something you only dreamed about at one time, it's hard to fight. No matter what logic and truth is in your face.

"He can really make you crazy." I jerked my head up at the voice to see a slim, beautiful woman reflected in the mirror. I could tell she was from eastern ancestry, but I couldn't put my finger on where, though with her graceful, thin figure, she could easily blend in here. Her red silk wrap suggested she might be "working." Prostitution wasn't blatant here; they were more subtle. A modern version of a *yiji,* which was akin to a geisha. "You look a little young and inexperienced for his normal type." She had a local inflection in her voice.

"Excuse me?" I twisted around.

"He has a talent for making you foolish in all the right and wrong ways, am I right?" Her red-painted lips smiled knowingly. A knot formed in my stomach. "It's impossible to ever stay mad at him."

"I'm sorry, who are you?"

"An old friend." She went to the worn mirror, fixing her perfect hairdo.

"I'll bet." I huffed. "Let me guess, another one of Croygen's *contacts.*" I curled my fingers in a mocking tone.

"Are you any different?" A single eyebrow arched up high.

"It's not like that." I shook my head. "Not between us."

"Yet." She turned back around to look at me.

"Ever."

"Let yourself believe that."

"I don't have time for this." I went for the door, done with his jealous old conquest.

"I want to warn you."

"Warn me about what?" I stopped, my hand on the handle.

"Croygen. Risking his life coming back here means whatever he's searching for must be very important." She tilted her head, almost daring me to deny or confirm her statement. "There is only *one* thing Croygen would ever risk his own skin for, and that's something for himself. If you think you have a deal with him, you don't. He will take it from you in the end."

My face gave nothing away, but inside, alarm bells bashed against my vertebrae.

"Sounds like you really know him. Maybe you should be speaking to him about this." I pulled on the door.

"I'm talking to you because you're the one he's going to screw over."

I whipped back to her. "You may know him from bouncing on his cock, but you don't know me."

"It is one *hell* of a ride. I fully recommend it." She didn't even flinch at my jab. "I'm telling you, from someone who has been deceived by Croygen before. It's in his nature. He will try to take whatever it is in the end. Pirates can't help themselves."

"Well, good thing I am a pirate too." I slammed out of the restroom, ire flaming off me, ready to walk out and leave Croygen to deal with his clinger. I got halfway to our table before my feet slowed as five angry men surrounded Croygen. Two of them were the size of sumo wrestlers, yet Croygen grinned. Cocky, unruffled, and arrogant.

I knew how deadly that swagger could be.

"You fucked my wife!" one of them yelled.

"Shit." I closed my lids briefly, popping them back open when the man yelled again. He was only a foot from Croygen's face. His average body bristled with aggression.

"Maybe if you spent more time with her instead of your

boyfriends here, she wouldn't be looking for someone else to make her come." Croygen finished his drink. "Though, the way she screamed, not sure she ever had a real orgasm before."

I inwardly groaned, knowing what was coming.

On cue, the man lurched for him. In one seamless move, Croygen grabbed the back of his head, slamming his face into the table, the man crumbling to the floor. He didn't hesitate, jumping up and smashing his fist into the next one as the other three attacked, turning over chairs, glass crashing to the floor.

One of the sumo wrestlers grabbed Croygen, chucking him into the next table, tipping it over and hurtling him to the floor.

"Dammit." Blowing out, I wagged my head with annoyance before leaping into the scuffle. The husband and the two wrestlers went after Croygen while I charged after the other two.

I had missed my boots, the sharp blades embedded in the soles, and the way my coat felt like a shield and a cape when I fought. Typhoon and Hurricane had limited my need to fight, but I never backed down from one. The power of seeing the captain herself slice a man's throat in seconds created more fear than anything.

My fist knocked into the back of a man with a goatee, toppling him into a table full of people, sending their drinks flying into the air. They scattered away like seagulls, squawking and flapping to get out of the way. He twisted, coming back for me, while his buddy in a white tank swung out for me.

I ducked as his arm swished over my head. Popping back up, my elbow rammed into White Tank as I kicked Goatee in the stomach, pitching him back. Spinning around, Croygen and I were back-to-back while the five surrounded us, working in tandem as Master Yukimura had taught us. Croygen had often jumped in with Killian and me, upping the

176

stakes in a fight and teaching us how to use each other's strengths and limit our weaknesses.

We slipped into this mode without even thinking or looking at each other, effortless and instinctive, as if we somehow knew each other's moves before we even made them.

One by one, we dropped the men, leaving only a sumo twin and the man who started all of this.

The husband snarled, yanking out a butterfly blade, jumping for Croygen as he fought off the sumo twin.

"Croygen!" My body jolted as I watched the blade slice into his side, blood spurting out. "No!" Fury took over me, my insides heating, my control slipping. Claws grew from my fingers, my teeth forming into sharp daggers. I pounced on the man, my nails tearing at his chest. A scream belted from him as my claws dug in, dragging over his skin. I went for his throat next, and he stumbled back, sputtering and grabbing his neck while blood dyed his white T-shirt. He dropped to the ground.

Whirling around, I leaped on the back of the enormous man, my arms strangling his throat. Croygen's knuckles cracked over his chin, whipping his head so fast to the side it snapped. My hold on his throat took even more oxygen from him. He stumbled over, his sausage fingers trying to pull me off, but he was losing consciousness quickly.

Croygen grabbed me before the massive guy took me down with him. Unconscious, the final man lay on the floor, a ring of comatose bodies around us.

My gaze lifted to Croygen's, both of us breathing hard, our eyes locking. It was only a moment, a flash, when the entire world could have stopped. Fire burned in his eyes, an emotion I couldn't name, but something stirred deep in my soul, a power overtaking me, not letting me think, only feeling the something between us, the lifelines on our palms weaving together in an unseen web.

177

"Chūqù!" Get out! The bartender yelled, his arms flurrying around, breaking us away from each other, snapping reality back into place. My attention drifted over the disaster the pub was in, the five unconscious bodies lying on the floor, the owner's voice pitching in the background.

Croygen sucked in sharply, looking at his wound, his brow furrowing, blood glistening his shirt.

I moved to him, my hand pulling his away to examine the deep slice in his side.

"Just a scratch," he grunted.

"Get out! Get out!" The bartender shooed us to the exit. "Do. Not. Come. Back!"

"Well, that was fun." He winked at me.

"Shut up." Glaring at him, I put my shoulder under his other arm, helping him get out the door and stepping into the torrential downpour as lightning cracked overhead.

I sighed. There was no way we could get back to the ship tonight.

"I know of a place we can go."

"No," I snapped. "I'm not going to any of your many fuck buddies' houses."

He opened his mouth.

"Or a whorehouse."

"Sucking out all the fun, Kitty-Kat."

"I'm gonna leave you here to bleed to death."

Croygen smirked cheekily, only fueling my irritation.

"Come on." I yanked him a little harder than needed, forcing a yip from him. The pregnant raindrops splashed down on us, soaking us completely as I took him to the only place I could think of. A spot I had used before when I ran into problems.

So much for staying out of trouble.

Night was seeping in, darkening the already heavy sky, thunder vibrating the cobbled ground.

Rushing us into a murky alley behind a market, which sold various types of meats—though meat here could mean a lot of things, like rodents and insects—I found the door an average pedestrian would walk right past if they didn't know it was there. My knuckles rapped the wood, hoping the owner would answer.

Several moments passed before the door squeaked open, yellow eyes glowing from the other side. A petite Asian woman stood behind the door, her expression stern, her body bristling with annoyance.

"Oh." Her lids narrowed on me. "You."

Mrs. Yang hadn't changed a bit in a hundred years.

"No, you go away." She waved me away. Croygen snorted, my own glare turning to him. "You cause nothing but problems!" She started to close the door.

"Mrs. Yang." I pushed back on the door, stopping it from closing. "Please. You know I wouldn't come here if I didn't have to. I'm under Yeo's protection."

Mrs. Yang's glower could have burned holes through me if she had the power. She was a Pallas cat-shifter—grumpy, secluded, territorial, and didn't like me very much.

Cats seemed to be neutral when it came to other cat-shifters. They either preferred to be part of a clowder or hated all other cats.

"Please, he's hurt." I nodded back to Croygen. "We need a place to stay tonight."

"Where's old boyfriend?" she huffed, her curious gaze on Croygen.

"Killian was just a friend, Mrs. Yang."

She rolled her eyes, not believing me for a second.

"You pirate too?" She flicked her chin at my companion, but wasn't searching for an answer. "You cause any damage, you pay," she declared.

"Of course."

179

She heaved a substantial exhale, wholly put out, opening the door wider for us. "You stay quiet. I will bring up healing herbs." She nodded at Croygen's wound as we stepped into the rundown entry. The room led to the shop and to her private flats above. The raw scent of meat twined with fish soaked into the wood, making my stomach growl. I would always choose a nice filet of fish, but eating meat was in my DNA, craving to sink my teeth into it.

"Go." She batted her hands, wanting us to get out of her way as fast as possible.

"Making friends everywhere you go, Kitty-Kat?" Croygen's cheeky grin could be felt through his words, but I ignored him, going up the stairs, annoyed at how easily he could get under my skin.

Opening the door to the room, my chest clenched. I'd forgotten how minuscule the place was. A sink outside a toilet closet, a few shelves on one wall filled with books, trinkets, and useless items like an old pre-Fae War microwave and hot plate, which no longer worked because of the magic in the air. On the other side, next to the windows overlooking the street below, the rain pelting against the glass, was a small double bed.

The time Killian and I had to use this place to hide, I didn't even think about the size or the one bed. Killian and I had shared beds all the time growing up, but now my skin tingled with awareness as Croygen shut the door behind us, two firebulbs the only light in the room.

"Cozy." Croygen's voice snaked up my spine. I tried to control my breathing, adrenaline still pumping in my veins, creating a frenzy in my blood. Normally, I would find someone to take my excess energy out on, a wealthy victim to seduce and rob, fucking him until I could think clearly again.

Needing to distract myself, I checked the room like I'd find some hidden ninja in the tiny place. I could sense

Croygen's gaze on me, but I ignored the feel of him as he moved to the bed. He sat with a hiss, and my head jerked back to him, noticing the blood still oozing from him.

"You okay?" I went to him. Leaning over, I rolled up his drenched shirt, trying to see his wound. "Shit, he got you good." My fingers grazed his side. Touching his skin was like striking a match, rushing heat through my body. His abs flexed under my touch, the air around us crackling while thunder boomed outside the room.

"I'm fine," he gritted, drawing my eyes to his, catching them like a trap. "It will heal," he muttered. The hoarseness of his voice pounded my heart. I couldn't remove my gaze from his. The air in the room curled around me with a thrilling hold. Our wet clothes clung to our skin, our adrenaline pumping, filling the room with tense energy. Need.

I bolted away from him when a knock rattled the door. Mrs. Yang stomped in, a tray in her hands.

"If you get blood on anything. You buy." She dropped the tray on the side table next to the bed. She looked between us. "And no hanky-panky," she barked, marching out the same way she came in, leaving the room in silence.

"Guess no hanky-panky, then." Croygen smirked, his humor trying to cut the odd strain in the room, but it only seemed to add more. Mrs. Yang had said it out loud and gave the unspoken topic life, drawing attention to the way my drenched shirt clung to my breasts. The way drops dripped down his heated skin. The way his erection was heavily outlined in his cargo pants.

Not wanting him to catch me staring, I jerked my head away, turning my attention to the packed tray. There were fae healing herbs, which were becoming more standard across the world, since humans realized how much better they worked than western medicine. Baijiu, a clear, potent liquor, swabs, rubbing alcohol, and a basket of dumplings.

My stomach gurgled with hunger, the scent of pigeon and other "unspecific" meat inside the cooked dumplings. Food was getting harder to find, and in places like this, you ate what you could get.

"Fuck, give me that." Croygen motioned for me to hand him the baijiu, downing a gulp when he unscrewed the cap.

"Strip," I ordered, grabbing the swabs and dosing them in disinfectant.

"Pants too?" He lifted an eyebrow, getting out of his shirt. "Want me naked, *Katze*? You just have to ask."

A seductive smile curled my mouth. Lowering to my knees, I moved in front of him, getting in a better position. He watched me intently, his nose flaring.

I swiped the cotton over his wound.

"Fuck!" he howled when the alcohol touched his open wound, his teeth diving into his lower lip.

My grin widened with mischief.

"Payback?" he gritted.

"You deserved it."

"You didn't have to join in the fight. I had it all handled."

"Yeah, I saw how you handled it. Getting tossed across the room was part of the plan?"

"Yep." He sucked in again as I continued to pat around his injury. "Get them cocky, thinking they have this won, and then come back and take them all down."

"Mm-hmm," I snorted. "I have a crazy idea... maybe stop sleeping with everyone's wives and girlfriends?"

"They come to me. *Beg me.*" He took another slug of baijiu.

"Like the *yiji* I ran into in the bathroom who wanted to warn me off you."

"*A yiji?*" He frowned. "I never sleep with hired professionals."

"Well, she remembered you. Seemed a little bitter."

"It was all a long time ago."

"What? Last month?"

"I haven't been on this side of the world in decades, and even if I had… I haven't slept with anyone, married or not, in almost a year."

"What?" My head jerked up, shock stilling me. Croygen wouldn't go a day without sex unless we were at sea. Sex was his gift, and by the number of women who used to plead at the ship to sail away with him, most might think he was an incubus.

That was just Croygen.

He oozed dominance, sensual confidence, and naughty energy, which everyone wanted firsthand knowledge of. He charmed and seduced, and would fully dominate once he had them in bed.

"That surprise you?" His dark eyes went down to mine.

"Yes." I suddenly was very aware of my position, down on my knees between his legs. I couldn't stop the thought, the impulse to unzip his pants, bow my head, and take him into my mouth, seeing desire fill his dark eyes, feel his fingers twine in my hair, gripping so hard as I sucked him down further. To be the one who made him come, to have the power to bring the illustrious Croygen to ecstasy.

As if he could see every thought going through my head, his nose flared, his jaw straining, hands rolling tight against the bottle.

"Kat," Croygen said my name so low, mixed with warning, need, and a question.

Fear overtook the desire scorching up my bones, and I leaped to my feet. I turned my back on him, busying myself with the items on the tray, not doing anything but moving them around like chess pieces.

"Get some herbs on that, and you should heal quickly." I spoke so evenly that I sounded like a robot. Clearing my throat, I grabbed what I needed before turning back around again, keeping my focus off his face. Spreading a healing paste over the wound, I covered it in a bandage, moving away from him as fast as I could.

What was wrong with me? In all the centuries I have lived, no man in the world made me feel as unsettled, unsure, and vulnerable as I did around him. He always had, even during the time I spent away from him. He was always there, under my skin, driving me forward. Preparing me. My devil and my angel. My villain and my hero.

"So, how about you?" His deep voice scratched up my back.

"What about me?" I twisted to face him, guarded and cold.

He held out the liquor bottle to me, waiting for me to take it before he continued.

"I told you, so it's only fair you tell me when the last time was for you?" He watched me guzzle down the liquor. I was about to crawl out of my skin.

"Think that's appropriate to ask?" I was trying to keep a boundary between us, even if another part of me wanted to burn it to dust. "Aren't I just the little girl you watched grow up on your ship?"

"Except you haven't been a girl in centuries, Kitty-Kat."

I glowered at him, but I didn't seem to mind him calling me that, though it felt vastly different from how Killian used it.

"If you're grown enough to become the notorious Puss in Boots, the pirate who drops men to their knees with her pussy…"

Just him saying the word had my core pulsing, like it was conditioned to react to his voice, to know he was calling it. I downed more of the strong, floral-tasting liquor, needing this moment to not feel so out of control, my head already spinning from the potency of it.

"Come on, truth for a truth."

"Is that what we're doing?" I tipped my head, the alcohol giving me more confidence. "Fine. Truth for a truth, then." I strolled closer to him, handing the bottle back. "No matter what."

"You sure you're ready for that?" He leaned back against the headboard, his bare torso still damp from the rain. Why did he have to be so unbearably hot? And why did he feel like my weakness, forgetting everything I had trained for and planned for years.

"I should ask the same of you?" I grabbed the dumplings and dropped them on the bed, sitting as far as I could from him.

A feral grin hitched the side of his mouth in a challenge. "Only one topic is off the table."

I snorted, popping a dumpling in my mouth. "What?"

"Your father."

Every muscle in my body locked up, air halting in my lungs, anger drilling into the back of my neck. "Why?" I shook my head. "No! That's bullshit. A truth for a truth, you said!"

"You don't want to know that truth."

"Because we already know you murdered him? That I'm sitting here with my father's killer when I should have dropped you at the bottom of Davy Jones's locker the moment I saw you?"

He didn't move, unfazed by my reaction. "You have no idea what actually happened."

"Then tell me."

"That is not the story you will get from me tonight."

"Why?"

Croygen's lids narrowed. "Start with something else, or you get nothing from me at all."

"Typical Croygen, your way or no way."

"How it works on my ship, Kitty-Kat. And if I remember correctly, you're still my captive." He nicked one of the dumplings, biting into it, his gaze never leaving mine. "Why isn't Killian with you?"

Sucking down another sip of baijiu, my mind and mouth started to disconnect.

"He wanted something I couldn't give him."

"And *what* was that?" Croygen's intensity made me wonder if he already knew the answer, the response screaming from every molecule.

"A relationship. Love."

"And why couldn't you give it to him?"

I swallowed, drinking more, everything becoming a little fuzzy around me.

"Kat?"

"You."

"Me?" His brow curved up seductively.

I shifted on the bed, staring at the swollen drops of rain against the window, the room shadowy and humid, sticking my wet clothes to me even more.

"My obsession to become a better pirate than you—to best you in every way, to track you down, force you to see what you did—was more powerful than my feelings for him."

"Ouch." Croygen's lips pressed together, but he looked anything but compassionate for Killian. Smugness curled his mouth. "That had to hurt. Killian's only thought was always for you... and your only thought was of *me*."

"It wasn't like that." I glowered at him.

"Sure," he smirked

"Get over yourself."

"So you thought coming before me, showing what a better pirate you were, more ruthless, cutthroat, seductive, would do what?" He bit into another dumpling, his tongue sliding over his lip. "Make me ashamed I kicked you off the ship? That my actions turned you into the remarkable, powerful, and extremely clever woman you are now?"

His praise blossomed like flowers in my gut. The little girl who had lived for the approval of her captain was a grown woman who wanted to be punished for it now. A twisted sickness I couldn't seem to rid myself of.

"Sorry, Katrina. You failed miserably in that."

"You were the one that left me an orphan, not trusting anyone, turning away the only man who loved me because I was more consumed with killing you than being happy."

"And would you have been?" He took the bottle from me, the liquor hitting far below the halfway mark. "Would you be happy with a husband and children—the only time you get to yourself is in the bathtub, where you reminisce about the freedom of the open waves, the best years already in the past."

It was exactly what made me run from Killian. He had wanted to settle down and live this boring life like so many others. I had never wanted that. I never wanted to be contained.

Croygen smiled knowingly, no doubt hearing my unsaid thoughts. "We are too much alike. The sea is the only place we feel at home."

"Really?" I moved farther onto the bed, leaning against the wall, our legs grazing. "I heard you left the pirate life for a while. I can't imagine the great Croygen would turn his back on the open waves for a woman."

"Is there a question in that, *Katze*?"

"Yes. Was there a woman?"

"There were several."

"They were serious?" My stomach knotted, not liking the sincerity of his response. "Who were they? Full truth."

"Hmm." He leaned back further into the bed. "Full truth, huh?"

Was I ready for it? To hear him speak of women he might have loved? Did he still?

187

"Well, Amara came when I lost everything. Her drive to survive, no matter who she hurt or took from, was the epitome of the saying 'misery loves company.' When cruelty is the only thing giving you breath because life feels so ugly. And the more she twisted me up, the more I craved the pain. To the point, I could see nothing else, wanted nothing else, because I think she was the punishment I was seeking."

I sucked in; I did not expect his honesty.

"I only got over my toxic addiction of Amara was when I met Zoey."

Amara fired up my jealousy like an engine, but the reverence and respect in the way he said Zoey's name hit like a train.

"Were you…" My throat tightened. "In love with, Zoey too?"

"For a moment, I might have thought so." He flinched in physical pain, shifting himself higher on the headboard. "But later I realized she gave me something much better."

My brows furrowed.

"She gave me a family. A place to belong. A life I never imagined for myself. Friends, a home, an annoying *pet*." He shook his head with a chuckle.

"So what made you leave?"

He sighed, his gaze going out the window to the stormy night. "I wasn't meant for their world. I had been fooling myself."

"Full truth," I said quietly, sensing in my gut he was avoiding something.

He rubbed at his head. "I left because of Lexie."

Her name caused a strange fluttering in my chest, a twist in my gut.

"She was killed." His voice grew hoarse. "And I wasn't there to protect her as I told her I would be." I stayed silent, hoping he'd continue. "She was young. I had seen her grow up, and it felt all wrong. I never thought about her like that... Then she got older, and I could feel a magnetic pull to her. Sexually confident, she didn't hide her crush on me. It felt good to have her attention even when I tried to fight it. The night before the battle..." He took a long pause, lost in another time. "It was just a kiss." He swallowed hard. "After all she went through, losing her parents, being in a wheelchair, and being an experiment of Dr. Rapava's, she was so full of life and adventure. She wanted to explore the world with me. And for a moment, I let myself believe I could be that man for her. Show her my world." He huffed, head wagging. "I was naive."

Naive was never a word I associated with Croygen.

"Even if I hadn't let Lexie down, I realize now she never would have fit, no matter what we both wanted to believe. And I would have slowly destroyed her like I do to so many others because I am too selfish." His gaze met mine. "Deep down, I knew I could never love her the way she deserved. But I would have killed myself trying, pretending she would have been enough... and that's what wrecks me."

Staring down at my hands, a lump stuck in my throat, his torture so like my own. Killian was Lexie in my story. I would have played the part, both of us knowing I wasn't *in* love with him, no matter how much I absolutely loved him.

"We're quite a pair." I pulled my legs up to my chest.

"We are." He watched me. A long silence stretched out. "You half shifted into your cat form when I was about to be attacked earlier."

Embarrassment flushed my cheeks at the moment of weakness. I hadn't thought. Instinct had kicked in. I had worked hard to control my changes after the mortifying incident on his deck so long ago. A lot of shifters could partially change, but I learned to fight without doing it, so I didn't need to. But tonight, that had been lost in seconds. A single threat to him and I forgot it all.

"Yeah, so?"

"Just an observation." He sunk down in the pillows, drinking until about two inches were left, handing it back to me. "Takes skill to do that. I was impressed."

He didn't know that was a slipup for me.

"Think you need to rest." I finished off the bottle, dropping it on the side table.

"You never answered my question." His lids were lower, but the intensity of his gaze became even more powerful.

"What's that?"

"Last time you got laid, Kitty-Kat?"

A few words and he had me boiling, my body telling me it had been far too long, intuitively knowing he could make me purr.

"Full truth." His expression was full of trouble.

"Been a little busy lately."

"Still not an answer."

"A while," I stated. "And leave it at that."

"And did they make you come?"

Flustered, I changed positions, unable to look at Croygen, everything in me screaming how badly I needed sex now, the craving spinning my already drunk mind.

"Obviously not good enough."

"Takes a lot for me." *Shut up, Kat. Shut up.* "I'm not like other fae. It takes the edge off, but…"

"But no one has made you come so hard you blacked out?"

"No, I'm too busy robbing them."

"If you can even move after, they weren't doing it right."

My nipples hardened under my damp shirt, *his shirt*, arousal curling my hands as if I wanted to shift again.

"Let's not talk about this."

He shrugged, wiggling down further onto the pillow. "You asked first."

"Well, now I'm asking you to shut up and go to sleep."

He grinned, loving that he was needling me.

"Just letting you know." He nodded down at his trousers. "I don't sleep with clothes on."

I slanted my head, needing to get back on even terrain, my expression derisive.

"Me neither."

Chapter 16
Croygen

That completely backfired on me.

My jaw locked as I watched Kat slip out of her wet pants, trying to cover the fact that I was fully staring. She was trying to act smug, but I could sense her nerves, the line we were poking at, trying to play each other.

I shouldn't be participating in these games. It was wrong, but I couldn't get myself to stop.

She removed the empty dumpling basket, turning off the lanterns before clambering onto the bed wearing only my shirt, still damp from the rain.

"Move over." She crawled in next to me, flopping down on the pillow, our bodies far too close to put me at ease.

So we were doing this. Pretending we were unaffected, lying next to each other. As if we did this all the time.

Skirting the edge of the bed, I flinched at the tug of my healing wound. My pants chafed my thighs, and my cock painfully pressed against the wet fabric. I didn't usually sleep in anything but boxer briefs. The logical part of me understood it would be inappropriate to undress. The inebriated part didn't give a shit.

I was uncomfortable. Toeing off my boots, they dropped

to the floor with a plunk. I unbuttoned my pants, trying to tug them down, as a wave of pain struck me. I hissed as my head dropped back.

"You okay?"

"Fine," I gritted, trying again. The wet material gripped my skin, making it harder to pull down. "Fuck," I grumbled, my lesion breaking open again.

"You need help?"

"No," I shot out quickly, grinding my molars, giving up. "Screw it."

Kat exhaled. Sitting up, she moved over me, the air in my lungs halting.

"What are you doing?"

"Helping because you're too stubborn to ask for it."

I scoffed. "Like you should talk."

She rolled her eyes, her small hands gripping my waistband. Her fingers glided over my hip bones, sliding down my V-line. The simple touch was an electric shock going straight to my cock. Biting back my groan, I forced my gaze from her. The intimacy of this act in the dark overwhelmed my senses, taking all the blood and logic away from my brain.

"Up," she whispered hoarsely. My hips lifted at her command as she peeled my pants down and off, dropping them to the floor. Her chest hitched, eyes blazing bright, locking on my erection. The tip pushed out of my boxer briefs, wet with pre-cum. Her attention on it only made it twitch more. The need to toss her on her back, spread her legs, and thrust into her rocked at my willpower.

I was on the verge, ready to snap if she even breathed my way. "Kat." My tone was angry, warning her to back away.

She didn't budge, her chest heaving violently, desire filling the room. We were both on the cusp, ready to fall over. The only things stopping me were the voice in the back of my head, Rotty's face, and knowing the truth of what happened that night. How this girl had always been my downfall, even then.

Karma was a bitch.

Because I was about to break, I climbed off the bed, brushing past her, needing to move. I strolled to where the tray was, wiping away the fresh blood with a swab, my shoulders rising and falling with each breath.

I hadn't slept with anyone in a year—and before that, it was more a transaction than anything—because I had lost my drive. My "magic." After Lexie's death, nothing felt right or real. I no longer wanted to seduce for the fun of it. I didn't have the energy or need to put in the effort. No one sparked my interest. I thought something was wrong with me.

Nope... karma was out to punish me. Picking Katrina out of all the women in the world my dick throbbed to be inside of, needing it more than air, was cruelty at its finest. My magic swirled in me, dizzying me as it woke up, sizzling up my spine. I tried to ignore it, but from the moment she stepped onto my ship, she roused everything in me, including anger.

"Croygen?"

"Go to sleep, Kat," I ordered, finishing the tiny bit of alcohol left, craving anything to dull what I was feeling, what I wanted to do.

She scoffed. "Don't tell me what to do."

"For the love of the gods!" I barked, rubbing my head. "For once, do what I ask."

"You first."

A groan bubbled up as I slammed down the empty bottle. "Boarding school sure didn't work for you." I glanced back at her. She sat on the edge of the bed, her arms folded.

"Guess not, since I was barely there for two years."

I swiveled all the way around. "What are you talking about?"

"You think pirates are cruel? The school was horrendous.

They beat me, locked me in the basement, starved me, and encouraged the girls to bully me. I was suspended eight times. I hated it there, and the feeling was mutual with the students, teachers, and headmistress. So I ran away."

"But your father got letters from you…"

"Yeah, I let him believe I was still there. I knew he'd talk me into going back if he found out." Her lip lifted. "And I was never going back to that nightmare."

"Where the hell were you the whole time?"

"Surviving with other kids my age on the street. Getting better at thieving, fighting, at being a pirate, so when I came back, there would be no way you could turn me away again."

My mouth parted in shock. I believed she had been in school that whole time. Safe. Fed. Warm. I knew life on the streets and how much more she had to fight being a petite, pretty girl.

"I had just received word from Father that he would be coming to visit me. I thought then I could show him how much I had grown, gained control over my shifting. I hoped he would be proud of me." She stared at the ground, swallowing hard. "He never came."

Because he died. I wasn't sure how to respond or what to say now that I knew how she had been living at such a young age.

"Killian found me not too long after." She wouldn't look at me. "From there, it was all about becoming the best pirate who ever lived, no matter what I had to do."

She desperately wanted to avenge her dad. To make me pay for all she lost.

She sniffed, quickly wiping at her eyes. "I'm tired." She slipped under the covers, her back to me, ending the conversation.

I didn't know how long I stood staring at her, the weight of guilt and fatigue weakening my legs. With a heavy sigh, I quietly went back to the bed, crawling in next to her. Lying still, I listened to her breathing.

"He was always proud of you, *Katze*," I whispered. "Don't ever question that. You were his entire world. There was *nothing* he wouldn't do for you."

She didn't know how true my statement was.

And I didn't want her to know.

My lids popped open, an itch at the back of my head dragging me from a deep sleep with alarm. The darkness in the room told me it was still deep in the night.

The consciousness of not being on my ship, alone in my own bed, barreled into me. I was in a cramped room, on a small bed, surrounded by the scents of raw meat and fish. And a warm body pressed into me, a purr coming from the figure engulfed in my arms.

Holy fuck.

My hand was up Kat's shirt, my palm cupping her bare breast like it was the most natural thing to do. Panic poured into my bloodstream as I realized how calm and content I was snuggled into her, my cock cradled between her ass, happy as shit.

I didn't cuddle. Ever. Especially with someone I wasn't supposed to be touching. Not like this. The only time I ever laid next to someone without sex was Lexie on her last night. And then, unlike now, I hadn't had the urge to slip her panties to the side and enter her while she slept, waking her up with an orgasm.

A noise downstairs nipped at the back of my neck. I twisted my head to the door, my stomach knotted up at the realization that the warning bells came from something other than Kat.

Staying still, I listened, anxiety clawing at my throat. My heart started to slow when nothing reverberated, thinking it was all in my imagination.

I became aware Kat had awoken; her body locked up, my hand still holding her boob, my dick still nestled in her ass. Before I could move away and apologize, her head popped up, nose wiggling, eyes going to the door. Her reaction had nothing to do with me.

"Kat?" I knew she could smell and hear far better than me.

She took another sniff, her head swiveling as if her ears were tuning in.

A creak of wood from the stairs below sounded like a scream in the silent house.

Kat scrambled out of bed, flaring terror into my veins. It wasn't Mrs. Yang coming up the stairs. I scrambled up right as the door slammed into the wall, banging on the wood. Four men dressed in dark clothes rushed into the room, crowding the already tight space. My survival instincts kicked in, and I attacked with no hesitation.

Katrina sidled up to me, and we worked in unison as Master Yukimura taught us. It felt like more than that, as if something connected us outside our teachings. It was beyond anything I could explain, but with each spin, punch, kick, and block, it was there. We worked in tandem, a harmony I never had with anyone else, which felt more intimate than it should have.

She could take care of herself, but the connection made me more possessive, growling with retribution when one man lunged for her, his knife ready to cut her.

My heel struck his chest, tossing him back. His body flew into the window, shattering the glass as he fell through, his cry ending when he hit the cement below.

Kat blinked at me before going back to fighting. Her elbow rammed into the neck of one, hurtling him back, his

197

fingers grasping at his throat as he gasped for air. Ducking out of the way of another strike, she punched another man in the crotch, dropping him to the ground in agony.

"That's my girl." I grinned, winking at her as I fought the last guy, realizing a moment later what I said.

I slammed my knuckles into the largest guy, a bottle shattering near me as I took him to the ground. Kat came up next to me, the jagged edges of the liquor bottle touching the man's neck, her heavy breathing in my ear.

"Who the hell are you?" she seethed, her force only turning me on. "You know what happens to those who go against Yeo? I am under his protection."

"You didn't say that when I was attacked at the pub," I exclaimed.

"Because you deserved to get your ass kicked."

"Brutal." A huff of laughter came up my throat, my head wagging.

"Please tell me you're not here because he fucked your wife?" She turned back to the man. He was fae, but I couldn't feel a lot of magic.

His dark eyes narrowed, spitting at her.

Snarling, I gripped his throat harder, forcing him to gasp for air.

"Answer her, motherfucker."

"Gǔn kāi." Fuck off.

Kat squatted down, cutting the glass deeper into his neck. "You answer or you join your friend out the window."

Hatred flared his nose, his lips pinning together.

"Alrighty, here we go." I yanked him up, pulling him to the window.

"We were paid," he spat.

"Who paid you?"

"I don't know. We never met face-to-face."

"For what?"

198

It took another push to the broken window to get him to speak again.

"To dissuade you."

"Dissuade us from what?" My patience thinning, I dragged him over the broken glass on the sill, cutting into his back, his head hanging outside. He cried out in pain, sweat dripping down his head.

"From going after something called the nectar," he croaked. "That's all I know."

Cement pooled in my gut. Not only did someone else know about the substance, but they somehow knew we were after it too.

"Fuck," I muttered, peering over at Kat. She had the same trepidation in her eyes.

"You broke!" a woman cried out, jerking our heads back to the doorway. Mrs. Yang stood there, her arms flaying, her expression pinched. "You destroy my place again! Blood all over. You buy!" She motioned to an upended side table and broken glass on the floor, not caring about the men's bodies strewn over the ground.

Ignoring her, I looked back at Kat. Without having to say a word, she understood. We had to get back to the ship. Yeo's protection no longer helped us.

The one thing I was certain was fictitious at one point was becoming very real.

And so was the threat on our lives.

The morning sun rose, the humidity only slightly decreased after the storm, and the streets puddled with water as we slipped through the alleys. People were setting up market carts, the streets cramped with horses and wagons jaunting down the lanes.

Katrina stayed close to me, both of us on alert. We hadn't talked much after we left Mrs. Yang's. The old woman was shrewd as fuck, and we left her purse heavier than the damage we did. But to be fair, we also left her to clean it up.

My nerves were coiled, ready to react to anything. I kept us moving, paranoid we were being followed. Ducking and weaving through the city to lose any tails, we took longer than I wanted, finally getting back to the dinghy when the sun was high in the sky.

My shoulders relaxed at my ship in the distance, knowing it was still there. Drifting our small boat next to it, Scot tossed us down a line from the deck.

"Hey, Captain." Scot leaned over, hauling Kat up the rope ladder with no effort, a strange smirk on his face.

"What?" I climbed up, another prickle of energy running up and down my spine, his strange grin unsettling me. I climbed aboard, my gaze darting around nervously.

"We've been boarded." Scot stepped out of the way, gesturing to two figures behind him.

Shock stilled me in place, my eyes taking in the two blonds. The tall, ripped man appeared like some Californian surfer with an easygoing grin and chiseled jaw.

The small girl next to him had waist-length, wavy hair the color of soft gold and a face you'd picture on an angel. She was a punch to the chest, cracking it open with memories and love.

"Annabeth?" I croaked.

Her blonde hair floated in the wind like a halo. A smile of pure joy spread over her face, her blue eyes filling with tears as she ran for me.

"Croygen!" She leaped into my arms, and I felt like a piece I had been missing slotted back in place. A part of my family returned. "I have missed you so much."

I held her so tight as she sobbed, threatening tears of my own. Annabeth was like my little sister, part of the family

200

Zoey had created. Zoey had met AB after the devastation hit Seattle. She had lost her parents and had been kidnapped and put in a fighting/sex ring. Zoey saved her from that life and made her part of our "found family."

Annabeth and Lexie became like sisters, Zoey adopting them and adding her baby to the growing family. I had watched AB grow up alongside Lexie, then witnessed her fall in love with the Dark Dweller, Cooper, standing behind her.

The problem was that AB was attached to almost every memory of Lexie, bringing that part of my life back in a wave of emotion.

"What are you doing here?" I put her back on her feet, flabbergasted that she was standing in front of me. She wiped at her tears, still trying to calm down.

"Hey, man." Cooper approached, shaking my hand, his other one rubbing her back. "Good to see you."

Returning the handshake, I nodded. "It's good to see you guys too, but seriously, what the fuck are you doing here?" My attention jumped from AB to Cooper. "How did you even find me?"

"Lars has eyes everywhere." Cooper gave me a knowing look. "And since you are here, you probably know why we are too."

A sinking sensation set me back on my heels. "Oh, fuck..." I whispered. "The nectar."

Cooper grinned more.

"He knows." I swallowed.

"You know Lars makes it his business to know all."

"Knows all and wants it." I shook my head. My focus jumped back to Annabeth. She had grown more into herself since I had been gone, looking stunning. She'd definitely been training, but she was still a waif.

"Why would he send you guys?"

"Let's just say I made a bargain with him." Cooper's gaze drifted to AB. "If it does what it says..."

201

My lid closed for a moment as understanding dawned on me.

Annabeth was human. She was aging, would grow old and die, while Cooper wouldn't age at all. None of us around her would, not for eons. She was his mate, and he would do anything to keep her around forever.

Something I wanted for AB as well. To always be with us.

"And let me guess,"—I smirked at Annabeth, knowing her too well—"you wouldn't let him go without you."

Her familiar grin lit up her face with mischief. I blinked away my tears, pulling her into me again, ignoring the bag strapped around her digging into my wound, kissing her head. "Fuck, I've missed you."

"We've missed you too," she muttered.

"No! Stop! I have no more brains to suck! You promised you'd suck something else!" A voice jolted through me, causing me to stumble back, my gaze going to her bag between us.

"Oh. No…" I uttered, recognizing the tiny voice. "Nooo."

A furry brown head popped out, a honey package stuck to it. "What?" He peered around, rubbing sleep from his eyes. "This doesn't look like an all-you-can-eat buffet. But I'm starving. Am I dead? I have to be. I don't see any food. This is hell. I am in hell, aren't I?"

"Oh crap! Sprig! How did you get in there?" Annabeth slapped her hand over her mouth in shock, blinking at him as if he wasn't supposed to be here.

"Oh fuck. No." I shook my head. "No fucking way."

The monkey-sprite twisted to me, his eyes opening. "Oh, sprite biscuits. I was right. This is hell. I'm back with the butt-pirate and no honey. What did I do to deserve this?!" He waggled his arms up at the sky. "Why me?"

"What the hell is that? How is it talking?" Kat came up

next to me, staring in astonishment at the talking creature. Monkey-shifters couldn't talk in their animal form, so even in the fae world, this thing was a freak.

I blew out, my hands rubbing my face.

"An annoying *pet*."

"Pet? Pet!" The five-inch monkey squeaked, crawling further out of the bag, a pair of girl's black underwear around his neck like a cape, the honey packet still on his head. "How dare you, smelly ass-bandit! I'm the great *Spriggan-Galchobhar!*"

"Great at licking your own balls." I smirked at my old friend, pretending I didn't want to bundle him up in my arms and kiss his furry head.

"At least I have some."

"And here I hoped they'd donate you to a zoo by now."

"You two," Annabeth groaned with amusement. "Straight back into it, huh? Some things don't change." She plucked the wrapper from his fur. "Guess I can figure out why you got in my bag. How many did you eat?"

"One, *Bebinn!*" *Fair woman*, his nickname for her. He held up a finger. "Okay, maybe two or three..." He looked guilty; sprites could not lie. "Nine, I swear... okay, ten at most."

Sprig was an experiment from Dr. Rapava's labs. A sprite put into a monkey body. A prototype of bigger plans Dr. Rapava had conceived before we killed him and destroyed his labs. Sprig attached himself to Zoey, becoming another member of our little fucked up group.

"I'm gonna have to call Zoey before she freaks out."

"She knows you're here?" Her name dug into my heart, missing her more than I thought.

"Yeah." AB nodded. "She wanted to come too, but with Wyatt and the orphanage, there was no way for her to get away."

"How's Wyatt?"

"He just turned six." She gave me a look, a slight judgment. "So much like Zoey and Ryker. We think he's a Wanderer. He's showing magical signs of it."

"Oh, shit." I blinked, hating how much of the boy's life I missed. I should have been there—Uncle Croygen. Now he wouldn't even know me. "Ryker must be shitting his pants."

"Not as much as Kennedy and Lorcan are." Cooper laughed. The Druid Queen and the Dark Dweller had twins, their kids taking on both druid and dark dweller magic. A first for the fae world, which seemed like trouble waiting to happen.

"You also better call Rez. She's mad at you too," Annabeth chided.

Sign me up for the worst parent of the year. I missed the parenting window by a long shot, but I tried to stay in contact with her to establish some kind of relationship with her.

Commotion at the beginning of the pier caused my head to look around as a group of Ju's soldiers moved down, asking for papers and checking out the products on the trading ships.

"Oh, shit," I muttered. "Sorry to put this reunion on hold, but we have to get out of here." I found my first mate. "Scot, get the crew ready. Sail us out now."

Scot nodded, yelling to the guys to set sail. Water was neutral territory and a lot harder to attack.

"Go inside. I'll meet you in the galley once we're out to sea," I told Annabeth and Cooper, turning back to help my crew. Something jumped on my shoulder, a soft brown tail curling around my neck, his "cape" flapping in the wind.

"I did not miss you at all, pirate," Sprig huffed.

"*Tradesman*," I countered, our constant joke. "And I didn't miss you either, gerbil."

Fuck, even *I* didn't buy that lie.

Chapter 17
Croygen

"Honey bread? Honey nuts? Honey-covered mangos? Pancakes? Honey cake? You don't even have peanut butter and honey truffles?" Sprig exclaimed. He stood on the counter next to Zid, who was cooking lunch in the galley. "What kind of establishment is this? I'll even settle for cinnamon sugar churros! I'm dying here... I'm not kidding. Can't you hear my stomach?"

Zidane blinked at the tiny thing, clearly not sure how to react to the talking monkey. It had been over an hour since they boarded, and introductions had been made. Now we floated not too far away from Shanghai port, enough so Ju couldn't reach us.

"Cookies? Biscuits? Scones? Honey-drizzled chicken?" Sprig bounced on his toes. "Do you understand how desperate the situation has become? I. Will. *Die!*"

"There's a banana right there." I grinned to myself, waiting for the response because he despised the fruit.

"Murderer!" Sprig gasped, his eyes wide. "*Bebinn,*" he yelled for AB. "He's trying to kill me. I always knew you hated me, wanted me dead, but I didn't think you were so heartless."

I reached for the yellow fruit, peeling it and taking a large bite. "Yum."

He stared at me, blinking as if I had kicked a puppy.

"Stop traumatizing him." Annabeth scooped him up, handing him a granola bar. "Here, Sprig. Tide you over for a bit."

"Give us at least five seconds of silence," I scoffed.

"Masssmole," Sprig mumbled, flipping me off, the granola filling his cheeks like a squirrel.

"Yep, just like old times," I snickered, moving to the tables. I had my crew, minus Corb, who was on watch, down in the galley for a meeting.

Without even looking, I became aware of Kat coming into the space, sitting at the table, clean from a shower, her hair wet, and wearing one of my T-shirts again. At least she had on pants this time. My awareness of her had skyrocketed overnight, and it was disconcerting. We hadn't even talked about what happened or how we woke up; it was another ghost in this room.

With Annabeth here, so was Lexie because she had been there every step, witnessing the change in my and Lexie's relationship. Raw, strange guilt throttled my lungs. As if I shouldn't be conscious of Kat because Lexie was somehow still around. And if she hadn't died, she would probably be right here with me.

If she was, would I still feel this pull to Katrina? The squeeze in my gut told me what I didn't want to know. But that was with a different Croygen. Another man, another life, someone who was lost alongside her.

"Well." I clapped my hands together, walking to the front of the room. "Let's get right into this. We can do full introductions later." The introduction had been brief, the need to get away taking precedence. "Cooper and Annabeth have been sent by King Lars, confirming why we came here. He's quite sure the nectar is real."

"Shite." Scot sighed, probably still thinking this was a fool's errand.

"Wait, did you say nectar?" Sprig piped up, finishing his bar. "You mean honey of the gods?"

And our five seconds were up.

"Not that kind of nectar." I shot him a look. "And if you eat it, I will squeeze you like a bag of frosting until you pop."

"Man, someone needs to get laid," he grumbled. "Crabby butt bandit."

"Hey, talking rat? Shut up." Damn, did he feel like an annoying younger brother.

"I don't know. He's a lot more interesting than you, Captain," Vane goaded.

"I agree!" Sprig stood up, his hand in the air. "Who seconds he should walk the plank?"

"Shut the hell up."

"You know what? I second that." Kat held up her hand, a smirk in her eyes.

"I like you." Sprig bounded to her, leaping on her shoulder, pointing at his eyeball. "All say eye?"

"It's *aye*." My hands rolled into fists, trying to show the slight difference in the words.

"That's what I said. *Eye*. E-y-e!" He shook his head at Kat like I was losing my mind. Which I might be.

"It's A-y-e."

"Eye doesn't start with an A!" He threw up his arms. "You must walk the plank—on the decree of the one-eyed pirate named Matty. Because you're an idiot."

"Oh, my gods." My head fell into my hands. "That's not…" I gave up, knowing he'd never get it. Breathing in, I rolled my shoulders back. "Can we get back to business now?" I pointed at him. "You open your trap again and I will gag you with your tail."

"I won't kink shame you."

Taking another deep exhale as Vane and Scot snickered and snorted, I let my gaze drift to Katrina. A familiar sensation dropped to my dick, wanting to take every one of my kinks out on her.

It was a moment, a flash, a picture of what I could do to her. Her bent over the helm as I spanked her. Heat burned up the back of my neck before I slammed the door on that thought, disgusted with myself for even thinking it. Especially with AB here.

Moving my gaze away from her, I spoke. "Kat and I were attacked this morning."

"Wondered how you got your wound." Zid sat down, waiting for our meeting to be over. The smell of stir-fry coming from the kitchen was enticing us.

"Uh, that was from another fight."

"Another pissed-off husband?" Scot questioned, a grin on his lips.

"Fuck off."

He let out a burst of laughter, hitting the target.

"The latest attack was not, and the little information we could get out was they wanted to scare us. Stop us from going after this nectar."

"How the hell did they know?" Scot sat up at the seriousness of this. "Did you tell anyone?"

"Only person I said anything to was Duan Ru. And I know he wouldn't talk."

"Are you sure?" Zidane kicked his boots up on a bench.

"He was freaked out and wouldn't help us." Kat lifted the shoulder Sprig wasn't on. How fast she seemed comfortable with him being there. "He practically ran out. What if it was him? He's the only one who knew."

"Makes no sense, though. He seemed almost scared of it. Wanted nothing to do with it." I shook my head.

"Unless it was an act and he's going after it himself,"

Cooper said, tying up his shoulder-length blond hair in a knot. "The awareness of this substance is growing, at least with the people dealing in black-market items and who can afford to be in the know."

Like Emperor Batara.

Like Lars.

The Demon King had a history of going after powerful mythical items. His need to obtain the four treasures of Tuatha Dé Danann led to so much destruction and death in the past. Why was I surprised he would go after this, too, after all that happened? He was happy with his mate, Fionna and their daughter, Piper. Why would he go down this road again?

"Only thing that makes sense," Vane added his opinion.

Duan Ru sending people to scare Kat and me didn't fit right, but I couldn't think of anything else. How else would anyone know we were pursuing it?

"Well, whether it was him or not, people know we are after it, which puts a very large target on our backs." I perched on the top of one of the tables, my brain racing to figure everything out. "Now where do we go from here? Any clues on where it is located? Lars tell you anything?"

"Just that there was a report it was in this area, and he knew you had at least figured out the same thing." Cooper leaned on his forearms, his muscles bulging. "The last report Lars received said a Dr. Novikov had it. Lars tracked him down here in China."

The Dweller was even bigger than I remembered. Since he had become second in charge after Eli left, the guy had packed on more muscle. Not that Dark Dwellers needed it because they were born to kill. To slip up behind their prey and tear their throat out with their sharp dagger teeth. I had seen them shift before, and they were scary as shit, a cross between a prehistoric wolf, black panther, and monster rolled into one. They were fortified with claws, teeth, and poisonous daggers that grew down their backs when they shifted.

My body froze, ice pouring down my veins.

"What?" I struggled to speak. "What did you say his name was again?"

"A scientist by the name of Dr. Jansug Novikov."

The name scraped down my spine, taking me back to the horrors of Rapava's testing labs, where that name had come up. My charm had gotten a lot of information from the nurses who worked for Dr. Rapava, thinking they were doing some heroic deed while we "lab rats" were tortured and tested on.

My time there with Zoey, and then later Lexie, still haunted me, waking me up in cold sweats. And no matter how hard I tried, I couldn't forget a detail of that place.

Including that name.

He had worked with Dr. Rapava back in their home country of Georgia before Rapava ventured to the States to really chase his demented beliefs. Novikov went a different path in the pursuit of saving humans from diseases.

That path had circled around and ran straight back into me.

Dr. Rapava might be dead, but it seemed like he had returned. Another fucking ghost from my past coming back for me.

"Croygen?" Annabeth's voice stirred me out of my painful thoughts, drawing my gaze to her. The girl was one of the kindest souls you'd ever meet, helping with disabled kids, assisting Zoey with the orphanage, and looking like some Disney princess come to life. But considering her past, there was steel behind her sweetness. She had been in hell down in his labs too, though what she went through had been horrific. She hadn't been there long and clearly didn't recognize the man's name. "Are you okay?"

"Fine." It took everything I had to nod, to pretend everything was all right. Sprig, me, Zoey, Lexie, Ryker, and Annabeth had all been down there. We all were experiments

210

of Rapava's. But I was probably the only one who knew about Dr. Novikov since he had no connection to the Dr. Rapava we knew in Seattle. I flirted with the nurses, getting them to talk and tell me things. Learn all about the man who was torturing us.

"We know anything else?" I shook off the sickness I felt, pushing forward. "Batara give you anything else?" I glanced at Kat.

"He had the same intel. Somewhere in China, last seen with this scientist." Kat pinched her lips together, her gaze directly on me as if she could sense something going on behind my façade, peeling back the layers.

Irritation with that intimacy turned me away from her. "We need to find something more!" I barked. "China is a big fucking place, and this guy could already be in hiding." Everyone stared blankly at me. "Does anyone have one intelligent thought?"

"Ohhh!" Sprig's hand went up.

"Open your mouth, and I will thread your tail through your esophagus." I pointed at the monkey.

"Okay." Kat clapped her hands. "How about we get some food and take a break." She still stared through me, once again tearing at my walls.

"Take a break?" I belted. "We have Ju's soldiers breathing down our backs and people trying to kill us."

"Sounds like a normal day for you, pirate." Sprig leaped off Kat's shoulder onto the table. "Plus, we need food. Bad things happen when I don't get food… ohhhh… Do you have fried honey noodles with ice cream? Or how about double-fried ice cream with honey drizzle? Or maybe—"

"Sprig. Shut up," I growled, pinching my eyes closed. A soft thump sounded. "I need to fucking think."

"Holy shit!" Kat yelled, jumping up, my head darting to her, my heart fluttering in panic.

She stared down at the monkey lying on the table, appearing dead.

"Oh, my gods, what just happened? He-he was just talking! Is he dead?" She reached over, prepared to give him CPR.

"Don't worry about him." I breathed out in relief.

"What?" Her head jerked to me in shock.

"Another thing you should know about him besides having ADD and an addiction problem." I snorted as his mouth puffed, a soft snore coming from him. "He's a *narcoleptic* monkey-sprite with ADD and an addiction problem."

The rich, tawny liquid burned down my throat, the smoky aroma coating my tongue, doing nothing to ebb my tension. The stars shined brightly out of my chamber window, though my brain circled around the same situation over and over, coming no closer to a plan than we had earlier.

We had nothing. No leads, no clues, no nothing.

Being the captain came with lots of responsibility and with that, guilt and blame. Right or wrong, it all fell on my shoulders, and with Cooper and AB, I felt it was my fault even more.

"Pam is mad at you." A voice jolted me out of my thoughts.

"Holy shit." I jerked to see Sprig on my desk, holding up his girlfriend. A small stuffed goat named Pam. "You scared the crap out of me. How in the hell did you get in here?"

"I'm five inches, which, unlike what women probably tell you, is small. I can get in anywhere." Sprig pushed Pam closer to me. "Apologize."

"Get that fucking stuffed sheep out of my face."

"How. Dare. You." Sprig sucked in with a loud gasp, covering Pam's ears. "Don't listen to him, baby. You are not a sheep." He glared, hissing at me. "You know I will hear about this for days. And she's already mad at you."

Snorting, I took another drink. "Okay, I'll give... Why is the donkey mad at me?" Sprig had spent a lot of time alone in Rapava's labs; his only friend then was a stuffed animal, a tiny bear he had to leave behind. To him, she and Pam were real. It was sad and adorable all at the same time.

Sprig sniffed, turning his back to me. "You're right, Pam. He doesn't deserve forgiveness after what he's done."

Setting down my glass, I watched him for a while, his tiny shoulders slouching with disappointment, digging at my cold, dead heart.

Groaning, I rubbed viciously at my forehead. "Okay, what do I need to apologize for?"

"Not talking to you," Sprig huffed.

"Normally, that would make my day, gopher." I poked at him. "But talk."

Sprig circled back to me.

"For leaving." I felt the stab instantly. "For hurting *Bhean*." It was what he called Zoey, meaning woman. "*Bebinn*. Even the Viking, and... Pam." Meaning him.

Emotion wound around my vocal cords. In my own pain, how many I had hurt when they were mourning too? Losing Lexie was devastating to them all. And then they lost me as well.

Swallowing the knot in my throat, I rubbed my thumb over the top of his head.

"I don't say this often, or at all... I'm sorry, furball."

"Not me you need to apologize to. I personally was happy you were gone." He shoved Pam into my face again. "Apologize to her... like you mean it."

I let out a light growl as I clenched my teeth, Sprig poking Pam into my nose.

"Nice and loud, boot humper."

"Please, forgive me…" I gritted through every syllable, forcing out the last word like it might actually kill me. "Pam."

Sprig tilted his ear to her mouth.

"She doesn't believe you. Now again, but from the heart."

"I'm going to use her innards as toilet paper," I snapped.

"Someone is being a massive Viking." In Sprig code, that meant asshole. "Pirates and Vikings aren't all that different, I suppose." He shrugged.

"But unlike Ryker, I don't need my food separated. I can eat a goat and a monkey at the same time."

"Don't threaten us with a good time, pirate! We're still mad at you."

A groan pinched my lids together as a sharp knock thrummed my cabin door. "Enter," I called out, downing another swig, trying to get all visuals out of my head, figuring it was Scot. I did a double-take when Cooper entered.

"Hey." He peeked in. "Have a moment?"

"Yes." I nodded eagerly. "Otherwise, you might have to tell Zoey I chucked her pet hamster overboard."

"Hamster?" Sprig yelped. "I'll have you know, bootleg-humper—"

"Hey, Sprig, I think Annabeth is down in the galley making tea with *honey*." Cooper motioned at the door.

"What?" He stopped midsentence, his eyes growing wide. "Honey?"

"And some sugar cubes."

"Gotta go, ass-bandit!" Sprig flew off the table, his cape of underwear flapping behind him, Pam in his arms, as he scrambled off the table. "Honeyhoneyhoneyhoneyhoney!" He chanted all the way out of my door, and Cooper closed it behind him, smirking back at me.

214

"He'll be passed out in five minutes."

"I give it three."

Cooper stepped farther into the room. "Have another one of those?" He nodded at the drink in my hand.

"Like that should even be a question." I got up, yanking out a large bottle of Scottish whiskey Scot got from his homeland. Pouring Cooper a drink, I handed it to him, gesturing to a chair on the other side of the table I used for a desk. "Everything okay?"

Cooper sat down, his gaze not meeting mine, his hand brushing his hair back. Something in his expression sent a warning down my limbs, my chest tightening.

"She doesn't know I'm here." He gulped the entire glass, setting it back down on the table, and poured himself another.

"Who doesn't?" Trepidation slid down my gullet.

"Annabeth." He took a moment to look at the whiskey before taking another huge gulp, only adding to my nerves. "She'd kill me."

"What the fuck is going on?" Anything having to do with AB had my complete and full attention. There were only a handful I would kill and die for, and she was one of them.

"She doesn't want you to know." He frowned. "Anyone to know."

"Cooper." My spine straightened. "If you don't fucking tell me what's going on. Right now…"

"She's sick."

"What?" I froze.

He shifted in his seat, visibly agitated and upset.

"Cooper—" It rattled in my throat, almost a threat.

"We found out a few months ago." He swallowed. "She has cancer."

My blood stopped in my veins, dread submerging me with so much fear I couldn't move or speak.

"We're pretty sure it's from the experiments, what

Rapava did and gave to her down in the labs." His eyes filled with liquid.

Emotion filled me like a volcano. I popped out of my seat, moving around the room, ready to explode. My brain could not wrap around the fact that she had cancer. It wasn't fair. She had been through so much cruelty, horror, and loss, yet she radiated goodness and light. It was just like her to not want anyone to know. She wouldn't want anyone to fuss over her, only over the kids at the orphanage.

I opened my mouth to ask something, but Cooper seemed to know, answering my next question.

"It's incurable."

"FUCK!" Fury bubbled under my skin as I erupted. I picked up a chair, chucking it across the room, roaring with anger as it crashed into my shelves, dumping books and trinkets onto the ground. I wanted to destroy everything in this room, tear the world apart with my hands if I had to. Plead with the universe to save her.

Not her... anyone but her.

Cooper didn't move from his chair, not reacting at all to my outburst, taking another drink as I stared at him, wondering how he was so calm.

"You think I haven't already broken everything in our house? Been so fucking angry at the world I had to be locked up for a bit so I didn't kill everyone?" He shook his head, his light-brown eyes flashing with red, a sign the Dweller wasn't far underneath. "I've cursed the world and tried to fight everyone I encountered. But it didn't make her better." He rolled his head back, blinking at the ceiling for a few beats. "She needs me strong, at her side, not throwing a tantrum." He curved his head toward me. "She needs you too."

Grief balled up in my throat, the reality of it hitting home.

"It's why, even more, we have to find this nectar. It was easy to convince Lars to send me; he understands, out of all people, if it exists, I *will* find it." His jaw set with determination, hiding the fear and pain flicking in his eyes. "Because if it's not... if there is nothing we can do..." His hands rolled up into fists. "That's not even something I can contemplate." He stood up, his shoulders tight. "I wanted to tell you since I thought you deserved to know. I knew, like me, you would do anything for her."

Not even a question.

"Please act like you don't know. Let her tell you in her own time, okay?"

I tried to nod.

"I think she's hoping that if this nectar is real and cures her, no one will even have to know. She doesn't want people upset for no reason."

"Typical AB." I could barely talk, struggling to get sounds out of my throat. "Always thinking of others and never about herself."

Cooper dipped his chin in agreement, strolling closer to where I was.

"Just know, I love her more than life. More than *anything* else. I will do *everything* to save her. Either you have me as your best ally and fighter." He looked me dead in the eyes. "Or you have your greatest enemy if you get in my way."

"For her." I stared back. "There is nothing I won't do."

Cooper took me in one more moment, then nodded his head at the truth in my expression. "Good."

I had already lost Lexie, failed to save her.

I would *not* lose Annabeth too.

Chapter 18
Katrina

Lights from the city glowed on the horizon, wispy clouds slithering over the stars, the smell of rain in the air again. The breeze flapped the flags high on the masts, the wind gliding over my skin, ebbing the humidity in the air. The taste of salt and brine layered on my tongue, making me exhale with the peace the water always gave me.

Most thought it was strange for a cat to love the water so much, but anything could be normal if you grew up around it. And since I was a toddler, I lived and breathed the pirate life.

I left the galley, most everyone else in bed at this late hour. I had spent a while talking to Annabeth and already adored her. She was taller than me by a few inches, yet her delicate frame made her feel small and younger than her twenty-five years. I might look the same age, but I was many centuries older than her human age.

She could easily be mistaken for fae, having an almost ethereal quality. The girl was the nicest and gentlest person I'd ever met. That had to be why she had nothing but good things to say about Croygen.

"We're talking about the same guy, right?" I had tipped

my head at her, my nose twitching at an odd, sour smell I couldn't place. "Croygen? The pain in the ass pirate who probably seduces himself in the mirror?"

"All a front." She batted her hand in the air, sipping her tea. The monkey, Sprig, was passed out on the table next to her, spooning what looked like a stuffed goat, with a honey packet in his other arm. "Croygen is one of the most faithful, good-hearted people I know."

"Seriously, we can't be talking about the same man."

"For those he loves, he will do anything. He purposely put himself in hell, going down into Dr. Rapava's labs *twice*. If you had any idea what hell, what depravity, went on down there, you would understand his love and dedication."

Envy flinched through me because he would never do the same for me.

"He let himself be experimented on and tortured for both Zoey and Lexie so they wouldn't be alone down there." Her expression darkened as if she was experiencing a memory. "He purposely put himself there. Believe me, I know what kind of sacrifice it must have been."

"Lexie?" I stilled at the name, having heard about her the night before. "You knew her well?"

"She was my sister. I mean, not by blood, but that wasn't important" Sadness flooded her eyes. "I lost my biological family in the devastating electrical storm that hit Seattle years ago. Zoey found me in a bad situation, took me in, and raised Lexie and me when she didn't have to. But she made us all family. And Croygen was part of that..." She stared down at her tea. "That was, until Lexie was killed. He didn't handle it well. None of us did...he left right after."

Was it sick to be slightly jealous of this Lexie? He'd so easily sent me off, never looking back, and never having any remorse for what he did, while this girl still tortured him. So much he had yet to return to his family after many years.

"He really loved her?" Was I fishing? No. Certainly not. I was just curious.

Annabeth looked up briefly, her mouth pinching in thought. "I know she loved him." She twirled her tea bag around. "And no doubt he loved her. Absolutely adored her. There was no way you couldn't. Lexie was filled with so much life, almost like her body couldn't contain it all in this life."

I swallowed.

"But was he *in* love with her?" Her blue eyes met mine as if she sensed something more in my question. "Until I met Cooper, I would have said yes. But now I understand fae better, and what mates mean to them. How it feels, the intensity and deep connection between us. There are no words in the English language to describe the bond." A blush colored her pale skin. "To experience it. To witness it firsthand with Ryker and Zoey and so many at the Dweller ranch." She paused, her gaze boring through me. "No." She wagged her head. "Croygen loved her, but he wasn't *in love* with her. Not the way she would have wanted him to be."

A strange mix of sadness for this girl flowed over me because I knew how it felt to be so in love with him and for him not to feel the same, and also relieved that he wasn't. Which only made me feel guilty because this poor girl was dead. What kind of person was jealous of a girl no longer living?

A loud fart whistled in the air, a sigh coming from Sprig. Annabeth and I both laughed, watching him curl up tighter around the goat, smacking his lips.

"I better get him to bed." She scooped him up, smiling at me. "It was good talking with you, though I feel like I've somehow known you forever." Oddly, I felt the same. "See you in the morning."

"Night."

AB took off toward the cabin she and Cooper shared, that bitter scent still lingering. My nose wiggled. Must have been Sprig farting the whole time. Cats had an excellent sense of smell. It was how I knew we were being attacked this morning; the men coming up the stairs had a strong magical stench I knew wasn't from anyone I had met before.

This morning...

A flush warmed my cheeks, recalling how I woke up. I swear I could still feel his massive cock tucked in my ass, his hand up my shirt, his thumb absently rubbing at my nipple.

Desire slid down between my thighs, pulsing fiercely.

Jumping up, I needed to move, get some fresh air to flood out my thoughts. Taking deep breaths, I let my feet take me to the quarterdeck, trying to regain my composure.

My skin prickled, my senses knowing who was here before I even acknowledged them. My nose and eyes picked up on the figure standing at the railing.

The draw to the spot was a habit I had learned from him. When the pendulum swung too high and nothing made sense, the ocean would always center me again.

I was sure he was aware I stood there, but he didn't react when I stepped up next to him, leaning on the rail, the impending storm rocking the ship.

I could feel turmoil whipping around inside him, his jaw clenched, his muscles tight, and his gaze far away.

"When I was young, late at night when no one was awake, I used to sneak out of my bed and spy on this pirate," I spoke, my attention on the swells. "He'd come to this same spot when he felt the world on his shoulders."

"Really?" he said flatly.

"I could hear him talking to the sea, telling it all his woes. And one time, I asked him if it ever answered him back."

"And what did he say?"

221

"He said, 'the sea always answers.'" My eyes stayed forward as I repeated the words he had told me in the past. "Maybe not directly. It keeps many secrets, but it will always guide you."

His mouth hinted at a sad smile.

"Sounds like this pirate of yours was full of shit."

"Oh, he was definitely that." I grinned at his lips twitching again. "But he also was one of the wisest I've ever known."

"Was that a compliment, Kitty-Kat?"

"You're assuming you were the pirate I was talking about."

His head twisted to me, our gazes catching. I could see and feel his sorrow, like he was adrift and had no raft to hang on to.

"You never snuck up on me. I always knew you were there," he breathed. "I think you were one of the things that calmed me."

I hated this sensation in my gut, this need to forget all the stuff between the time he sent me off the ship to when I climbed back on. Pretend he wasn't the reason my life had been so rough, that I didn't miss my father every minute. That I hadn't spent every day for centuries planning my revenge, becoming a notorious pirate to spite him.

"I need you to tell me about my father."

He blew out a breath, his head wagging. "This is not the time, Kat."

"Yes, it is." My voice rose, desperate to get my answers. "I need to know the full truth. I think you owe it to me."

"No!" He turned to me, rage flaming behind his eyes, his body almost pressing into mine. "When I tell you it's not the time..." He leaned in close, his nose almost touching mine. "I mean it. I'm hanging by a thread here. Don't push me."

"And what if I do?" I defied him, pretending I didn't feel

the rush of fear and fury. Wanting to push him past the point of cracking, needing to crack the unbreakable Silver-Tongue Devil. Somehow I knew in my gut he needed it more than anything. "What are you going to do to me?" I inched forward, getting a hair's breadth from his face, his nose flaring at my nearness, his eyes dropping to my mouth, then darting back up again. "Kill me?"

"Kat," he warned me, only fanning the flames of my own anger. He made me forget my grief, my father, because being near him short-circuited my brain. He was the reason I had no family. I had nothing but memories of struggle and pain, of being beaten at the boarding school, of fighting to stay alive in the streets not intended for girls. Even though I was an excellent fighter, when I was up against a gang of boys, there was no way of winning. At night I went to sleep curled into a ball, wearing his coat, beaten, bloody, and starving, wishing for death to take me by morning.

However, morning always came, and, needing to face another day, I got back up. I practiced and trained even harder, determined to make every one of those boys who hurt me pay.

Including Croygen.

He was the only one left to pay his debt.

"Come on, Croygen." I challenged him as thunder rumbled, the storm skirting across the sky. "So far you seem to be all talk. Has the devil lost his touch?"

"Katrina." His teeth gnashed together, his tendons straining at his neck. "I'm not joking."

"Neither am I." I slipped up to him, my fingers wrapping around the handle of his sword at his waist. The sound of the blade leaving its sheath sizzled through me, revving me up like only fighting and sex could do. "Come on, Croygen. Show me what the illustrious pirate can do." I tossed his sword back to him, the devil catching it with one hand.

Emotion thumped off him, the desire to combat the world. I could feel his need to fight, to taste the blood of his victim, to dance close to the edge.

It spurred my own emotions, needing to give him what he desired. What we both craved. I yanked my sword out from my sheath. Even in the modern world, he and I were still old-school pirates. We had guns for protection, but our swords were for battle.

Gripping the handle, I stepped back, watching his gaze roll over me as the storm brewing inside him rumbled as loud as the one rolling over our heads. His eyes latched onto mine, filled with hunger.

Hunger for a fight.

Moving back, we began circling each other.

"You sure you want this, Kitty-Kat?"

"Oh, yeah."

He shuffled forward, his blade chinking against mine. A crack of lightning boomed overhead, almost as if the storm felt our energy. Pushing his blade to the side, he retreated, our feet moving quicker.

I could easily take on the best of the best. However, Croygen was unsurpassed, even beating Master Yukimura when they trained. He went from my role model to my nemesis.

"This how you killed my father?" *Clank. Clank.* Our swords sparked off each other. "Oh right, you stabbed him in the heart with his own dagger."

Lunging, he tried to nick my side, but I spun out of the way.

"How fast did Killian run to you? Couldn't wait to tell you, could he?" he mocked. "And I bet you believed him without question. Your boy was so in love with you, he would have told you the sky was red if you wanted him to."

Clank. Clank. Clank.

"Are you saying he's lying?"

"I'm saying not every story is black and white." He regripped his sword, circling.

"I didn't know killing my father, your own right-hand man, was considered a gray area."

"You ask for a truth you are not ready to know."

"Yes or no. Did you kill my father?"

"Yes." He slanted his head. "And no."

Rage pumped momentum into my muscles, a grunt coming from me as I lunged for him. Our swords crashed together, thunder responding as rain started pouring down, the skies opening up, dumping their tears on us.

"Hah!" I bellowed, twirling, my sword slicing for his unwounded side. Croygen twisted away, noting the slight tear in his shirt, a trickle of blood sliding down. His lids narrowed, a noise working up his throat. He swung for me and I spun, the blade nicking my arm.

The pain of his hit spurred the ire inside my chest. In an instant, everything changed. Our fighting went from serious to severe as we both felt the drive increase to purge our demons, harbor our egos, and prove our dominance.

The loud clanks of our blades rang in the air like chimes against the drums of thunder and the tambourine of rain. We danced across the slick deck, droplets pasting his shirt to his sculpted chest, his pants sticking to his toned thighs, adding a carnal potency to every strike of his sword.

My arms burned with the weight of the weapon, but anger fueled me, driving me forward. Moving around the deck, Croygen spun, coming right in for me. Leaping up on the rail, I used the shrouds, swinging myself down feet away from him.

"Joining the circus, are we?"

"Think Sprig already has a trained monkey."

Glowering, he lurched for me, the rain pouring down

225

harder, making it more difficult to see. He lunged one way, my body already moving to block him when I realized my mistake. How many times had Yukimura trained us with this fake out move? He reversed, twisting to the other side, his blade nicking the back of my leg.

As the edge sunk in, my nerves screamed in pain, but the adrenaline kept me from truly suffering, bursting more anger through me. I itched to change, my claws digging into my handle, my teeth sharpening. Twice now, my control had wavered, and both times around him. Hissing, I swiped out with my claws, gripping one of his wrists, my nails sinking in. Croygen inhaled sharply, momentarily distracted. Not giving him a moment of hesitation, I pitched forward, my blade pressing up against his neck with force. Blood trickled down his throat, the sharp edge cutting into his skin.

Breathing heavily, I paused, keeping my sword tight against him.

"Go ahead." His chest pumped in and out, his wet hair hanging around his face, water trailing down his cheeks and over his lips, his dark eyes alight with vigor. Like for one moment, he actually felt alive. "You want your revenge? Take it."

I stood on a precipice. Everything I had worked for, everything I had planned and trained for, was here. The revenge I sought. The blood I needed. The life I had wanted to take for so long.

"This is the only chance you'll get, Kitten."

My nose wrinkled at his challenge, daring me to do it. It was all right at the tip of my blade. One move, and I could accomplish all I ever set out to do. My father could rest in peace.

His elbow came down on my arm, knocking the sword from my grip, pushing me up against the railing, his own sword hovering close to my neck.

"Once again, you hesitated." He licked the water from

his lips, pulling my focus for a moment. "Remember, you *never* hesitate. Kill or be killed."

"So, what are you waiting for?" I spat. "If you're going to kill me, then do it. What are *you* afraid of?"

His lips lifted, his gaze narrowing, and he stepped into me.

"Killing you is not what I'm afraid of," he growled. "This is." Dropping his sword, the metal reverberating on the wood deck, he gripped the back of my head, yanking me to him.

His mouth took mine with bruising strength. It was like he lit a match on dry kindling and then doused it in gasoline. Fire exploded through my bones, sparking magic through my nerves. I became ravenous, angry, and wrathful, and his lips were just as greedy to hurt and take all he needed. We battled and attacked. Our kiss was savage, my tongue seeking his, my nails dragging up his chest, needing to mark him like an animal.

With a groan, his fingers curled through my wet strands, tugging my hair tightly, his body pressing harder into mine. I arched into him, needing to rub against him, feel his erection burning through my wet clothes. The smell of blood dripping from his neck boiled in my veins, tasting the aggression we carried.

"That turn you on, Kitty-Kat?" He growled in my ear. "Pain? Blood?" His teeth scraped down my neck. "You liked waking up to my dick hard against you, didn't you?"

Fuck, yes.

"You wanted me to slip your underwear to the side and thrust into you, fucking you so deeply until you screamed, making you break into pieces. Am I right?"

I swallowed back the yowl in my throat, my cat too close to the surface, my nails clawing deeper into his arms.

"Can't lie to me. I feel your heat, can already taste it on my tongue, Kitten."

Normally, I hated those pet names, but my body responded with feral need to the way he rumbled over them. My hips pushed back into his like I had no control. We kissed with the same violence we fought with. Taking what we could.

This was how we battled each other, how we sought our revenge.

His free hand moved under my T-shirt, exploring every curve, reminding me how it felt waking up to his touch this morning. How much more I wanted.

Our mouths devoured—biting, nipping, and sucking, causing each other to bleed, the pain only driving our desire higher. The rain and blood slipped between our hungry mouths, our wet clothes creating friction against our skin, his thick cock rubbing against my pussy.

"Katrina." He rolled his hips into me, my fingers digging into his ass, pushing him harder into me.

I lost all thought. The only thing speaking was need.

All I wanted was him sinking inside me. Claiming and destroying me at once.

"Captain?" Scot's voice broke through the darkness, and Croygen leaped away from me. "Oh shite, sorry." Scot appeared, his expression telling me he saw more than he wanted to. "I'll come back."

"No, what did you need?" Croygen moved back further, clearing his throat, sounding cool and unaffected.

"Tsai wants to confirm which port for the morning."

"Yes." Croygen nodded. "Tell her I'll be right there."

Scot nodded, his gaze jumping between us, a slight smirk on his face before he turned and left.

Tension filled the space he kept putting between us, expanding the silence. Desire still clung to the clouds, but regret danced on the tide.

His brow crinkled, his wet hair almost hiding his face.

"That was wrong of me." He spoke like he was some professor and I was a pupil. "I wasn't in my right mind. It won't happen again." He swiped up his sword, striding away, not looking back.

I watched him disappear into the darkness, almost becoming it. Rain pattered my face as I tried to rein in all the emotions colliding.

Anger. Hurt. Disappointment.

No... relief. It had to be.

Because he was right, it was a mistake.

A mistake I didn't slice his throat when I had the chance.

Chapter 19
Croygen

I stomped across the deck and sheathed my sword. My fists were so tight at my sides that my knuckles popped.

What the hell did I just do? What was I seconds from doing?

There was no doubt if Scot hadn't stepped in, I would be fucking Katrina against the railing right now, not thinking about the consequences.

I never used to care about those things, but Katrina was different. She wasn't some woman I could bed and walk away from with no strings attached.

I almost screwed everything up, and 99 percent of me wanted to turn back around, strip her bare, and push inside her, already sensing she could take me to my knees.

But it was wrong. I shouldn't look, touch, or feel that way about her.

"Fuuuuck!" I bellowed up at the sky, rain trickling down as the storm skated by, moving on. My body throbbed with anger, desire, and confusion, but what mostly pissed me off was the sense of peace I felt when I was near her. A calmness that felt reckless and turbulent. It made no sense. Everything in me was agitated and feral, but deep in my gut was a serenity, as if Kat could pinpoint exactly what I needed, what was plaguing me, easing the pressure inside like a bloodletting.

I had needed the fight to forget about Annabeth's disease, to push away all the unknowns of our mission, and get lost in the bloodlust and battle.

And fuck, it felt *so* good dueling with her. The sword to my throat had my cock hard as a rock, experiencing the power she held, the moment she could take my life, and the moment I could take hers. She could actually challenge me, which hadn't happened in a long time. The girl was a force. Strong, confident, and sexy as hell. She enticed me like no other, and fighting her was better than sex with most of the women I had been with.

That's what scared the shit out of me.

Rotty's daughter should be the last person I should feel anything for. And when she learned the truth about that fateful night?

I grunted, my fingers digging into my eyes, trying to regain some sensibility and draw the blood in my dick back to my brain.

Pirates didn't live by many codes of conduct. We had minimal rules, and most could be broken. There were a few we took seriously. And fucking your first mate's daughter had to be on the list.

The moon peeked through the clouds, and a snicker found me through the dark. The silhouette of a small figure stood not far from me.

"My dear boy. You are so screwed."

"I could've been," I muttered to myself, pinching at my brows, wanting to take that back.

"What stopped you?"

"You know what." I clenched my jaw. "Plus, I knew her as a kid. It's wrong."

"You would've been a kid when I was around your age, and I'd fuck you now."

A laugh coughed out of my chest, my head shaking. "We need to put a warning label on you."

"Too hot to handle." She grinned, showing off her few teeth.

"With all those layers, you really are."

"This one is different. That troubles you." She grew serious. "Release the past, or it will always keep you from a future." She clicked her tongue. "Or peace."

"Getting philosophical on me?"

"My way of saying get your head out of your ass." She rolled her milky eyes to the sky. "You already know the truth; you are simply too scared to face it."

"Too scared of what?"

"Being owned by a pussy." She snorted, shuffling by me. "Confirming we are headed for Hangzhou?"

"Yeah," I grumbled. Hangzhou was run by fae, a stunning, prosperous place at the head of the Hangzhou Bay, sitting between Shanghai and Ningbo, controlling a lot of imports. The fae in power made gambling a huge part of the city. They created a playground for the wealthy and the desperate, hoping to win some kind of fortune to survive in these times, only to return home more destitute than when they went in.

It was also the best place for shady deals. Ju didn't reign there, making it a perfect place to get supplies and regroup.

Stomping into my cabin, I slammed into my bathroom, stripping and stepping into my shower before it even heated up. Cold water stung my skin, and I welcomed it, wanting the torture, craving the pain. Anything to take away my thoughts, lessen the need still throbbing in my dick. My hands went to the wall, and I leaned under the stream. I could still feel her heat, hear the moan she tried to hide from me, see the way she bowed into me. My gaze caught where she cut into my side and her nail marks on my arm. She had enjoyed inflicting pain as much as feeling it.

"Fuck," I hissed, my hand wrapping around my shaft. It was so tight it hurt, making me go insane. I was a breath away from tracking her down, bending her over whatever surface we were near, no matter who was there, and fucking her so hard I'd make sure Killian, wherever he was, heard her cry out *my* name, knew it was *my* cock inside her, claiming her.

Did he fuck her? Know the feeling of sliding into her?

A growl gurgled in my chest, my molars crunching down. A violent possessiveness washed over me, my hand stroking harder. The vision of her on her knees, her mouth sucking down my cock as her cat teeth dragged faintly down my shaft.

Grunting, I clamped down, rubbing firmly. Sex was always something I was up for. Even bad, it was good. But I was *always* the one in control. The one to dominate, even if my lover got out her whip and toys. I took lead. Whatever they were into, I was down for, but I was never out of my league or too desperate not to walk away.

Katrina was twisting me up. I had no willpower. My awareness of her, even when she wasn't in the room, was worrisome. The yearning to always find her, challenge her, fight her, was not something I was used to.

Why her? Why, out of all the women in the world, was she the one who had woken something in me?

My aggravation with her only increased my need, my balls tightening as I pictured myself pumping into her as she held the sword to my throat, the blade cutting into my skin the moment I released inside her.

"Shiiiit!" My cum gushed over my hand and onto the tile, my legs unsteady under me. Taking several pulls of air, I fell against the wall. Reality slowly set in, and with it, chagrin over who had gotten me off.

Not seeing Katrina as the little girl I knew, but as the woman she had become, was a problem. I needed to keep her squarely in the box marked "Do. Not. Open." Because as much as Kat said I was the one who wrecked her life, she was the one who took everything from mine.

"Land Hoe!"

"It's land *ahoy*."

"There's just one hoe?" Sprig sat on my shoulder, nibbling on a pancake Zid had made this morning. "That doesn't seem good for business."

"Ahoy... not a hoe."

"I still say, one hoe for the whole place? She must be exhausted. You'd think there'd be a couple of hoes by now."

My hand going to my face, I exhaled. Why was I even bothering?

"Don't you have a stuffed pig to go hump?"

"Pam is to be spoken about with respect and love," he exclaimed, looking around, nestling closer to my ear. "Let me tell you, I know from experience that she *does not* like being called that in or out of the bedroom. She got so mad at me. Though she didn't mind being the pony one time."

My eye twitched. "I walked into that one," I muttered to myself. "That was my fault."

Scot, Corb, and Vane prepared us to dock. The bustling port was getting ready for market day in the slums of the city. Humans and fae moved in and out of this area freely, unlike a lot of other countries, but mainly fae lived here. Only a sliver of land was left to the servants and workers of the fae elite to inhabit.

How fast, when the world divided, class and money took

all, forcing the middle class to fall into poverty. There were only two races, fae and human, and two classes, rich and poor.

"Is it breakfast time yet? I'm starving." Sprig licked off the last bits of butter and pancake from his fingers, syrup in his fur and covering his mouth. There was a reason Zoey and Ryker hand-fed him. The sprite was a natural disaster around food.

"You literally just ate." I wiped off his fingers and face with my shirt. "Like two seconds ago."

"Us sprites need to eat constantly or we whittle away and die."

"Could I be so lucky?" I picked him up, plopping him on Tsai's shoulder behind the helm. "Here, you're now on babysitting duties."

I left it up to them to figure out who I was referring to.

Cooper strolled up to me, the heat already dampening his brow. He wasn't used to this kind of humidity coming from the Pacific Northwest. Rain, yes, but the type of heat that strangled you, clogging your lungs, wrapping around you like a wool blanket with the heater fully blasting, no.

"You coming?"

"Yeah." Cooper nodded. "Need to get a few supplies. Better clothes for this weather. And AB wants to see if the long-distance walkie-talkie Lars gave us will work on land. She needs to tell Zoey she has Sprig."

Lars was trying to create new devices to work in this magic-infused world. He had the best engineers, scientists, and doctors leading the way, and they were making good leaps, but still, there would be hiccups and setbacks along the way.

"I'm coming too," a voice slunk up my back, her statement reminding me of a fantasy I had last night. I wanted to say the shower was a one-time thing, but I had woken up in the middle of the night, my body craving hers like a drug. Half-asleep, I had no guard up, letting my mind free, and fuck, did we get dirty. It felt so real, like I could feel her weight on me, smell her, taste her.

My muscles locked up, my walls rising.

"No, you're not." I scowled at her.

"I'm sorry?" She cocked her head, folding her arms.

"I'm out," Cooper scoffed, giving me a look that said, *Good luck, pal.* "Meet you on the dock."

I barely heard him. I faced Kat, my arms mirroring hers.

"There is no need for you to go. You're going to stay here and out of trouble."

She stayed quiet, but she was anything but silent, and I had the urge to run after Cooper.

"Not only do you have no say in what I do—"

"Technically, you're my prisoner."

"Nor do I give a fuck," she continued, ignoring my assertion. "I need some underwear, pants, and a shirt that doesn't stink of you."

"I've been told I smell good."

She stepped up to me. I clamped my hands tighter on my arms because all I wanted to do was grab her hips and drag her all the way into me.

"It amazes me someone hasn't killed you yet."

"Must be my charm." The side of my mouth hitched up, and I inched even closer to her, forcing her to tilt her head back. My body towered over hers, my mouth so close I could almost taste her lips again. The impulse to lean down and kiss her, like it was something I did all the time, almost overtook me.

Stepping back, I pushed past her. "Fine."

"I wanna go," Sprig chirped.

"No," I barked, my fury turning on him, freezing him before he jumped. "You will only attract attention. Even now, a talking monkey would create hysteria."

"I promise I won't talk." He pretended to zip his lips. "See? Silent as the dead," he pledged, pointing at his mouth, which was moving freely.

"I said no."

"Wow, someone really needs to get laid. You're acting like a Viking again. I can always tell when he needs to club his seal."

Both my eyes twitched.

"Sprig, just stay here this time. I promise I will bring you back something yummy." Annabeth rolled up her hair in a topknot.

"Better be fried and covered in honey!" He stomped his foot on Tsai's shoulder. "Ohhhh, like honey cookies, or honey noodles, pastry. Oh, deep-fried honey knots with honey dip rolled in sugar. Oooo, how about—"

"We get it, chinchilla." I started down the plank.

"You get me anything with banana, and I will poop in your boots again!"

Kat's eyebrow lifted at that as we hit the dock.

"Yeah, he did that. And in my jacket pocket too."

"Speaking of jackets. Can I get mine back?"

"You mean mine?" I glanced over at her, Cooper and Annabeth already taking off ahead of us. "You took it from *me*."

"Possession is nine-tenths of the law."

"And it is now in *my* possession again."

"I want my jacket and boots back."

"You mean the boots you could slice a man in half with? Most likely me? No fucking way."

"Seriously, how has no one killed you yet?"

"Lucky, I guess."

She ran her hand through her hair, pretending to be more irritated than she was, but I could see the amusement she was trying to hide.

"Come on, there's a clothing stall." I didn't think, my hand threading through hers, pulling her with me as I wormed through the crowd to the cart, where AB and Cooper were already picking through stuff.

When we walked up, Annabeth's gaze dropped to where my hand was holding Kat's. I instantly let go as guilt and embarrassment flooded me all at once.

I was not a hand-holding kind of guy. That was an intimacy I had no affiliation with. I courted to seduce, took their hand in a dance, kissed them to command. I didn't hold hands in the middle of the day just because. It was weird for me. Except with Kat, it had come way too easily.

Turning away from them, my attention returned to the crowds, watching all the different characters and types of people moving along with their lives.

Scanning the area, my gaze stopped on two men buying survival gear—knives, boots, camping items, rope, compass. Something about them caught my attention, a tick in the back of my brain.

One turned to his buddy, nodding his head.

"Holy. Shit," I breathed.

"What?" Kat's response was instant, her head darting around, searching for whatever caused my reaction. She looked at me, following my gaze to the two men. "You know them?"

"Not really." My gaze stayed intently on them. "But I know what they're after."

Her head jerked to me.

"Those are the guys from the pub." I nodded at the two men. "They're the ones I overheard talking about the nectar."

Of all the places in all the towns, Tiger and Hammerhead were standing only feet away in this one. A link to the nectar.

"I think we just found our break."

Cooper was tall enough to see above most of the crowd, his head nodding, telling me the men were coming our way.

"Keep your distance," I whispered to Kat.

"Croygen," she snapped, my head turning to her. "I'm a cat-shifter. I *know* how to stalk prey without them knowing. I can do it in my sleep." She placed her hands on my chest. "Now shut up and calm the fuck down. I got this."

Shit. Was it bad that I was turned on by her remarks?

She slipped out from the cart, trailing the two men who were loaded down with stuff, not paying attention to their surroundings, oblivious to who shadowed them.

We couldn't let them out of our sight. They were our only clue as to where the nectar might be.

It took everything I had to wait, to let the men drift out of view. Cooper and AB stood out too much around here, their golden hair recognizable. And there was a very slight possibility the men might recall me from the pub.

Like Kat, I had a talent for disappearing easily, blending in with my surroundings and almost vanishing in front of your eyes. It was how I got out of many sticky situations when husbands came home while I was in bed with their wives.

Five minutes later, Kat was back, slinking up beside me.

"That was fast." I nodded to Cooper and AB to join us. "Did you lose them?"

"No." She frowned at me, waiting for my friends to circle in. "They're staying in a room above a bar. Third floor, on the corner."

"Bar," Cooper repeated. "Good chance they'll be drinking there tonight?"

"Hopefully, and leaving the room unguarded." I hoped it would be that easy. Otherwise we'd have to do it when they were asleep. "We get in, take note of everything they have. Maps, documents, pictures. Anything."

"Easy enough." Kat tucked her hair behind her ear.

"Uh. Did I say you were going?"

"Uh, do I care?" she countered. "What don't you get? I'm a cat. Why do you think we're synonymous with thieving? I know you're having an issue seeing me as a competent woman." That was *not* what I was having trouble seeing her as. "But I became the pirate PIB for a reason. Maybe this is hard on your ego, but I'm amazing at what I do. So stop being an egotistical jerk and get over yourself." She slammed into my shoulder, stalking by me, leaving the three of us.

"I really like her." Annabeth curled her arm around Cooper's, both of them nodding in agreement, grinning like fools.

Cooper was loving that I just got my ass reamed. "Think someone got put in their place."

"Shut up," I mumbled, tramping back to the ship as their laughter followed me.

The problem was I didn't disagree with them.

Chapter 20
Katrina

The night brought even more people to the streets. The craving to block out life came with a plenitude of vices: drinking, gambling, sex, drugs. It was gifted to you everywhere here. The fae had fewer restrictions on sin, and humans and fae alike were drawn to it. Except there was definitely a divide here. The poor man's area and the rich's. The elite fae stayed away from the dock, protected in the clean, upscale gambling establishments in the wealthy part of the city, while the disadvantaged stayed in the seedy zone.

Slinking through the stacked, dirty, cramped lanes full of shops with apartments above, the smell of cooking spices and mystery meats wafted through the confined streets.

I slipped by people without notice, sticking to the shadows. Normally, this wasn't even a thought. Human form or cat, sneaking around was instinctual. Except my head wasn't entirely in the game tonight, too conscious of the figure staying right up on me, pressing against me every time we came to a stop.

My lashes fluttered at his breath at the back of my neck, his presence making me jittery and distracted. My skin prickled with the memory of his touch.

His kiss.

As a preteen, I had dreamed about kissing him, but it was always sweet and simple, having no idea the true pleasure this man could bring with a simple kiss. Because with him, it wasn't just a kiss. It was a command of your body, a seduction of all your senses. Why did I think I'd be immune when all other women, fae or human, had failed? I was shown my folly.

Tortured by it, the kiss looped in my head on repeat since he walked away. I couldn't seem to let it go, to chalk it up to our emotions running high and needing an outlet. There was a shame in knowing I not only enjoyed my father's killer kissing me, but I craved it like nothing else. I couldn't face the fact I had to get myself off in the shower later, and in the middle of the night, I woke up like I could feel his energy surrounding me, skating over my skin, and weaving through my soul, bringing me to climax again. It had felt so real, like he was there with me.

I had to get myself off twice when we got back from shopping, my body so tight, my need to go to the cabin he slipped off to was almost too tempting. I wanted to blame him, to turn this all on him because I had never experienced this before. The number of men I had been with in my life was astounding, yet I couldn't remember their names or faces after I left. A few here and there had stuck around a little longer, but I would get bored, my focus solely on my need to become a successful pirate.

I had Killian and my crew. I didn't need anything more. The men were to either steal from or take the edge off, preferably both.

Then Croygen, the devil himself, strolled back into my life and turned me into a fool again.

"Where to, Kitty-Kat?" Croygen's sultry voice grazed my ear. A shiver ran over my skin, my lips rolling together, keeping in my response. This man made me weak, and I hated it.

Stepping away, my irritation increased. "A block up." I didn't even glance back before taking off, wishing it was more than just me and Croygen on this mission.

Cooper wanted to come but was sensible enough to understand that more people brought more attention and risks. Croygen and I had the skills to slip in and out of places, blending in with the night, robbing people blind. It was what we did.

Croygen hadn't even fought me when I showed up dressed in black with a backpack, ready to go. Instead, he motioned for me to take lead.

Music and voices spilled from the bar, people and prostitutes packing the small watering hole. Croygen and I moved closer to it, hoping the shark-shifters were there enjoying the warm night.

We had two plans, depending on if the men had or hadn't left the room. No matter what, we were going in. One plan left them unconscious on the ground but aware they were being tracked. The other left them unaware anyone was even in their room, going on their way, easy to follow.

Hood up, Croygen slipped into the bar, his magic helping him blend in, and within twenty seconds, he was back out.

"They're there."

"Good." I breathed out, heading around the building. The bar was on a corner with rooms above. Theirs was the top one. We ducked into the boarding house's entrance. Because electricity no longer worked, there were no alarms or buzzing people in, just good old-fashioned locks.

I opened my palm, waiting for Croygen. Without a pause, he pulled lock picks out of my bag and placed them in my hand, the interaction automatic, like we had been doing this for years. There was also no question that while I broke in, he would be on guard, watching for any other inhabitants coming the stoop.

It took me barely two minutes before the lock snapped open, and I grinned over my shoulder, pushing the door.

"Could have been faster." Croygen winked, strolling past me.

Rolling my eyes, I trailed after him, heading up the three flights of stairs.

"The end one." I pointed down the hall, our legs taking us to the door. I sensed it the moment we walked up, disappointment lowering my shoulders. "They magic-locked it."

"Shit." Croygen's head fell back on an exhale. "I was hoping these two weren't so smart."

"What do we do?" Normal locks were easy, but magic locks, which had become the rage after the Fae War, were not. No one had come up with anything to counter the spell yet, making them one of the hardest things to break into. If not impossible. "We can try going up the balcony?"

"And what are the chances they haven't spelled that door too?" Croygen scoured at his forehead.

"Still worth a shot." I shrugged, looking back at the door like the spell would magically be gone this time.

Movement caught my eye, a tiny hand reaching out by my hip, coming from a pocket on the side of my backpack.

"Holy shit!" I jumped, tearing off my pack.

"What?" Croygen jerked to me, watching me with confusion as I held it up, a furry arm sticking out.

"Nooooo," Croygen groaned.

"Hi!" The hand waved.

"No, no, no, no, no!" Croygen paced in a circle, his head wagging, before turning back. "No!"

"Yes, Captain STD." Sprig crawled out of the pocket to the top, and I noticed this time he didn't have the underwear, but a tiny backpack on instead. "You Neanderthal fae forget the mighty power of us sub-fae." He stood up, his hands on his hips.

"Don't do it."

"Behold..."

"Don't do it."

"Ta-da-da-da..."

"Do. Not. Do. It."

"Suuuuper Sprig! Coming to your rescue!"

"You did it." Croygen blinked up at the ceiling.

"You know you need me." Sprig held up his fingers, spreading them out. "Magic hands!"

"Oh, my gods." It dawned on me what he was getting at. I never had that much interaction with sub-fae, but I was aware they had qualities typical faeries didn't. Some might call them a weakness because sub-fae had far less magic than fae. Limited. Because of that, they were neutral to some magic. Like fae locks. "You can get through a spelled lock, can't you?"

"Duh. That's why I'm called *Super* Sprig."

"Holy shit. You are a godsend."

"Hear that, assbuckler? I'm godsent. Ohhhh, speaking of godsent. You don't happen to have any honey in your tits, do you?"

"Huh?"

Croygen groaned, though a smile slipped over his mouth.

"Is that only a *Bhean* thing? I praise her honey tits all the time. The Viking and Scurvy King over here do too."

"I'm sorry?" My head shot to Croygen.

"We don't have time for this." Croygen stepped up. "If you're here to help, then help, fur-ball, or I'm gonna use your honey bag as a muzzle."

Sprig hopped on my arm, motioning for me to hold him near the lock.

"Is that a Winnie the Pooh backpack?" I stared at the bag in the shape of a honey pot with the goat's head sticking out.

"Pam prefers riding in there."

245

"I can't believe you brought her," Croygen grumbled.

"You know how mad she gets when I leave her." His eyes widened like she turned into a fire-breathing monster. "In contrast to you, I like to please my woman."

"He's got you there." I shrugged.

Croygen's dark eyes shot to mine, sparking with heat, causing my lungs to slow, his kiss still searing my body. The intimacy in his look was daring me, challenging me. I knew perfectly well he could not only please a woman, but he would shatter them into pieces.

Not able to hold his gaze, I went back to Sprig as Croygen huffed at his win.

"Almost there..." Sprig worked the lock, his brow furrowing in concentration.

A door slammed from below, tensing both of us.

"Hurry up, gerbil, or you won't get any honey later."

"What?" Sprig's eyes grew big.

"I'll plant your face in a huge bowl of smashed bananas with dried banana chips."

Sprig stared at him like he gutted Pam in front of him.

"Try positive reinforcement." I shook my head. "Sprig, I will find you some honey if you hurry up."

"See, butt-pirate?" He stuck his tongue out at Croygen. "And you wonder why your only friend is your hand. She's nice."

"She's not very nice, believe me." His voice went low, suggesting more than what he said.

Click.

The lock broke free, the door swinging open. We rushed into the room as footsteps came up the stairs. I hoped it was anyone but the men staying in this room.

"They're gonna know someone was here now," I whispered.

"By then, we'll hopefully be long gone." Croygen shut

the door behind him. A firebulb was left on, giving the room enough dim light to see.

"Sprig, keep watch," Croygen ordered. "Listen for anyone coming."

Sprig leaped off my arm to a dresser near the door.

The room was a box with twin beds and a nightstand on a tile floor. There was a sink, one dresser, and a bathroom down the hall. The balcony was on the opposite side of the main door. Basic and low budget.

All the items they purchased at the market sat in one corner, but none of them captured my notice. It was the map and papers strung across one bed.

I beelined for the cot, Croygen coming up beside me, our gazes locking on a map of China. Red symbols marked a path from Shanghai, heading inland, toward a small landlocked province called Hubei.

"Hubei?" My forehead wrinkled. "What the hell is there?" I had many adventures and had seen a lot, but I stayed close to the sea. I wasn't big on being places without access to the ocean. "Why would the nectar be there?"

Croygen leaned further over, his finger stopping on an area that was underlined.

"Oh... wow."

"What?"

He huffed, shaking his head.

"What?" I stressed louder.

"Lichuan, Enshi City... is where the Tenglong Caves are."

"Annndd?"

"Tenglong means soaring dragon."

"Still not following."

"Maybe someone should've stayed at school, Kitten."

"I'm going to gut you in your sleep."

"We can get into your kinks later."

My cheeks heated, causing my hands to clench. This man could so easily make me blush, and no one had been able to do that in a long time, if ever. I had heard all the innuendos, the blatant sexual comments, the dirty talk, and never even batted an eye, but he could have me flushing like a schoolgirl in an instant.

"Croygen…"

"It's called that not only because of the size, but since dragons used to inhabit those caves at one time."

"But they've been extinct for a long time now."

"Yes." He licked his lip, pulling my attention for a second. "However, their magic lingered in the places they lived."

"If you could get to the point quicker, Professor Croygen."

His gaze skipped to me, heat flaring in his eyes at the moniker, causing me to look away again, my head spinning.

What the hell was wrong with me?

"What are dragons known for?" He probed me.

"Collecting treasure."

"Fuzanglon." Treasure dragon. "Deep in their caves, they hid and protected treasure, their magic shrouding their horde from the world finding it."

Understanding dumped down on me. "And if their magic still lingers in those caves…"

He grinned when I got it.

"What a perfect place to hide one of the most sought-after objects in the world from others."

"Holy shit," I muttered.

A door banged. Men's and women's voices echoed in the building, and unsteady footsteps could be heard coming down the hall.

"Hoooppee yooou didn't foorgett thhee sppell," an Australian accented voice slurred right outside the door, followed by a woman's drunken giggle. I could sense four of them out there, smelling the whiff of the women's perfume and the smell of cheap beer and tobacco.

They had come back… with friends.

Fuck.

Panic dumped down on me, my wide eyes catching Croygen's, the same alarm on his face.

The rustling of a wrapper drew our attention to the monkey over by the camping gear, not at the door where he was supposed to be on watch, stuffing a granola bar into his mouth.

"Sprig!" Croygen hissed.

"What? I got bored." He munched on his treat, holding it up. "But look what I found. It has honey in it."

"I'm going to kill that mole rat," Croygen sneered as the doorknob wiggled, another man's voice slurring over an incantation to unlock the door, sounding like nothing but gibberish, not noticing the spell was already broken.

The doorknob twisted. There was no way to get to the exit and off the balcony before they entered.

The instinct to shift tingled over my skin as Croygen grabbed me, yanking me down with him under the twin bed. His body rolled into mine, the twin bed high enough but barely wide enough to hide us.

"Sprig?" I mouthed, worried he would be caught.

Croygen shook his head, his muttering barely audible. "He'll be fine."

He was so tiny he could hide anywhere, probably in one of the men's packs, finding another power bar.

The two men and two women stumbled into the room, so drunk they knocked into the furniture.

"Oops…" The tiger shark-shifter tumbled onto the bed above us, laughing, dipping the springs into Croygen's back.

"Ohh, what's this?" A woman with a deep Russian accent spoke, making it almost impossible to understand her. Croygen's head slanted, like something alerted him, his brow furrowing, his head slightly shaking as if he was rebuffing something.

I could hear the crinkle of paper. "What's in Hubei?"

Paper being snatched echoed in the small room, the map fluttering to the floor beside us. "Nothing to worry about, *bokkie.*" *Sweetheart* in Afrikaans. His accent was very light, but his use of the term of endearment revealed he was from South Africa.

"Looks like you are going on an adventure." Her weight added to his as she got on the bed, which pressed Croygen down harder into me, making sure I felt every inch of him. "Without me," she whined. "I've always wanted to go on a quest for treasure. The idea of it makes me *wild.*"

The sound of kissing and a bed squeaking as the other man and woman fell onto the opposite cot made it harder to understand the woman's dialect.

"Reeeaaally? Wild, huh? What does that entail?" Tiger-man murmured with insinuation. "And how do you know I'm hunting for treasure?"

"Because dangerous men like you always are." I could hear a zipper being pulled down; Tiger's breath hitched. "It gets me so hot."

"Oh, gods." The tiger shark moaned. "Put your mouth around my dick, *bokkie.*" A loud grunt came from him.

My body stilled, my eyes widening at what was happening. Croygen's gaze met mine. The small room shrunk down to nothing, the air dissipating. The strain and intense awkwardness gripped my lungs as I tried to pretend this wasn't actually happening. This was only a mission, and I wasn't thinking about how he kissed me the other night, how so many times his touch rained fire through my body. Nope. Nor did I notice his weight on me, the closeness of his mouth, the feel of his cock between my thighs.

"Tell me all about your adventure." The woman's knees hit the floor right by us, settling between his legs. "While my mouth sucks you off."

"*Fok*." Tiger hissed. The sound of her working him shot through my blood, my nipples hardening, heat flushing my whole body. "That's it. Take me deeper."

Oh. Please. No. This couldn't be happening.

"Tell me... I get so wet when you men talk about your exhilarating adventures." She hummed, creating another boisterous response from him.

"I'm-I'm going to Hubei to find my brother..." The shark-shifter's voice was strangled. "*Fok* yes... Oh, gods, you are so good at that." He breathed out. "He-he-he told me about something him and a doctor found before he disappeared." A deep, guttural moan tore from him. "Something so rare, so powerful, and so dangerous, it's worth even more than the four treasures of Tuatha Dé Danann." He struggled through his words, gasping and grunting. "They disappeared after leaving here... I need to find my brother."

The cot next to us with the hammerhead started to squeak, the couple's noises growing louder, adding to the power filling the cramped space. The force sank into my skin, possessing me from the inside out. My body responded to the sexual energy in the room; the need had me arching, my cat too close to the surface.

Croygen sucked in, his dark eyes piercing mine, tension webbing between us. His erection pushed into me, throbbing, the heat causing wetness to seep from me, my nipples hardening, my hips widening.

It was natural—a basic, rudimentary response to hearing or seeing sex. And fae responded to it even more intensely than humans. And for fae like Croygen and me? It was kryptonite.

Sex was our vice, our power. With him, it also felt like a weakness.

"Tell me more... Will there be danger?" The Russian woman encouraged him. "Feel how wet I am."

His hand reached down between her thighs, generating a swear from him.

"Very dangerous," he touted. "I think when they disappeared, they were trying to hide it in the Tenglong caves, where dragons used to live."

"There haven't been dragons for centuries." She was getting harder and harder to understand.

"They say," he huffed, trying to sound tough. "But how do we know they haven't been in hiding? No one who's gone deep into those caves, far beyond the tourist area, has ever returned." I could hear a throaty reverberation followed by a slurping sound. "Oh *fokkkkk*."

"Yes! Yes!" The other woman across the room screamed, the bed bouncing as the other couple started to fuck.

I was in hell. I had to be.

My clothes scratched my skin, the heat inside burning me up while I tried to pretend I wasn't affected by it. No matter what I told myself, it didn't take away the twisted desire, wanting to shed my clothes, regardless of where we were, open my legs, and feel him push inside me. Lose myself in the cloud of bliss.

As if he read my thoughts, Croygen's nose flared, his breath stilted, his throat bobbed. His hand gripped my hip, his fingers sprawling over my stomach. He watched me, waiting for any reaction telling him no. Whatever he saw in my expression encouraged his continued exploration. His fingers trailed the waistline of my pants.

"Harder!" The woman in the other bed demanded, their cot slipping over the tile, while violent moans came from Tiger above us.

Croygen watched me, still gauging my response, slowly pushing up my shirt. He ran his hand over my skin, tracking sparks everywhere he touched. He stopped at my pants zipper, giving me one more chance to stop him. I stared boldly back, almost challenging him. Deftly unfastening my pants, his artful hand moved down, his fingers gliding above my underwear and over my pussy. My mouth parted, Croygen's touch sparking magic through my system, twisting up my mind, taking away any control or logic.

His eyes were on me while his hand traced over me again, feeling how soaked I was. Such overwhelming desire surprised me, knocking out any alarms trying to rise. My ass tipped up, giving him the green light he needed. A noise rattled his throat as he skated under my panties, his fingers sliding through my wetness, parting me. I sucked in sharply; the same electrical shock I felt every time he touched me made my body twitch.

I was always the one in control, never fully satisfied, getting off on my own power, aware of what I did to my lovers. In a blink, Croygen flipped everything on its head. I was at his whim; I could no longer stop or tell the difference between right and wrong.

I rolled into him, yearning for more, my body trembling with need.

"Kat." He growled low in my ear, two fingers rubbing my clit before plunging into me. My body bowed, a groan working up my throat, my eyes rolling back. His hand covered my mouth, stopping the moan from escaping.

My hips opened more, bucking into his hand, his caresses stimulating every inch of my body without having to actually touch it, my clit throbbing to the point of cruelty. He added another finger, his thumb rubbing my clit like he owned my body, knew it better than me, controlling me. And right then, I didn't care.

"You're so fucking wet," he rumbled into my ear like he was in pain. His fingers were magic, pumping in deeper. A cry built up in my chest, my nails needing to claw and scratch. Reaching out, I unbuttoned his trousers, desperate to touch him, to make him feel even half of what I was, putting us back on even terrain. My palm wrapped around his thick cock, biting my bottom lip to keep from audibly purring as I took in his length. There was no doubt why he had so many women on their knees pleading for more. Now I understood the swagger. The man had to counter the weight and size he was carrying.

My hand greedily explored him, my mouth watering, craving his taste.

"Kitty-Kat," he gritted, his eyes going all black, his fingers pumping deeper, muscles on his neck straining like he was trying to hold back his own groans, his dick growing harder under my hand. My thumb rolled through his pre-cum. His hips jerked forward, his fingers curling deeper inside me, hitting the spot that had my animal yowling, his hand buffering the noise.

My lashes fluttered as I fucked his hand, no longer caring if we got caught. I needed him inside me. The sound of my wetness was obscene, though it seemed to be drowned out by the others above. The room was reaching a fever pitch, the gasps and screams more clipped, the beds protesting.

"*Fok. Fok, bokkie*, I'm gonna come!" Tiger shark hissed.

A growl came from Croygen. With the little room we had, he somehow pushed me up to the top of the bed, his body wiggling down, yanking my pants down my hips as his head moved between my legs.

His tongue sliced through me.

Oh. Holy. Fuck.

I became frantic. I turned feral.

My body jackknifed, my hand slapping over my mouth, my cry no longer in my control. His mouth consumed, his tongue licking deep through me. Everything around us blurred out. All I could feel was him, something in my soul tugging, magic spilling from me, my hips bucking wildly.

"Oh, gods! Oh, gods!" someone screamed in the room.

I hoped it wasn't me.

His hands gripped my hips, pinning me down as he feasted on me like he was starving. My nails dug into his shirt, clawing at his back, drawing blood.

A noise came from him, and I swear I could feel it through my soul. His actions intensified, sucking hard on my clit and nipping down.

Everything exploded, light flashing behind my lids, my body locking up as the abundance of sensations ripped the air out of my lungs.

Loud moans and cries charged the room, pitching me into another sphere as I convulsed, pleasure rupturing every cell, no longer in my own body. Though, I could feel *him* hovering around me, finding me in the void.

The intensity was so violent I couldn't even scream, his power singing through my veins. Croygen hungrily lapped me up as I shuddered violently before he lifted himself, his hot cum spurting over my stomach. The claiming action pulsed another orgasm through me.

The entire room moaned together in release, falling back down from the high in stunned silence.

I couldn't move, barely able to breathe, because I had never had an orgasm like that before. Not that I hadn't had amazing sex before, but this felt *so* different. Like I had been blind all my life and now could make out all the vibrant details. Taste, hear, and feel them.

My chest heaved for air, my attention going to Croygen, his eyes burning, his mouth glistening with my release. Every second, reality sank back in. I swallowed back the contented purr in my chest as his gaze dropped to my stomach, taking in where he marked me, then down to where I was still exposed to him.

The vulnerability of his gaze was a sucker punch. I yanked up my pants, using my shirt to wipe off his cum.

What the fuck did we just do?

"Wow." The girl in the bed over gushed out.

"Bloody hell, that was amazing. Worth every fuckin' penny."

"Speaking of." The Russian woman rose from the bed.

"Yeah, yeah, take it all. *Fok*, you deserve it," Tiger slurred, sounding like he was a hair away from passing out.

After the rustling of clothes and movements, the women departed.

"That had to be the best sex of my life. I've never felt magic so intense before. That's like mate-level shit."

His wording caused me to freeze, needing to get out of this room more than anything, needing to run.

"Best blowjob I ever got. I think I spoke in tongues."

The men laughed, the cots squeaking as they both settled in. Alcohol and an orgasm had them blacking out quickly.

The strain between Croygen and me became louder as we waited for them to be fully asleep. The awareness of his proximity twisted me between disgust and desire, only adding to my self-loathing.

Croygen. The pirate I worked so hard to train myself to hunt down and kill just had his tongue between my legs, giving me the best orgasm of my life. His cum drenched the front of my shirt, and my inner kitty was pawing and purring inside, which pissed me off.

I let my dad down.

I let *myself* down. I hated that I was no different from any other girl who succumbed to his charm, begging him to take her again.

When the guy above started to snore, I pushed away from Croygen, slipping out from under the cot. My anger rose as he followed, buttoning his pants, reminding me that it was I who had undone them, who had been desperate to touch and taste his cock.

Humiliation and anger propelled me toward the door,

only doubling down when Sprig leaped onto my shoulder. A witness to what had happened.

We easily walked out; the men were passed out cold. Keeping several feet in front of Croygen, I didn't look back to see if he was there. I didn't need to; I could feel him. His presence pumped in my veins, propelling me to walk even faster, to lose him in the streets.

But somehow, I felt it would be pointless. He would be able to find me.

"Soooo?" Sprig said into my ear, his tone full of implication. "You and the pirate, huh?"

"There's no me and the pirate."

"Huh. That's funny because from where I was, it looked like he was digging for treasure... with his fingers and tongue."

Embarrassment burned my cheeks, wanting to slip away into the tiniest place and hide.

"The buccaneer got the kitty purring?"

Ignoring the remark, I darted faster through the lanes.

"He swab your deck? Loot the booty? Shiver thy timbers?"

"Sprig." My voice grated. "Please stop."

"Don't worry, *Bhean chait.*" Cat-woman. "The whole room really enjoyed your energy."

"Ours?"

"You and the bootlegger," Sprig replied. "That sex power was *all* you guys."

"What are you talking about?"

"The other four barely had any wits about them, so drunk and low-magicked they couldn't have sparked a candle between them all, let alone boinked so hard," he uttered.

I shook my head, wishing we were already back at the ship, this conversation tapping at something I did not want to discuss.

"Well, just saying, they owe you thanks. Pam says thank you too."

257

I squeezed my lids, stopping my mind from going to a very bad place and grateful when we got back to the dock.

Cooper, Scot, Tsai, and Vane waited for us to return, their gazes moving over me when I walked up the plank. Sprig leaped over to Cooper, whining about being starved to death.

Vane strolled closer to me, smirking, his gaze going to the large damp spot on my shirt.

"Took care of business, I see." His eyebrow lifted.

"Yes, we got the information we needed. We know exactly where they're headed."

"Not what I was talking about, *bonita*…" He leaned in. "I have a nose for sex… I can smell it all over you."

"Vane," Croygen barked, a warning to back away.

"Someone's feeling possessive." A full grin broke out over Vane's face, his eyes moving over me with glee as he stepped away.

"You have no idea what you are talking about."

"Sure."

The shame I felt on my own seemed to crush me as I took in everyone's perceptive looks. They all knew.

My revenge became pathetic, my core beliefs nothing but words, my fight all hiss and no claws. I was hollow, and my word was worthless.

I couldn't stand being there one more minute, needing to wash him off me, get away from the scrutiny.

I took off for the stairs, leaving him to call after me.

"Kat?"

I didn't stop, didn't look back, disappearing into the crew's quarters.

How could I hate someone so much, desire his suffering, and at the same time crave him, feel a peace with him I had only felt when I was his pupil? He had always been my home. I was safe, secure, and nothing could harm me when he was around.

Until he became the one who hurt me.

I could never trust him, never concede to what fluttered in my gut like a promise.

Croygen and Kat could have been friends.

The Silver-Tongue Devil and Puss in Boots would always be enemies.

Chapter 21
Croygen

My eyes stayed on where she had disappeared, an uncomfortable pressure resting on my chest. The entire way back, she couldn't seem to get away from me fast enough, though at the same time I felt like she was calling to me, pulling me along the streets without even trying. I knew before she turned where she was going. I knew, by a twitch of her cheek, she was just as aware of me as I was of her.

I couldn't even describe what happened back in the room, what possessed me to do what I did. I was out of control. Touching her, making her come, was something I needed more than air.

People fucking in the same room had me hard, but it wasn't the first time I've been trapped with people having sex. Ryker and Zoey were fucking fiends, and I had lived with them. The last night before our fight against two powerful entities a few years ago, the entire castle was fucking like it was their last rites. I could hear them, feel them, and Lexie was undoubtedly hinting at it, encouraging me to cross the line with her, begging me, but I had kept it in my pants, able to restrain myself.

Where the hell was that restraint about forty minutes ago?

"Captain?" Scot's voice yanked my head away from where she had gone. I turned to him as if I hadn't been staring after her like a lost puppy.

He tried to hide his expression. "Everything okay?"

"Yeah, fine." I peered at the faces around me.

They all knew something had happened. We reeked of sex; the intensity from the room clung to me like a second skin.

That had to be the reason. I just ate out my old first mate's daughter, a girl who had plagued me, bringing me bad luck since the day she left my ship.

Rotty's face came into my head. I imagined his expression at finding out what I did to his baby girl. "Fuck." I rubbed at my head, self-loathing knifing up my chest.

"Captain?" Scot called me again, making me more irritated at myself that I was so inattentive.

"You might need to try again. Some of his brain cells were dumped out on the floor earlier." Sprig munched on something Cooper had given him.

My lashes lowered, and I glared at the sprite. He shrugged. "Am I wrong? You left your nuts and cream all over the place."

"Shut. It." It was more than a warning, my mood plunging quickly.

"I'm sure if you wring out her shirt, you can get them back."

My gaze flashed, going from Sprig to Cooper.

"Sprig, why don't you go downstairs," Cooper suggested, hiding his smirk. "Annabeth was worried about you. Plus, I think she has your honey-covered mango chips."

"Ahhhh!!!!" Sprig leaped off, zooming around the deck. "Honeyhoneyhoneyhoneyhoney!!!" He zipped down the stairs, his voice echoing after him. I wouldn't be surprised if we found him passed out on the stairs, never making it to the room. Narcolepsy usually followed his zoomies.

Taking a deep breath, I walked farther onto my main deck before facing the men. "The shark-shifters are heading to Lichuan, Enshi City."

"Where the hell is that?" Vane asked.

"Inland, about a week or so by horse. It's where the Tenglong Caves are."

"The dragon caves?" Scot ran his knuckles over his beard, his eyebrows wrinkling in curiosity. "Isn't that place still supposed to be teeming with dragon magic?"

"Yep. A great place to hide treasure," I responded.

"You know no one searching for dragon treasure there has ever come out." Scot leaned against a mast. "Old dragon magic is not something to mess with."

"There is no other option." My gaze went to Cooper's, his eyes saying the same. For AB, there was no other choice, plus Katrina couldn't go back on her promise. All we could do was move forward.

"Cooper and I will head out tomorrow... with Katrina." I muttered the last part. Her vow put her right in the game; she couldn't stay back. "The rest will stay here."

Voices instantly refuted, heads shaking.

"No," Scot exclaimed. "I'm not letting you go off someplace like that with no backup."

"Scot, this isn't up for debate. You are my first mate; I need you here, in charge. And if anything happens to me, this is your ship... you are the captain. The flag on this ship will never be lowered." That was the rule of the sea: the pirate might die, but the name and the ship would continue on.

Scot's jaw rolled, but he knew this was how it went. He took on the role of captain if I was off ship.

"Then Zid and I go with you," Vane stated.

"No." I wagged my head. "The more people, the more we draw notice. Cooper and I have fought things you guys could never imagine." Like the creatures Rapava made from

Zoey's DNA, turning things like strighoul into smarter, harder-to-kill monsters. Strighoul were the bottom feeders in the fae world. They were what humans thought of as "vampires," but they were far worse. They didn't just suck blood; they were cannibals, eating fae to contain powers.

Zoey's "kids," as we called them, had escaped and were still out there. They were so good at hiding that even the bounty hunters, Ember and Eli, couldn't find them.

"And Katrina certainly can hold her own. We'll be fine."

"I'm going too." Annabeth's voice came from the stairs, a sleeping monkey in her hoodie pocket.

"No," I refuted. "No way."

"Yes," she stated sternly, her attention flashing to Cooper, daring him to defy her too.

"AB…" He sighed. "It's too dangerous. And you're—"

"If you say human, I will punch you," she volleyed. "And you know Zoey has taught me to fight."

Zoey was an ex-street fighter who used to go by the moniker "Avenging Angel," and, fuck, I had seen her drop people in seconds. She scared the crap out of me and totally turned me on at the same time.

"I'm not weak or fragile."

"Babe, I'm sorry, but compared to us, humans are fragile," Cooper countered.

"Where you go, I go." She spoke directly to him, the link between them palpable. "Would you let me leave you behind?" We all knew he wouldn't. "And just think what it would do to me if you didn't come back."

"I'm a Dark Dweller, baby. I always *come* back."

She rolled her eyes, her hands going to her hips. "I'm going. If we're a team, then we're a team in everything. Don't put me in a cage and suffocate me because *you're* scared. Not. Now." She stressed the last two words, meaning more than most here understood. "I want to live every moment. With you."

Cooper's shoulders lowered, his white flag waving.

"What? No." I stepped up. "You can't! If anything happened to you…" Fear tightened my throat. "I can't let you."

Annabeth stepped up to me, her blue eyes seeing right through me, seeing the terror Lexie went through all over again.

"You would have never kept her from that battle. No matter what you did. No one could have." Her hand squeezed mine. "If Lexie taught me anything, it was to go after what I want, not cower away, because in life, fae or human never know how long they have left in this world."

Tears burned my lids, my teeth clenching.

Shit, I think I just surrendered too.

Sipping my whiskey, I stared at the moon in the sky. I needed to get some sleep, but my mind wouldn't let me.

It wasn't about the treacherous journey we were undertaking across this perilous land, the fact Annabeth was coming, or what was ahead…

No, all I could think about was her.

Downstairs, on the other side of the ship, I swear I could hear her heart beating, feel her calling to me, the ache in my cock becoming more distinct.

No matter how much I drank, I could still taste her on my tongue, feel her coming, her body convulsing, orgasming so hard I almost drowned in it.

A low growl hummed in my throat, and I slammed down my empty glass, my feet pacing the floor. The turmoil in my mind kinked up like eroded gears, stuck, repeating the same scene over and over.

She made me lose control. Sex had always been a game

for me, one I was excellent at. I could handle my urge and draw out the woman's pleasure until she went blind and passed out from the intensity. Many times, when seducing someone, I walked away without coming. I made it all about them. They felt special, prized. Wanted.

With Katrina, I had no such constraint. Something had possessed me—the need to soil her, claim her. My cock stiffened again when I saw my seed on her, wanting nothing more than to drag my fingers through it and push it into her pussy.

"RRRRRRRRRRRR." A noise gurgled in my throat, my hand hitting my bed frame in aggravation.

In all the situations I put myself in during my long life, the terrifying, deadly, and dangerous things I had done, I had always stayed calm. I was the guy that nothing seemed to faze. Threatened, tortured, and almost killed a thousand times? Whatever.

Alone under a bed with a petite cat-shifter? Fucked.

I paced back to my table, leaning over it, trying to regain my sanity.

Think of Rotty. What would he think of your actions?

My attention went to his dagger on my belt. Slowly I pulled it out, laying it on the desk in front of me. I stared at the blade I carried with me. As punishment. As remembrance. As a tribute to the man who loved his daughter more than anything.

The memory of that day replayed freely in my head. Over and over, torturing me. The smells, sights, sounds, and tastes coming back to me like it was yesterday…

The stench of black powder smothered the air, burning my nose and coating my tongue. Clanks of swords, blasts of rifles, and yells of men fighting clashed over the deck.

The glorious Silver Devil flag whipped in the wind above us, still declaring that this was my ship, my crew, and my home. But for the first time in my life, genuine fear iced my heart. My guard had been down, thinking we had an understanding. A truce.

He had three times the men I had and trained them to be barbarians like him. Cruelty was the point, and he loved inflicting pain and terror.

"Lowe?" I bellowed at the man coming aboard who was trying to take my ship.

Ned snapped his head to me. The apathetic deadness in his eyes told me there was nothing left in him except for greed, fame, and malice. He knew what ship he was raiding and didn't care.

Ned Lowe was known across the sea for being merciless, a pirate who got off on brutality and torture. Except we had known each other for a long time, been crew together in our youth, drank in pubs, fought pirate hunters, and raided merchant ships. I saved his skin more times than I could count.

Not exactly friends, but certainly not enemies. A comrade who would help me in an attack, not be the assailant.

I was wrong.

"Is this who you are now?" I motioned around, our men at war, though mine were already falling.

"Nothing personal, Croygen." He sneered. His scarred, bearded face, worn clothes, sharp broadsword, and filthy, knotted hair made a frightening figure. He wanted to look savage, someone you'd fear for his cold ruthlessness.

"Not personal?" I regripped my sword, moving closer to him. "It feels very personal to me. After everything, you come for me?"

"I'm here only for what is mine."

"Yours? I have nothing here for you." Nor much bounty. I hadn't had much luck lately with pilfering merchant ships.

Bangs and screams circled around me. Several of my crew were already dead, their blood staining the wood red.

"Get off my ship, Lowe."

"But your ship was part of the deal."

"What deal?"

Lowe's grin was haughty, like there was something I was missing.

"Oh, Croygen. At one time, I used to respect you. Looked up to you. Now all I see is a washed-up, gullible man whose own crew doesn't even respect him." He wagged his head. "A man about to lose everything."

A boom blasted in my ears. A cannonball cropped the quarterdeck, throwing me back, my head smacking hard against the deck before everything went black.

Shaking my head, I shoved the memory back, the anger still curdled in the back of my throat. That day altered my life forever. Ned's words stuck like a sword because he was right—I had lost everything.

Collapsing in my chair, I threw my feet on the table, exhausted but too riled to sleep. The journey ahead was going to be fraught with danger, harsh conditions, and arbitrary fae doors we could disappear into.

In a land of lawlessness, one would find out exactly the kind of person you were when everything was about life and death.

The horse's hooves clipped along the road, my ass aching with every bounce. My mood had soured somewhere in the fifth or sixth hour of our fifteen-hour ride, and we'd barely made a dent in the land we needed to cover. The sun was stifling, but eased as it lowered over the horizon. Days like this made me realize how much I missed modern conveniences—cars, trains, motorcycles, planes.

What used to take hours now took a week or two, going back to the days Genghis Khan used to ride these same trails.

My horse kept a strong pace, leading, while Katrina or Cooper took turns watching our backs. Even in the daylight, we weren't safe anymore. When there was no right or wrong, no police to run to, why wait for darkness? The only thing that made traveling in the day safer was the raiders were probably staying indoors and out of the heat.

When the sun disappeared, the thieves would start to hunt.

"I think she looks like a Sally? No, maybe a Gertrude?" An annoying voice grated in my ear, his fur brushing my hot, sticky skin.

"Not naming the horse," I grumbled. We had taken the burden of caring for these horses off some rich asshole in the suburbs, where the elite had moved to, trading their high-rises for farms. The elite outright stole homes with land, farming, and animals, while the original farmer was usually forced to work his own land, living in a hut away from the main house while the new owners took the profits.

"That's rude. No one wants to be called *Whatcha macallit*. Oooohhh, do you remember those? Sweet caramel, peanut crisps, and chocolate goodness. They would have been better if they dipped them in extra honey too, but still, they were good. Why they never gave them a name, I don't understand.

"That was their name."

"What was?"

"*Whatchamacallit*." I knew where this was going.

"See? You don't even know their name," he exclaimed. "So do you have one?"

"Why would I have one?"

"Why *wouldn't* you?" he asked. "Did you hear me? They have *caramel* in it. We should find some."

"Sure, next convenience store we pass."

"Really?"

"Very next one." I grinned smugly. There wasn't any kind of store like that out here, probably not even on the main roads. Not like there would be American candy in them anyway, since all that stuff disappeared fast after the war. A few lodgings popped up between towns for weary travelers, the only money to make once outside the city. Yet so far, since we left the suburbs, I hadn't seen anything open. Just remnants of life that once existed, nature already whispering at the edges, taking back the land.

"Oh, I know. I'll call him Caramel, then." He pointed at my horse. "That one, Chocolate." He pointed back to Cooper's dark horse, then went to AB's horse. "That one, Churro. Oh, I miss those. And that one..." He pointed to Katrina's. "Tootsie Pop." He leaned in, nudging me with his elbow. "Get it?" He snickered. "How many *licks* does it take to get to the center?"

I stared straight ahead, wondering how long it would take before I snapped. Sprig's endless stream of chatter only stopped when he was sleeping.

"I thought I banned you from my shoulder." I took a deep breath.

"That was your right shoulder. I'm on your left," Sprig replied, his backpack holding Pam pressing against my neck. There was no way we could have left without him. Not only did Annabeth feel the need to keep him with her, but he also had the ability to open magic locks and sneak into small places we couldn't. When Zoey and I were in the basement labs together, I couldn't deny Sprig had gotten us out of some tense situations.

He had spent the first three hours reminding me of that, singing "magic hands" and wiggling his fingers in front of my face.

Why he wasn't gagged and bound by now was a mystery to me.

"Croygen?" Kat's horse got even with mine, my body

269

stiffening at her nearness. I had done well all day with keeping away from her. Only talking when I had to and trying not to look at her. Maybe if I was a mature adult, I would talk to her about what happened, but I was fine with ignoring it.

"We should find lodging soon." She glanced over her shoulder, her voice lowering. "Annabeth isn't looking too good. Think she needs a break till morning."

Glancing quickly back, I saw what Kat meant. AB kept her head up, but fatigue made her body limp, heat burning her pale cheeks bright red, yet she was still pale. She looked beyond exhausted, barely holding herself up.

Any human would have reached their limit by now, and still, she kept her mouth shut, pushing on with us.

I had stopped many times during the day when we didn't need to, making sure she was hydrated and okay, paranoid about her illness. She'd always pin on a smile and tell me she was fine.

AB was stronger than all of us combined.

"Yeah." I nodded. "The town of Nanxun is not far."

I clicked my tongue, encouraging my horse to go faster, needing to get away from Kat.

I now knew how badly it hurt to be on a horse with an erection.

Her release was still on my tongue, my fingers tingling with the memory of being inside her. Only a thread of reasoning had kept me from kissing her again last night. I wouldn't have been able to stop from completely falling over the edge, getting us caught.

The four of us rode into the old town, firebulbs flickering off the canals of this once prosperous village. Nanxun sat on various canals, like Venice, south of the Yangtze River, and was established for the silk trade. It was a stunning village, but it was obvious the glory days were far behind them. It was like stepping back in time over 750 years, with its ancient buildings, arched stone bridges, temples, and gardens.

Since the barrier fell, this place had become a haven for fae and humans. A stop before heading out into the more treacherous, lawless lands of China. It reminded me of an old frontier town men frequented for supplies before heading into the mountains to mine for gold.

I swung my leg off my horse, my boots hitting the ground as I took in the old inn, which hadn't changed. Red Chinese lanterns hung along the patio, reflecting off the water, and voices from the tavern/restaurant on the ground floor suggested it was packed. I had come to this place a lot in the past. Silk was an excellent trading commodity.

In the past, the inn only had a few places to sleep, and I doubted it had gotten better.

"Let me see if they have room for us. Coop, take the horses to the stalls in back." I handed Sprig back to AB, sauntering inside. The small dining/bar area was packed. The smells of meat, steamed buns, and beer had my stomach growling.

The human family who ran the inn had gone through so many generations in my lifetime, I forgot who was in charge now. They were people who always knew about fae and magic, seeing so many of us not age a day while they grew from children to a hundred.

Two women looking like mother and daughter took orders while father and another daughter served the plates and drinks. The small kitchen staff tried to keep up.

The older man spotted me first, his lids narrowing in recognition.

Shit. Did I do anything last time? I couldn't remember if I got into a fight or broke a bed or something.

"Croygen." He broke my name apart in English. "You have returned."

"I have." I glanced around, but not one table was free.

"You do not remember me. I was a boy when you came last."

A good reason I didn't recognize him.

"My father, Baihu, ran it. I'm Fang."

Baihu. Now I remembered. And I recalled the four-year-old little boy he had. That boy was now in his sixties, at least.

"Yes." I bowed my head in respect. "Your father was always kind."

He bowed back.

"Have room for four and a meal?"

"No rooms left." He shook his head. "No rooms left in this town. Very busy."

It was *much* busier here than I had ever seen it, even in its prime, which seemed odd to me.

"Oh. Okay." I bowed my head, about to turn away. Maybe we could find a horse stall to hunker down for the night.

"Except." His words stopped me. "My room and girls' room." He nodded to his kids running around the place, only in their early preteens. "You pay price. You can have."

"What's the price?" I wasn't even going to pretend to talk him out of giving up his own rooms. He wouldn't offer if he didn't mean it. Most people in these parts didn't do "nice" for politeness's sake, putting themselves out for strangers. This was a trade.

"Six hundred yen."

"Six hundred yen?" I coughed. My eyes widened at the price tag. Equivalent to $80 in the West. At one time, that might have seemed like nothing, but things had changed. Money was a lot harder to come by. "That's extortion!"

"That is the price." He shrugged.

"How about three hundred yen?"

"Good luck finding someplace else." He twisted to leave, my gut twinging at the thought of AB not getting a good night's sleep. I recalled how fatigued she looked, her illness hanging over me like a hatchet.

"Fine." I huffed, pulling out the money pouch hidden under my shirt, grumbling as I forked over the bills, cutting into our funds.

"Always good doing business, Croygen."

"And they say I'm the thief," I mumbled.

"Come." He headed for a table of four, shooing them out before they could even finish.

"There. Sit."

Retrieving the group, I slipped into the tight space, the tables practically on top of each other.

"Oh, my gods, I am starving." Sprig's voice hissed from Annabeth's bag, his head popping out just enough to see him. "Do they have honey chicken? Or maybe honey fried rice? Honey-duck skewers? Honey drizzled pork?"

"Shut up," I hissed. "Or I'll be frying you up in honey and skewering a stick up *your* ass."

"But you're saying I would die in a bubbling bath of honey?"

"That's not really a threat to him." Cooper snorted, pushing Sprig's head down into the bag.

The wife plonked down baijiu, and I grabbed it instantly, pouring the clear liquid into the cups and pounding mine down. It wasn't long before the dishes arrived. This wasn't a place customers ordered from a menu; we ate what they cooked. But honestly, that made it even better. The homemade food was scarfed down between us—okay, everyone but Annabeth. She ate very little, her body only sinking more into her chair.

"*Bebinn!*" Sprig whined, not getting food delivered fast enough to him.

"Here." My arms reached out, collecting the bag from AB. Putting it on my lap, I shoved a Chinese crepe into the hungry monster's mouth.

Through my lashes, I saw Cooper and AB grin, the same knowing smile on their lips.

"Fuck you both." Shit, I had become Ryker. I remembered in South America, years and years ago, watching Zoey and Ryker trade him off like a couple with a baby. I howled with laughter at how domesticated the barbaric Viking had become.

Now look at me.

From my years living with them, I knew what feeding time was like with this tiny tyrant. It was like prepping for war because he nipped at our fingers if we didn't feed him fast enough.

My memories strolled back to the times Zoey or Lexie would hand him over to me with a bottle of honey, like it was my turn to feed the baby before his nap.

I thought I had run from that life. Left it all behind. Funny how fast it can step back in.

I peered down at Sprig as his lids began to lower, his chewing slowing. The food coma was taking him down.

"Here, let me clean him." AB noticed the same thing I did, but all I saw was exhaustion in her own expression.

"I got it." I dampened my napkin, wiping his mouth and hands as he completely nodded off. Tucking him deeper into the bag, I ignored the eyes on me, witnessing my vulnerability as I cared for the lab rat.

"Is it okay if I go to bed? I seem to be very tired." Annabeth looked only moments from passing out like Sprig.

"Yeah, of course." I started to rise.

"No. You guys stay." She motioned us to sit. "Enjoy the rest of the meal."

"I'll go with you." Cooper leaped up, his hands grasping her to keep her steady. "Just point us where we're supposed to go." He looked at me.

Catching the owner's eye, I nodded at Cooper and Annabeth. Fang motioned his wife over. "She'll show you."

"I'll get her settled and come back," Cooper told me, reaching over to take the carrier with Sprig back.

The owner's wife waved them to follow, disappearing upstairs.

Leaving me alone with Katrina.

I downed another cup of baijiu, tempted to go up with them just to escape the awkwardness.

"Sit." Fang ordered two men to take the seats of our absent friends, the place so busy they put customers where they could.

A tall, lean man with brown eyes, black hair, and a beard nodded, pulling out the chair Cooper had vacated. A shorter man with blond hair stood beside him, looking around cautiously.

"Drink?" Fang demanded.

"Just baijiu," Beard guy said. His facial structure looked Russian, but his accent was Hungarian with what sounded like a touch of Czech.

Fang nodded, disappearing into the busy restaurant.

"Kaptain?" the blond guy called his friend, his Czech accent very thick.

"Yes, go check on the others and water the horses. See if you can find us some kind of accommodation." He ordered his companion, who was now looking more like a subordinate.

"Yes, Kaptain." Blond man dipped his head, marching out on the order.

I lifted an eyebrow, and the man called "Kaptain" shifted around in his seat, his brown eyes meeting mine. He was human, but had the confidence of a fae, like was used to being in charge.

Fang dropped off a huge bottle for the whole table, nodding at us to share.

Guess my 600 yen came with a few perks.

"Suppose there is no pretending why we're all here."

Kaptain poured us all a portion and lifted his cup. *"Egészségére!"* Cheers in Hungarian.

Kat and I lifted our glasses.

"May the best man or *woman* win." He winked at Kat, sipping back his alcohol, his gaze coming back to us.

"Win?" Kat asked.

"I'm figuring you two were after what everyone else here is going after." Kaptain motioned around before turning back to us, studying us. "Maybe we can help each other out."

"And what would we be helping each other with?" A knot formed in the back of my throat.

The man sat back, his lids narrowing like he was trying to figure out whether I was messing with him.

"Probably the biggest find this world will ever know."

Kat's hand squeezed my knee under the table, both of us having the same thought.

Did they know about the nectar?

There was no way I was playing my cards and saying it out loud until he did.

"And what is this find?"

"Come on, you guys can't be that clueless." The man laughed like we were idiots, digging in his pack and tossing a newspaper on the table.

"This." His finger stabbed into the print. "Is why everyone in this room is here. Heading inland."

Acid burned down my esophagus as I picked up the paper, Kat leaning in to read.

Dr. Novikov Goes Missing After He Is Said to Have Found the Nectar of The Gods.

Dr. Novikov, a well-known scientist and partner of Dr. Rapava, has disappeared in China after claims of finding the fae nectar, which is said to give humans fae qualities. This nectar is reported to make humans stronger and faster and end disease, sickness, and aging. For a long time, the idea of fae food was considered a myth, which died when the barrier between the Otherworld and Earth fell. But before his disappearance, Dr. Novikov claimed he had found the last known object to give humans eternal life, along with strength and power similar to a fae's.

The last reports of him were in Shanghai, rumored to be heading east. Some have claimed to have spotted him near Wuhan and Enshi City...

The article went on, but I read all I needed to. 6

"When was this printed?"

"Printed first in Georgia a week ago, then in Czech and Hungary a few days later. It won't be long until word spreads throughout the world."

Holy. Fuck.

The nectar was no longer a secret. This reporter may have published the story of his life, but he didn't realize what it did. My gaze went up, looking at the packed room differently, noticing most were European-looking, not from around here. Everyone was now an enemy, a potential competitor, getting between me and saving my family.

This would be worse than any gold rush because gold could be found in many places, making many rich.

Only one could win this prize.

A cold-blooded game of kill or be killed, where the last person standing took all.

Chapter 22
Katrina

Croygen's boots shuffled over the wood floor of the bedroom. The insistent thumping was clawing down my spine.

"Stop. Please." I grabbed his arm, holding him in place. The room was already small. Cooper and Annabeth had fallen asleep in the parents' bedroom, leaving us in the girl's tiny twin beds. "You're making me crazy."

"That's what is making you crazy?" he exclaimed, his energy so frazzled I could feel it nipping at my own, rubbing against my soul like an agitated cat. "Not that the entire eastern bloc probably knows about this nectar and is out hunting for it?"

"Not the *entire* bloc. Yet."

Croygen's dark eyes narrowed on me.

"Yeah, I know it's bad." Everyone in the restaurant wasn't from here, suggesting the newspaper had circulated fast and far. This disreputable newspaper was known for printing fake stories. Even so, there would be enough who believed it.

"Do you *get* how bad this is?" He faced me, his voice

rising. "This situation? How much more dangerous and dire this is?"

"Yes!" I barked back. "Of all people, I *do* understand! My crew, my ship, everything I have in this life is riding on whether I get this nectar or not."

"Fuck your ship," he roared. "You can get a new one."

I jolted back. To pirates, our ships were part of the crew. We might pilfer and steal them, but we were faithful to the one we christened.

"Get a new one? That is my home. All I worked for!"

"And it's just a fucking ship," he yelled back. "You can live without it... Annabeth will die without this nectar. And soon."

"What?" I stepped back.

He blew out a heavy breath, his hand riding over his hair. He didn't speak for a long time, his throat bobbing.

"She's sick."

I went still, the food in my stomach turning.

"Cancer." He stared at the floor. "Incurable."

"Oh, gods." My hand went to my mouth. I realized the sour odor I smelled wasn't Sprig farting; it was the disease consuming her body.

"She doesn't want anyone to know. Cooper told me in confidence."

The probable reason Croygen was extra tense lately, hovering over her.

"Her life was limited anyway because she's human. But now?" He swung his arm, starting to circle again. "I can't lose her."

"I know."

"No, you don't. I *can't*..." he stressed. "I already let Lexie down. I *will not* let Annabeth die." His gaze drilled into me. "Whatever it takes. I will get the nectar for her. She is my family, and I will kill anyone who gets in my way. Do you understand?"

His words were a pledge. As good as a promise.

"Yes, I understand! I have the same oath. For Gage, Zuri, Hurricane, Typhoon, and Moses. Getting the nectar saves their lives and returns them to me!"

"They are already dead," he seethed back. "It's too late for them."

"What?"

Take what you can. Give nothing back.

Chapter 23
Katrina

Misty rain tapped at my leather coat, the clop of horse hooves drumming against the creak of my saddle while nature's noises sang a chorus in the background. The same song I had been hearing for over a week now. My body ached, exhaustion and boredom fatiguing my mind. At the same time, we could never let our guard down, keeping us all anxious and agitated.

Which didn't help the already tense situation.

Every day was filled with new scenery and beauty. I didn't realize how much greenery and water the middle of China had. Canals, lakes, rivers, and streams were surrounded by crags, mountains, and deep fissures everywhere. Yet, I grew restless just the same. I longed to feel the salty sea on my face, the freedom and vastness of the ocean. The creak of wood, not a saddle.

The dreary, humid day was darkening the trail quicker than usual, the hidden sun lowering behind the horizon, turning the late afternoon to night.

I glanced behind me, a shiver of alarm wiggling up the back of my neck, scratching my skin. For days now, it seemed we were being followed. Watched. But when I tuned in, listening for any sound, waiting for something to show itself or attack, nothing but silence responded.

"I'm soooo bored," a voice bellowed, yanking my head back to the tiny monkey dramatically lying between my horse's ears. "It's dinnertime, right?" Sprig whined. "My stomach is eating itself."

My horse neighed, flicking his head.

"Right? Tootsie agrees!" Sprig patted her head.

"You had a granola bar five minutes ago." I rolled back my shoulders as they cracked and popped.

"Exactly! Five zillion trillion minutes ago! Do you know how long that is in sprite time?"

"Five minutes?" Cooper snorted in front of me. He and I switched off watching the back, though, since Nanxun, I had volunteered to stay in the last spot. Croygen and I were trying to give each other a wide berth, staying on opposite sides if we could.

Though with four of us, two being a couple, it didn't always work well.

My eyes lifted to where he was, his strong, muscular back and tight ass drawing my attention far more than the views ever did. Even when I was young, he had this pull, an energy I couldn't seem to resist. And I had grown no tolerance against it as an adult either.

During the long, boring hours, my mind drifted off a lot, going to dark, erotic places. Like the fantasy of him not walking away from me the night in Nanxun. Imagining his hand choking me while he drove into me, rattling the hinges on the door, howling through the small inn.

"Hello?" A small hand waved in front of my face, Sprig's face about an inch from mine. "Anyone in there? Think you were purring there, *bhean chait.*" *Cat-woman.*

"No, I wasn't!" I quickly countered, my cheeks heating, wondering if I really had been. It would be absolutely mortifying if I had. Cat-shifters used our throat vibrations for many things—healing, seducing, communicating, and when we were content. The purest was when it came unconsciously, letting down our guard, our cat taking over, our purr out of our control.

In all my life, a man has never made me purr after sex. I never was with anyone I could completely let down my guard. It was always just sex, or sex and a thieving opportunity.

"You sure?" Sprig nudged me with his elbow, his cape over his backpack, keeping Pam dry. "Any swabbing of the deck below?"

"Sprig." I clenched my teeth, more images coming back to me. The night hiding in the hotel room, under the tiny twin bed. My core clenched at the memory of him licking through me, how the Silver-Tongue Devil had me orgasming so hard I went blind. Every time I shut my eyes at night, my thoughts went right back there, craving him so badly I had stopped sleeping the last couple of nights, staying on watch because I was afraid of what I might do. How natural it seemed to want to crawl into his sleeping bag just to feel his warmth surround me.

How could I crave and hate a man so much at the same time? This man, once again, was destroying my life, taking away all my hard work and carefully made plans. I had sacrificed and turned away from so much on my mission for revenge. To be the pirate who killed the legend himself. To feel fulfilled in my retaliation. Have him understand his crimes, feel his remorse, and know he was getting his just desserts.

Except none of that happened. Not only was I working with my father's killer, but I had kissed him, and his devil of a tongue had made me come. Hard.

I was a cliché, another one to fall under his spell.

And now we were partners in the quest for this nectar.

Along with the rest of the world.

"Croygen?" Cooper called out to the pirate, flicking his

head at Annabeth. It wasn't cold, the humidity mixing sweat and rain together, but AB shivered as the sun lowered, her back curling more and more over her horse. Exhaustion riddled her thin body. Though the girl tried to pretend otherwise, it became increasingly obvious how sick she was.

Cancer.

The word triggered an ache in my chest. I hadn't known her long, but I already cared for her. The internal battle to help my own family or to help her was already waging war inside. The nectar could save her life and turn her fae, but then I would be forgoing my own crew, leaving them to die in Emperor Batara's hands, if they hadn't already. Going against the vow to get him this substance would be suicide for me as well.

Croygen's dark, sensual eyes went to AB, taking her in before he dipped his head. "We'll stop here for the night."

"I'm fine." Annabeth waved him on, her arm barely lifting. "Keep going."

"I need to stop," I spoke, having this urge to take the burden off AB. "I'm tired. And hungry."

"Did someone say food?" Sprig chirped. "Yes, I vote yes on food! Maybe honey BBQ chicken wings? Sausage-stuffed honey buns, or fried chicken biscuits with honey drizzle?"

"How about canned beans and rice." Croygen slid off the horse Sprig had named Caramel, leading us off the path under some trees.

"Ugggg… This is like being back in the labs!" Sprig exclaimed. "The cruelty and torture! At least there, *Bhean's* tits came filled with honey."

"You are free to join your kind at any time." Croygen motioned to the dense forest around us, the trees filled with wildlife. We had seen a few troops of gibbons, macaques, and leaf monkeys on the way.

"How. Dare. You!" Sprig stood on his hind legs on top of Tootsie's head. "I am a sprite, not a monkey."

"Looks like a monkey, talks like a baboon…" Croygen shrugged.

Getting off my horse, I stretched my muscles before taking the saddle off Tootsie and giving her a good rubdown. She scrubbed her head into me affectionately. I hadn't grown up with horses, never having a reason to encounter them, but I was getting very attached to this one. We were a team. Her ears were in tune like mine, always twitching and listening, as if while I was guarding everyone else, she was looking out for me.

Churro, AB's horse, seemed to know she was more delicate than us. He was so gentle and slow with her, trying to keep his steps as even as he could for her over rough terrain, staying steady when he sensed her drifting off, nuzzling her leg when he needed her to wake up. I had a deep respect for these majestic creatures.

And they were always the first thing we took care of when we stopped, getting them food and water before we set up camp.

The camping and food supplies we got back in Nanxun were starting to dwindle, the beans and rice becoming a staple. Croygen wanted to stay off the main paths. Too many people were out here now, and that brought more raiders to the roads, picking off what they could from travelers.

Night came fast under the thick layer of clouds and the canopy of trees, blocking out light and making us rush to set up camp. Croygen built a fire as AB cooked, while Cooper did a fast sweep of the area, making sure the only things out here with us were other animals. I had yet to see him shift, but I could feel the magic every time he did, and even though I knew him, I was still terrified of what he was.

My cat form wouldn't even be a snack to something like him.

"I'm gonna go get some water." I nodded toward the

creek not far from us. Retrieving a bottle, I headed down to the creek, the night crackling with sounds from the campfire and the buzz of animals just waking up to hunt or heading home so they wouldn't become the prey. Shadows circled around me, the light from our camp barely visible through the trees, making me feel completely isolated from my group.

There was something about the forests in China. I couldn't explain it. The fog clutching the trees was like the ghosts of long ago, haunting the territory.

Or hunting.

Squatting down, I splashed water on my face, the icy chill zinging down my nerves. My skin itched with the sensation of eyes being on me. My gaze scrolled over the woods, glad I could see better than most in the dense darkness, but no figure moved, nothing to note other than small rodents scurrying around, which matched the awareness crawling over me.

My intuition was usually spot on, something I not only learned from my captain, but from living on the streets. Being a petite girl had put a target on my back, and my skills became as sharp as my claws.

Muscles along my back twitched, the need to shift scraping my skin. Looking back over my shoulder, I saw the glow of the fire and heard the distant sound of Annabeth talking, oblivious to anything else out here, feeling safe in her bubble.

Standing up, I stepped away from the creek before my body transformed, my clothes falling around me onto the rocks. Sleek and black, I blended in with the darkness like it was my own, a creature designed for the shadows, a hunter of the night.

My ears and nose twitched, taking in the abundance of smells, trying to pick a single thread out of them. Slinking through the brush, my tiny frame trotted through the forest, my nose picking up on a particular odor.

Male. Fae.

Magic had a smell, a weight that lined the nose. Some had a vanilla, sweet scent, and some had an earthy smell. It varied, but I could always tell when they were human or fae.

Men's voices ticked at my ears before I spotted them. A mile or so back from where we stopped, three men sat around their own campfire. I could see a dozen more at a firepit not too far away, as if these men were generals and captains while the others were lowly soldiers.

"He said to keep close," a big brute of a man with light-brown hair and a chiseled jaw spoke, his language taking me a moment to understand and translate in my head.

Hungarian.

"Follow them."

"Why them?" another asked, his Hungarian accent even thicker. From here, he looked to have rich, dark skin and short, cropped hair. "We don't even know why we're here."

"Not for you to question, Connor," the first one spoke, sounding like he was their leader. "We follow orders."

"Can you not be a tight-ass for a moment?" The man he called Connor scoffed. "I'm just asking."

"That's like asking Sloane not to breathe," the third guy laughed. I could see he was attractive, with blond hair and high cheekbones.

"I do my duty, Vale. My *job* without bitching," the leader, Sloane, countered, his shoulders pulled back. "Unlike you."

"We have no idea where he came from, who he even is." Vale stood up, grabbing food off the grill they set up.

"Doesn't matter. He's our ruler now." Sloane let out a breath, setting down his mug. "I believe he will be better for our country. For our people."

"Good thing since you helped him kill the other guy." Vale laughed to himself.

"Sometimes sacrifice is how the world can move forward."

287

"Including the people we're following?" Connor downed the rest of his drink, the hair over my body prickling, telling me we were those people.

"If he orders us, then yes."

Fingers pinched at the back of my neck, lifting me off the ground. Fear tore through my cat body, strangling a cry in my throat as my body shifted back to human in terror. A hand slammed over my mouth, a huge body pressing me back into a tree.

Croygen's dark eyes penetrated mine, his finger at his lips, his frame hard against mine. My heart slammed against my ribs, fright still making me want to claw and hiss.

"Don't make a sound, Kitty-Kat," he muttered against my ear, his hand clutching my hip, holding me firmly against the bark, making me very aware of his clothed frame against my naked one. Terror turned quickly into something else, pebbling my nipples against his shirt. My body reacted without my say, salivating at the memory of his touch, the power he had over me. It was nothing I had ever experienced before, and as much as I hated myself for it, I wanted it again.

"You will do exactly what I say." His lips brushed over the sensitive spot behind my ear. "Am I right, Kitten?" His teeth grazed down my neck, compelling me to swallow back my refusal, my head nodding. He dropped his hand from my mouth, gripping both my hips. His thumbs slid down low, hinting at how close he was to touching me again. "Follow me. We're not going back to camp."

"But-but my clothes," I stuttered, forcing my body not to curve into him.

"I have them." He lifted his head, his eyes capturing mine, as we both watched each other like we were waiting for the other to act, to give an invitation. There was barely a thread of logic left in my head, my willpower gone. The need for him overtook everything. I wouldn't care who heard. Who saw us.

Croygen's eyes trailed down my naked body, his jaw ticking, desire filling the space between us.

A loud pop from the fire jolted his body, his lids closing for a moment.

When he opened them back up, a different man looked back. He flicked his head, stepping back, moving quietly and quickly through the woods, not stopping until we were a good distance from the men. My clothes sat in a heap on a log, and I could smell our horses, Cooper and Annabeth close by.

"Here." He leaned over to a pile of fabric, chucking my clothes at me.

"How did you even find me?" I grabbed for them, anger replacing my fear. "How did you know where I went?"

"You weren't hard to find, Kitty-Kat."

My lids tapered. "Yes, I was. There was no way you could've found me so easily."

"I don't know." He ran a hand through his hair, tension riding his shoulders. "I just did."

"Just did?" I yanked on my underwear. "I was in cat form, the size of a shoe. In the middle of the dark forest, hiding under brush. There is no way you should have found me!"

"That's not important right now." He headed away from me.

"Not important?" I pulled on my top. "What? You're running from those three guys? Please, we could take them without even trying."

Croygen glanced back. "They aren't the only ones following us right now."

"What?" Tugging on my boots, I followed Croygen through some thick brush to discover Cooper and AB waiting on horseback for us, all our gear packed up, Tootsie saddled and ready to go.

"Cooper found another group trailing us." Croygen nodded at Cooper, climbing on his horse. "That man we met at the pub a week ago, the one called Kaptain? He and his group are camped only a half mile from us."

"He's human. He poses no real threat."

"Not about them attacking us." He pulled the reins, trotting Caramel out. "It's about who gets to the nectar first. And I don't want parasites attaching to us." He heeled the horse, taking off down a trail, Cooper following.

AB handed me the lead to Tootsie.

"He's a stubborn man." She shook her head with a smile.

"Is that what you call it?" I grumbled, climbing up on Tootsie.

"He does it because he loves too much."

"Too much?"

"Croygen is all-or-nothing. But once he lets you in, he will die for you." Annabeth adjusted the bag on her shoulder, the outline telling me Sprig was probably sleeping inside. "And when he loses one of those he loves? He never forgives himself for being the one who lived." She tapped at Churro, galloping after the guys.

Pain settled in my chest. The version of Croygen Annabeth spoke of was the one I had once known as a child. Or thought I had. But it had been several hundred years since my view of him changed. I remembered the cruel, narcissistic pirate who had destroyed my family and taken everything from me.

Yet, some moments I fell right back into believing in this man again. Trusting the pirate who used to hold me so tight in his arms as waves splashed down on the deck, my giggles singing over the ocean, my arms open and wide, wanting life to be like that forever.

Feeling so safe and free at the same time.

But even if a world full of magic and fae, there was no such thing as fairy tales.

Chapter 24
Croygen

It was well past 1 a.m. by the time we rode into Enshi City, though people still strolled around the city, the pubs exploiting all the travelers. It was the last town before we went up into the mountains. A mix of modern and ancient, parts of the city dated back to around 750 BC, showcasing traditional style temples, dramatic curved roofs, and wooden tiered structures of the Tujia culture.

The town was set between dramatic mountainscapes, nestled by the Qing River, not too far from the deep fissures, waterfalls, skyscraping pillars, and the breathtaking Enshi Grand Canyon. The Tenglong Caves were only half a day's ride away.

If it were me, I might have pushed on, but the guilt of even driving AB this much twisted my gut. Cooper had put her on his horse, holding her up when she could no longer stay awake, tying Churro's halter to Chocolate.

Fuck, I'm actually referring to the damn horses by name now.

I scrubbed my head, fatigue giving me a slight headache. It had been a long day, but my thoughts wouldn't shut down, cranking my brain into knots.

The groups following us weren't what bothered me. Katrina was right. We could take them on. Cooper alone could wipe them out in seconds. Though, leaving them behind in the middle of the night gave us a slight edge on them. I'd love to see them wake up and realize we are long gone and that we tricked them, not the other way around.

It was more than that. Something kept nipping at me, though I couldn't put a finger on what. A nagging feeling in my gut, like something was right in my face and I wasn't seeing it.

The incident with Katrina unsettled me more than anything. When Cooper came back after finding Kaptain's group, I went to locate Kat, retrieving her clothes by the river.

I sent Cooper to get our gear together and meet me a mile down the trail while I headed out to find Kat. I couldn't even tell you how I found her. I just did. My feet moved to her, something pulling me to the exact place she was.

It reminded me of something both Ryker and Eli had said to me about Zoey and Ember—their connection to their mates. They could track them down wherever they were in the world without even thinking. Like an internal GPS set directly to them. Instinctual.

The thought terrified me. Nope, there was no fucking way. Just a coincidence.

First, I never wanted a mate. I enjoyed all women too much to have *one* for the rest of my life. That sounded horribly boring.

But does it? You haven't had sex because you're bored now. I shook my head, rejecting the thought.

All the mated pairs I knew seemed to feel the exact opposite of bored. They *only* wanted one. And shit, they were all horny as hell, fucking nonstop, and desiring that person even more after years together, the bond between them only strengthening.

Second, it seemed impossible for me to want only one forever. I was usually over someone after the first or second time we had sex. Amara was the one exception because I knew deep down she didn't want me. She was a challenge. And at the time, I loved how fucked up she was, allowing me to be the worst of myself too. Wallowing in the ugliness of my life.

I stopped my horse in front of an old inn, the firebulb outside still lit, suggesting they still had room.

"I'll go check." I got off my horse, my attention falling on AB as even more tension built along my shoulders. Her lids barely parted, Cooper kept her tight in his arms, and she used his bicep as a pillow. Her body and mind had given up hours before, unable to keep up with our stamina.

No human could, but I knew this was more than that. The disease was sucking the life out of her more and more every day.

Cooper nodded, cradling her in his arms, unable to hide the adoration, love, and pain in his expression.

As much as I didn't want a mate, I was also envious of them. To be so in love with someone. And have them feel the same about you.

Strolling inside, I spied an old man standing behind a counter, folding towels.

I greeted him in his native tongue, and he nodded at me.

"Do you have rooms left?" I asked in Mandarin.

"Yes. One."

"One?" I sighed. "Can it fit four?"

"It can fit how many you pay for, but only one bed."

Of course.

"Fine, we'll take it." I pulled out money, exchanged it for a key, and headed back outside. "Here." I tossed the key to Cooper. "Get her in bed. I'll take care of the horses."

He didn't hesitate to lift her into his arms, sliding off the horse and taking AB inside. Sprig was settled somewhere in the bag she had on.

Stroking Caramel's nose, I watched Kat in my peripheral vision, overly aware of every move she made. Something had shifted between us. I could sense all the tiny connections between us.

"I'll take them," I said gruffly. "Go ahead inside. You girls can have the bed."

Kat stood there, her head down, staring at her boots. A strange awkwardness threaded the air, reminding me it wasn't just finding her that was notable; it was how every time I was around her, I couldn't stop touching her. Craving the taste of her skin, craving the taste of *her*. My cock was so desperate to be inside her, I stopped breathing. I needed whatever this was to end. To go away and never return.

"Go." I reached for her horse's reins, stepping into her. Kat didn't move when my boots hit hers, my body looming over her. Her nearness did something to my brain, keeping me from moving back. I stood over her, watching her chest move up and down. Her long, silky hair tempted my fingers to tangle through it, to take what was *mine*.

I sucked in at that thought, and her head tipped up, her gaze looking straight into me.

"How did you find me?" It was practically a whisper. She was begging me for a good explanation, something we could both chalk up to nothing. A reason I could track her down over a mile and pluck her almost invisible tiny black body from deep in the bushes.

My mouth opened, but no answer came out. I had nothing.

Her eyes went back and forth between mine, tearing at every barrier I was trying to keep up.

"Go inside," I huffed out, looking away. "I'm gonna sleep in the barn tonight." I clutched the leads and tugged the four horses toward the stalls out back, my gaze shooting away for a moment, making sure Kat did what I asked. My body knocked into something, and I whipped my head around to a thin, hooded figure stumbling to the side.

"Oh shit, sorry," I said in Mandarin, reaching out to grab them.

"I'm fine," a woman replied in the same language, holding up one hand, keeping her body and face turned away from me. "Wasn't watching where I was going," she muttered, moving away quickly.

I watched her hustle away, disappearing into the shadows, her cloak hiding her completely. Something triggered in me, her voice and her movements, but once again, I couldn't say what had bothered me about them. Her accent was slightly off, as if she wasn't from here, but neither was I. Many people here weren't.

Turning back for the barn, I tried to shake off the odd feeling, knowing I was tired and over-stimulated. Everything was off, and I blamed that on Katrina.

Why the fuck couldn't I stop thinking about her? I spent centuries without thinking of her...

That's a lie. She was always there in everything you did. Especially the bad shit, like you needed to exorcise what you did to her from your soul.

Trudging the horses in, the nagging sensation still worming through me. My dick ached, my body hurt, and my mind wouldn't shut down.

I needed a fucking drink.

The thought triggered something, my hand slapping over the pouch I kept the money in.

Empty.

"No. No. No." I searched the bag. "Fuck!" I bellowed, my head tipping back. "That fucking thief." Anger and embarrassment roared through me. *I was* the thief, not the other way around. That woman had meant to run into me, playing it off as if it was my fault, while she took my money.

"Dammit!" I barked, hating how easily she had stolen

from me because my attention had been on Katrina. It was my fault, but it showed how weak Kat made me. How nothing else seemed to matter when she was around.

I was a chump.

Caramel huffed, rubbing his head into me like he was patting me on the back and saying, *Yep, you're a chump.* What had happened to me? Once a legend of the sea, the infamous Silver-Tongue Devil, who could steal women's hearts and panties along with their husband's bank accounts, was now getting pickpocketed by a street urchin.

The barn door clicked softly behind me, and I heard people entering the barn.

The back of my neck prickled with alarm, and my muscles tightened along my shoulders, my hand going to the handle of my sword.

There was a moment, a single breath, before the calm serenity of the barn flipped. Swinging around and yanking my blade from the sheath, I took in the four men dressed in black, their faces covered, all holding huge Dadao swords, which were basically meat cleavers on the end.

Being robbed and attacked within minutes was no coincidence. They had come for more, possibly the horses.

"Look at you guys, all dressed like each other. So cute," I mocked, silence rebounding back. "No introductions? It's really hard to tell you guys apart."

The men lunged for me.

"Guess not." My blade clanked against one as I swung, kicking the stomach of another, flinging him back into a stall. "Fine, You're Thing One, Two, Three, and Four." I nodded at each one. "I know, not very creative, but somehow, it fits your cheery personalities."

Advancing, deflecting, we moved through the small barn, startling the horses. They reared up, filling the barn with their frightened noises.

Thing Three let out a holler, swiping down for me. I darted out of the way as three more descended on me. I had no time to think, relying on my teachings. The hours and decades I had conditioned my body came back to me like breathing. Rotating, I countered a blow from Two while my elbow slammed into One, causing him to stumble back.

"Nǐ huì sǐ!" You will die. One hissed in Mandarin, leaping back for me, his sword swinging.

The Dadao sword was swiped over me, kissing my spine, nicking my jacket. *Fuck. This is one of my favorites.* Dropping to my knees, I swung my leg out, knocking One off his feet as I jumped up, rushing Thing Two.

"Uhhh," I grunted, slamming his spine into a grain barrel with everything I had as a figure came at me. The blade skimmed over my head when I ducked, piercing Two through his chest, the blade slicing all the way through him and sticking in the wood cask. Leaping up, I twirled around as the other two men pounced.

The space was too tight to use my longsword, so I grabbed the dagger on my belt. Yanking it out, I darted in close. Rotty's blade sliced along Three's neck. Blood squirted out, his body hitching over for air before falling to the ground. Four hurtled at me with a cry. Dropping the small blade, I flipped the longsword in my hand, smashing the hilt into Four's face. The sickening crunch of bone and cartilage reverberated down my limbs, his body falling at my feet.

My attention was off the last guy for a moment. That's all it took. A sharp cleaver went to my throat from behind, the serrated edge cutting into my skin.

"You will die tonight," one said in English.

I swallowed. A simple drag across my neck, and he could decapitate me.

"What do you want?" I gritted. "You already robbed me. You want the horses?"

"No," the man replied. "We're here to kill you."

"Did I sleep with your wife?" I paused. "Girlfriend?" I lifted a brow, trying to nettle him. "Boyfriend?"

"No," he huffed in disgust. "This is not personal."

"People keep saying that, but because I'm the one dying, I'm taking it kind of personally."

"She paid for you to die. You die."

She.

It had to be the same *she* who tried to kill us in Shanghai.

His hand started to move the blade across my throat. My lids squeezed together as a trickle of blood dripped down my neck. This was how the great pirate would die? Beheaded in a barn, surrounded by horse manure.

Fucking figures.

A click of a gun being cocked echoed in the space.

"I don't think so."

My eyes burst open at Katrina's voice. Out of the corner of my eye, I could see her pressing her gun into my attacker's temple, looking deadly and badass.

"Drop the sword," she ordered the man. "Now."

He hesitated, his throat bobbing. "She'll kill me anyway."

"She may kill you,"—Katrina moved in close to him— "but I will track down your family, everyone you care about, and kill and torture them while you watch. Then I'll slowly cut out your lungs so you can see yourself take the last breaths." *Fuck. Am I turned on by that? Yes. Yes, I am.* "Now drop the weapon."

With a heavy sigh from the swordsman, the Dadao cluttered to the floor.

Picking it up, I circled around. My gaze locked with Kat's. Desire coursed through my bones at the feral glow lighting her eyes. We both thrived in life-and-death situations, feeling the high of walking on the edge.

And she was here… like she *knew* I needed her.

Reaching over, I tugged down the cloth covering his

mouth. I didn't recognize him, giving me no more insight into who he was.

"Why are you trying to kill us?" Kat asked.

His expression hardened, not speaking.

"Who hired you?" I ordered.

His mouth clamped together, reminding so much of the guy we questioned in Shanghai. Whoever "she" was, they feared her.

"Tell us or you join your friends." Kat threatened, her gun pressing harder into his head.

"I will die either way. But at least I will die with honor," he stated, snatching a hidden blade at his side and lunging for me, the tip heading straight for my jugular.

Bang!

Blood sprayed over me, and the man stilled, his limbs going limp, his eyes wide with shock. Then his body fell to the ground.

I blinked in surprise, my gaze lifting to the person behind him. Kat still pointed her gun where the man was, covered in his blood as well, her jaw set, a ruthlessness in her eyes.

Holy. Fuck.

She didn't hesitate. She didn't question. She just killed him…

To save me.

Chapter 25
Katrina

Adrenaline hummed through my ears, my body pumping with energy, the gun still hot in my hand. Everything around me was hazy and distant, focused on the man lying in a heap at my feet.

The one about to kill Croygen.

There was no thought. It was completely instinctual. As the blade was about to cut through Croygen's neck, a guttural cry came from the depths of my soul.

Mine.

The sensation rattled through me, tearing at my chest like a battle cry. I didn't just want to stop whatever was hurting him—I wanted to destroy it.

The air echoed with our heavy breaths while the realization of what had just happened stunned me. Not the awareness of what I did, but how I knew he needed me.

I couldn't even say how or why, but it was there. A tug in my gut, a restlessness in my bones, an icy feeling prickling the back of my neck. Anxiety. Terror. There was a sensation a part of me was about to be lost. I couldn't fight the pull. As if deep in my soul, I knew he was in trouble. And he was calling to me.

Needing me.

Lowering my gun, my chest heaving, my eyes slowly lifted, already feeling the weight of his stare.

His shoulders rolled forward, his jaw tight, but his eyes were electric with life. Hunger. They pierced mine, shredding any barrier I was still trying to keep up. The blood of my victim trailed down his face, rendering him fierce and animalistic. I knew I was covered in the same blood.

Fear, anger, hate, and desire boiled like lava under us, the edge of life and death hemorrhaging out into the air, stabbing my lungs like thousands of daggers. I needed to be marked. To drink the blood of our enemy, to taste his, to make him roll in mine, like some barbaric ritual.

A feral growl echoed from him, as if he could read every one of my thoughts.

My gun dropped from my hand, his sword from his, both of us moving at the same time, our bodies colliding.

He grabbed the back of my head, yanking me to him, giving me no time before his mouth crashed down on mine, his lips vicious and bruising. I could taste the blood, taste him. It incited me, flared my need to punish back. To take everything he stole from me.

A noise worked up his throat, the vibration humming through my bones as I clawed my nails through his hair.

With a groan, he hitched me up, my thighs squeezing his hips, his hard cock throbbing against me. He slammed me back into a horse wagon, stealing my breath and turning my cat fully feral.

I craved the hurt, the desire to lose all control, to be so primal there was nothing else in this world that mattered. To make each other bleed.

To leave permanent marks.

"Croygen..." I groaned against his mouth, my fingers tugging off his jacket. I needed him inside me, to feel my heat wrap around him, feeling him stretch me.

Both of us were gifted at seduction, tempting, and teasing. But it had always been for a purpose. A game. Always in control, always with an objective. None of that existed here. Even when we fought on the ship weeks ago, there had been a power play, a need to be better, to bring the other down.

I still wanted to bring him down, but this time I would go with him.

His fingers tore off my jacket, dropping it to the ground, his mouth only leaving mine for a moment as he tugged my shirt and bra over my head together while I ripped his shirt off, exploring his ripped torso. His large hands cupped my bare breast, and his bloody fingers rubbed at my nipple, causing my head to tip back.

"Like that?" His eyes flashed as his mouth covered my breast, sucking and flicking at my nipple with his tongue, smirking as he caused a low moan from me. His palm wrapped around my throat, pinning me harder against the wagon, his mouth taking the other breast. "Fuck, I can feel your heat, Kitten. Sense how wet your pussy is." He moved up my neck, rumbling in my ear. "Does it need to be licked, Kitty-Kat?"

Heat flushed through my body, and I curved into his, my nipples hardening more as they brushed up against his chest. His hand still held my neck roughly, keeping me in place.

"Tell me," he demanded, his teeth scraping against my neck, his voice gravelly. "Want me to make it purr, Katrina?"

I reached for his pants, flicking the buttons, my fingers sliding into his boxer briefs. I wrapped my hand around his hard, thick cock, a desperate cry rising in the back of my throat.

A low groan came from him, his hips moving with my hand as cum leaked out the tip. My mouth watered; I wanted to taste him, to bring him to his knees.

"No." He gritted his teeth, dropping me to the ground and twisting me around, his breath hot in my ear. "I get to break you in first."

Croygen ripped down my pants, picking me up then bending me over one of the saddle racks, widening my legs, displaying how wet and needy I was. For once, I got off on being out of control, the one completely at his will.

Reaching over me, he grabbed a bridle. "I'm gonna make you yowl. I'm gonna make you scream." He leaned over me, his hand running down my body, stimulating every nerve. "And then I'm gonna make you purr."

The rein slapped across my ass. A cry escaped my throat, and searing pain sizzled into pleasure. His fingers slid through my folds as he did it again.

"Oh, gods!" I choked, jarred from the stimulation, my pussy squeezing around his fingers.

"Fuck." Croygen growled, his fingers working me deeper, whipping me again, closer to my pussy.

A deep moan shivered from me, wetness dripping down my leg. My nails shifted into claws, the base of my spine tingling, hinting at a cat tail.

"Croygen..." I didn't care how desperate and needy I sounded, which I had never been before. What the hell was he doing to me?

My ass curved up, pushing back into him, groaning louder as he curled his fingers inside me, the rein striking again. "Ohhhh, gods... please." I begged, my desperation bringing me close to tears.

"Want my cock in your pussy, kitten?" He removed his fingers, and the sound of him undoing his pants zipped up my spine, my body so frantic I rubbed back into him.

"Yes." My words and body were no longer my own; something beyond was controlling me. Like it understood far more than I did.

He grabbed my chin, turning my face to him while his hips curved into me, running his thick erection through me, the tip hinting at my entrance. "How bad do you want it, Kitty-Kat?"

I could feel the game, the sudden need to be in power. Little did he know, I was even better at this. Dropping men, human or fae, to their knees, begging for more.

With a snarl, I rolled my hips back, forcing him slightly deeper, squeezing my heat around him, my magic.

A strangled cry came from his throat, his legs dipping, his grip on me loosening. His eyes lifted, flaming with fire, meeting mine. A slow smile curved my face. "How bad do *you* want it, tradesman?"

I could feel the switch, the violence in the air, the blade we were about to fall on.

Croygen's jaw clenched, his hand running up the back of my head, gripping my hair roughly, yanking back at the same time he thrust into me brutally.

A scream stuck in my throat, electricity charging through me. I gasped in pain as his size shredded me in half. One side was agony, the other implausible pleasure.

"Fuuccckkk!" Croygen bellowed, huffing as he pulled out, pushing in even deeper this time.

"Oh, gods!" I clawed at the saddle, my nails ripping into it, trying to grapple for air. My body shook, magic exploding through me like I was being electrocuted. He stretched me, filling me to the point I lost all humanity. I no longer understood sympathy or kindness.

Untamed and feral.

"Fuck, fuck…" Croygen pulled on my hair harder, his body curving over mine like he no longer had the strength to fully stand up, pushing his cock deeper with severe strokes. "I need to fuck you deeper. To feel my cock inside you for decades to come." He growled, his fingers digging into my hip, pounding harder. "To know it's mine."

My legs widened at his words, craving that more than air, pushing back into him with the same brutal energy.

"Shit. Katrina," he hissed. "Gods... nothing has felt like this."

I had to agree. We were both *well* experienced with sex, thousands of years with thousands of partners. Sometimes it was good, other times amazing, but nothing had ever felt like this.

There was no close enough because I needed to crawl inside him, to feel his raw pleasure rub and stroke against mine, to have him mark me so deeply, I could feel it burning into my bones. To have his insignia glowing from under my skin.

The sensation was overwhelming, my actions out of my control.

His cock slipped out of me when I whirled around, my legs hooking around his calf, pushing him down. He dropped into the hay with a huff. I gave him no time to respond. Straddling his hips, I plunged down on him, watching him enter me, spearing me deeply.

"Fuck!" he bellowed as my own cry howled out, my claws raking down his chest. Croygen grabbed my hips, pushing up into me, his eyes rolling back. "Fuck the gods!" he groaned, a vehement need straining his features, his dark eyes flashing with magic.

He slammed up into me. A deep yowl came from me, pitching the air loudly, my body freezing with the abundance of sensations. *What the fuck?* I had never heard myself make that sound before. Ever. Nor had I even felt like every neuron in my body was being electrocuted.

Electric currents tore through my muscles, my spine curving as I rode the fuck out of him. My nails turned more into cat claws, and I scraped them deep into his chest, like I wanted to mark his skin with my own tattoos. He hissed as blood pooled from them, growing harder inside me.

I leaned over, my rough tongue lapping at the blood. The healing magic trailed over the cuts, and I kissed the skull and crossbones tattoo on his chest.

He reached up, dragging his thumb across my bottom lip, picking up the smear of blood left there. My mouth wrapped around his finger, sucking it hard, tasting more of his blood on my tongue.

His nose flared as he let out a low growl.

That was my only warning.

A snarl lifted his lip, and he tossed me onto my back into the hay, his body moving between my legs, spreading me wider. He grabbed my wrists with one hand, stretching them over my head. "Want me to draw blood too?" he growled. He drove back into me, hitting so deep he pushed me up, the hay scraping my back. "I can make you bleed." He lost all inhibitions, fucking me so violently I couldn't do anything but let him have full command of my body.

"Oh, gods… more!" I reveled in the sound of him railing me, our pleasure resonating off the barn walls, the smell of hay and horses. I had never felt so out of control and so alive.

He grunted, his mouth sucking at my bouncing tits. Letting go of my wrists, he reached down with one hand, rubbing my clit as his other hand wrapped around my throat, the same thumb I sucked pressing into my airways.

It was like I had been hooked up to a battery, the charge frying through my body. A strange sensation, as if for a second, I could feel him, had gotten inside him, feeling his own pleasure, his soul brushing against mine, adding to the intensity.

It broke me into pieces.

His eyes met mine, as if he felt the same. The connection hit every molecule in my body, claiming me.

My mouth opened on a cry, sounding more cat than human. The intensity ruptured across my vision, suspending me in time. My pussy locked around him, an orgasm tearing through me. I bit down on his neck, my teeth sharpening at his bellow, tasting his skin, his essence. He pushed in so deep I jolted, shrieking like a feral animal.

"Kat!" His hot cum released inside me, drowning me in utter ecstasy. And I let myself go under, sinking to the bottom of Davy Jones's locker. A moment of absolute peace and tranquility while I could still feel my body greedily milking and pumping his cock, taking all it could, leaving nothing.

His release trailed down my thighs as he continued to pump inside me. His fingers dragged up my leg, scooping his release and rubbing it over my clit, exploding another orgasm through me.

My spine snapped back, a deep moan sticking in my throat, losing my last bit of hold on this Earth, my grip around him strangling.

A loud, guttural noise came from Croygen, holding him in place for a moment, his body quaking, his muscles contracting. "Fuck! Katrina!" he bellowed. I felt it more than I heard it, experiencing his bliss as well as my own, making me black out for a moment.

His body collapsed over mine, cocooning us, our lungs heaving together for air, unable to move or speak. I let my eyes close, coming down from the high, the intensity causing me to tremble and jerk as though I were cold. Magic liquefied my muscles, and my mind completely splintered.

For a long time, we stayed like this, not able to speak or move.

Shiver me timbers... What the hell was that?

A sea of emotion tumbled me around like clothes in the washer as I came back to myself. My mind was stunned, my soul calm, my body completely content. Blissfully sedated. Which had never happened to me before.

Fear and reality started to trickle in, my heart pounding for other reasons.

"Fuck, Kitten." Croygen exhaled, his breath brushing down my neck, slipping over my skin. Slowly he lifted his head, our gazes meeting, both of us searching for an answer to a question we didn't even know. But I could feel it, the look in his eyes mirroring back in my own.

What just happened? This wasn't normal, right?

Croygen adjusted his weight on his arms over me, making me feel him move deep inside me. My core fluttered around him, still gripping him tight, like it couldn't get enough, hanging on for dear life, wanting more.

"Your pussy doesn't want to let me go, Kitty-Kat." A low moan emanated from Croygen, his lashes dropping, his teeth digging into his bottom lip. "And I told you,"—his mouth brushed mine— "I could get you purring."

Oh. Gods.

My entire body locked up suddenly at the low vibration coming from my lungs, the hum of pure contentment, not even realizing I had been doing it.

Cat-shifters purred for various reasons, vocalizing different moods. Sex was different. Separate vocal cords were used, displaying a deep intimacy. Bonding. Something I had never felt or would show any previous lover. It was vulnerable and exposing. To do it with Croygen had humiliation burning my cheeks, dropping reality on me with a thud.

Pushing him off, I scrambled away. The instant his cock pulled out of me, his cum gushed down my leg, and what we had just done hit home even more. How *incredible* it had been. How *impossibly* good.

And this made it worse.

"Oh gods," I whispered. Sitting up, I turned away from him. I grabbed the closest piece of clothing, covering my chest, hiding the thing that made me weak, displaying such a vulnerability.

"Kat?" he spoke behind me, his voice sparking an instant response.

My gaze scanned the room, taking in what led us to this—naked in a horse barn, covered in blood, sweat, hay, and sex, surrounded by dead assassins. My attention went to the one lying face down, not too far away, the back of his head gone.

I had killed many men, but when he lunged for Croygen? All I saw was red. Death. The thought of him taking Croygen from me had me ready to chop him up into little pieces. The bullet was too quick and easy.

"Katrina?" Croygen's fingers grazed my spine, making me bolt up. I needed to get away because if he touched me again, I would be lost, fighting the deep craving to curl up against him, letting him cover me like a blanket and bury inside me again.

I scrambled to find my clothes, rustling the hay. Croygen got to his feet. A groan worked up my throat, but I quickly swallowed it back.

He stood there naked, his thick cock coated in my arousal, his sculpted body covered in tattoos, cuts, blood, and scars, his dark hair a mess with hay sticking out of it. He looked like a pirate god come to life, ready to demonstrate his command over me.

Again.

My ass stung where he whipped me, making my thighs clench, stirring arousal through me. I had always been the more dominant one in bed. Some of the men I slept with may have thought they were in charge, but in the end, they were the ones babbling nonsense and screaming to me like I was a god, blacking out from the orgasm.

It had never been fair before, on equal terrain. But Croygen cut me at my knees.

I not only let him dominate me, but I had loved it. It was the most intimate thing I had ever done. Besides purring…

Embarrassment covered my cheeks, causing me to rush faster, tugging on my pants and top.

"Stop." He grabbed my shoulder, turning me to him, bubbling terror up my throat because I had no resistance to him. Defenseless. His dark eyes pierced me, his naked body calling to mine. He loomed over me, causing me to tremble with desire, the need to press into him, to feel his body against mine. To lose myself. "Giving me a complex, Kitten." His voice rumbled low. "*Never* had anyone running out on me... especially after I fucked them senseless."

My lungs hitched.

"Well, I guess if you did it right, I wouldn't be walking at all, would I?" I lashed out, jerking away from him.

His jaw clicked, lids narrowing, like he could see right through me.

"It was a mistake. Our emotions were heightened." I gestured around to the dead bodies. "I was not myself."

"And you liked it." He grabbed me, yanking me into him, his cock hardening against me. My head spun, throbbing with stimuli. Magic filled and sparked through my entire body, causing me to shake more. "You liked being out of control."

"No, I—"

"You can't lie to me." His mouth skated over my ear. "I can hear you purring again, Kitty-Kat. I can feel it."

Humiliation. Weakness. They both scorched me to cinders as my body betrayed me so acutely. It was low, almost inaudible, but somehow, he heard it. Just his nearness had me vocalizing something I could not face.

I retreated, my bare feet stepping on something cool and hard. I looked down, my gaze landing on an item.

Air stuck in my throat, and ice slithered up my spine, spearing into my veins. As if my father's ghost rose from the depth of the sea, to remind me of my promise to him.

His dagger, smeared with blood, lay at my feet. A symbol of his life. An omen of his death. And what did I do? I slept with his murderer, insulting his memory, his honor.

Everything I had lived, fought, and killed for, and I had cast it all aside in one moment. When I spread my legs and let my enemy in.

Croygen's physique tightened, his gaze locking on the same object and then lifting to mine.

"Katrina…"

"No." I stumbled back more.

"You don't understand—"

"Understand?" My voice pitched higher than I expected. Anger bulldozed through my hollow chest. "There is nothing to understand." My teeth gritted, emotion tumbling from me. "Did you or did you not kill my father?"

His mouth opened, pain creasing his face.

"Tell me!" I screamed.

"You want to know if I stabbed that dagger through your father's heart?" Croygen barked back, his own fury matching mine. "Is that the *only* thing you want to know?"

"That is the only thing I need to know!" I was unraveling, wishing more than anything he would tell me no so I could find an excuse for what I just did. Absolve myself of my despicable crime. But I didn't deserve that. I earned the penance.

"A slice of a fact is not truth." Croygen snarled.

Frustration and ire gurgled up my throat. Swiping up the dagger, I got in Croygen's face, the blade lining up with the cut already across his neck.

"What are you gonna do, Kitty-Kat?" His gaze darted to the blade, his lips wrinkling, his erection hardening as I pushed it against him. "Have the guts to finally do it?"

"No more skirting the question," I ordered, wrath oozing off every word. "Killian saw you kill my father. Did you stab him like he said?"

Croygen peered down at me with a scowl.

"You want a villain? I'll play the villain for you." He inched closer, the knife cutting deeper. He leaned in, his mouth near mine. "Yes, Kitten. I was the one who stabbed him through the heart. I felt his life bleed from him."

A strangled noise twisted in my throat, and I felt like he dropped me off a cliff. Though I had seen it coming for a long time, known it was there, it still ripped the air from my lungs when I went over it. Death to what was and what could've been. My worship of him as a little girl and my respect for him as an adult crumbled under my feet. Replaced with the heartache and shame of hoping I was wrong.

"Go ahead," he growled, only leaning into the blade more. "End me, Katrina. It's what you always wanted, right? Take your vengeance. I won't even fight you."

The struggle inside, the emotion of everything I felt, leaked tears down my face. The pain. The torment. The battle between what I thought I should do, what I had trained to do, and what my soul screamed out, feeling even more pathetic because I knew what would win out.

Crying out, I shoved away from him, my head falling forward. I let my family down. I was a disgrace to my father.

Turning on my heels, I ran out, needing to get far away from him. And myself.

Outside, the warm air only suffocated my lungs more, my body shaking, my mortification devastating as Croygen's seed trailed down my leg with every step.

I had spoken of Croygen's betrayal for so long, spouting how I wouldn't hesitate to kill him, when in the end, I was the one to betray my father.

Slipping into a side alley, I leaned against the wall, sobs hiccuping up my throat. Sliding down the wall with my father's dagger clutched in my hand, I experienced every sore muscle, reminding me of what I did and how much I liked it.

My heart shattered into dust.

Small. Lost. Like I no longer had ground beneath my feet. My entire world had been structured around Croygen. Around my revenge.

And now I was nothing. My entire belief system was nothing but a façade.

"Oh look, a stray." A woman's voice came from the depths of the alley, jerking my head to the side. I could barely make out her slim silhouette before a handful of figures moved in on me, dressed the same as the men who attacked us in the barn.

I leaped up, the blade in my hand, turning toward them, ready to fight.

Crack!

Something struck the back of my skull, toppling me to the side with a cry. My body and mind instantly retreated, going hazy and useless. I dropped to the ground. Through my hazy vision, she stepped closer, bending down to peer at me, her dark eyes narrowing on me, her nose wrinkling with disgust. Something about her nicked at my mind, but it quickly fled out of reach. "Guess he'll learn to not let his pets out at night where they can be eaten." She stood, nodding at the men. "Let's move."

The men picked me up, and I tried to fight, to call for him, but only the soft whisper of his name glided from my lips before darkness took me under.

Chapter 26
Croygen

I couldn't move, my gaze still on the door Katrina escaped from. My voice locked in my throat, her name on my tongue to call her back, the need to run after her burning my spine.

Yet, I couldn't.

My body reacted like it had been traumatized—sweating, trembling, heart racing, unmoving. But all for the opposite reasons. It wasn't from a bad experience, but from a phenomenal one, short-circuiting my brain. My head couldn't catch up with what just happened, the turn of events which went from me almost getting my neck sliced by a ninja, to fucking Katrina over a saddle.

How it felt sinking into her, the magic I could feel as I drove in and out of her. Fuck...

My legs wobbled under me, my dick hardening at the thought. What the hell just happened? It was as if I had no power or control, which had never happened to me. Ever. Sex was fun, but most of the time it was just a game to me. A power play. An amusement for the evening. A competition with myself at how crazed I could get them. And in my time, I've had some really kinky and mind-blowing sex. Not much I hadn't done.

Kat was different.

I never once felt challenged. At one time, I would've said Amara had, but really, I was in a fight with myself, going after someone who didn't want me. We were never on the same playing field.

Kat stood toe to toe with me, gave back just as fiercely, but when her magic wrapped around my cock—*shit*—I would've done anything she asked... *anything*. I blacked out, my lungs halting for a moment, my body trembling like some cold street urchin. Nothing had ever felt so good. I couldn't even come up with a word for it, but I could feel it rattling in my bones, braiding in my muscles, and absorbing into my skin.

Her presence was everywhere.

My hand brushed over the throbbing in my neck where she had bitten me, my gaze scanning over the red claw marks carving into my torso and stinging my back. My cock was still covered in her release. My mind echoed with her cries, the way she yowled...

And purred.

Fuck, that sound vibrated through me, cocooning me in such a blissful bubble. It was so content I couldn't even explain it. Like I could stay there forever. I was torn between wanting to wrap around her and fall asleep or fuck her all over again, slow and deep.

Then, like being thrown into the icy sea, Fredrich's blade, covered in blood, and dead bodies littering the space around us, splashed reality back with a vengeance. I could see her grief, feel her shame and agony because of what she thought I had done.

If she only knew the whole truth.

It was like Rotty made his presence known, his ghost filling the room, building the wall between us, making me realize what I just did.

315

I just fucked my first mate's daughter. The girl I had promised to protect. I failed at protecting her from myself, turning her into another victim of the Silver-Tongue Devil because I couldn't keep my dick in my pants. Except I hadn't put my cock in anyone lately. She was the first one to make me feel something in a long time. And from the moment she stepped on my ship, she was a siren song, pulling me down into the depths of the sea, drowning me.

She made me feel vulnerable. Weak. As if I could lose everything. Again.

The splash of water slapped across my face, my lungs choking up sea water, my lids bolting open as the sounds of fighting, cannons, and the death cry of a ship.

Lifting my head to the men battling over the deck, screams and clanks of metal pierced my ears. The waves rolled the ship, tipping it slightly to the side and crashing water over the bow.

Terror wrapped around my gut like an octopus, sucking and squeezing the air from my lungs. My ship was flailing, my men were dying. Everything I had built was about to sink to Davy Jones, another sacrifice to the pirate god.

A growl rose from my throat, fury pushing me to my feet, and I grabbed the sword at my side.

"Lowe..." I cursed his name, my knuckles tightening over the handle, searching for the man, my old friend. Pirates were funny. In some things, we had no code of ethics, and in others, we lived and died by an unspoken rule.

Ned Lowe and I had been allies. Comrades at one time. And in a world of pirate hunters, governments, and empires ready to hang your body up as a trophy, we had an implicit understanding.

We left each other alone.

Ned broke that, attacking and boarding my ship. I knew he was ruthless and cruel, but I didn't realize how far he would go.

Creaks moaned from my ship; the ocean was turbulent, as if it could feel the grievance.

"But your ship was part of the deal." Ned's statement played back in my head. I figured that meant he was going to steal it, put his flag high on the mast. He was sinking it instead. Destroying my legacy, taking the infamous vessel, and putting it in a grave.

So I could never take it back.

Moving across the deck, I hunted for Ned. Most of the men were already dead. And for the ones still alive, I uttered words I never imagined, heavy and foul in my mouth. "Retreat!" I ordered them, motioning to the dinghies. "Go!"

Water crashed down on us, the ship listing more to one side. "Now!"

"What about you, Captain?"

"Don't worry about me," I yelled through the squall and commotions, my soaking hair hanging around my face, my mouth spitting out salty water.

I was ready to go down with my ship, but I would take Lowe with me.

At the helm, Lowe gripped another man by the collar, pressing a sword to his throat, both of them in a heated conversation.

Dread paused my heart as I recognized the man he held, looking desperate and scared.

"Rotty!" I ran for my first mate, the man I considered a friend. Family. He was not a fighter, but the brains of my operation. The one that had everything running like clockwork, who worked out every possible outcome, every way to defeat an enemy or achieve our goal. He was the reason I became the notorious pirate I was, because his process never failed us. His mind was unequalled.

But he could not physically battle Lowe.

"You assured me!" Rotty's voice barely hit my ears. "I would see her!"

"And you believed me?" Ned's laugh was cruel and belittling. *"Never trust a pirate, mate."* He moved in closer to Fredrich. *"You are a gullible fool. And you provided me exactly what I wanted. Sinking this ship, killing Croygen's crew. I will be a legend evermore. I will be feared and worshipped. No one will touch me. I am the greatest pirate of all time. And it's all thanks to you."*

"Lowe?" I bellowed. He turned his head to me.

It gave Rotty a moment, his expression crunching in wild fury, something I had never seen before. Grabbing the dagger from his belt, he lunged for Lowe.

In a blink, Lowe seized the handle, twisting it around. The sharp edge sank into Rotty's chest.

There was a moment of shock. Rotty's eyes went to the blade in his heart, then back up to Lowe. A profound grief carved into Fredrich's features. It went beyond pain or sadness. Like he understood something I did not. Slowly his body sagged to the ground.

"Noooo!" I leaped up the stairs to the helm, my sword ready to taste Lowe's blood, to kill this man.

Crack!

Wood groaned from deep in the bowels, tipping the ship over more, gliding me away from my target. Landing hard on the deck, my body slid, knocking into the side, water breaking down on me.

Spitting and shaking the water off, I searched for Lowe, my blood boiling with the need to kill.

The wave had tossed him back onto the main deck, yards away from me. Getting to his feet, swaying as the ship tittered, sinking further under, he looked back at me. *"How fitting. The illustrious Silver-Tongue Devil goes down. But this time into a watery grave."* A malicious smile grew over his lips. *"One thing about betrayal. It never comes from your enemies. It's always those who are closest to you."*

The neigh of a horse snapped me back to the present, my head shaking away the memories of my past, only feeling more disgusted about what I had done.

Though, in a way, it was very apropos. I fucked the person who has been fucking me for centuries.

A groan worked up my throat, my hand rubbing over my head, brushing out the straw. Tugging on my pants, I searched for my shirt, only finding hers.

Kat had mine.

A noise hummed in the back of my throat, my hand sliding over the stiffness in my pants. Why did the idea of her in my clothes fucking make me so hard? Normally, I avoid that kind of shit like the plague. It was too "couple-y," a possessive reaction from both parties, signaling to everyone they were "mine."

Glancing around at the four dead bodies, I sighed because I would have to get Cooper up to deal with this shit. No doubt it would circle around to why I was shirtless and barely able to walk.

Stepping into my boots and clutching the rest of my stuff, I made my way back to the inn next door. When I reached for the door, a shiver brushed up my spine, making my head turn around. The warm, humid night clung the clouds close, making it muggier. Ice wormed down into my veins, alarm dancing on my nerves, feeling like I heard my name being called, tugging at my gut.

Something felt off. Wrong.

Darting inside, I took two stairs at a time, peering behind me before I went into our tiny room, exhaling when I saw Cooper and Annabeth lying on the small bed against the window. His huge physique, which barely fit, circled around her sleeping form like a blanket. His head popped up instantly at my entrance, ready to attack and protect if he needed to.

Fear gripped me again when my gaze went over every

corner, noting Kat's sleeping pad was still rolled up and she was nowhere to be seen.

"Where's Kat?"

"She left a while ago, I thought to help you," Cooper responded, sitting up.

"She didn't come back?" Panic plucked at my vocal cords.

"No." Cooper watched me, picking up on my distress. "Why?"

I couldn't even tell him why, but my intuition was screaming. I felt a pull to her, as if I knew she needed me. Anxiety whisked me around, and I ran out of the room as Cooper trailed after me down the stairs, not even hesitating.

"When did you last see her?" Shirtless, he came up next to me, sniffing the air, his eyes flashing red, an indication the Dweller was right at the surface, trying to pick up her scent.

"About ten minutes ago," I responded, but my full attention was on every nook and cranny of the dark street. "Can you smell her?"

"I'm trying, but all I can smell of her is on you… along with blood and sex." He peered at me, his eyebrow curving up. "Could she just be needing a moment?"

I wanted to believe, yes, that's all this was, her needing some air after what had just happened. But the sick feeling continued to tug at my gut, my muscles itching to move. The desperation to find her had me running down the street.

"Kat?" I bellowed. The low murmurs from a bar on the corner were my only response. "Katrina?" Every second that ticked by without hearing her voice in return only drove my panic higher. A moment ago, I swore I could hear her, feel her near. Now all I could feel was empty space.

My pulse pounded in my ears as I darted further down the lane, wanting so badly for her to step out and tell me what I sensed was all in my head.

"Croygen!" Cooper's call whipped me around, my legs

already running toward his voice. My boots hit the pavement. I came up behind him. He stood at the entrance to an alley not too far from the inn.

"Look." He pointed, my focus following his finger.

Dread bricked up the back of my throat.

A dagger lay near the wall, dried blood on the blade, the gold handle facing me as if it had been dropped.

Fear gurgled in my stomach, the bricks crashing down.

Kat would never leave her father's blade behind.

"Coop…" His name came out a whisper, but he instantly understood. Not even waiting to take off his pants, his body shifted into his Dweller form. I had seen it many times, but it never ceased to amaze me to watch. With a roar, his bones popped, his muscles expanding, black fur covering his body as he dropped on all fours, claws protruding like scythes, sharp poisonous blades popping out of his spine like a mane. His teeth were longer than my hand, and he came up to my chest.

In the Otherworld, they were the ones you hired to kill. And if you saw one, you were already dead.

Cooper's eyes flashed red again, a low growl vibrating in his vocal cords as his huge head lowered, smelling the ground. His claws scraped across the cobbles, tearing off down the alley.

Running after him, I tried to keep up, his body blending in the darkness, disappearing before my eyes. Reaching the other end of the alley, I came out to find nothing but a quiet street.

"Fuck." I peered around, trying to pick a direction to go, though something told me it was pointless. Kat was no longer here. "No." I batted back the thought, picking up my pace. I would not give up.

Hours went by as I wove through the city, looking for any sign of her. When dawn hinted on the horizon, I headed back to the inn, defeated, angry, and terrified. Was she alive? Dead? Who took her? Was it more of those men?

When I reached the inn, the early light cast a slight glow on the figure at the door, his blond hair pulled back in a knot. He was dressed in a new pair of pants and a shirt.

"Cooper!" I jogged up. "Did you find anything?"

"No." He shook his head. "I lost her scent not too far out of the alley." His expression was somber. "I kept going out, trying to pick it up again, but I couldn't."

"What does that mean?"

"Once she left this alley, her feet never touched the ground again. I tried to track the men's and the horses' scents, but they stopped up the road, and a bunch of other smells basically washed out anything specific."

"Really?"

"It's like they knew how to disguise and end their trails." Frustration wrinkled his brow. "Though there was something familiar there, but I couldn't place it. It wasn't strong enough."

Disappointment built a headache behind my eyes, my hand absently rubbing at the claw marks starting to heal in my skin. Just hours ago, she was riding me. Now she was gone.

"I need to check on Annabeth... and you know Sprig will be up soon."

"Yeah." I nodded, swallowing, feeling lost and broken, not having a clue what to do next. I followed Cooper into the inn, and the man behind the desk stopped us.

"Here." He tossed an envelope to me.

"What's this?"

"I don't know," he snipped. "Not your maid. Said to give it to you."

I picked up the envelope. "Who?"

"Wearing hood, didn't see the face, but sounded like a woman."

Ripping the envelope open, my throat closed around itself as I unfolded the paper, scanning over the blocky nondescript writing.

Lost your pussy?

If you want her back, you will get the nectar. Find it and she might be returned to you...

If not, your little kitty has no more lives.

I won't hesitate. (But you already know that about me.)

I read it again, looking for any clues, the last line furrowing my brow.

"What?" Cooper leaned in.

I shoved the paper at him, letting him read it. His gaze met mine with understanding.

"Get Annabeth and Sprig," I ordered. "I'll get the horses ready. We're heading for the dragon caves now." I gritted my teeth, slamming through the door.

The bitch took what was mine. Possessive, raw anger boiled under my skin. The need to destroy everything in my wake hummed over me.

My tongue may have been sharp, but my blade was deadly. I would do whatever it took to get Katrina back. I would get this nectar, and then I was going to kill this woman.

And as you know...

Dead women tell no tales.

The Adventure Continues Soon!
***Devil in Boots* (Devil in the Deep Blue Sea #2)**

Thank you to all my readers. Your opinion really matters to me and helps others decide if they want to purchase my book. If you enjoyed this book, please consider leaving a review on the site where you purchased it. It would mean a lot. Thank you.

About the Author

USA Today Best-Selling Author Stacey Marie Brown is a lover of hot fictional bad boys and sarcastic heroines who kick butt. She also enjoys books, travel, TV shows, hiking, writing, design, and archery. Stacey is lucky enough to live and travel all over the world.

She grew up in Northern California, where she ran around on her family's farm, raising animals, riding horses, playing flashlight tag, and turning hay bales into cool forts.

When she's not writing, she's out hiking, spending time with friends, and traveling. She also volunteers helping animals and is eco-friendly. She feels all animals, people, and the environment should be treated kindly.

To learn more about Stacey or her books, visit her at:

Author website & Newsletter:
www.staceymariebrown.com

Facebook Author page:
www.facebook.com/SMBauthorpage

Pinterest: www.pinterest.com/s.mariebrown

TikTok: @authorstaceymariebrown

Instagram: www.instagram.com/staceymariebrown/

Goodreads:
www.goodreads.com/author/show/6938728.StaceyMarie_B
rown

Stacey's Facebook group:
www.facebook.com/groups/1648368945376239/

Bookbub: www.bookbub.com/authors/stacey-marie-brown

Acknowledgements

Kiki & Colleen at Next Step P.R. - Thank you for all your hard work! I love you ladies so much.

Mo - Thank you for making it readable and your hilarious comments!

Jay Aheer - So much beauty. I am in love with your work!

Judi Fennell at www.formatting4U.com - Always fast and always spot on!

To all the readers who have supported me: My gratitude is for all you do and how much you help indie authors out of the pure love of reading.

To all the indie/hybrid authors out there who inspire, challenge, support, and push me to be better: I love you!

And to anyone who has picked up an indie book and given an unknown author a chance.

THANK YOU!